DRAGON EYRE BLACKRO

Christopher Mitchell is the author of the epic
in Edinburgh before living for several years in the Middle East and Greece, where he
taught English. He returned to study classics and Greek tragedy and lives in Fife, Scotland
with his wife and their four children.

Brigdomin Books Ltd
First Edition, May 2022
ISBN 978-1-912879-75-5

For Jadon

ACKNOWLEDGEMENTS

I would like to thank the following for all their support during the writing of the Magelands Eternal Siege - my wife, Lisa Mitchell, who read every chapter as soon as it was drafted and kept me going in the right direction; my parents for their unstinting support; Vicky Williams for reading the books in their early stages; James Aitken for his encouragement; and Grant and Gordon of the Film Club for their support.

Thanks also to my Advance Reader team, for all your help during the last few weeks before publication.

THE TWELVE REALMS OF DRAGON EYRE

The Twelve Realms of Dragon Eyre (in 5252, when *Dragon Eyre – Badblood* takes place)

The archipelagos and island chains of Dragon Eyre were traditionally split into twelve ancient realms. Geographically, the realms were also separated into two 'Rims', denoting the eastern and western edges of the ring of archipelagos. The invasion of Dragon Eyre by Implacatus began in 5228 (twenty-four years before *Badblood* begins), and was completed by 5231, when the last rebel, Queen Blackrose of Ulna, was defeated.

The Western Rim

1. **Alef** – *80,000 natives; 40,000 settlers; 25,000 Banner forces.* Alef consists of hundreds of tiny islands, most of which are uninhabited. It has large oil reserves, which are administered and protected by Banner garrisons. 200 dragons remain, living on the remotest islands.

2. **Olkis** – *300,000 natives; zero settlers; 45,000 Banner forces.* The most unruly and chaotic of the Twelve Realms, Olkis is a haven for rebels, surviving dragons, and pirates, who roam the seas around Olkis. The Realm of Olkis used to include the semi-independent island of **Tankbar**, whose entire population was annihilated by Banner forces following an uprising in 5248. 2,500 dragons live in relative safety in the mountainous regions of the south-west.

3. **Ectus** – *50,000 natives; 150,000 settlers; 60,000 Banner forces.* Converted by the occupying forces into a vast complex of naval and army bases, with the main shipyards of Dragon Eyre located on the northern coast. Heavily-forested mountains provide the wood to construct the fleets of the Sea Banner. No dragons remain.

4. **Gyle** – *800,000 natives; 600,000 settlers; 40,000 Banner forces.*
   Traditionally, Gyle was the main island prior to the invasion,
   and remains the capital of Dragon Eyre. Its foremost city is
   the settler-built Port Edmond, named after the Blessed
   Second Ascendant. Includes the islands of **Mastino** and
   Formo. No dragons remain.

5. **Na Sun Ka** – *100,000 natives; 100,000 settlers; 30,000 Banner
   forces.* The former spiritual home of the dragon-worshipping
   tradition of the Unk Tannic. For administrative purposes, the
   outpost of **Yearning** is considered part of the realm of Na
   Sun Ka, despite its location in the Eastern Rim. No dragons
   remain.

Note – under Banner occupation, the group comprising **Ectus**, **Gyle** and **Na
Sun Ka** are referred to among the settler population as the '**Home Islands**'.
Despite the presence of rebel Unk Tannic cells, there are no dragons remaining
on the Home Islands, meaning that they are relatively safe locations for the
settlers to dwell.

The Eastern Rim

1. **Haurn** – *zero natives; zero settlers; zero Banner forces.* Occupied
   by greenhides following an uprising in the Eastern Rim in
   5239. 500 dragons live in colonies on the southern cliffs,
   while a small number of natives live on the scattered islands
   to the north of Haurn.

2. **Throscala** – *100,000 natives; 80,000 settlers; 30,000 Banner
   forces.* The main Banner base of the Eastern Rim. 200
   dragons hide in the mountain peaks on the east coast of the
   island.

3. **Ulna** – *70,000 natives; zero settlers; zero Banner forces.* The
   realm where **Blackrose** was Queen prior to the invasion.
   Devastated by greenhides following an uprising in the
   Eastern Rim in 5239. A few overcrowded colonies of refugee

humans live on the southern isles of Serpens and Tunkatta, along with 200 dragons.

4. **Enna** – *60,000 natives; 20,000 settlers; 20,000 Banner forces.* Houses a large Sea Banner base, from where the Eastern Fleet patrol the seas between Geist and Throscala. Includes the smaller island of **Meena**. 400 dragons remain, mostly in the mountains of Meena.

5. **Geist** – *50,000 natives; 20,000 settlers; 13,000 Banner forces.* The borderlands of the occupation. Home to a large garrison of Banner forces, who defend the island from attacks by the dragons of Wyst. 1,000 dragons live on the islands between Geist and Wyst.

6. **Wyst** – *zero natives; zero settlers; zero Banner forces.* The only realm of Dragon Eyre where all attempts at colonisation or invasion have failed. Even prior to the invasion, Wyst remained aloof from the other realms, and has excluded any humans from living there for centuries. The 7000 surviving dragons of Wyst despise all humans, whether native or settler, and have successfully resisted the occupation.

Note – the distance between **Alef** in the Western Rim, and **Wyst** in the Eastern Rim, is further than the maximum flying range of any dragon. Consequently, Alef and Wyst can be seen as the two ends of a single, long chain of archipelagos.

Central Region

1. **Rigga** – *50,000 natives; zero settlers; 7,000 Banner forces.* Out of reach of any dragon, Rigga was traditionally the only human-dominated realm of Dragon Eyre. The resource-poor islands of Rigga are in the centre of the Inner Ocean, and can only be reached by ship. Prior to the invasion, it was considered by most dragons as exceptionally backward and primitive. A Banner garrison subdues the native population. No dragons have ever reached Rigga.

NOTE ON THE CALENDAR

Note on the Divine Calendar – Dragon Eyre

The Divine Calendar is used on every world ruled by Implacatus. As all inhabited worlds were created from the same template (and rotate around their sun every 365.25 days), each year is divided into the same seasons and months as that of Implacatus itself. Dragon Eyre differs from other worlds in not having four seasons – instead, the world has two distinct periods that share the same warm, sunny weather, but have alternating wind cycles.

In 'summer' (the first six months of the year), the wind blows anti-clockwise round the Inner Ocean.

In 'winter' (the last six months of the year), the wind blows clockwise round the Inner Ocean.

Each month (or 'inch') is named after one of the Twelve Ascendants (the original Gods of Implacatus). Through long years, the names have drifted some way from their originals, but each month retains its connection to the Ascendant it was named after.

In the Divine Calendar, each year begins on the 1st day of Beldinch.

Dragon Eyre Summer:

- Beldinch (January) – after Belinda, the Third Ascendant

- Summinch (February)– after Simon, the Tenth Ascendant

- Arginch (March) – after Arete, the Seventh Ascendant

- Nethinch (April)– after Nathaniel, the Fourth Ascendant

- Duninch (May) – after Edmond, the Second Ascendant

- Tradinch (June)– after Theodora, the First Ascendant

Dragon Eyre Winter:

- Abrinch (July) – after Albrada, the Eleventh Ascendant

- Lexinch (August) – after Leksandr, the Sixth Ascendant

- Tuminch (September) – after Tamid, the Eighth Ascendant
- Luddinch (October) – after Lloyd, the Twelfth Ascendant
- Kolinch (November)– after Kolai, the Fifth Ascendant
- Essinch (December) – after Esher, the Ninth Ascendant

DRAMATIS PERSONAE

The Haurn Rebels

Sable Holdfast, Avenging Witch

Blackrose, Queen of Ulna

Deepblue, Tiny Dragon

Millen, Deepblue's Rider

The Five Sisters

Ani'osso (Ann), Captain of the *Flight of Fancy*

Elli'osso (Ellie), Based in Olkis

Adina'osso (Dina), Based in Olkis

Atili'osso (Tilly), Captain without a ship

Alara'osso (Lara), Captain of the *Giddy Gull*

Olkian Pirates & Associates

Maddie Jackdaw, Blackrose's Rider

Oto'pazzi (Topaz), Master of the *Giddy Gull*

Ari'anos (Ryan), Carpenter's Mate

Vizzini (Vitz), Seaman and Settler

Ito'moran (Tommo), Young Master's Mate

Wyat, *Gull's* Bosun

Olo'osso, Legendary Pirate Patriarch

In Ulna

Shadowblaze, Blackrose's Suitor

Ahi'edo, Shadowblaze's Rider

Ashfall, Daughter of Deathfang

Greysteel, Blackrose's Uncle

Austin, Rebel Demigod

The Colonial Gods

Bastion, The Eldest Ancient

Ydril, Commander of Throscala

Kolai, Blessed Fifth Ascendant

Vettra, Fire Goddess

Others

Ata'nix, Leader of Unk Tannic (Eastern Rim)

Redblade, Dragon of Skythorn

Tallius, Banner Captain

Dragon Eyre - Western Rim

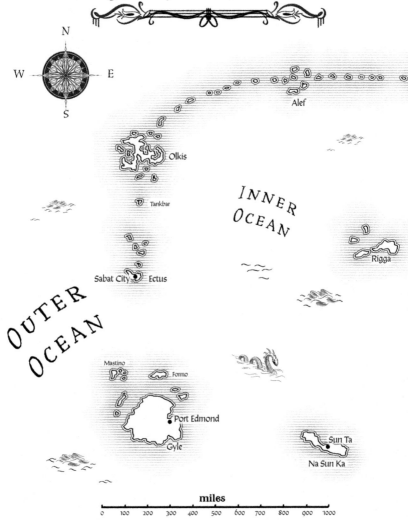

N
W E
S

Alef

Olkis

Tankbar

INNER OCEAN

Rigga

Sabat City · Ectus

OUTER OCEAN

Mastino

Formo

Port Edmond

Gyle

Sun Ta

Na Sun Ka

miles

0   100   200   300   400   500   600   700   800   900   1000

Dragon Eyre - Eastern Rim

N

W   E

S

Wyst

Geist

INNER
OCEAN

Enna

Meena

Ulna

Serpens

Throscala

OUTER
OCEAN

Yearning

Haurn

miles

0   100   200   300   400   500   600   700   800   900   1000

Dragon Eyre - Ulna

ULNA

MINIG ISLES

PLAGOS BAY

Costin
Point

Gliden

Plagos

Udall

Alg

Seabound

Gundra

USTEDD

ALG
BAY

SPEEN

SOUDANA

TUNKATTA

Arclas Heights

SERPENS

Legend

× GREENHIDE
NESTS

• TOWNS

▲ VOLCANOES

N

W — E

S

miles

0   25   50

Dragon Eyre - Olkis

OLBAN

FANSKA

QANA

Cape
Endu

Yafra

TANROE

Cape
Atar

Nankiss

THE KOLETI
ISLES

GARTMUN

Luckenbay

Aipura

MUCKLE
SKERRIE

The Skerries

Skythorn

Vipara

Langbeg

Cape
Keru

Pangba

OLKIS

Cape
Unco

ONSAR

N

W   E

FELJIRA

S

NAGELI

0   10   20   30   40   50   60   70   80   90   100
miles

CHAPTER 1
TAKING OWNERSHIP

Nan Po Tana, Haurn, Eastern Rim – 28th Beldinch 5255 (18th Gylean Year 6)

Sable stood bathed in the first rays of dawn. Her eyes were not directed towards the glorious sunrise that split the horizon; instead, she was gazing out towards the north-west. Across the hundreds of miles of empty ocean, far beyond the range of her vision skills, lay Ectus. Upon a tower on the north coast of that island, in between the huge shipyards and a vast complex of quaysides, she had slain an Ancient. She had crushed the Governor of Dragon Eyre's skull and stolen his Quadrant. It was one of the greatest feats of her life – an achievement that even Daphne Holdfast would have had a grudging admiration for, if she ever learned about it. Sable wondered if she had killed more gods than her half-sister. There had been Maisk on Lostwell, and then the three demigods that she had decapitated on the ships of the Sea Banner in the lead up to the battle for Alg Bay. Should she include Seraph in her tally? Shadowblaze had been the one to rip the god's head from her shoulders, but Sable had done the hard work that had made it possible. She would assign herself half a point for that one. Governor Horace had been all hers; there was no denying that. Five and a half.

It wasn't enough.

It would never be enough.

She heard someone appear next to her on the cliff-top path, but didn't turn.

'Blackrose wants to know if you're ready,' said Millen.

Sable nodded.

'This is a bad idea,' Millen went on. 'It's only been a few days. You need more time.'

'Time for what?' said Sable.

'Time... to recover, I guess.'

'If Blackrose is ready, then I'm ready too.'

'Blackrose is a dragon, Sable,' he said. 'They react differently to death. I worry that you... well, you know, your state of mind. You're still in shock.'

'I promised Blackrose that I would help rescue Maddie. The wounds she picked up on Ectus have healed, and her harness has been repaired. There's nothing else keeping us on Haurn.'

Millen lit two cigarettes and passed one to Sable. 'What about me and Deepblue?'

'You should be safe here.'

'That's not what I'm talking about. We want to help you, but you keep leaving us behind. Deepblue worries; she's devastated about what happened. We all are, but she's taken it very badly. Sanguino... sorry. I meant Badblood. Badblood was her best friend, and...' His voice tailed away, as Sable continued to stare out towards the horizon.

'I just think,' he went on, his words strained, 'that you need more time.'

Sable said nothing. She turned her head, and saw the sun rising above the ocean to her right. The sky was blue, with no clouds anywhere in sight, and she loosened the heavy cloak that she had been wearing to keep her warm through the night. She took a final draw from the cigarette, then cast the butt into the waves that were rolling against the shore beneath them.

'You're going to ignore my advice, aren't you?' Millen said.

'Yes.'

'You can be the one to tell Deepblue.'

'Maddie could be suffering,' said Sable. 'A promise is a promise.'

'She's been missing for months. Will a few more days make any difference?'

'They might.'

She rolled her shoulders, exhaled, then started to walk back down the path towards the temple compound. A shadow flickered overhead, as Deepblue circled, watching out for any stray greenhides that might be in the area. The small blue dragon swooped as Sable and Millen approached the gates leading into the complex. She hovered a few yards above them until they had passed through the gates and locked them behind them, then she landed onto the grass.

'Good morning, Deepblue,' said Sable.

'Good morning,' said the dragon. 'Have you eaten anything, Sable? You look tired. I caught a few fish before dawn – would you like some?'

Sable attempted a smile. 'Thank you. I think we'll wait until we get back from Olkis.'

Deepblue's eyes tightened. 'How can you think of travelling again, so soon after Ectus? Blackrose is pushing you too hard. I will speak to her. She is thinking of her own rider, when she should be thinking of all that you have lost. It's only been a few days, Sable. You need to rest, and...'

'Don't tell me what I need,' said Sable. 'If I keep moving, then maybe... I have to keep moving. If I don't, then I'll sit here and fester. I can rest once we have Maddie back. Where's Blackrose?'

Deepblue looked angry for a moment, then she glanced down. 'By the pyre.'

'You two wait here,' said Sable. 'I'll speak to her, alone.'

She walked away, leaving the small blue dragon and Millen by the gates. Sable crossed the neat little fields that made up the majority of the space enclosed within the walls of the temple. Orange blossom drifted by on the breeze, the delicate petals swirling by Sable's boots as she passed the orchard. Ahead of her, she saw the scorched and blackened circle of earth. Not a trace of Badblood remained; not a bone or scale – all had been reduced to ash by the flames of the pyre, assisted by dragon fire. Blackrose was sitting by the edge of the circle, her repaired harness strapped over her broad shoulders.

Sable walked up to her, but said nothing.

'Badblood would want us to find Maddie,' said the black dragon. 'I know that this is hard for you, Sable; it is hard for me too, but we must carry on.'

'I know,' she said. 'You don't have to try to persuade me. I'm ready.'

'Millen and Deepblue are of the opinion that...'

'I know what they think. It doesn't matter. We shall go to Olkis today, and do what needs to be done.'

Blackrose tilted her head. 'Thank you, Sable.'

'Let's get a few rules out of the way first.'

'Rules?'

'Yes,' she said. She withdrew the Quadrant from where it had been tucked into her clothes. It had been wiped clean of the blood that had covered it in Ectus, and she gazed at the embedded jewels, and the strange engravings that covered its surface. 'In Lostwell,' she went on, 'I stole one of these, and gave it to you.'

'Yes, but...'

'I hadn't finished. I am aware that I delayed handing it over to you, but the fact remains, that I stole a Quadrant, and gave it to you, so that you could return here, to Dragon Eyre. This cannot be denied. I don't think that you ever actually thanked me for what I did – you were too busy calling me a liar to show any gratitude, but that doesn't bother me. But what I will say is this – I am the sole owner of this new Quadrant. I killed an Ancient to get it, and I will not be handing this one over to you. It is mine; do you understand? I will help you find Maddie, because I promised to, and because Maddie is also my friend. That does not mean that I will be making the Quadrant available to you, to use whenever you feel like it. I have my own plans.'

'What plans?'

'You will see. I will also be keeping my own counsel. Some of our aims are aligned, but not all. Once we have Maddie back, safe and sound, then I will be going my own way. We are not friends, you and I. We never have been. You don't like me, and that's alright; because we are not enemies either. Do not turn me into an enemy, Blackrose. I will not harm your interests, unless you harm mine. Are we agreed?'

'How can I agree, when I do not know what you are planning?'

'Because the alternative is that we do become enemies. However, I promise you that I will leave Ulna alone, if you leave me alone.'

Anger passed over Blackrose's features. 'I accept that the Quadrant is yours,' she said after a while. 'As for the rest, we shall see.'

'That's good enough for me. Shall we go?'

'Now?'

'Yes.'

'Very well, witch. Climb up onto my shoulders.'

Sable glanced up at the back of the dragon. She had been dreading this moment. She had flown on Blackrose's back once before, when they had attacked a Sea Banner vessel before leaving for Yearning. At the time, she had sworn to herself that she would never ride on any other dragon again, apart from Badblood.

'I sense your reluctance,' said Blackrose; 'however, if we arrive above the ocean, you may fall into the sea and drown, and you and the Quadrant would be lost forever. Believe me, I would rather not carry you, but Maddie is the priority, not our own feelings.'

Sable frowned, then pulled herself up onto the black dragon's shoulders. She settled into the saddle, and buckled the straps round her waist, her eyes focussing on the new sections of leather that Millen had stitched into place. He had done a good job, replacing the parts that had been ripped and burnt over the shipyards of Ectus. Sable turned her attention to the Quadrant in her lap. She had never been to Olkis, and would have to make an educated guess about where they would appear.

'Get ready to fly,' she said, then glided her fingers over the copper-coloured surface.

The air shimmered around them, and they appeared high above the ocean. Blackrose fell for a few seconds, her wings extending, then she levelled out.

'Where are we, witch?'

'If you look north, you'll see the coastline of Olkis in the distance,' said Sable. 'I've brought us to the south-western peninsula, exactly where Meader told me that the pirates and dragons live. Fly north, and I'll use my vision to decide where we are going next.'

'Very well.'

'Did you know that I had just learned how to use my powers while remaining connected to Badblood's mind?' she said, as Blackrose sped off to the north. 'Think of what Badblood and I could have achieved together.'

'There is much to regret, witch.'

Sable nodded, but said nothing. She tried to push her feelings to the side, before regret swallowed her whole. Maddie, she thought; she was doing this for Maddie. She allowed her vision to leave her body, and sent it hurtling northwards, outpacing the speed of the black dragon. Her sight reached the ragged cliffs of southern Olkis, then began to cross the high, forested peaks that dominated the south-western peninsula. Tiny villages, surrounded by terraced fields and farms, were dotted across the landscape, by the banks of fast-flowing mountain streams, but she saw no large settlements until her vision reached the northern coast of the peninsula. A huge bay opened up in front of her, full of sharp rocks and hundreds of tiny islets. The Skerries, she thought. It must be Luckenbay. Her sight homed in on a large town nestling within a bay. A few miles to the west of the bay, a tall solitary peak rose up, around which dragons were flying. If the town was Langbeg, then the peak must be Skythorn, she thought to herself.

'Angle a little to the west,' she said to Blackrose. 'Do you have any objections to me placing the location into your mind?'

'Not if it will help.'

Sable entered Blackrose's thoughts, and imprinted an image of the town and mountain into the dragon's mind.

'Have you seen Maddie in this place?' said Blackrose.

'No. That would be too difficult at this range.' She glanced down at the Quadrant. 'Get ready; I'm going to move us a lot closer to the town.'

She moved her fingers across the surface of the device before Blackrose could object. The air shimmered again, and then the town of Langbeg appeared right in front of them. Below, the large harbour was full of ships, and Sable noticed a castle perched on the top of the cliffs to their right. She sent her vision back out, and entered the mind of an armed guard by the gatehouse of the castle. She lingered for a moment, gleaning what she needed from the man's head.

'Take us to the castle,' she said. 'It's called Befallen, and it's where the Osso family lives.'

'The family of the Five Sisters?'

'Yes.'

'Have you seen Maddie?'

'Not yet. Land by the castle, and we'll question someone.'

Blackrose soared over the town. Several humans looked up at them, but there was no sign of alarm or panic. They must be used to seeing dragons overhead, Sable thought, and probably found it difficult to distinguish one black speck in the sky from another. Blackrose swooped over the castle, circled once, then landed in the centre of a large court-yard within its walls. Guards stared at them from the gatehouse, then one shouted, and, within moments, Sable and the black dragon were surrounded. The guards had crossbows, and each man was pointing his weapon at Blackrose.

'Do nothing hasty,' said the black dragon. 'I have not come here to kill anyone, but I shall, if provoked.'

An officer among the guards stepped forwards, his eyes wide. 'I do not recognise you, dragon. Have you come unannounced from Skythorn?'

'I have not,' said Blackrose. 'I have come from Ulna, and am here to seek my rider – Maddie Jackdaw. Have you seen her?'

At once, the colour drained from the officer's face. 'Maddie Jackdaw?'

'That is what I said, human. Is she here?'

'She was,' said the officer, 'but…'

Blackrose's eyes gleamed. 'But what?'

'Please wait here,' he said. 'I shall fetch Lady Adina'osso. She is the only member of the family currently in Befallen. She will be able to tell you what happened.'

The dragon watched as the officer ran into the largest of the three squat towers that ringed the fortress.

'I know what happened,' said Sable. 'I read it out of his mind. They didn't believe Maddie; they thought she was lying about being a rider, and so they decided to sell her into slavery.'

Flames erupted around Blackrose's jaws, and the guards surrounding them edged away.

'Slavery?' roared the dragon. 'I will kill them all!'

'Wait,' said Sable. 'Something went wrong. I think someone might have rescued Maddie. The officer's thoughts were confused.' She unbuckled the straps holding her to the harness, and slipped down to the smooth flagstones. 'His mind was more occupied with the idea that you were about to kill him.'

'Don't move!' cried one of the guards, his crossbow pointed at Sable's chest.

Sable rolled her eyes. She glanced up, and noticed that a large red flag was being raised over the central tower.

'I think we should expect a few more dragons,' she said, lighting a cigarette.

'Why?' said Blackrose.

Sable pointed towards the flag.

'I see,' said the black dragon. 'Very well. I am prepared for all comers.'

A young woman emerged from the largest tower, a cluster of guards around her. Sable glanced at her. She looked nothing like Ann, but Sable could see a trace of Lara in the woman's eyes.

'You must be Dina,' she said.

'I am Adina'osso,' said the woman. 'What do you want?'

'You know what I want,' said Blackrose. 'What have you done with my rider?'

The young woman swallowed. 'It wasn't our fault; I swear it. The dragons of Skythorn told us that Maddie was lying, and we had to go along with their judgement. We had no choice. My father only did what he thought was for the best…'

'He thought that selling my rider into slavery was for the best?' cried Blackrose. 'I should burn this castle to the ground. Where is he?'

'He's not here!' wailed Dina. 'He and my sister Ann set off a couple of days ago. Lara and Tilly overtook the *Giddy Gull*, and stole it, along with your rider. My father is chasing them in Ann's ship.'

'Lara rescued Maddie, eh?' said Sable. 'Where are they going?'

'Back to Ulna,' said Dina. 'They're taking Maddie back to Ulna. They killed my cousin; that's why father is chasing them. They shouldn't have done that. Dax was stupid, but he didn't deserve to die. I thought Lara was going to kill me too, I…'

'Be quiet,' said Blackrose. 'I am going to ask you some simple questions, and you will answer them. First, when was this? When did Lara steal the ship?'

'Four days ago,' said Dina.

'Will your father have caught up with them by now?'

'Not a chance,' said Dina. 'The *Gull* is much quicker than the *Fancy*. If Lara's headed straight for Ulna, he won't catch them until they stop somewhere in the Eastern Rim. Please; I've told you the truth – Lara is taking your rider home.'

Sable smiled. 'I can read minds; you should know that.'

Dina's hands began to shake. 'Are you a god?'

'No. I'm a Holdfast. I can see your part in the sordid little scheme. Lara made you row all the way back to Langbeg, eh? Good for her. And Topaz was involved too, was he?'

'Who is Topaz?' said Blackrose.

'A sailor I met in Throscala. It was his boat that I led Lara to before Alg Bay. According to Dina's memories, she seems to think that Topaz is in love with Maddie. That's why they rescued her. That, and because Lara wanted her ship back.'

'Maddie has an admirer?'

'So it seems.'

'And this Osso girl – is she guilty? Does she deserve to be punished for her part in this?'

Dina fell to her knees. 'Please don't kill me,' she cried. 'I'm sorry.'

A dragon swooped over the castle, then landed in the midst of the courtyard. Blackrose tensed, her claws ready.

'Who are you,' said the strange dragon, 'and what do you want here?'

'It's Queen Blackrose, Redblade,' cried Dina. 'She's come for her rider. Maddie was telling the truth.'

Redblade's eyes widened, and he backed away a step from Blackrose.

'Well?' said Blackrose. 'Is it true? Did you falsely accuse my rider of deceit, leaving her to be sold into slavery?'

Redblade said nothing. His eyes glanced up at the sky, as if hoping more dragons would appear.

'Answer me,' roared Blackrose, 'or I will rip you to shreds and burn Befallen to the ground!'

Redblade lowered his head, and made a whimpering sound. 'Please forgive me.'

Blackrose eyed the young man upon Redblade's shoulders. 'Should I take your rider in exchange?' she said. 'A life for a life? Is your rider precious to you?'

'I am sorry,' said Redblade; 'please don't harm my rider. We made a terrible mistake. We assumed that Maddie must be lying, as she is not from Dragon Eyre. We thought she was an imposter, but we didn't tell Olo'osso to sell her into slavery. We left her fate up to him.'

Blackrose turned to Dina. 'Is this the truth?'

Dina's mouth opened, but no words came out.

'It's true,' said Sable. 'Her father made the decision. The dragons of Skythorn didn't want to take any responsibility for what happened, and Olo'osso wanted Maddie sent far away.'

Blackrose roared in frustration, and flames roiled about her jaws, as her claws ripped up the flagstones of the courtyard.

'Take us back to Haurn!' she bellowed. 'Otherwise, I will kill and burn everything here in this den of snakes.'

'I am so sorry, Queen Blackrose,' said Redblade, his gaze not rising from the ground.

'Do not speak another word, coward,' said the black dragon.

Sable pulled the Quadrant from her cloak and traced her fingers over its surface. The air shimmered, and, in an instant, she was standing next to the scorched circle of earth within the temple complex on Haurn. Next to her was Blackrose, while, still kneeling, was Dina.

Blackrose glanced down at the Osso woman. 'Why did you bring this girl with us, witch?'

Sable shrugged. 'I hadn't finished going through her mind. If we need to search the vast ocean for a tiny ship, then I'll need all the help I can get.'

Dina stared around, her whole body trembling.

Millen emerged from the temple. 'Back already? Where's Maddie?' He squinted at Dina. 'Who's that?'

'Her name's Dina,' said Sable. 'She's one of the Five Sisters, and she's now our hostage.'

An hour later, Sable was sitting at her dining table, playing with Meader's metal lighter. Outside, the sun was reaching its noon peak, and the island was baking in the heat. The thick stone walls of the temple were keeping the interior fairly cool, but Sable wasn't paying attention to the temperature. Instead, her thoughts were going round in circles, as she tried to work out their next move.

Millen appeared at the front door. 'Can I come in?'

Sable nodded.

'I've secured Dina in a room in the next building, where Meader used to stay,' he said, sitting at the table. 'She's not too pleased about being here.'

Sable shrugged.

'What now?' he said.

'I don't know,' she said. 'We have to assume that Lara will have chosen the most efficient route to Ulna, which means that she'll be sailing up by Alef and Wyst. The trouble is my vision doesn't reach as far as there. Shit. I remember trying to locate Ann's ship, after I rescued Lara from jail. It took me almost a month, and I was only searching a limited area of ocean. Dina seems to think that it'll take at least twenty days for Lara to reach Ulna – twenty damn days.'

'The answer seems simple to me,' he said. 'You wait that length of time, and then you take Blackrose to Ulna.'

'I can't sit here idle for twenty days, Millen.'

'You should. I keep telling you that you need some time to sort yourself out, Sable; and events seem to have conspired to grant you that time.'

'Banner reinforcements are arriving in Gyle as we speak. Thousands of them. I need to act.'

Millen nodded. 'And what exactly are you planning to do?'

Sable choked out a bitter-sounding laugh. 'Kill people.'

'Who?'

'All of them.'

'All of whom?'

'Every Banner soldier on Dragon Eyre, every sailor serving in the Sea Banner, and every god that has been sent out from Implacatus.'

Millen blinked. 'What? You can't be serious, Sable.'

'Oh, I forgot to include the Unk Tannic. Every one of those bastards too.'

Millen leaned his elbows on the table, and looked Sable in the eye. 'Listen to me. You, along with Deepblue and Maddie, are pretty much the only friends I have left. I know that you are in pain. Badblood was... well, he was great. I loved him too, you know. Not like you, but I can understand how you're feeling. Maybe, just maybe, it's time to leave Dragon Eyre. This war has nothing to do with us. If you wanted to go home, you know, back to your own world, then take me and Deepblue with you. If we stay here, then nothing good will come of it. Find Maddie, and then take me to meet the rest of your family.'

Sable sparked the lighter, and watched the oil-powered flame flicker in the shadows. 'No.'

'Why not?'

'If I went home, Millen, the rage would follow me. The anger, the pain; all of it. I would take it back with me, and then I would regret it. I can't rest, not until I have my revenge.'

'But, you killed Governor Horace,' he said. 'You killed the god who took Badblood's life.'

'It's not enough.'

'And killing every soldier and sailor would be? I don't get it, Sable.'

'I have a hole in my heart. A hole that is so wide, I think I might fall in and never be able to crawl my way out. I need to fill the hole. I need to fill it with the blood of my enemies. If you want to leave, then that's up to you. I would rather you stayed, so that I have someone to come home to every day, but I'm not going to force you.' She stood. 'I'm going to Alef, to start the search for Lara's ship.'

Millen gazed at her. 'I can't bear to see you like this. It breaks my heart to know the pain you're carrying.'

'It's all my fault, Millen. If I hadn't pushed everyone so hard, then Meader, Evensward and Badblood would still be alive. The dragons of Haurn know the truth – I've seen the way they look at me. You, Deep-blue and Blackrose are too polite to mention it, but I know I'm to blame for everything. It's only right that I try to make up for it. It's what Badblood would want.'

'Is it?'

Sable said nothing. She felt her eyes well, and took the Quadrant out from her clothes.

'Tell Blackrose that I'll be an hour or so,' she said, then activated the device.

The air around her brightened, and she found herself standing on the summit of a low hill, with trees around her, and a view of the shore a hundred yards away. A golden beach stretched out for miles, and a few small vessels were sailing in the distance. She tried to collect her thoughts, to prepare herself for a long vision search of the ocean, but the tears that she had managed to suppress in front of Millen won out, and she sank to her knees on the soft grass, weeping.

Would Badblood want her to bathe in the blood of her enemies? Would he be happy to know the course she had chosen? For all her talk to the contrary, she knew the truth. Badblood would have wanted her to be safe. He would have agreed with Millen, and advised that she go home, to try to find peace.

She hardened her heart and wiped her eyes.

No. There would be no peace for her. She didn't deserve peace. She would fight, and she would kill.

She would kill them all.

CHAPTER 2
MULLING IT OVER

South of Wyst, Eastern Rim – 10ᵗʰ Summinch 5255 (18ᵗʰ Gylean Year 6)

Maddie smiled as the warm breeze brushed her face. She took a deep breath of ocean air, as her hands gripped the side railing of the *Giddy Gull*. Behind her, the crew was busy. Some were high up in the rigging of the sails, while others were doing things that made little sense to Maddie. She didn't care – on days as beautiful as this one was, she was happy just to be alive.

Lara appeared at the top of the bow hatch, and was followed out to the main deck by the ship's bosun. She noticed Maddie standing by the bow, and walked up to her.

'Another five or six days of sailing, Miss Jackdaw,' Lara said, 'and we'll be nearing Ulna.'

'Is that all?' said Maddie. 'The days have flitted past so quickly on board. Alef went by in a blur, and we're at Wyst already. I'm looking forward to being back in Ulna, but I'll miss the *Giddy Gull*.'

Lara shrugged. 'It's not like you'll never see us again. As long as you make sure Blackrose doesn't eat us, then I intend to sail the *Gull* in Ulnan waters for quite a while. Tilly and I can't go back to Langbeg, not for a year or two. That goes for Topaz, too.' She grinned. 'So, how are you and my master getting along? That was a rhetorical question, by the way. It's a small ship – I know fine well what's been happening; or, what's not been happening, if you catch my drift. You've been leaving the poor lad all frustrated.'

Maddie frowned. 'That's none of your business.'

'It's my ship, little lady; everything that happens on the *Gull* is my bleeding business. So, what's up? Do you not like him?'

'I like him.'

'Then why haven't you even kissed him?'

Maddie's face went red. 'I'm not ready.'

Lara laughed, long and hard. 'Dear gods. What's a boy got to do, eh? If you ain't careful, you'll end up being friends.'

'I want to be his friend.'

Lara pulled a face.

'I want to get to know him first, that's all,' Maddie went on. 'And I don't care what you, or anyone else, thinks. I do like him, but I'm worried about making a mistake.'

'You should see if he's any good in bed. That'll give you more of an idea.'

'I can't.'

'Why not?'

'Well, for starters, everyone on board would know. As you've pointed out, nothing remains a secret on a ship, and I can't stand the thought of everyone looking at me, and judging me. And, I feel... Malik's ass; what's wrong with me? Anyway, I feel like, if I sleep with him, then my heart will be his. I don't do casual relationships. I'm not like Sable. I want love, and commitment, and I don't know if I'm ready.'

'Gods above, Maddie; we're not talking marriage or anything. And, what did you mean about Sable? Does she have a habit of jumping into bed with strangers?'

Maddie hesitated, remembering that Tilly had told her that Lara had been involved with Sable.

'I see,' said Lara, her eyes darkening.

'Sable's impulsive,' said Maddie. 'But, in all the time I've known her, she's only slept with two guys, not including you, obviously. And both of those were strictly one time only. Do you, ummm, do you still have feelings for her?'

Lara shrugged. 'I don't know. She broke my heart when she sent me back to Ann, and it took me a while to get over it. I don't know what I'll feel if I see her again.'

'You're quite similar to her, in some ways,' said Maddie.

'Enough about Sable,' she said. 'We were talking about you and Topaz.'

'Does he speak to you about me?'

'You're joking, yeah? He never shuts up about you. Maddie this; Maddie that; it does my bleeding head in. Gods know what will happen if you actually kiss the lad. His damn head might explode. Anyway, I'm heading up to the quarter deck. We'll need to stop off at Wyst for a bit, to refresh our water supplies.'

'I thought dragons controlled Wyst; dragons who hate humans.'

'Oh yeah, that's true. However, there are a few coves where they let us anchor for water. We don't bother them; they don't bother us. It's a useful agreement. Come on.'

She turned for the stern of the ship, and Maddie followed her, keeping her steps in time with the rise and fall of the ocean swell. Far off to their left, the coastline of Wyst was a hazy blur of grey in the distance, and Maddie's thoughts went to the thousands of wild dragons who called the island their home. They reached the quarter deck, where Tilly was speaking to Vitz and Topaz, who were standing by the wheel. Topaz's eyes met Maddie's gaze, and they both glanced away. Lara laughed, and shook her head.

'We're going to be pulling in to Wyst,' she said. 'Master, take us closer to the coast; there's a small cove a few miles away, where we can collect fresh water.'

'Yes, Captain,' said Topaz. 'Vitz, we'll need the top sail on the mizzen brought down, then I'll tack thirty degrees to the east.'

Vitz saluted. 'Yes, sir.'

The young man ran off, racing down to the main deck.

'I'm glad we kept that lad,' said Lara. 'If only all settlers were as accommodating as him, eh?'

'I still think he'd run if he had the chance,' said Tilly. 'He's a farmer at heart.'

'He won't run, ma'am,' said Topaz. 'He's got nowhere to run to.'

Tilly narrowed her eyes. 'And what about you? You're not thinking of jumping ship when we get to Ulna, are you?' She nodded in Maddie's direction. 'You wouldn't be the first sailor to desert over a woman.'

'If he did,' said Lara, 'then we'd know where to find him.'

'I'm the master of the *Gull*,' he said. 'I ain't deserting, ma'am. But, I'd like some time ashore when we arrive at Udall; if that's alright with Maddie.'

'That's fine with me,' she said, trying to ignore her embarrassment. She hated when others were present when she was with Topaz, especially when both Tilly and Lara were wearing smirks on their faces.

'Old Ryan's going to be disappointed,' said Lara. 'Are the days of you two cruising the brothels over, eh?'

'You never told me that you went to brothels,' said Maddie.

Lara laughed, as the red on Topaz's cheeks deepened.

'He's a randy sailor,' said Tilly. 'What else would you expect?'

'I have never paid for a woman in a brothel,' Topaz said. 'We went to that place in Pangba because it was safe, and they had good food. Ask Ryan, if you like.'

'I will,' said Lara.

'I was talking to Maddie, ma'am.'

'You know,' said Lara, 'Ryan was asking me if we could collect some fresh timber supplies from Wyst when we stopped. I was thinking of sending a team out to cut down a tree or two. You can go with them, Maddie, so you can question Ryan about Topaz's brothel activities. Deal?'

'Will it be safe?' she said.

Lara shrugged. 'From who; Ryan? Probably. Tilly, you should tag along, to keep an eye on them.'

'I ain't your bleeding lieutenant,' said Tilly.

'Did I say you were? Dear gods; fine. Tilly, darling, would you please be a dear and accompany the landing party ashore? I would be frightfully grateful.'

Tilly smiled. 'Yeah, alright.'

Lara rolled her eyes. 'I cannot wait until you get your own ship again; then you and the lads from the *Sneak* can finally get off my *Gull*. Hey, what are you going to do about a master? You ain't taking Topaz.'

Tilly frowned. 'Can I have Vitz?'

'You can have Vitz, if I can have your cook.'

'Hmm, I dunno,' said Tilly. 'My boys might mutiny if they had to eat the slops your cook produces. We needn't worry about it, though; there are bound to be willing volunteers in Udall, if, you know, Blackrose doesn't kill us all as soon as we arrive.'

'That's if she's even there,' said Lara. 'I've heard many stories about dragons who ended up searching the world for their missing rider. Maddie, do you think Blackrose will be looking for you?'

'I don't know,' she said. 'I guess I'd like to think so, but she has a realm to rule; her queendom of Ulna. That's probably kept her busy. She also had lots of suitors trying to mate with her, and the deadline for that passed a while ago. She might have a new husband by now.'

'She'll be looking for you,' said Topaz. 'Dragons can't function without their riders. She won't be interested in her realm, or by any suitors; not until she's found you.'

Maddie smiled. 'Thank you for saying that. I hope you're right, but I also hope that Blackrose isn't too upset. If she is in Ulna, then let me talk to her before you march into Udall. I'll make sure she understands that you helped me.'

Tilly glanced down. 'I might hide in the hold while that's happening. If Blackrose is looking for revenge, it'll be me she picks. Lara will be the hero, and I'll be the villain.'

'You nearly got blown up on the *Little Sneak* trying to save me from slavery, Tilly,' said Maddie. 'You'll be fine.'

'As long as we're all honest with the dragon,' said Topaz; 'that's the important thing. We'll be alright if we tell her the truth.'

Vitz appeared back on the quarter deck, and Topaz leaned over to pass on a few more instructions to the master's mate. Maddie watched them for a moment, then turned to gaze out over the sea. The coastline of Wyst was much closer, and she could make out a series of narrow inlets, where rivers rushed down from the mountains and ragged cliffs.

Lara pointed at a cove. 'That's the one, Master. Take us in there.'

Several hours later, Maddie was standing by Tilly on a narrow stretch of golden beach. The *Giddy Gull's* rowing boat had been hauled up onto the sand, and sailors were unloading a collection of empty barrels next to a small stream that led into the ocean. Ryan was rubbing his chin as he gazed at the treeline a few dozen yards ahead of them, while a small team was waiting next to a pile of rope, saws and axes.

'Pine and spruce,' muttered Ryan. 'Not ideal, but it'll do. One of each, lads, I reckon.'

He strode off towards the edge of the forest, and his team picked up their tools and followed him.

'I'll wait here,' said Tilly, 'and make sure the water barrels are filled. You go with Ryan, Maddie.'

Maddie nodded, then tramped over the beach, her sandals filling with sand. She entered the forest, and felt the humidity increase under the burning sun. Ryan was wandering around, eying the trees, then he pointed at one that had been blown over by a recent storm.

'This one first, lads,' he said. 'Knock the branches off, then rig it up to the ropes and we'll drag it back down to the beach.'

His team nodded, then Ryan lit a cigarette as they started to work in the heat. He glanced at Maddie.

'Smoke?' he said.

'No, thanks.'

He smiled. 'So, I guess you're here for a reason, eh? Did Captain Lara put you up to this? Did she tell you to interrogate me about Topaz, eh? Well, you're going to be disappointed, because I don't tell tales about my mates. However, I do have a few questions for you, Miss Jackdaw.'

Maddie's face flushed. 'You do?'

'Aye; I do. Like, what's the deal, eh? I hear you've been holding out on the lad. I hope you ain't leading him on.'

'I just want to get to know him a bit better before I... you know.'

'But you do like him?'

She nodded.

Ryan frowned. 'Just as well. He's given up everything for you. He illegally commandeered the *Sneak*, and then he disobeyed orders and boarded the *Gull*, and then, worst of all, he goes and kills Olo'osso's damn nephew.'

'You're hardly innocent,' she said. 'You disabled the *Gull's* rudder.'

'That is correct. But, I did that to force the *Gull* to stop, so that the survivors of the *Sneak* could be picked up. My offence is forgivable. Killing Dax? Not so much. I've heard Captain Lara talk about lying low for a year, as if she thinks it'll all blow over, but the chances of that are exactly nil. There's no way that Olo'osso is going to forgive Topaz for killing Dax. Not a bleeding chance. He's burned his bridges – for you.'

Maddie glanced down at the floor of the forest, unsure how to respond. She had intended to ask Ryan about Topaz, expecting to learn a few nuggets about his personality, but, instead, it was Ryan who was grilling her.

'He saved me from being sold as a slave,' she said.

'That he did, miss,' said Ryan, his eyes on the sailors as they hacked off the limbs of the fallen pine. 'And now he's waiting patiently, for you to make up your damn mind.'

'Has he... has he had many girlfriends?'

Ryan squinted at her. 'Did you not hear what I said before? I ain't spilling any gossip about Topaz. That lad has a heart of gold, and if you mess him around, then you'll have me to deal with. Tell me, what will happen when you're reunited with your dragon, eh? I ain't never heard of any rider who had the time for both a dragon and a human in their lives. What will Blackrose think about it all? Have you thought of that? What if she forbids it?'

'She wouldn't do that.'

'Yeah? Are you sure? Dragons can get very jealous, and Blackrose is a bleeding queen. What will her royal court think about her rider shacking up with a common sailor, eh?'

'Most of the dragons in Ulna already think very little of me, because I'm not from Dragon Eyre. Quite a few tried to persuade Blackrose to abandon me.'

Ryan stubbed out his cigarette. 'Maybe she has. How long have you been parted for?'

'About three months.'

'Well, if she has abandoned you, at least you'll be free to see Topaz, eh? Otherwise, I can't see it working out, if I'm honest. Topaz will be at sea, while you'll be in Udall.'

'If you're trying to depress me, it's working.'

He shrugged. 'I'm just looking at the practicalities.' He gestured to his team. 'Right, lads; that's enough. Rope up the trunk and haul it back to the beach. We'll chop it up down there.'

The sailors nodded, sweat dripping from each of them. They secured the long trunk with the ropes they had brought, and began dragging it from the forest. Ryan set off after them, pausing to pick up an axe that had been left behind. Maddie stayed where she was, trying to think through what Ryan had told her. If any relationship with Topaz was doomed before it had even started, then it would be better to tell him that; to let him down before it got out of hand. She wished she could be more like Sable. The Holdfast woman would have already slept with Topaz, if she had been in the same situation; she leapt into things without any concerns for the consequences, while Maddie hesitated, trying to weigh up every possible scenario before committing herself. Was this why she had always failed to find anyone? As she had told Lara, she couldn't cope with casual relationships. She wanted love, and that meant she had to be careful about whom she opened her heart to. If she was reckless, then she would be hurt. She liked Topaz, and had found nothing so far about him that put her off. If she turned from him now, then she would be sad, but she would get over it. She tried to imagine what it would be like to sit in the palace in Udall while he was away sailing; how often would she be able to see him? What if Lara decided to move the *Giddy Gull* further from Ulna? What if she decided to go back to Olkis?

'Hey!' cried Tilly from the edge of the forest. 'Get your ass down here, Maddie.'

Maddie trudged back to the beach, where the sailors were all staring upwards. She glanced at the sky, and saw three dragons overhead.

'What's going on?' she asked Tilly.

'I'm not sure,' she said. 'The Wyst dragons never usually come this close.' She turned to the sailors. 'Keep working! Get the full barrels on the boat; come on.'

One of the dragons started to descend, and Ryan's team scattered as it landed next to the stripped tree trunk. The dragon stared at the sailors.

Tilly stepped forward. 'Greetings, dragon,' she said. 'We just stopped off for some water and timber.'

'I can see what you are doing, insect,' said the dragon. 'It must cease, immediately.'

'I thought we had an agreement,' said Tilly. 'We're not doing any harm.'

'The agreement is over, insect,' said the dragon. 'Things have changed in the Eastern Rim. The only reason that I have not incinerated you all is that I assume you are unaware of these changes. The Sea Banner and the settlers from Implacatus have fled Geist and Enna, and the dragons of Wyst are reclaiming what was ours in times past. There will be no more cooperation with human sea-going vessels. You have five minutes to get off the beach, or you will die.'

Tilly's eyes widened. 'But, without the fresh water of Wyst, the voyage from Olkis to the Eastern Rim will be almost impossible.'

'That is not our concern, insect. You now have four minutes.'

'Get those damn barrels loaded!' cried Tilly to the sailors. 'Quickly. Petty Officer Ryan, abandon the timber and get into the boat with your team.'

Ryan frowned. 'But...'

'But nothing!' shouted Tilly. 'Move!'

Maddie approached the dragon. 'May I ask something?'

The dragon regarded her, but said nothing.

'Is Blackrose in Ulna?' Maddie said. 'Do you know that?'

'The Queen of Ulna is absent from her realm,' said the dragon. 'Three minutes.'

'Where is she?' Maddie said.

'I know not, and care not. Why would her location be of interest to a mere insect?'

'I'm her rider.'

The dragon laughed. 'Is that so? You foolish girl – you shall be remaining here, I think. The Queen of Ulna is absent because she is searching the entire world for you. She would pay dearly to have you back. Yes; you shall make a most useful hostage.'

The dragon reached out with a giant forelimb to snatch Maddie, but she was shoved to the side before the talons could reach her. Maddie fell to the sand, then looked up to see Ryan standing over her, the axe in his hands.

'Stay clear of her, lizard,' he said; 'or I'll chop your bleeding claws off.'

'How dare you?' roared the dragon, rearing up.

The sailors on the beach paused, each one of them staring at Ryan standing up to the dragon.

'Everyone,' whispered Tilly; 'back away, slowly. Get into the boat.'

'I should render you all to ash for this impertinence,' cried the dragon.

'Our ship has pisspots and ballistae,' said Tilly. 'You told us to leave, and we're leaving. You wouldn't want to break your word, now, would you? Dragons don't break their word, or so I heard. Ryan, lower the axe, and escort Miss Jackdaw to the boat, if you please.'

The dragon stared at them as they edged back across the sand. Ryan helped Maddie to her feet, and pushed her towards the rowing boat, making sure he kept himself between her and the dragon. Maddie got into the boat along with the sailors, and sat between two full barrels. Tilly was the last to board, walking backwards across the sand away from the dragon. As soon as she stepped into the boat, two sailors pushed it into the water with long oars, and they began rowing back towards the *Giddy Gull*.

'Holy shit, Ryan,' muttered one of the sailors, as they moved away from the coast. 'You coulda got us all killed, mate.'

Ryan shrugged. 'Better dead than having to tell Topaz that we let a dragon take his missus.'

'Thank you,' said Maddie.

Ryan eyed her. 'Maybe you shouldn't tell all and sundry that you're Blackrose's rider, eh? Shit on a stick; I could do with a drink after that. My bleeding hands are shaking.'

'We'll break out the gin when we're back on the *Gull*, lads,' said Tilly. 'I think we all need a drink.'

'This is outrageous,' said Lara, as she stood by the railings of the quarter deck. The three dragons were circling overhead, watching the *Gull* as it prepared to sail.

Tilly sighed. 'It is what it is, sister. Damn Wyst, and damn dragons. This is going to make any return voyage to the Western Rim tricky.'

'Maybe things will have changed again in a year or two,' said Maddie.

Lara frowned at her. 'And I hear you were almost kidnapped. Again.'

'Yeah. Sorry about that.'

'Worse,' said Tilly; 'Blackrose ain't on Ulna. That dragon said she was away, searching the world for little old Maddie.'

The lead dragon swooped down towards the quarter deck, then

hovered above their heads, his enormous wings covering the deck in shadows.

'This was your final warning, insects,' he called down to them. 'If you return to Wyst, your ship will be destroyed the moment any of you step ashore. Pass on this message to any other ships you encounter. Do you understand?'

'We understand,' cried Lara. 'Now, piss off.'

The dragon eyed the captain for a moment, then soared away to join his colleagues.

'We have enough water to get to Geist,' said Lara, watching the dragons continue to circle overhead. 'We'll have to collect more there.'

'When Tilly abducted me,' said Maddie, 'Blackrose was on Geist. She was there because the Wyst dragons were claiming the island as their own. We might have the same problem when we get there.'

'Wyst has wanted to get their hands on Geist for centuries,' said Lara. 'They seem to think it belongs to them, but the Sea Banner kept them from making any moves. Tens of thousands of humans live on Geist, even after we exclude the settlers who have apparently all fled. If the Wyst dragons have moved in, there could be carnage. We should be prepared for the worst.'

She and Tilly looked at each other, their expressions grim. Maddie glanced over at Topaz, who was on the wheel, talking to Vitz. She walked across the quarter deck, and Topaz nodded to Vitz, who got the message and went down to the main deck.

'I heard all about it,' Topaz said to Maddie as she reached his side. 'Good old Ryan.'

'He was very brave.'

Topaz nodded. 'Did you ask him about the brothels, then?'

'No.'

'I thought that's what you were going to do?'

'That's what I had planned to do, but Ryan had other ideas.'

'He did, did he? I dread to ask, but what kind of ideas?'

'Oh, the kind where he thinks our relationship is doomed. He doesn't see how it could work.'

Topaz's face fell. 'I see. Do you agree with him?'

'Do you?'

'No. Ryan is many things, but he ain't an expert on relationships. He's grand at picking up girls, but they never last. The lad doesn't know how to commit.'

'Are you not fed up with me by now? I've made you wait all this time while I try to decide what to do.'

'I've waited all my life for someone like you to come along, Maddie. I can wait a little longer.'

'I'm not sure I can manage a relationship with Blackrose, and one with you at the same time. I want to think I can, but it's all so complicated. Why is it so complicated?'

'I come off duty in an hour,' he said. 'Let's grab something to eat and talk about it.' He frowned. 'In the meantime, I'd better stay clear of Ryan. There are a few things I'd like to say to him about sticking his nose where it don't belong.'

CHAPTER 3
PATIENCE

West of Geist, Eastern Rim – 12th Summinch 5255 (18th Gylean Year 6)

Maddie glanced up from her breakfast bowl. 'Seven?'

Topaz nodded. 'Yeah.'

'Your mother sold you when you were seven?'

'That's right. She didn't have enough money to feed me and the rest of my brothers and sisters, so one of us had to go. I was lucky, though.'

Maddie pulled a face. 'Lucky? It doesn't sound lucky.'

'I could have been sold as a slave, but I was picked up by a ship's captain instead, and impressed into his service. Of course, it meant that I never saw my mum again.'

'Would you want to after that?'

He put his feet up onto a wooden chest and lit a cigarette. 'I don't know. I sometimes wonder how my brothers and sisters are getting along. They were all younger than me – two sisters and two brothers, from three different dads. I can't risk making contact with them, though. I assume they still live in Nankiss, and it's too dangerous for me to go there. I have a price on my head.'

Maddie blinked. 'You do?'

'Yeah. It's not as much as the bounty for Lara – she's got the highest price out of the Five Sisters, and she loves to let the others know about it. I figure that if my mum was prepared to sell me for a handful of gold coins when I was little, then she wouldn't hesitate to hand me over to the Banner for a thousand.'

'What about your father?'

'My old dad was a drunken waste of space. Well, that's what I remember; I hardly ever saw him. When I was put onto the captain's ship, after he bought me, I tried to forget all about my past. It wasn't too difficult, as I was kept busy for years. I started off as the captain's servant; you know, making his meals, polishing his boots, and doing his laundry, and then I was sent up into the rigging to learn the trade. When I was about thirteen, the captain started giving me more responsibilities, and sometimes let me take the wheel if the master was sick, or too drunk. It was a good life, and then, one day, when we were sailing out of Luckenbay, we were stopped by the Sea Banner.' He shook his head. 'It was the worst day of my life. The bastards picked me and a few others, and made me swear an oath to the Sea Banner. The next thing I know, I have a shackle round my ankle and I'm working for the damn occupation forces.'

Maddie coughed.

Topaz raised an eyebrow. 'The smoke getting to you?'

'A little bit. This cabin isn't exactly very big.'

He stubbed out the cigarette in an ashtray. 'People are going to gossip.'

'Why? We're only having breakfast.'

'Yeah, but we're in my cabin, alone. You know what sailors are like.'

'Have you spoken to Ryan about what he said?'

Topaz nodded. 'He was unrepentant. I guess he thinks he's looking out for me, but he needs to remember that I can make my own decisions.'

'I wonder what Blackrose will think of you.'

'Is she the jealous type?'

'I'm not sure. I do know her well, but I've never had a boyfriend since I became her rider, so I don't know how she'll react.'

He smiled. 'Is that what I am – your boyfriend?'

'Hardly,' she said. 'I mean, we haven't even kissed.'

'I'd like to, though. I dream about kissing you. You have extremely kissable lips.'

Maddie's cheeks reddened a little. Topaz suppressed a sigh. He longed for physical contact with her, and had been tempted many times to throw caution to the wind, take her in his arms and kiss her, but knew it would be a mistake. Maddie seemed to be evaluating him as if she were a prospective captain trying out a new ship. It was a massive investment, and you had to be completely sure before you signed the contract. Maybe Ryan was right; maybe he was deluding himself that he and Maddie could ever be happy together.

'Let's wait until we get to Udall,' she said. 'The *Giddy Gull* is your home, and the crew are like your extended family. That's it – that's what it's like. I'm in the midst of your massive family, who are all staring at me to see if I'll break your heart. I can feel their eyes following me wherever I go, and it makes me uncomfortable. It'll be different in Udall.'

'That's only three days away.'

She nodded. 'Have you ever been to Udall?'

'Ulna was crawling with greenhides the last time I saw it. The Sea Banner used to avoid the island, but I've seen the coast from a distance. What will you do if Blackrose isn't there when we arrive?'

'That's the big question, isn't it? It depends on who is running Ulna, I suppose. I hope it's Greysteel – he was one of the few dragons on Ulna who seemed to like me. On the other hand, the Unk Tannic were digging their claws into Udall just before I was taken away. If they're in charge, then there could be trouble.'

'Were there many of them?'

'A few dozen, I think.'

'Weapons?'

'Yes; crossbows.'

'We could probably subdue them, if it came to it. The *Gull's* armed to the teeth.'

'You'll need to watch out for Ata'nix; he was their leader.'

Topaz squinted at her. 'Ata'nix was on Ulna?'

Maddie nodded. 'Do you know him?'

'You could say that. A story for another time; I'd better get to work.'

They stood up in the cramped cabin, and Topaz collected the used bowls and mugs.

'Thanks for breakfast,' she said.

He gazed down at her face, startled by how beautiful she was. He tried to think of something else.

She opened the door to the cabin, and they walked out onto the lower deck. The night watch were getting settled into their hammocks, while a few hushed conversations were taking place. Several sailors turned to glance at Topaz and Maddie, but no one said anything to them. Topaz avoided eye contact, then dropped the crockery off at the cook's bench, and headed for the aft hatch. They climbed the steep stairs, and emerged onto the main deck, the morning sunlight dazzling after the shadows of the lower deck. Off the port bow, the coastline of Geist was visible, and a blustery wind from the north-west was guiding them closer to the shores. Topaz took a second to marvel at the speed the *Gull* could achieve in such perfect conditions. They must be travelling at close to fourteen knots, he guessed; almost twice the speed of the old *Tranquillity*.

Maddie stood by him as he gazed along the side of the ship.

'You like all this, don't you?' she said.

He nodded. 'I love it. It sounds stupid, but sometimes I think my mum did me a massive favour. If I'd stayed in Nankiss, I would have lived the rest of my childhood in poverty, fighting for scraps in the slums, while bombs went off every other day. She saved me from that life.'

'It's a funny way to look at it, but maybe you're right. If things do work out between us, you're not going to give up being a sailor, are you? I mean, if you love it, then I wouldn't want you to give it up for me. But, how would it work? You'd be away sailing all the time, while I'd be wandering the halls of the palace, waiting for you to get back.'

'I wouldn't be away all of the time. When we have a good place to base ourselves, we only sail for one day out of every three. I would be in Udall for two-thirds of the time.'

She nodded. 'That still doesn't sound ideal.'

He glanced over his shoulder, and saw Vitz on the quarter deck, waiting to be relieved.

'I'd best go,' he said. 'Being late for the start of your shift is unforgivable. I'll see you around, yeah?'

'Alright,' she said.

He left her by the railings, and hurried up onto the quarter deck.

'What bleeding time do you call this, Master?' said Lara. 'Poor Vitz has been waiting for nigh on five minutes.'

'Sorry, Captain; sorry Vitz.'

He took over his place at the wheel.

'It's alright, sir,' said Vitz, stepping away. 'We heard you had Maddie in your cabin, and...'

'Stop right there, lad,' said Topaz.

Lara cackled. 'Well? Give us the juicy details, Master.'

'Sure,' said Topaz, whispering. 'Come closer.'

Lara and Vitz leaned in.

'Are you ready for this?' said Topaz.

'Get on with it,' said Lara.

'Alright; if you're sure you want to hear about it. We were in my cabin, right?'

'Come on!' cried Lara. 'Tell us!'

'And then,' Topaz went on, 'and then, we had breakfast.'

Lara frowned. 'And?'

'That's it. We had breakfast.'

'I should slap you across the face, you miserable bastard,' muttered Lara. 'You were getting my hopes up.'

Vitz rolled his eyes. 'I'm going for a kip, sir, ma'am.'

'Come five minutes late for the next watch, lad,' said Topaz. 'I owe you that much.'

Vitz saluted, then left the quarter deck.

Topaz glanced at Lara. 'What are your orders, Captain?'

'I take it that you are familiar with Geist?'

'Yes, ma'am. Our frigate often stopped there.'

'I confess that I've never been to any of the harbours on the island. They were always packed with Sea Banner. Where would be a good place to stop for water? Ideally, it'll be a small, out-of-the-way location. Definitely not one of the bigger towns.'

'The northern coast sounds like the best bet,' he said. 'I guess it depends on what the Wyst dragons are up to down here.'

'Take us to wherever you think most suitable.'

Topaz nodded. He spotted a young midshipman, and called him up onto the quarter deck.

'Get me a chart of northern Geist, Middie,' he said.

The midshipman saluted. 'Yes, sir.'

Topaz turned the wheel as the midshipman ran off. He glanced up at the wind pennant, and made a few calculations in his head.

'Belay that,' said Lara.

'Ma'am?'

Lara pointed in the direction of the port bow. In the distance, four dark specks were closing with the ship, soaring through the blue sky towards them.

'Shit,' he muttered.

Lara strode to the front of the quarter deck. 'Battle stations!' she yelled. 'Unwrap the ballistae!'

Tilly emerged from a cabin behind the wheel, her eyes wide. She glanced at Lara and Topaz, then turned and saw the approaching dragons.

'You take the ballistae,' Lara said to her; 'I'll command from up here.'

Tilly nodded, then raced down to the main deck and began shouting out orders.

'Master,' said Lara, 'angle us back to the south-east. Let's not make it look as though we want to close with the coast.'

Topaz turned the wheel again. 'Yes, ma'am.'

'Shit, shit, shit,' Lara muttered. 'Why can't those bastards just leave us alone?' She turned towards Tilly. 'No loosing except on my express command, sister.'

'Got it,' Tilly yelled back.

Lara paced the quarter deck as the dragons got closer. They circled over the *Giddy Gull* a few times, then one of them descended, until it was hovering alongside the ship.

'Where is the captain of this vessel?' the dragon said, its voice booming out.

'I'm up here,' said Lara, raising her arm.

The dragon turned its head to stare at her. 'I am here to ensure you do not attempt to dock in Geist, insect. The realm is now under the authority of Wyst, and no humans are welcome here.'

'What about the humans who live on Geist?' said Lara.

'They are in the process of being removed,' said the dragon. 'Can you take any?'

'No,' said Lara. 'My ship has already collected the survivors from another vessel, and we're full up.'

'Very well. Continue on your present course. If you turn towards Geist, you will be attacked. There will be no more warnings.'

'This is ridiculous,' cried Lara. 'Geist doesn't belong to Wyst.'

'You are mistaken, insect. Geist has always been ours; we are merely reclaiming what was lost.'

'How are we supposed to get fresh water?'

'Go to Ulna, insect. Enna is also out of bounds to your kind. Go to Ulna, and be thankful that we have allowed you to live this day.'

The dragon soared back up into the sky. Two of its colleagues turned, and headed back towards Geist, while the other two continued to circle overhead.

Lara shook her fist at them, as Tilly bounded up onto the quarter deck.

'Cut the water ration in half,' Lara said. 'Effective immediately. We'll have to eke out what's left of the supplies until we get to Ulna. The rest of the water is for drinking only.'

'Shit,' said Tilly. 'We're all going to be a little thirsty by the time we get to Udall.'

———

For the next few hours, the mood on the *Giddy Gull* was sombre. The news of the cut in water rations had quickly spread among the crew, and many were staring at the coast of Geist in the distance, or cursing the presence of the two dragons overhead, who were continuing to shadow them as they pulled out of Geistian waters. Topaz could remember many times he and Ryan had enjoyed shore leave on the island. The Sea Banner had been detested by the locals, but there had been plenty of settlers around, and the facilities on the bases had always been welcoming. He wondered how the locals now felt about the withdrawal of the occupation forces. So many dragons had been slaughtered in the two decades of war, that the Wystians now outnumbered all of the other dragons on the Eastern Rim put together, and without the military might of the Sea Banner to restrain them, they were free to roam far and wide, and take whatever they pleased.

The sun was halfway down the western sky, when a sailor atop the rigging let out a cry.

'Ship off the starboard bow!' he yelled. 'Two miles and closing!'

Lara glanced up, her eyes squinting into the distance.

'Sea Banner?' she shouted up to the rigging.

'No, Captain. A merchant vessel.'

She glanced at Topaz. 'Set a course to intercept, Master. They might have water that we can, eh, buy.'

'Yes, ma'am.'

She disappeared into her cabin, then emerged a moment later, carrying the long eye-glass. She lifted it to her face, and peered through the lens.

'Some clinker-built piece of shit,' she muttered. 'Slow and sluggish. Damn it. I was hoping it might be suitable for Tilly, but I think she'd rather die than captain such a shitty vessel.' She lowered the eye-glass.

'We're going about three times its speed; we should catch up with it soon.'

Topaz summoned a midshipman, and plotted out their new course. It took less than half an hour to draw close to the old merchant vessel. Its crew had given up trying to outpace the *Giddy Gull*, and were standing on the deck with sullen expressions, as Topaz guided the brigantine alongside. Tilly organised the ropes, and the merchant ship was secured to the side of the *Gull*. Above, the two dragons were still circling overhead, but they made no move to intervene.

Lara rubbed her hands together, as she stood before Tilly and a small group of a dozen armed pirates.

'Right, lads; let's be quick about this. We'll take their water supplies, and any spare food and booze. I want the ship's captain brought over to the *Gull* as a hostage while we take a look around. Tilly, you are in command of the operation. No unnecessary deaths; let's keep this clean.'

Tilly nodded, then led the sailors towards the main deck. They jumped aboard the merchant ship, and Topaz watched as they took over the smaller vessel. After a few moments, two of the sailors escorted a man over to the quarter deck of the *Gull*.

Lara eyed him. 'I presume you are the captain of that shit-bucket?'

'This is an act of piracy, madam,' he cried.

Lara laughed. 'No kidding? Are you going to tell the Sea Banner? Twat. Right; what's your cargo?'

The man said nothing, his eyes betraying his nerves.

'We're going to find it anyway,' said Lara; 'so you're as well to tell me.'

'I refuse to comply with this criminal act.'

Lara slapped him across the face. 'You will refer to me as "captain"; got it?'

Tilly appeared on the quarter deck of the smaller ship.

'There's no spare water,' she called over to Lara. 'None worth drinking, anyway; their supplies are rank.'

'What are they carrying?' Lara shouted back.

'Refugees from Geist,' Tilly cried. 'There's a ton of them in the hold, packed like ship's biscuits in a tub. Women, children, you name it. It bleeding well reeks down there. There's no food, no water, and no sanitation. The refugees claim that the captain charged them a fortune in gold, and then crammed them below decks with the rats.'

'Have you found the gold?'

'I have, sister; a whole chest, full of the stuff.'

Lara turned back to the captain of the merchant vessel. 'Well?'

The man said nothing. Beads of sweat appeared on his brow.

'That's terrible,' said Maddie, arriving on the quarter deck. 'Those poor people.'

'Where were you taking them?' Lara asked the captain, who, again, did not respond. 'Are you refusing to answer me, you little prick? Right, that's it.' She glanced back at her sister. 'Tilly,' she shouted; 'you are now in command of the merchant vessel. I'm keeping its captain under arrest on the *Gull* until we get to Ulna. Give the gold back to the refugees, and make sure they have food and water; we'll escort them to Udall.'

Tilly blinked. 'Eh, alright. I'll need a few more crew.'

'Take your lads from the *Sneak*,' Lara said. 'Has that piece of crap got a name?'

'It's called *Patience*,' Tilly said. 'Presumably, someone had a bleeding sense of humour when they named it. I'll start transferring the crew now.'

Lara waved in response, then turned to the two pirates guarding the smaller vessel's captain.

'Take this asshole below deck and lock him in a tiny cupboard. Let's see how he likes it.'

The sailors saluted, then hauled the captain away.

Maddie beamed. 'You did a good thing, Lara.'

'Shut up,' muttered Lara. 'Why does everyone act all amazed when they discover I'm not a complete bitch?'

Topaz laughed.

Good afternoon. Words cannot express how relieved I am to finally track you down. Do you have any idea how difficult it is to find a ship on the ocean?

Topaz jumped, his eyes widening in fright.

I'm sure you can guess who this is, Topaz.

'Sable, is that you?'

You don't need to say it out loud; I'm in your damn head.

Maddie turned to him. 'What did you say?'

Answer her. Tell her that we're on our way. We'll be a minute or so.

The voice disappeared.

'Maddie asked you a question,' said Lara. 'Have you got something to say, Master, or are you just talking to yourself again?'

Topaz blinked. 'Sable Holdfast was in my head.'

'When?' said Maddie. 'Now?'

He nodded. 'Yeah; just a moment ago. She said I was to tell you that "we are on our way". I don't know who she meant by "we", though. Blackrose?'

'Sable's coming here?' said Lara.

'That's what she said, Captain. In a minute or so, apparently.'

Maddie glanced up at the sky, and the others did the same. The two dragons who had been following them since Geist were still circling above the ships. Lara stared upwards for a moment, then strode to the edge of the quarter deck.

'Tilly!' she yelled.

Her sister's head appeared over the railings by the side of the merchant ship. 'Yeah?'

'Get over here; quickly!'

Topaz watched the two sisters, then turned back to scan the skies.

'What else did she say?' said Maddie.

'That she was relieved to finally find the ship. Shit. That means they were looking for the *Giddy Gull*; which means they know what happened in Luckenbay.'

Lara raised an eyebrow. 'They actually made it to Olkis? Holy crap. Oh no, I hope they didn't kill father.'

'Look!' cried Maddie, pointing at the sky.

Topaz squinted, and saw a third black speck above them, where, a moment before, there had been nothing but empty sky. The new dragon approached the two from Wyst, and, within seconds, both turned, and fled back towards Geist. The remaining dragon then soared down towards the *Giddy Gull*, and Topaz stared at the approaching beast. She was enormous, and completely black.

'Blackrose!' yelled Maddie, waving her arms in the air. 'Over here!'

The huge dragon descended to the level of the quarter deck. Upon her shoulders sat Sable, her eyes on the ship.

'My rider,' said Blackrose; 'at last. Are you safe? Where are the two sisters?'

'I'm fine,' said Maddie, laughing as she leaned on the railings. 'Topaz, Lara and Tilly rescued me from Olkis.'

'We know,' said Sable. 'Hold on a moment.'

The Holdfast woman examined something on her lap, and then she appeared on the quarter deck. Lara shrieked.

'You got the Quadrant back, then?' said Maddie.

Sable shook her head. 'I had to get another one.'

Topaz frowned. Something about Sable seemed different, as if she was finding it hard to keep calm, or as if she was repressing some deeper emotion. She had barely glanced at either him or Lara, and seemed to want to get the rescue of Maddie over with as soon as possible.

'How are you, Sable?' said Lara.

The Holdfast woman eyed her. 'You should know that your father is on Ann's ship, and they're chasing you. You should also know that I have your sister Dina in my custody on Haurn. I'll return her, as long as Olo'osso behaves himself. Sail onwards to Udall, and we'll see you there.'

She swiped her fingers over the Quadrant, then both she and Maddie disappeared. Topaz turned back to Blackrose, and saw them both sitting upon the dragon's shoulders, then, a moment later, all three vanished, leaving the skies around the ships empty.

Tilly arrived on the quarter deck. 'What did I miss? Was that another dragon from Wyst? What did they want?' She frowned. 'Where's Maddie?'

Lara glanced down. 'Sable took her.'

'What? Sable was here?'

Lara turned towards her cabin. 'I'll be inside, getting drunk. Topaz, you have the command.'

She strode into her cabin, and slammed the door.

'Would someone please tell me what is going on?' said Tilly.

Topaz did his best to explain, then he sent a midshipman to fetch Vitz, as Tilly stood open-mouthed. The master's mate yawned as he was led up onto the quarter deck.

'Sorry, lad,' said Topaz. 'I need you to take the wheel for a couple of minutes.'

Vitz tried to smother a scowl, as Topaz stepped aside.

'Don't move the *Gull* until I get back,' said Topaz, heading towards Lara's cabin.

'Yes, sir,' said Vitz.

'Should I come with you?' said Tilly.

'I'd like to speak to the captain alone, ma'am.'

'Alright. I'll knock when the transfer has finished.'

Topaz opened the cabin door and walked in.

Lara glanced up from a seat, and quickly wiped the tears from her face. 'You're out of order, Master. You didn't even bleeding well knock.'

Topaz sat down close to her. 'Are you alright, Captain?'

'Fine,' she snapped.

'That was... weird,' he said.

Lara laughed, but it was a bitter sound. 'I am so stupid,' she said. 'When I saw Sable, my heart started to race, and then, she didn't even look at me. Did you hear the way she spoke? So cold.'

'Should we press on for Ulna, Captain?'

'We have no choice,' said Lara. 'We have to drop off the refugees and pick up water. There's nowhere else to go.'

'Understood.'

'You'll be happy. That's where Maddie will be.'

'I would have liked the chance to say goodbye to her before she was whisked away, but yes; I want to go to Udall. We should also be safe there from your father. Blackrose won't let him approach Udall if she thinks he's going to do something crazy.'

'We killed Dax, Topaz.'

'No. I killed him.'

'Yeah, but I tried first.'

'He had a knife to your throat, Captain. I have no regrets.'

'Somehow, I don't think father will see it that way.'

'We've got a few days, Captain. Even if your father left Langbeg right after us, they'll still take another seven or eight days to get as far as here. The *Flight of Fancy* is a good ship, but it's nowhere near as fast as the *Gull*. That will give us time in Udall to see where we stand.' He looked Lara in the eye. 'I'm sorry about Sable, Captain. This might sound trite, but don't take it personally. That wasn't the Sable I remember. Something must have happened to her. Something bad, I'm guessing. She looked as though the slightest thing would have made her explode.'

Lara frowned. 'Do you think so?'

'Definitely. Do you not agree, Captain?'

'She did seem different. I thought it might have been because of me.'

Topaz lit a cigarette, and offered one to Lara.

'Master,' she said, 'tell no one that you saw me crying. I don't want the crew to know.'

'I won't say a thing, Captain.'

'Thank you, Topaz. You're a good friend.'

'That means a lot to me, ma'am.'

She smiled, and wiped her eyes again. 'Yeah? Well, get your lazy ass back out onto the quarter deck, and give me some peace.'

He stood. 'Yes, ma'am.'

He strode out of the cabin, and gently closed the door behind him. Vitz turned to him.

'Go back to bed, lad,' said Topaz. 'You can start your next watch an hour later than normal; alright?'

'Thank you, sir,' said Vitz, as Topaz took over the wheel of the ship. 'Captain Tilly told me about Maddie, sir.'

'She did, did she?'

'Yes, sir. I hope it works out all right.'

Topaz gave a wry smile. 'So do I, lad; so do I.'

CHAPTER 4
STRIKING A DEAL

U dall, Ulna, Eastern Rim – 12th Summinch 5255 (18th Gylean Year 6)

Ashfall soared over the forested mountainside, her eyes scanning the trees for movement.

'Down there, Austin,' she said, 'by the side of the ridge – do you see them?'

Austin peered over the dragon's flank as Ashfall started to bank. Through the tree cover, three greenhides were crouching over the eviscerated corpse of an animal, too engrossed in devouring the remains to notice the presence of the dragon above them.

'I see them,' he said; 'hold on.'

He raised his right hand, and sent a powerful wave of flow powers down into the forest. One of the greenhides shrieked in agony, then all three collapsed, green blood streaming from their eye sockets. Their limbs quivered, then they lay still.

'Got them,' he said.

'That makes seventeen for this morning, Austin,' said the slender grey dragon, as she ascended into the blue sky.

Austin frowned. 'That's our lowest tally so far. They're getting harder to find.'

'That is not a cause for disappointment,' said Ashfall. 'They are harder to find, because so few remain. Between my eyes and your powers, we have cleared entire districts of the beasts. Even better, we have done so without having to burn down half of Ulna's forests; you should be proud.'

'I still worry that we've missed a few; lurking in caves and hiding out of sight.'

'That will indubitably be the case, demigod. It will be virtually impossible to locate all of the beasts.'

'I don't want to give up just yet; can we come back out tomorrow?'

'Of course. We can travel south to Seabound, and take another look there. Shall we return to Udall?'

'Yes; my stomach is starting to rumble.'

The dragon turned until she was facing the north-east, and set off with a burst of speed. The hills and valleys of southern Ulna flew past beneath them, then they emerged over the muddy and desolate landscape of the central lowlands. Signs of the land's recovery were everywhere, with new grass spreading out from the edges of the old field boundaries, while patches of wild flowers and gnarly bushes were poking up through the churned mud. No greenhides had been seen in the lowlands for over ten days, and the entire area was empty and silent. Ashfall kept on in a straight line, and they passed an observation tower on the edge of the inhabited area. A green dragon was perched upon the top of the tower, guarding the farms and the perimeter of the town. A few humans were out in the cultivated fields within the protected zone, and several glanced up at Ashfall as she flew by.

The town of Udall was bathed in sunlight, and the domes and spires of the bridge palace were gleaming. Work was going on down by the harbour to repair the damage wrought by the battle that had taken place nineteen days before. Several buildings by the quayside had been flattened by falling dragons – their bodies had been removed, and dozens of humans were labouring to clear up the remaining rubble. They were being supervised by a new militia, formed by Shadowblaze to replace the black-robed Unk Tannic, none of whom had been seen in public since Splendoursun's death.

Ashfall soared up to the highest tower platform on the bridge palace, and landed. The vines that climbed up and around the trellises surrounding the platform were heavy with dark fruit, and Austin started to salivate at the sight of so many grapes. He unbuckled the straps on the harness and jumped down to the paved ground. He plucked a handful of grapes from a trellis, and gazed out over the town as he popped them into his mouth. His eyes went to the place where he had been imprisoned within a cage. The quayside crane had gone, but he could see the marks on the ground where it had been. Next to it, the waters of the harbour basin were clear, and sparkling in the light. A few fishing boats were tied up along a rebuilt pier, while a large merchant vessel was being unloaded; its cargo of timber and oil being hauled down the wide gangplank by dock workers. The only other ship in the harbour had arrived the night before, bringing more hungry refugees from Geist to the shores of Ulna.

'It is quite a view, Austin,' said Ashfall.

'It's the only free place on Dragon Eyre,' he said; 'the only place not ruled by greenhides, the Banner forces, or by the dragons from Wyst. It's an oasis in the desert; beautiful, but vulnerable. And surrounded on all sides by enemies.'

'That is true, demigod, but do not denigrate what has been achieved here.'

'I'm not denigrating it. Udall has become dear to me, which is strange, as it's also the place where I was imprisoned for nearly two years. It looks a lot better from here than it does from the inside of a cell.'

'Come; let us report this morning's tally to Lord Shadowblaze, and see if he has any work for us this afternoon.'

They turned, and strode down the long ramp that led into the dragon-proportioned upper levels of the palace. The vast marble-lined hallways were quiet, and the few human militia on duty saluted them as they passed. They entered the huge reception hall, which was lit by a series of large skylights that allowed the sun to penetrate the interior. Shadowblaze was standing at one end of the hall, while Ahi'edo was sitting by his large forelimbs. The grey and red dragon was talking to Greysteel and a few others, who were gathered before him. He noticed Ashfall and Austin, and broke away from the discussion.

'Greetings,' he said. 'Did you have a profitable expedition today?'

'A mere seventeen greenhides, my lord,' said Ashfall. 'I think Austin is disappointed.'

'Only seventeen?' said Greysteel. 'Where did you go?'

'We searched the area to the north and west of the southern nest, my lord,' said Ashfall. 'Tomorrow, we shall move back to the vicinity of Seabound, to see if any of the beasts have escaped our attention.'

'This is excellent news,' said Shadowblaze. 'The greenhide numbers have fallen significantly since you two began your operations. You have our thanks. The humans can sleep easier at night, knowing that so few of the beasts remain on the loose.'

'I promised to kill them all, my lord,' said Austin.

'You did,' said Shadowblaze, 'but I will not hold you to that particular oath. Your abilities have allowed us to clear vast tracts of land, without the damage that dragon fire would have caused to the forests. Once again, we are in your debt, friend. If there is anything you require to make your life more comfortable, I hope you will ask. Now, I must return to my previous conversation. These dragons here have been scouting to the north, and have brought tidings from Enna.' He turned back to the dragons he had been speaking to. 'Please continue.'

'Yes, my lord,' said one. 'The news is not good. The Wystian dragons have moved their forces down from the north coast of Enna, and are now occupying the interior of the island, cutting off the remaining humans who dwell there. They are allowing ships to transport refugees to Ulna, but there aren't enough vessels to carry them all. I fear that the result will be another massacre, on the scale of what has already occurred on Geist.'

'Were you able to fly as far as Geist?' said Shadowblaze.

'No, my lord. The Wystians drove us away before we could reach the island. We saw a few ships, heavily laden with refugees, but we were unable to ascertain what is happening upon Geist.'

Greysteel lowered his head. 'So, Enna has also fallen? Meena will be next, unless we do something to stop the Wystians, my lord.'

'There is nothing we can do to save either Enna or Meena,' said Shadowblaze. 'Our resources are already stretched, and our primary duty is to care for the refugees. We must feed and house them, and then put them to work, each according to their abilities. If we attempted military action against Wyst, we would not only fail to repel them from Enna, but we would weaken our own defences. Ulna must be a bulwark; only then will the Wystians think twice before trying to invade this island.'

'I have other news, my lord,' said one of the scouts. 'This time, I do not know if it is good or bad. While we were investigating Enna, we came across several large communities of humans sheltering on the southern coast. Among them, we saw many armed men wearing the black robes of the Unk Tannic.'

'The Unk Tannic are on Enna?' said Shadowblaze. 'That would explain their absence from Ulna.'

'We cannot be sure that all Unk Tannic fled there, my lord,' said Greysteel. 'It is likely that some merely discarded their robes in Udall, in order to blend in with the rest of the human population. We must remain on our guard.'

'I agree,' said Shadowblaze. 'The Unk Tannic have expertise in infiltrating themselves into the general body of humans. I suspect that several of our new militia may, in fact, contain some of their agents. However, unless they act, we have no way of identifying them. Therefore, we must carry on with our plans to fortify Udall. To that end, I propose...'

His voice tailed off as a loud cry came from outside the hall. The large doors swung open, and Blackrose strode in, with two humans upon her back.

'My Queen!' cried Shadowblaze, emotion tearing through his voice. 'Praise all that is holy; you have returned to us.'

Austin and the others stared in silence as the huge black dragon approached them. The scouts bowed their heads low, and Ashfall did the same.

Greysteel roared with delight. 'Your Majesty! You found your rider, I see. Congratulations. Are you hungry? Do you require to rest?'

'I am fine, thank you, uncle,' said Blackrose. 'I have travelled over much of Dragon Eyre, and am happy to be back in Ulna, at last. Maddie is safe, and well; and I have also brought Sable, without whom I would have failed in my task.'

Ahi'edo's face fell as he glanced up. 'Sable?'

Shadowblaze gave his rider a glance.

'I declare the feud with Sable Holdfast to be over,' said Blackrose. 'We may still have our differences, but she has suffered much to help me find Maddie, and she is under my personal protection while she stays on Ulna.'

Up on the black dragon's harness, Sable said nothing, her expression guarded. Maddie unbuckled the straps holding her to the saddle, and climbed down. She staggered as she stepped onto the solid ground, then swayed.

'Oops,' she said. 'I'm not used to standing on ground that isn't moving.' Her eyes glanced over the occupants of the hall. 'Hi, Ashfall. Austin?'

The demigod bowed his head. 'Maddie.'

'Listen, everybody,' Maddie said. 'We have some bad news.'

'Wait,' said Sable. She slid down from Blackrose's shoulders, while avoiding eye contact with anyone in the hall. She took a breath, and lifted her face. 'Badblood is dead.'

'No!' cried Ashfall. 'My poor Sable; my heart breaks for you, and for all of us.'

Sable started to cry, and Maddie embraced her, holding the Holdfast woman close as she wept into her shoulder.

'He died bravely,' said Blackrose, 'fighting an Ancient in Ectus. I could not have been prouder to call him my son, and his loss will tear at my heart forever. Sable's grief is to be respected by all in Ulna – she has lost what was dearest to her, and my wrath will descend upon any who insult or belittle what she has suffered. Badblood gave his life so that we could obtain a Quadrant, a Quadrant that was essential to rescuing my rider.'

Sable pulled herself away from Maddie. 'A Quadrant that we had no business needing. What happened to the Quadrant on Ulna? If we'd had that, then Badblood would still be alive.'

'We failed in our task,' said Ashfall, her head bowed. 'The Unk Tannic had stolen the Quadrant that was left here.'

'And how were the Unk Tannic able to get their hands on it?' said Blackrose.

'Much has happened in Ulna these past few months, my Queen,' said Greysteel. 'It will take some time to explain it all.'

'Do they still have it?'

'No,' said Austin. 'Ata'nix destroyed the Quadrant, upon Splendoursun's orders. I watched him do it.'

Blackrose glared at the demigod. 'And you did not think to stop him?'

'I was severely wounded at the time, Queen of Ulna,' he said. 'Where is Meader? Is he still on Haurn?'

Sable and Blackrose glanced at each other. Sable wiped the tears from her face, then walked towards Austin, pulling the Quadrant from her clothes as she approached the demigod.

'We won't be long,' she said, then she swiped her fingers over the surface of the device.

The air shimmered, and Austin found himself standing on the side of a high mountain. A strong wind was gusting from the north, and he shivered. Sable was standing next to him, and she placed the Quadrant back into the folds of her clothes.

'Where are we?' said Austin.

'We are high in the mountains of Ectus,' she said, 'near the eastern end of the island.'

'I don't understand. Is Meader here?'

She glanced down, then nodded. Austin felt a chill grip his insides.

His lips quivered, and he tried to keep his composure, as dread and fear threatened to paralyse him.

Sable lifted her hand, and pointed to a large cairn that sat upon the side of the high ridge.

'I'm sorry, Austin; I'm so sorry.'

Austin fell to his knees next to the heap of rocks. 'My brother.'

Sable crouched down next to him, and put her arm over his shoulder. 'My friend.'

Austin let out a painful sob, pulled from somewhere deep within him, then he fell into Sable's arms and wept. Her tears were also flowing, and they sat by the cairn for a long time, saying nothing as the cold wind bit through their clothes.

An hour passed, maybe longer. Time seemed to stand frozen to Austin as grief flooded him. Eventually, Sable moved away from him, and lit a cigarette, her eyes red.

'Was it quick?' said Austin. 'Did he suffer?'

'No,' she said. 'It was over in an instant.'

'Who did it?'

'The Sea Banner. He was struck in the head by a ballista bolt, when we were flying on Badblood's shoulders. Ectus is as far as we got. Evensward was also killed here, along with a dragon she brought from Haurn to help us. It was a disaster.'

He rubbed his eyes, barely taking in what she was saying.

Sable raised her hands, and pulled a ring from a finger. She dropped it into Austin's palm.

'This belongs to you now,' she said.

Austin gazed at the ring for a few moments, recognising it.

'Thank you,' he said. 'Why was my brother with you?'

'He wanted to help. He had decided to become a rebel, and he wanted to fight the gods and the Banner forces. I know that you don't agree with what he believed in, but he was trying his best to do the right thing.'

'You're wrong,' he said. 'I do agree with what my brother was fighting for. I wasn't completely honest with you about the old Quadrant. I managed to steal it from the Unk Tannic, but I didn't know how to use it properly, so I went back to Implacatus.' He glanced at her. 'Did you already know that? Have you read my mind?'

She shook her head. 'You've lost your brother; I'm not going to intrude into your thoughts. If you went to Implacatus, though – why did you come back?'

'Have you ever been?'

'No.'

'Well, there are two great cities on Implacatus, high up on the side of an enormous mountain range; a bit like up here, I suppose, only even higher. Serene is where the mortals live, while most of the gods live in Cumulus. I say most, because many gods also stay in Serene. They govern the city, and organise the Banners. Hardly any mortals ever get to see Cumulus, which is where I lived. Every Quadrant can take you back to Implacatus, and...'

'Can they?' she said. 'I don't know how to do that.'

'It's one of the only things I was taught. Do you know how to make a Quadrant take you back to the last place it was used?'

She nodded.

'There's a similar action, which takes you to the first place it was used, which will be somewhere on Implacatus. All Quadrants originated there. I'll show you.'

Sable took the Quadrant from her clothes, and held it out, without passing it to Austin. He leaned over, and pointed to a tiny engraving.

'You activate it here, to go back to the place where this device was first used.'

Sable nodded. 'And it will take me to Implacatus?'

'Yes, though where on Implacatus is anyone's guess. There used to be hundreds of the devices in existence, and they were used all over Implacatus. Did this device belong to Lord Horace?'

'Yes. I killed him, then took it.'

Austin blinked. 'You killed Lord Horace?'

'I broke his skull open and ground it to a pulp. He deserved it. He killed Badblood.'

'Oh. You know, I'm very sorry about that. I know how much you loved him.'

'Never mind that. Go on with what you were telling me. Where did my old Quadrant take you?'

He quietened for a moment. 'I wish I could tell Meader what I saw. He was always wondering why Implacatus invaded Dragon Eyre, and now I know. The Quadrant took me into the middle of a vast desert, where the wind never stopped, and where the air itself was poisonous. Just breathing it in nearly killed me. My self-healing took a battering. At first, I thought I'd made a mistake – that I couldn't be on Implacatus, because I'd always been taught that the lowlands beneath the mountain cities were green and fertile.' He frowned. 'They were lying. Implacatus is a broken, toxic, wasteland. That's why they want Dragon Eyre. The Ascendants have destroyed their own world, and want to move to another one.'

Sable glanced away. She tossed her cigarette butt over the side of the ridge, then lit another.

'Don't you have anything to say, Sable?' he said. 'This is the greatest secret the gods on Implacatus are keeping. No mortals in Serene know the truth.'

'It might have interested me once,' she said, 'but I'm not sure I care any more. They're not getting Dragon Eyre. I'm going to stop them. Your brother did me a favour. He persuaded me that I needed to use my powers to help free this world, and I'm going to honour that. He was one of the very few friends I had.' She shook her head. 'He forgave me for what I made him do in Alg Bay. He didn't need to, but he did.'

'You still have Maddie,' he said. 'It must have felt good to rescue her.'

'We didn't exactly rescue her, Austin. Two of the Five Sisters had already done that for us by the time we were able to track them down.

We made it to Olkis, with the Quadrant, to find that they'd left several days before. All the same, I'm relieved that she's alright. Now that Badblood's gone, she and Millen are all I have left.' She smiled, but her eyes remained sad. 'It was Maddie and Millen who saved Badblood from the fighting pits on Lostwell. I manipulated them both, just as I manipulated Meader. And then, somehow, they became my friends. Before Lostwell, I had no friends – no one. I lied and tricked my way into people's affections, but none of them were my friends. I would pretend to be their friend, but it was always to gain some advantage. Perhaps I should have stayed that way. If I hadn't opened my heart, then I wouldn't be feeling... the way I'm feeling now, as if everything's broken. I feel lost without Badblood, Austin, and all I can think about is revenge. These twisted thoughts keep going through my head, of what I'd like to do to every Banner soldier on Dragon Eyre, and I can't make them stop. All I see is blood.' She bowed her head and started to cry again.

Austin watched her in silence. What could he say? He remembered hating Sable, when she had killed the gods on Seraph's fleet, and that hatred had only intensified when he had learned what she had forced Meader to do in Alg Bay. Looking at the tears on her face, he realised that he no longer loathed her. He pitied her, despite everything she had done.

'I had another motive for going to Implacatus,' he said. She didn't look up, so he continued. 'I wanted to search for my mother. Meader told me that she had probably been sold as a slave; kicked out of my father's harem after I left to go to school. She's another reason why my heart has turned against the gods. I longed to tell Meader that I have changed, that I now agree with everything he was saying. The Ascendants were wrong to invade Dragon Eyre, and I want to help this world fight back. That's why I stayed in Ulna. I want to help.'

She nodded. 'You want to fight?'

'Yes.'

'And you also want to find your mother?'

'Yes,' he said, relieved that she had been listening.

'I have plans, Austin. Will you help me? With your flow and healing powers, we would be unstoppable. If you help me, then I will help you. I could take you back to Implacatus, and use my vision powers to track down your mother.'

Austin's eyes widened. 'You would do that?'

'Yes. If you help me first. It won't be pleasant. I intend to wade in the blood of the Banners, and kill every god that the Ascendants send to fight me. I'm also going to wipe out the Unk Tannic. I'm going on a rampage, Austin, and I'm not going to stop until every one of my enemies is lying dead at my feet; do you understand?'

'You're going to bring down the colonial government?'

'No. I'm going to annihilate them.'

'What about the settlers?'

'I won't touch civilians, not unless they attack me first. You have my word.'

'What about the dragons of Wyst? They're sweeping through the Eastern Rim, slaughtering humans as they go.'

'Let's concentrate on the occupation forces first. What do you say?'

Austin said nothing for a while. He tried to imagine what it would be like to accompany Sable around Dragon Eyre, killing.

'Alright,' he said. 'But, if I can't take it any more; if the bloodshed becomes too much, will you still take me back to Implacatus?'

She nodded. 'Just do what you can; that's all I ask.' She stubbed out her second cigarette. 'I'll take you back to Ulna now, and then I'm going to Haurn for a few days to rest. I need some time away from Blackrose, but I'll be back. I want to see Lara, to apologise for the way I spoke to her earlier today, and then we shall begin, you and I.'

Austin got to his feet. He approached the cairn, and placed his right hand upon it, his left clutching the ring Sable had given him.

'Farewell, brother,' he said. 'I miss you. There's so much that I wanted to say to you, and now I never will.' He glanced at Sable, who was standing by his shoulder. 'Will you bring me back here, now and again?'

She nodded.

He slid the ring on to his finger. 'Then, I shall see you soon, brother.'

Sable swept her fingers over the Quadrant, and they appeared back in the huge, cavernous reception hall within Udall's bridge palace. Blackrose and Maddie were still there, listening to Greysteel, Shadowblaze and Ashfall tell them what had been happening in their absence. They all turned their heads at the sudden arrival of Sable and Austin.

'I'm sorry about Meader,' said Ashfall.

'Thank you,' said Austin.

'I'm going,' Sable said. 'I'll be back when the *Giddy Gull* arrives.'

She vanished.

'Must she be so abrupt?' said Ashfall. 'I wanted to say a proper goodbye.'

'She is in terrible pain,' said Blackrose. 'Did she take you to Ectus, Austin?'

'Yes,' he said. 'I saw the cairn you built.'

'We did not build it,' said the black dragon; 'Sable did it, with her bare hands.'

'My brother was her friend.'

'I am worried about the Holdfast witch,' Blackrose went on. 'She is allowing her grief and rage to control her actions, and I fear that Millen and Deepblue are not strong enough to restrain her.'

'I have agreed to help her,' said Austin. 'When she returns, I'll be leaving with her.'

Ashfall stared at him. 'And where will you be going?'

'I don't know, exactly. She has plans.'

Ashfall's eyes widened, and she looked uncomfortable.

'Is Austin your rider now?' said Maddie.

'No,' said the slender grey dragon. 'I have no rider. Austin is my friend.'

'I'm going for a walk,' he said. 'I need some fresh air. Do you need me here to fill in any of the details about anything that happened?'

'No,' said Shadowblaze. 'You are free to go, Austin. We were still in the midst of our discussion; we had barely reached the part where

Splendoursun forced the other suitors to withdraw. We have a long way yet to go; I will send someone to find you if necessary.'

Austin nodded. 'I'm glad you're back, Queen of Ulna, and you too, Maddie.'

He turned, and strode across the floor of the hall. Behind him, Ashfall glanced at Blackrose, then hurried after the demigod.

'Wait,' she said. 'May I accompany you, Austin?'

'If you like.'

They left the hall, and walked back up the ramp that led to the high, open platform.

'I do not want you to be alone,' said Ashfall, as they gazed over Udall. 'My heart is heavy, and I also do not wish to be alone. Meader and Badblood; I can barely believe it; and now you are planning on leaving with Sable. What am I to do?'

'What do you want to do?' he said.

'Follow you, my friend.'

'Do you mean that?'

'Of course I mean it. But, is it the right thing to do? Queen Blackrose and Lord Shadowblaze might require my presence here, but I won't be able to relax for a moment, knowing that you are roaming Dragon Eyre with Sable Holdfast. She is going to be drenched in blood, that much is clear. Must you go with her, Austin?'

He frowned. If his leaving Ulna was going to upset Ashfall, then how would she feel if he told her that he was intending to return to Implacatus? With a start, he realised that Ashfall was bonding with him, whether she could admit it or not. He knew that dragons formed unbreakable bonds with their riders – was that what was happening?

'I'm going to help her defeat the forces of Implacatus,' he said. 'I can kill, and I can heal.'

'Will you take me with you?'

'Of course, but I don't know what Sable is intending. She might want to only take me along on any operations. Would you be happy staying in Haurn with Deepblue and Millen, while Sable and I are off fighting?'

'Happy? No; but I would rather be there than here. I can watch out for your return each day, and if Sable requires a dragon to help her, then I will make myself available.' She lowered her gaze. 'My father would laugh if he could hear me, and so would Frostback, my sister. I have lost count of the number of times I have ridiculed other dragons for being over-fond of humans, and yet, here I am, unwilling to be parted from you. I should be ashamed, but I am not.'

'You have nothing to be ashamed about, Ashfall. We have a few days before Sable comes back; we can talk about it later.' He took a breath, and tasted the ocean air. 'Right now, there's only one thing I want to do.'

'And what is that?'

'I want to fly. I want to feel the sun on my skin, and the wind in my face. Will you fly with me?'

'Austin,' she said; 'it would be a pleasure.'

CHAPTER 5
THE SUITORS

C ostin Point, Ulna, Eastern Rim – 15th Summinch 5255 (18th Gylean Year 6)

Blackrose alighted on the top of the high stack at Costin Point, and pulled her wings in. She gazed around for a moment, and Maddie did the same. To their right, the crystal clear waters of Plagos Bay stretched away to the horizon, while the mountain peaks of the northern range rose up behind them. Out in front lay the lowlands of central Ulna, shimmering in a heat haze.

'It makes me happy to be back in my favourite place in Ulna,' the dragon said, 'and even happier that you are with me, rider. I don't know if you will ever understand how much I missed your company.'

'I think I understand,' she said; 'after all, I missed you too. These last few days have been so hectic that I can hardly keep my thoughts straight. First, we had to listen to Shadowblaze and the others tell their story, and then they had to listen to us. Your tale was the saddest, though.'

'Indeed. The only good thing to come of it was that Sable and I have reached a new understanding. The cost was too high, but at least we are no longer enemies. Now, my rider, there is something I have been meaning to discuss with you, but, as I wished to do it in private, I have waited until now.'

Maddie unbuckled the harness straps and clambered down onto the uneven slabs covering the top of the tall stack.

'Oh dear,' she said; 'that sounds ominous.'

'It may be nothing. While Sable and I were in Olkis, we questioned one of the Five Sisters – the only member of that family who happened to be present in Befallen Castle. Dina, her name is. Sable has her held captive in Haurn, but that is by the by. Sable read her mind, and gleaned from it that you have an admirer – a man called Topaz.'

Maddie smiled.

'Am I to deduce from the expression on your face that this is true, my rider?'

'He does like me, yes.'

'And how does that make you feel? Was he on the same ship as you were?'

'He was. His job is to turn the ship's wheel, so you would have seen him on the quarter deck of the *Giddy Gull*. Your other question is a bit harder to answer. I guess the simple answer is yes – I do like him.'

'I sense you wish to make a simple thing more complex, but go on.'

'Well, it is complicated. You know me; I'm not the kind of person who falls in love easily. I don't flit from man to man, swooning over them, and always thinking of marriage. I'm just not like that. If Topaz and I are destined to be together, then I want to take my time, and get to know him, rather than jump in head first, only to discover that I've made a terrible mistake. I feel that... I don't know; I feel that, if I fall for him, then I'm going to love him forever. I don't do things in a half-hearted way. It's all or nothing. So, I have to be sure.'

'There is nothing wrong with taking your time, rider, especially if this Topaz turns out to be the love of your life.'

'You know, I think he might. If, that is, he can be patient enough to wait for me to make up my mind.'

'If he is not patient, then he is not the one for you.'

Maddie sat down on a flagstone. 'Can I say something? You

mentioned that he might be the love of my life, and I agreed. He might be. But you are the love of my life, Blackrose. One of Topaz's friends tried to put me off, you know – asking difficult questions about how it could possibly work; and one of the things he said was that a dragon rider cannot also be involved with a human.'

'I do not think Topaz's friend is correct. Look at my situation, rider – I returned from searching for you, to find that the only suitor left with a claim turns out to be my oldest friend. If it is possible for me to have a rider and a mate, then why shouldn't it be the same for you? I know that some dragons get jealous about these things; look at the way Shadow-blaze tried to prevent Ahi'edo from mixing with girls his age.'

'I wanted to ask about that,' said Maddie. 'What are you going to do about Shadowblaze? Do you like him?'

'We were talking about you and Topaz, rider. I am still working through my thoughts and feelings regarding the suitor situation.'

'But, presumably, you'll have to either reject him or accept him? The deadline passed a while ago.'

'That is true. However, under the circumstances, I have decided to delay my decision. Shadowblaze shall remain the sole suitor for now.'

Maddie smiled. 'It's funny how things work out. No boys were inter-ested in either of us before, and now we both have suitors.'

'There is a curious symmetry to it,' Blackrose said, her eyes on the horizon. 'This view gives me much pleasure. The lack of greenhides heartens me.'

'Nice change of subject.'

'I have decided to forgive my uncle for his previous transgressions. He appears to have done a good job in my absence, and I believe he made a genuine mistake.'

'You really don't want to talk about you and Shadowblaze, eh?'

'No, Maddie; I do not.'

'Fine. Should we talk about Sable?'

Blackrose turned her long neck to look at Maddie. 'I do not know what there is to say. You saw the Holdfast witch with your own eyes; you must have detected the turmoil that is afflicting her. She barely spoke to me during the many long days she was searching the ocean for the *Giddy Gull*. At times, I thought her impatience to wreak revenge and slaughter upon our enemies would compel her to give up the search, but she remained true to her word, and persisted until she had located your position. Now that you have been found, I fear that she will unleash herself upon Dragon Eyre. Perhaps she wishes to join Badblood in death.'

'What about Austin? Are you going to let him go off with her?'

'I cannot stop him, my rider. Austin has proved himself a worthy ally, but he is under no obligation to stay in Ulna. I want to believe that he will be a restraining influence upon Sable; someone to whisper words of caution into her ear. On the other hand, she could be of great assistance to our cause, if she strikes at the heart of the occupying forces; so, perhaps, I should merely be content that she is on our side.'

'Are you sure that your aims are aligned?'

'She has promised to leave Ulna alone, and I am prepared to take her at her word. My attention will be focussed on preventing the further spread of the dragons of Wyst, and upon the possible conquest of Throscala. Anything Sable can do to distract the occupying forces will be of benefit to Ulna. She can go with my blessing.'

Maddie nodded, but she wasn't sure if she agreed. Sable might well turn out to be useful to Blackrose, but not if she got herself killed in the process. She had tried speaking to the Holdfast woman during the brief time they had travelled from the *Giddy Gull* to Udall, but Sable had been locked within her own thoughts; a silent, brooding presence on the dragon harness next to her, like a kettle about to blow. Maddie had never been afraid of Sable, despite her formidable range of powers, but when she had looked into the Holdfast woman's eyes, she had felt a twinge of fear.

'There it is!' Maddie cried, pointing down into the harbour, as Blackrose circled overhead. 'The *Giddy Gull*. They made it.'

'I see the ship,' said the dragon. 'Do you wish me to land, so that you can escort the senior officers to the bridge palace? I feel that a meeting with the two sisters is necessary, and I would like to meet Topaz.'

'Umm, alright.'

Blackrose started to descend, and Maddie gazed down at the activity on the main deck of the *Gull*. Next to the brigantine, the slow merchant vessel *Patience* was also berthed, and Tilly was organising the stream of refugees that was emerging from the hold of the vessel. On the quarter deck of the *Gull*, she could see tiny figures glancing up at the dragon, and she felt her heart race. She had often thought about Topaz in the few days since she had seen him, and took that to be a good sign. She wondered if he had been thinking about her.

Blackrose landed in the remains of a demolished harbour building. The rubble had been cleared, and there was just enough space for the dragon to fit. Maddie climbed down from the harness.

'Any instructions you want me to pass on?' she said.

'The crew are free to take on water, and to visit the town,' said Blackrose. 'I require only Lara, Tilly and Topaz to accompany you to the palace. I shall be waiting for you, rider.'

Maddie nodded, and Blackrose lifted back into the air, then soared away from the harbour. Maddie squeezed past a heap of rubble, and stepped out onto the quayside. The docks were busy, with dozens of labourers repairing buildings, while workers were attending to the two new arrivals. A mobile kitchen had been set up by the base of a pier, and the refugees from *Patience* were lining up to be fed. Several children were crying, while the adults looked hungry and exhausted. Tilly was down on the quayside with the refugees, and she saw Maddie approach.

The Osso sister smiled, and kissed Maddie on the cheek.

'You got here in one piece, then?' Maddie said.

'Yeah, though the damn *Patience* handles like a pig. And it leaks like an incontinent drunkard.' Her eyes flashed with tense nerves. 'So, have you cleared it all up with Blackrose? I'm not in danger of being eaten, am I?'

'Blackrose wants you, Lara and Topaz to come with me to the

palace. She wants to talk to you, but you'll be fine. She doesn't bear you or Lara any ill will.'

'Even though I was the one who kidnapped you in the first place?'

'She blames the Unk Tannic for that.'

'And what about the gold? Does she want it back?'

'She hasn't mentioned the gold; not once. To be honest, I don't think she concerns herself with that sort of thing. It's like mere gold is beneath her, or something.'

'That's just as well, seeing as how I don't have it to hand back. I gave it all to my father.'

'Did you see any sign of Ann's ship?'

'Nah. They'll be another few days. They'll be lucky to have reached Wyst by now. Shall we go to the *Gull*?'

They moved through the crowds of queuing refugees, and strode up the gangway of the brigantine. Sailors were gazing out over the town as they worked, and a few saluted Tilly as they walked onto the main deck.

'Well, here we are,' said Lara, striding down to meet them. 'Udall's looking fine; what a difference from a couple of years ago. So, Miss Jackdaw, here's the big question – are we welcome here or not?'

'If you weren't,' said Maddie, 'do you think Blackrose would have allowed me to come down here on my own?'

Lara shrugged. 'Good point. She can't think that we're likely to abduct you again. How are things? You left the *Gull* so abruptly that we weren't sure what was going on.'

Maddie wondered if Lara was angling for news about Sable.

'Things are alright. There's the trouble with Wyst, but you already knew about that.'

Lara nodded.

'Sable left almost as soon as we got to the palace,' Maddie went on. 'We haven't seen her since, but she said that she would be coming back when the *Gull* arrived.'

'She said that, did she? Well, we'll see, I guess.'

'Queen Blackrose wants us to go and meet her,' said Tilly.

Lara raised an eyebrow. 'When?'

'Now,' said Maddie. 'Topaz too.'

'I need to organise the crew. What's the water situation?'

'Blackrose said you're free to take on water, and that the crew can visit the town.'

Tilly shrugged. 'Give them all shore leave, sister. They deserve a break.'

Lara chewed her lip.

'It'll be fine,' said Tilly. 'Let's just get it over with.'

'Fine,' she sighed. 'You can go and fetch lover-boy, Maddie. He's up by the wheel. Vitz can watch the quarter deck while we're gone.'

'It that wise?' said Tilly. 'You know I think there's a risk he'll do a runner?'

'Where's he going to go?' said Lara. 'I trust him, because Topaz trusts him.'

Maddie glanced at the two sisters, then hurried up the main deck and climbed the steps to the quarter deck. Topaz and Vitz were smoking by the wheel, their attention on the harbour of Udall.

'Good morning, boys,' she said.

They turned, and a smile lit up Topaz's face.

'Maddie,' he said; 'it's good to see you. You settled back in?'

'I'm getting there,' she said. 'A lot has changed since I was last here, you know, and it'll take time to get used to it all. The bridge palace is the same, except I've had to change apartments. There was a horrible bloodstain on the floor of my old one, and the place has too many bad memories. Listen; Blackrose wants to see you, along with Lara and Tilly. Are you coming? Lara said that Vitz can look after the quarter deck.'

Topaz chuckled. 'Hear that, lad? You're being left in charge. You've come a long way since being tied to the mast.'

Vitz frowned. 'Yes, sir.'

Topaz's expression darkened for a moment. 'Don't do anything stupid, eh?'

'I'll try not to, sir.'

Topaz nodded. 'Right; let's go to the palace.'

Maddie and Topaz walked back down to the main deck, where Tilly and Lara were waiting for them. They went down the gangway, and began striding along the quayside.

'I could see the *Gull* staying here for a while,' said Lara, as they walked. 'We could use it as a base to hit shipping around Throscala. Serpens would be closer, but it'll be safer here. That's if her Queenship agrees, of course. Would Blackrose be prepared to come to an arrangement, Maddie?'

'We'll have to see about that,' said Maddie. 'For this first meeting, it'll probably be better if you let her do the talking.'

'I need to ask her about Dina, though,' said Lara. 'She's a cow, but she's still our sister.'

'I think she's safe; but, as I said, we haven't seen any sign of Sable for the last few days.'

'Where is she?' said Topaz.

'On Haurn, I think. She has a place there.'

'I know it,' said Lara. 'I stayed with her there for a while, along with her big red dragon.'

Maddie put a hand to her mouth. 'You don't know, do you? Badblood died on Ectus.'

'Shit,' said Lara. 'Poor Sable.'

'That explains a lot,' said Topaz. 'We thought she was being cold and unfriendly, but she's clearly grieving for her dragon.'

They walked past the end of the quayside, and took the main road that ran by the river.

Maddie pointed ahead of them. 'There's the bridge palace.'

Tilly nodded. 'We could see it even when we were still out at sea. It looks big enough to fit a thousand dragons inside.'

'Most of it's lying empty,' said Maddie. 'You can walk about the halls and corridors and hardly see anyone.'

'How many dragons does the Queen have on Ulna?' said Tilly.

'Altogether? Umm, about two hundred and fifty? But, they're not all from Ulna. There are dragons here from Geist, Enna, Throscala, and even a few from as far away as Gyle. More seem to arrive every day, along with boatloads of refugees.'

'And why is Topaz coming along with us?

'Blackrose wants to speak to him too.'

'Why?'

'Because she knows about... ummm, she knows...'

'She knows Topaz gets a cold sweat whenever he thinks about you?' said Lara.

Maddie's cheeks flushed.

'She wants to see what my intentions are,' said Topaz. 'I understand that. I'd be lying if I said I wasn't nervous about it, but I understand it.'

They entered the palace through a human-sized gateway, and ascended a long flight of stairs to the upper levels. A few militia were guarding various junctions within the palace, but the place was quiet, and their footsteps echoed off the marble floors. Maddie led them to the enormous reception hall, where several dragons were waiting for them. Blackrose stood in the centre, with Greysteel, Shadowblaze and Ashfall flanking her. They paused their conversation when the humans entered.

'Welcome to Udall, Osso sisters,' said Blackrose.

'Thank you for allowing us to berth safely, your Majesty,' said Lara.

'Wait,' said the black dragon. 'I remember you. You were in Seabound Palace two years ago, and you insulted me.'

Shadowblaze growled.

'Eh, yes,' said Lara. 'I happened to disagree with one of your decisions.'

'I feel an apology is in order, pirate,' said Greysteel. 'The Queen has graciously decided to overlook the crimes of the Five Sisters, a crime that includes the abduction of her beloved rider.'

'Sorry about that!' cried Tilly. 'That was me. I swear I didn't know she was a dragon rider; the Unk Tannic lied to me.'

'I accept your apology, Captain Tilly,' said the black dragon. She turned to Lara, waiting.

Tilly rammed an elbow into her sister's waist.

'Fine,' spat Lara. 'I apologise for calling you... what was it? Oh, yes, a filthy coward. I shouldn't have.'

'I forgive you,' said Blackrose. 'You happened to be correct. I should not have trusted the Unk Tannic; therefore, I choose not to hold a grievance against either of you.'

'Thank you, your Majesty,' said Tilly, bowing her head.

'Over the next few days,' said Blackrose, 'I intend to strike a deal with you. My uncle, Lord Greysteel, shall negotiate on my behalf; therefore, it would be wise for you to take some time to consider which conditions you wish to apply. Until then, your crews have the freedom of Udall. You may take on water, without any cost to yourselves, and the town militia will guard your ships. You must, however, keep your men disciplined. I want no disturbances to break the peace that has been established.'

'Thanks,' said Lara. 'I'll authorise shore leave when we get back to the harbour.' She smirked. 'Now, there's a certain Topaz standing here, who we've been politely ignoring while we dealt with the important stuff. Come on, Topaz; don't be shy. Is there anything you want to say to the Queen of Ulna?'

Blackrose regarded the sailor, her eyes tight as she peered down at him.

'Your Majesty,' he said, inclining his head. 'Thank you for the welcome.' He swallowed.

'Is that it?' said Blackrose.

'No,' he said. 'I'm in love with your rider.'

Maddie blinked. Love? That was the first time she had heard him use that word.

'Are you, indeed?' said Blackrose. 'You will be well aware, I am sure, that Maddie is extremely dear to me. What makes you think you deserve her?'

The air crackled, and Sable appeared in the middle of the hall. Most people gasped, but Maddie noticed that Topaz seemed relieved.

Sable tucked her Quadrant away and glanced around. 'Where's Austin?'

'The demigod has gone for a walk,' said Ashfall. 'Would you like me to look for him, Sable?'

The Holdfast witch shook her head. 'It can wait.' She glanced at Lara. 'I'm sorry about before; on the ship. I had... things on my mind.'

'It's alright,' said Lara. 'I heard about Badblood.'

Sable looked down, and nodded. 'Can I speak to you alone?'

'Sure.'

'Wait,' said Blackrose. 'Sable, we need to discuss the future.'

'I thought we had discussed it,' said the Holdfast woman. 'I will be going my own path, with Austin.'

Lara narrowed her eyes. 'Who's Austin?'

'Meader's brother,' said Sable. 'I need his flow powers to assist me.'

'I am not happy about this,' said Ashfall.

Sable shrugged. 'Tough. What's it to you, anyway? I thought you didn't like humans.'

'I don't, on the whole. You, I had believed to be a friend, but now I am not so certain. However, Austin is my friend, and I do not like the idea of you leading him into danger.'

'It's his decision.'

'Let's return to the main point,' said Blackrose. 'Sable, there may be times in the future where we could help each other. For example, Throscala remains occupied by Banner forces, and Lady Ydril continues to defend the island. If we could remove her, and her soldiers, then the entire Eastern Rim would be clear of the occupiers.'

'I see,' said Sable. 'You need my help in getting rid of the god? I could do that for you. I intend to kill every last Banner soldier on Dragon Eyre, so I would have got round to Throscala sooner or later.'

'Let's make it sooner,' said the black dragon. 'If we coordinated our attacks, we would be more assured of success.'

'Alright. I have a few things to take care of first, then I'll be in touch.' She glanced at Lara. 'Let's get out of here.'

She touched the Quadrant, and both women vanished.

'Holy shit!' yelled Tilly. 'Where's she taken my sister?'

'I know it is wrong of me to be upset,' said Ashfall. 'I know we need to make allowances for Sable's behaviour, but I am hurt by her brusque manner. She cares not for Austin's welfare; she merely wishes to employ him as a weapon.'

Ahi'edo shook his head. 'She was a bitch then, and she's a bitch now.'

'Silence, rider!' roared Shadowblaze. 'Do not utter another word about Sable in my presence.'

'But, master,' he said, 'have you forgotten what she did to us? She almost sent me mad, and she forced you to attack the Queen. Everyone's feeling sorry for her, because she got her dragon killed, but she hasn't changed.'

'Leave this chamber, rider,' said the grey and red dragon; 'and do not return until you are ready to make a full apology. The Queen has declared the feud to be at an end, and I will not tolerate you trying to spark it back into life.'

Ahi'edo glared around the hall, then strode away.

'He's lucky Lara wasn't here,' said Tilly. 'I doubt I would have been able to stop her from punching him in the face.'

'I would like to apologise to you all for my rider's words,' said Shadowblaze. 'I have told him many times to make his peace, not only with Sable, but with Maddie as well.'

'He still doesn't like me?' said Maddie.

'No, he does not,' said the grey and red dragon. 'I confess that our bond is under great strain at the moment.'

'Now that Sable has once again come and gone,' said Greysteel, 'I would like to hear Topaz answer the Queen's earlier question.'

Tilly laughed. 'Yeah. I'd like to hear it too.'

Topaz glared at her, then took a step forward. 'I don't know if I deserve Maddie,' he said. 'She seems perfect, and I'm just a sailor, with no great riches, and no noble blood.'

Blackrose gazed at him. 'Do you wish to mate with her?'

Topaz's face went red. 'Umm...'

'I shall rephrase that for human ears,' said Blackrose. 'Do you want to marry my rider?'

'It's a little early to be talking about marriage,' he said. 'I guess I want the chance to see if we work well together. I think we might, but there's only one way to find out.'

'Your Majesty,' said Shadowblaze; 'if you are going to allow your rider to mate, then there are many young men among the riders in Udall. Would one of them not be more appropriate for Maddie?'

'My rider is free to choose whomever she pleases,' said Blackrose. 'My role is to ensure that she is not led astray by a boorish lout, or by someone trying to take advantage of her kindness. Maddie's heart is full of love; I know this, because she loves me. If she decides to love you, Topaz, then I will be watching closely. If you abuse her love, I will kill you.'

Maddie took Topaz's hand, and began to pull him away from Blackrose.

'That's enough for now,' she said. 'Topaz answered your questions, and I don't like hearing talk about him getting killed. I'm going to show him round the palace. See you later.'

She hurried from the hall, dragging Topaz along with her. When they emerged into a vast corridor, she let go of his hand.

'Sorry about that,' she said. 'Blackrose can be very... protective.'

He laughed. 'It's fine. She's a dragon. I'd be more worried if she hadn't threatened me. I think that went well.'

'You do?'

'Yes. Blackrose didn't dismiss me out of hand, and she didn't seem bothered that I'm not a rider.'

'You said something in there that surprised me.'

'Yeah?'

'You said that you were in love with me.'

'I did say that. Sorry; I should have told you first.'

'Do you mean it?'

He nodded. 'I wasn't sure before, but as soon as Sable took you from the quarter deck of the *Gull*, then... I knew.' He took her hand again. 'Maddie, I love you; I adore you. Every time I look into you eyes, I can feel the world around me stop, as if nothing else matters.'

She stared at him. 'No one's ever said things like that to me before.'

'Then every man you've ever met is a complete fool. Maddie, my heart belongs to you.'

She felt a rush of desire for him. She wanted to kiss him but, with an effort, managed to resist. She swallowed, then smiled.

'Let's go for a walk.'

CHAPTER 6
YEARNING

Udall, Ulna, Eastern Rim – 16th Summinch 5255 (18th Gylean Year 6)

Sable pulled the thin blanket aside, and slid out of bed. The first rays of dawn were filtering through the shutters, and she placed her bare feet onto the floorboards of the cabin, then reached for her clothes.

'Are you leaving me again?' said Lara.

'I thought you were still asleep,' said Sable.

'No. I've been lying awake for a while.'

'I have to leave. I have things to do.'

'Things that involve blood and death?'

'Yes.'

Lara leaned up on an elbow, her figure wrapped in the blanket. 'Will you be coming back?'

'I hope so. Thank you for last night; it was a great comfort to me.'

'I want to be more than just a warm body next to you, Sable.'

'Don't get your hopes up. I'm not in the right frame of mind for any kind of commitment just now. But, if you can put up with me coming and going, and don't try to dissuade me from doing what I need to do, then I'd like to continue from where we left off.'

'Damn it, Sable; are you asking me to beg?'

Sable pulled her tunic over her head. 'Those are my terms. Take it or leave it.'

'Are you deliberately trying to hurt me?'

'No. I'm saying that it won't be easy.' She turned to face Lara as she pulled on her boots. 'I guess I'm trying to warn you off. I can't guarantee that I won't hurt you, but it won't be deliberate.'

Lara said nothing, and Sable finished getting dressed. She pulled her hair back, and tied it into a pony-tail, then reached down and picked up the Quadrant.

'No,' said Lara. 'Don't use that. I want you to walk out of this cabin, and I want the crew to see you do it. If you slip away with the Quadrant, then it'll feel like you weren't even here.'

Sable tucked the device onto her clothes. 'Alright.' She leaned over and kissed Lara. 'I'll see you around; take care.'

She walked across the cabin, then opened the door and left. Outside, the harbour was in semi-darkness. Udall had few streetlamps, and the shadows lay thick over the town. To the east, the sky was brightening, and Sable took a deep breath. A few sailors turned, and watched her as she crossed the quarter deck. One of them whistled at her, and she stopped. The sailor was repairing one of the ship's railings, and had a cigarette hanging from his mouth.

'Did you whistle at me?' she said.

He grinned. 'I sure did. You're Sable, yeah? I'm Topaz's mate – Ryan. Nice to meet you.'

'If you whistle at me again, I'll slit your throat.'

He raised his hands. 'Woah; steady. It's just nice to put a face to a name, eh?'

She narrowed her eyes. 'Give me a cigarette.'

'Sure, doll,' he said. He rummaged in a pocket, and produced a bundle of cigarettes.

'Some of those look like weedsticks,' she said.

'You have a good eye.'

'I'll take some keen and dream, if you have any. I can pay.'

Ryan rubbed his chin. 'How about five of each, and we'll call it two gold pieces?'

'Deal.' She held her hand out.

He counted out a few weedsticks, and handed them over.

She gave him the coins. 'And a cigarette.'

He passed her one, and she lit it with Meader's metal lighter.

'Where did you get that?' he said, his eyes widening. 'They don't make anything like that anywhere on Dragon Eyre; not as far as I know.'

'A friend of mine bought it off a trader in Haurn. I think it came from Implacatus.'

'Is it for sale? I'd give you a decent price.'

'Not a chance. Thanks for the weed, Ryan.'

She shoved the smokesticks into a pocket, and strode along to the gangway. The quayside was quiet, and she kept her pace brisk. It felt good to walk. She had been using the Quadrant for even the shortest journeys, as if she couldn't bear to be delayed in any way. She glanced around at the town as it started to wake up. A handful of market stalls were being set up in a little square close to the harbour, and a few civilians smiled at her as she passed them. She avoided eye contract, feeling envious that they were able to get on with their lives, while her mind was trapped in a pit of rage. Lara had helped her crawl out of it for a night, but she could feel the same old thoughts returning – thoughts of death and violence. Today was the day, she said to herself.

She entered the palace, and stole through the deserted hallways, slipping past the few guards on duty, until she reached Austin's set of rooms. She frowned. Sitting outside them was Ashfall, as if on sentry duty.

'Good morning, Sable,' said the slender grey dragon. 'You're up early.'

Sable eyed her. 'Are you going to be a problem, Ashfall?'

'That depends, Sable.'

Sable placed a hand on her hip. 'Upon what?'

'Whether or not you agree to let me come along with you and Austin.'

'I see. What does Austin think about this little arrangement?'

'He seemed happy for me to accompany you, when I asked him about it. Well?'

'You've seen where I live on Haurn. It's not exactly set up for dragons; especially compared to the comforts of the palace.'

'Deepblue seems to manage.'

'She has Millen, and she doesn't care about the basic facilities.'

'Have you forgotten that I lived in the Catacombs for years? I doubt Haurn is more basic than that place.'

Sable considered for a moment. 'It's not enough. I might also need you to help me, now and again. Some operations would be simpler with a dragon working alongside me. Would you be prepared to obey my orders without question?'

'I would, but I have one condition. I will not obey an order that will lead to Austin being harmed or killed.'

Sable snorted. 'Are you sure he isn't your rider?'

Ashfall lowered her gaze. 'It's just a word. If you insist upon calling him that, then so be it.'

'You have fallen hard for the demigod, haven't you? Don't answer that. Fine, you can come along; I accept your condition. Now, kindly get out of my way so that I can go and wake him up.'

Ashfall moved to the side, and Sable pushed the door open and walked into Austin's apartment. She strode through to the bedroom, and hauled the shutters clear of the window, letting the dawn light enter.

Austin groaned from the bed.

'Time to get up,' she said. 'We're leaving. Grab your shit and stuff it into a bag.'

'Sable?'

'Move. You have two minutes.'

'Uh, what about Ashfall?'

'Don't worry; she and I have had a little chat. She's coming too.'

'Is she? Great. Em, would you mind leaving the room? I'm naked under this blanket.'

'Fine. I'll be in your kitchen, stealing all the coffee and booze I can find. We have plenty of food on Haurn, but we lack a few of life's comforts.'

She walked out of the bedroom, and closed the door. She listened for a moment, to make sure that he was getting dressed, then entered the small kitchen. She opened every cupboard, and tipped the contents into a sack. Coffee, wine, cheese, salt – all of it disappeared into the sack, along with a collection of plates and cutlery. She swung the sack over her shoulder as Austin emerged from his room.

'Right,' she said. 'Let's get started.'

Twenty minutes later, Sable had gathered everyone bar Dina in the courtyard next to the temple on Haurn. Deepblue had been happy to see Ashfall, but the grey dragon's mood was sombre, while Millen seemed suspicious of Austin's presence. It was another beautiful morning in Nan Po Tana, and the sun was shining in the clear blue sky. Sable stood in the shade of a cypress tree, and lit a stick of keenweed.

'Today's target is Yearning,' she said. 'I'll be taking Austin, and only Austin, on this operation; the rest of you will be remaining here. Millen, could you fetch the armour I ordered?'

Millen stood. 'You mean, the armour I've been making is for Austin? I thought it was for me.'

'It was, originally,' said Sable. 'Now, it's for Austin. You're pretty much the same size as him, so it should fit.'

'But...'

'No buts, Millen. Austin is immortal.'

'So was Meader.'

Sable's frown deepened. 'You're not coming, Millen; it's too dangerous.'

The two dragons glanced at each other, but neither spoke, and

Millen trudged off into his workshop. Ashfall dug her claws into the surface of the courtyard, her frustration plain to see. Millen emerged from the workshop carrying a stiff, leather cuirass.

'Help Austin put it on,' said Sable.

She watched as he muttered something, then he walked up to Austin, who stood. Austin put one arm through a loop, and then Millen fastened the buckles down the other side, securing the leathers to Austin's torso.

Sable nodded. 'Thank you.'

She checked her sword was attached to her belt, even though she knew it was there, then pulled out the Quadrant.

'Stand back to back with me,' she said to Austin, 'then get ready.'

'Alright,' said the demigod. 'Yearning, eh?'

'Yes,' she said, 'but not quite yet. We have to collect something first.' She glanced at the others. 'This will only take a few minutes.'

She brushed her fingertips over the Quadrant, and they appeared in the midst of a massive pack of greenhides. The beasts were everywhere, spread out across a large plain in the centre of Haurn. Austin cried out in fright, as several turned in their direction, then Sable raised a hand.

'Don't use your flow powers, Austin,' she said, as she entered the minds of as many greenhides as she was able.

Do not attack us. Stand still.

She strained with the effort, fighting off a growing sense of revulsion. Around them, a few dozen greenhides were obeying her orders, but beyond them, the other greenhides were trying to push their way through to the humans.

She focussed, and sent her powers out wider.

You will obey me. Do not attack us.

'What's happening?' cried Austin. 'Why are they just standing there, staring at us?'

'I'm controlling them,' she said. 'Did you think I was going to personally kill every Banner soldier on Dragon Eyre? I need an army, and these ugly brutes are my soldiers.'

'You're controlling them? That's impossible – only Ascendants can do that.'

'Believe what your eyes are telling you, Austin. Alright, *now* we're going to Yearning.'

She swiped her hand across the Quadrant. The air shimmered, and then Sable and Austin appeared within the walls of a huge harbour, along with at least a hundred greenhides, who were packing out the quayside. Screams arose from the dock workers and sailors who were in the harbour, but the greenhides did nothing.

Sable smiled. *Kill them all.*

She activated the Quadrant, and they appeared back at the temple in Nan Po Tana. Austin fell to his knees, trembling and panting.

Sable glanced at Millen. 'Fetch me the four explosive devices we have left over.'

Millen frowned, then strode back to his workshop.

Sable crouched down by Austin. 'Get a grip, demigod. We haven't even started yet.'

'You... you took a hundred greenhides to Yearning, and unleashed them on unarmed sailors.'

'Yes. And now we're going to get more, and deliver the explosive devices at the same time.'

Millen came out of his workshop, pushing a wheelbarrow. Inside, were the last four ceramic explosive devices that she had taken from the *Lord Sabat*. He wheeled them over to Sable.

'Thanks,' she said, standing. 'Get up, Austin; our work is only just beginning.'

Austin stumbled up onto his feet, and Sable triggered the Quadrant. They appeared inside a tall, stone tower in the heart of the huge Sea Banner base of Yearning, the wheelbarrow next to them. Screams from the harbour were echoing off the thick walls, along with the high-pitched shrieks of the greenhides. Sable drew her sword.

'Austin, kill anything that moves. Follow me.'

She kicked down a door and ran through. Inside, a group of gods and officers were gazing out of a window at the carnage unfolding in the harbour below them, and no one noticed Sable at first. Austin raised his hand, then hesitated for a second. He closed his eyes, and the heads of every mortal in the chamber exploded, coating the walls and ceiling in blood. Three gods were also hit by the blast of flow powers – they fell, but began to heal. One got up onto a knee, and lifted his own hand; and Sable leapt over the large meeting table, and hacked his head off with the blade of her sword. She leaned over before the other two gods could recover, and removed their heads with two powerful lunges.

'Eight and a half,' she muttered.

She glanced around, ensuring that everyone was dead, then she heard the sound of footsteps climb up the stairs of the tower towards their level. She ran back out of the chamber, dragging Austin with her. She sheathed her bloody sword, then took out the lighter and lit the fuse of one of the devices. As soon as the flames took hold, she triggered the Quadrant, and they arrived back in the plains of central Haurn. A greenhide charged them. Austin shrieked, then lifted his hand, and the beast fell, blood exploding from its eyes.

Sable drove her powers into the greenhides' minds, and the creatures halted, staring at her with their insect eyes. She activated the Quadrant again, and transported another hundred greenhides to Yearning, this time placing them inside a huge barrack block. She listened for a moment, and heard the flames coming from the stone tower.

Kill everything, she ordered the greenhides, then she took herself and Austin back to Haurn.

Millen raised an eyebrow. 'You could have brought my wheelbarrow back. It was the only one I had.'

'I'm afraid it's been blown up, Millen,' she said. 'I'll get you a new one.' She glanced at Austin. 'Well done. You killed one rear-admiral, a commodore, two major-generals, and three captains. The entire command structure of Yearning has been eliminated, along with their three resident gods. How long did that take?'

'About twelve minutes,' said Deepblue.

Sable nodded. 'Gyle now has no way to communicate with

Throscala. We have separated the Western and Eastern Rims. A decent start.'

Austin stared at her. 'You're insane.' He looked at the others. 'Did you know she could control greenhides?'

'Millen and I knew,' said Deepblue. 'We've seen her do it.'

'I didn't know,' said Ashfall; 'but nothing Sable does has the capacity to surprise me any more.'

'Do you want to burn some ships, Ashfall?' said Sable. 'Come on. We're not quite finished with Yearning just yet.'

'I thought you said my services wouldn't be required for this operation?' said the dragon.

'I've changed my mind. There are no gods left there, but you'll need to watch out for ballista bolts. Austin, I'm relying on you to kill anyone who looks like they're going to loose at us.'

She and Austin climbed up onto Ashfall's shoulders, and strapped themselves into the harness. Sable activated the Quadrant, and they appeared in the clear blue sky, high above the fortified harbour of Yearning.

'Should I dive?' said Ashfall.

'No. Wait,' said Sable, as a wave of paralysing fear washed over her. Images of Meader's death flashed through her mind, and she tried to control her breathing. Panic reared up from the pit of her stomach, and she began to sweat. 'Just circle,' she said.

'There are a lot of ballista positions down there,' said Austin, leaning over to squint down at the harbour.

'Too many,' said Sable.

'Look at the mess where the tower was,' Austin said, pointing. 'You brought the entire building down.'

'And I can see greenhides rampaging through the harbour,' said Ashfall. 'Blood is flowing down the streets like a river. Are you sure you don't want me to dive? There are several ships that the greenhides cannot reach.'

'No,' said Sable.

Austin frowned at her. 'Are you alright? I thought I was the one who was feeling the strain.'

'It's too much like Ectus,' she said.

She swiped the Quadrant, and they re-appeared over the temple in Haurn. Ashfall glided down, and landed in the courtyard.

'Did you burn the ships?' said Millen.

Sable shook her head, then jumped down to the ground, her hands shaking.

'No?' said Millen. 'Why not?'

'Sable lost her nerve,' said Ashfall.

Sable put her hands on her knees and tried to breathe. Her head was pounding, and she felt sick. Millen thrust a lit cigarette into her fingers, and she took a draw.

'What happened?' he said.

'I made a mistake,' she gasped. 'I should have stuck to my original plan.' She straightened with an effort, and a tear rolled down her cheek. 'Sitting on Ashfall with Austin beside me, looking down at all those rows of ballistae pointing up at us – all I could think about was Ectus.' She wiped her cheek. 'I think we're done for the day. I'm going to get drunk.'

The skies remained clear into the night, and the stars shone down on the temple complex of Nan Po Tana, as Sable and the others sat out by a roaring fire. Millen was sitting on one of Deepblue's forelimbs, while Austin was next to Ashfall. Millen had cooked dinner for the four humans, from a large fish that Deepblue had caught in the little bay next to the temple's jetty. He had taken a full tray up to the rooms in the temple where Dina was being held, and had returned to report that the Osso sister was in good health, despite being imprisoned against her will. While the others chatted, talked, Sable had remained silent throughout the meal, and the several bottles of wine that had followed the food. Austin had recounted their trips to Yearning in great detail, while Ashfall had spoken of what she had seen.

Sable watched them, feeling lonelier than ever – the absence of Badblood like a void in her heart. She considered going back to Ulna to see Lara, but she didn't want to inflict her misery upon the young pirate captain.

'I know what went wrong,' she said, after a long spell of silence.

The others turned to her.

'I need to avoid replicating anything that reminds me too much of Ectus. If I had kept to the original plan, then I would have been fine. I can't risk feeling that sense of panic again; it'll only get us killed.' She lit a stick of dreamweed. 'From now on, I'll need to think carefully about each operation, to see if there's anything that might trigger the memories. I'm sorry.'

'You hardly need to apologise,' said Austin. 'You were magnificent. Insane, but magnificent.'

'You did your part too, Austin. You were very helpful.'

He raised an eyebrow. 'Was I? You talk about panicking, but I was the one who nearly wet himself when we arrived among all those greenhides. You know, Ashfall and I have been killing greenhides for days, back in Ulna; but that was the first time I've been so close to any of them. So, where's next?'

'I'm still thinking about that,' she said.

'I have a few ideas,' Austin went on. 'Do you want to hear them?'

Sable nodded.

'Right,' he said; 'we want to bring down the colonial government – yes? From what you've said so far, it's like you're thinking only in terms of action against military sites.'

Sable raised an eyebrow. 'You made me promise not to target civilians.'

'I know, but I'm not talking about civilians; I'm talking about hitting areas that are crucial for the economy of the Home Islands – and that means oil. Have you considered targeting the refineries on Alef?'

'Would that hurt the government?'

'Absolutely. The settlers use the oil from Alef for a hundred different purposes – heating, lighting, water-proofing Sea Banner vessels; their economy would be crippled without it. They can't import the quantities they need from Implacatus either.'

'I'm not sure I like you encouraging Sable in this manner,' said Ashfall.

'Look at it this way,' he said; 'the sooner we bring the government to its knees, the sooner our job will be done.'

'Burning the oil refineries would send a powerful message,' said Sable; 'one that even Lord Bastion might notice.'

Austin blinked. 'Excuse me?'

'Did I forget to mention him?' said Sable. 'He's on Dragon Eyre.'

Austin jumped to his feet. 'What? Bastion is here?'

'He's just another god, Austin. There's no need to wail.'

'Bastion is not "just another god", Sable. He's the most powerful Ancient in existence; more powerful than several Ascendants. This changes things.'

'No, it doesn't,' said Sable. 'I'm trying to attract the bastard's attention, so that he'll come looking for me. When he does, I'll kill him. Sit your arse down, Austin.'

Austin glanced around, his eyes wide, as if expecting Bastion to appear at any moment. He sat back down on the ground, and put his head in his hands.

'Did you think the Ascendants were going to give up Dragon Eyre without a fight?' said Sable. 'On Lostwell, they sent Leksandr and Arete, and then Edmond and Bastion also turned up. I'm expecting them to do something similar here.'

Austin stared at her. 'Did you kill the two Ascendants on Lostwell?'

'No,' she laughed. 'Belinda got one, and Ashfall's father got the other one. I did see Bastion, though, not long before the world disintegrated. I'm not afraid of him.'

Austin turned to Ashfall. 'Your father killed an Ascendant?'

'So I believe,' said the dragon.

'Why didn't you tell me this?'

'I wasn't there when it happened; I was with Blackrose, preparing to leave for Dragon Eyre, while Sable and Badblood flew to the city of Alea Tanton. I only know because Sable told me.'

'I don't understand,' said Austin. 'How could a dragon kill an Ascendant?'

'My niece was there,' said Sable. 'Kelsey Holdfast. Her presence alone is enough to negate all powers. Leksandr wasn't able to use any, and Deathfang reduced him to a smear of ash.'

Austin was still staring at Ashfall. 'You truly are a princess.'

Ashfall tilted her head. 'Please don't start with that nonsense. My father was the mightiest dragon on Lostwell, but he wasn't a king. I was born a slave, in the fighting pits of Alea Tanton. Not in a palace.'

'You were born there?' said Sable. 'I didn't know that.'

'Why would you? It's not something I particularly enjoy telling people. However, if it will stop you calling me a "princess", then it will be worth revealing the truth to you.'

'Sable's a princess,' said Millen.

'Are you?' said Austin.

Sable gazed into the embers of the fire. 'Not exactly. I'm the illegitimate daughter of Queen Miranda of the Holdings; the product of a sleazy affair between her and Godfrey Holdfast. It was quite the scandal, apparently. My mother kept my birth a secret, and when she died, her brother took the throne.'

'Is he still the king?' said Austin.

'No. His body was taken over by Nathaniel, the Fourth Ascendant, or, as I used to call him – the Creator. That was who I worshipped for years, and it was in his service that I committed all of the atrocities for which I will never be forgiven. I thought he was a real god, you know – all powerful, all knowing, and benevolent. It was bullshit. I saw his body on Lostwell; his real body, not the one he took over on my home world. A withered old corpse. About as far from a real god as you could imagine.' She glanced up at the stars. 'That's why I'm not afraid of the Ascendants; let them come. I hope they come.'

The others said nothing. Austin puffed out his cheeks, his eyes betraying his anxiety.

'You were right, Austin,' she said. 'Destroying the refineries will definitely attract Bastion's attention; however, to blow them up, we'll need more explosives.'

'Where will you get them?' said Millen.

Sable's eyes darkened. 'In the one place where they make them. Ectus.'

CHAPTER 7
MEMORABILIA

Udall, Ulna, Eastern Rim – 18th Summinch 5255 (18th Gylean Year 6)

'I'm going to buy up all the weed I can get my hands on, mate,' said Ryan, 'so that when Sable comes back, I can position myself as her supplier.' He glanced at the bar steward. 'Two more ales.'

Topaz frowned. 'And you reckon you'll make decent money from this?'

'Nah, but it ain't about the money, mate,' said Ryan; 'it's about the respect that comes from being Sable Holdfast's weed dealer. She's a bleeding hero, and folk'll be like, "there goes Ryan – he knows Sable."'

'But I know Sable.'

'Yeah, but you're dating a bleeding dragon rider, and that gives you a certain reputation. All I want is some of that shine to rub off on me.'

'I'm not exactly dating Maddie.'

Ryan groaned. 'Still? Holy crap; that bleeding girl's taking her time. You kissed her yet?'

Topaz shook his head as the bar steward deposited two more ales onto their table.

'Cheers,' said Ryan, and lifted his mug. He took a sip. 'Hey, this Ulnan ale's alright. I was half expecting rat piss.'

'You're on your third,' said Topaz.

'Yeah, but you need a few to gauge the taste properly, eh?' He waved his arms around. 'Just like this tavern. It'll take a few more visits before I can judge whether I like it or not. But, back to the topic at hand – the lads in the carpenters' workshop are well impressed that Sable spoke to me.'

'She threatened to kill you, mate.'

He grinned. 'I know. Amazing, eh? And then I sold her weed. And, more importantly, I was right – she's a damn fox, *and* she was sneaking out of the captain's cabin at dawn. Old Lara's got herself a right doll, eh?'

The tavern door opened, and Vitz walked in.

'Morning,' he said.

'Take a seat, lad, and join the party,' said Ryan. 'We were just discussing my burgeoning business relationship with Sable Holdfast. Did you hear?'

Vitz rolled his eyes. 'I heard. Listen, I can't stay. The Captain wants you, Master.'

'But it's my day off,' said Topaz. 'I have plans to go up to the palace later; I'm meeting Maddie for lunch.'

'I'm just the messenger, sir. Captain Lara told me to fetch you, and here I am.'

Topaz groaned, and placed his half-full mug back onto the table.

'You'd best go, mate,' said Ryan. 'You know how the captain gets if you keep her waiting.'

'Are you staying?'

Ryan gestured towards another table, where several off-duty seamen from the *Gull* were gathered. 'I'll sit with those guys,' he said. 'I'm sure they'll want to hear all about my new friend. Oh, and if the captain mentions Sable, be sure to let her know that I'm happy to keep her well-stocked in weed, eh?'

'I'm not sure how I'll manage to squeeze that into the conversation,' said Topaz, 'but I'll give it a try.'

He stood, then he and Vitz headed for the door. They emerged into the warm sunshine, and Topaz lit a cigarette.

'How are you finding Udall, lad?'

Vitz shrugged. 'It's better than Pangba, sir, but I kind of miss Langbeg.'

Topaz nodded as they started walking along the quayside towards their ship.

'There are one or two on board, lad,' Topaz went on, 'who seem to be under the impression that you might be thinking of doing a runner. Tell me it ain't so.'

'We're stranded in the middle of the Eastern Rim, sir. Where do these people think I'm going to go?'

'I don't know. Throscala, maybe?'

'What, so they can hang me for being a pirate? It's no secret, sir, that I never wanted this life. When my father first suggested that I try to earn a commission with the Sea Banner, I hated the idea. But, it's too late now. I've gone beyond the point of no return. I have assisted in the ransacking of a dozen merchant vessels, and have stood by while Sea Banner personnel have been executed by our beloved captain. My court martial would be over in thirty seconds.'

'Yeah, but on the plus side, you're turning into a fine master's mate. You could easily be a master with the Five Sisters in years to come. You might even end up with your own ship.'

'That would turn me into one of the most notorious traitors in Dragon Eyre history, sir. The son of a settler aristocrat, captaining a pirate vessel? My father would die of shame.'

'Well, it's something to aim for, at least.'

Vitz gave him a look.

'You're at a crossroads, lad,' Topaz went on. 'The captain is just starting to place her trust in you, and, if you seize that opportunity, then there's no limit to what you can achieve. But, if you let her down, then you'll slip back into obscurity, where you'll stay. She won't be handing out any second chances.'

They reached the gangway to the *Giddy Gull*, and Topaz paused to stub out his cigarette.

'Just think about it, lad,' he said, as Vitz stared at the ground.

They boarded the ship, and strode along by the railings to the quarter deck, where Lara and Tilly were talking to a few of the senior officers.

Lara noticed Topaz approach, and turned to him.

'How much ale have you had, Master?' she said.

'A pint and a half, ma'am.'

'Praise the gods for that,' she said. 'I need you sober. I was worried that you'd be on your eighth by now.'

'I'm supposed to be meeting Maddie for lunch, ma'am, so I wasn't planning on getting too drunk.'

'Cancel your lunch plans,' she said. 'We need to go to the palace. Lord Greysteel wants to go over our agreement. With any luck, we can hammer out a decent deal with the dragons of Ulna.'

Topaz glanced at the officers. 'Are we all attending, ma'am?'

'No,' she said. 'Just me, you, Tilly and Bosun Wyat. Wipe that look off your face, Master; this is important. You can have lunch with Maddie any day.' She glanced at Vitz. 'You stay here and look after the *Gull* while we're away.'

Vitz saluted. 'Yes, ma'am.'

Lara turned to the rest of the officers. 'You ugly buggers are dismissed. Go and enjoy some shore leave with your lads. The purser has a kitty for expenses; see him on your way off the ship.'

The officers saluted, then dispersed.

'Tilly has dealt with Lord Greysteel before,' Lara said to those remaining. 'She knows what he's like.'

Tilly nodded. 'We have to be very careful – Lord Greysteel is a cunning negotiator; he'll try to wring every conceivable concession out of us, so don't offer him anything that we haven't already agreed.'

'Do you have our list, Bosun?' said Lara.

The grey-haired man patted his coat. 'In here, ma'am.'

Lara nodded, and they set off. They left the ship, and walked towards the palace, through the crowds of dock workers and sailors by the quayside.

'If this goes well,' said Lara, 'then I want to depart Ulna at dawn tomorrow.'

Topaz raised an eyebrow. 'So soon, ma'am?'

'We're running out of money, Master. We can't survive on dragon charity, not while there are so many refugees needing fed. We need to get to work, so that we can pay our way. I was thinking of a ten day voyage, down to Throscala and back. If we can pick off one of the supply ships sent out from Na Sun Ka, then we'll be able to live off that for a good while.'

'And I want to find a new ship,' said Tilly. 'Don't forget that.'

'How could I?' said Lara. 'You bleeding remind me about it ten times a day.'

'What happens if we run into the *Flight of Fancy*, ma'am?' said Topaz.

'Then we wave at father, and speed away, laughing our asses off. The *Gull* can run rings round Ann's piece of shit.'

'Did you find out more about Dina, ma'am?'

Lara chewed her lip and glanced away. 'No.'

Tilly narrowed her eyes. 'But you were with Sable for a whole bleeding night, sister. I thought you were going to ask?'

'I didn't get round to it.'

Tilly sighed. 'That Holdfast woman has melted your tiny brain. Our sister is lying chained up somewhere, and you can't even be bothered to find out if she's still alive, or when Sable plans to release her. I know you didn't get on well with Dina, but...'

'I'm not going to discuss this,' snapped Lara.

'Promise me you'll ask Sable the next time you see her.'

'I will. *If* I see her again.'

Lara and Tilly scowled at each other. Topaz remembered Ryan's request, but decided not to bring it up. They reached the palace, and were greeted by a pair of militia guards, who allowed them to enter.

'I need to let Maddie know that I'm going to miss lunch,' said Topaz, as they ascended a long flight of stairs to the dragon levels.

'Do it now,' said Lara, 'and don't stop for a cheeky wee cuddle; be quick.'

'Yes, ma'am.'

He left the others at the top of the stairs, and hurried down a cavernous hallway. He descended a short flight of steps, and knocked on the door of Maddie's apartment. A moment later, she opened it, wearing a dressing gown, with a towel wrapped round her head.

'Oh,' she said. 'Hi. I wasn't expecting you until later. Come in.'

He walked into Maddie's untidy apartment.

'Excuse the mess,' she said. 'I would have tidied if I'd known you were coming. Actually, I probably wouldn't have. I have to be honest; I like mess. A messy house feels like a home.'

He glanced around at the piles of clothes and belongings scattered about the main room. 'The state of untidiness is quite impressive. I'm the opposite. Living on a ship means you have to be tidy. How do you ever find anything?'

'It can take quite an effort; I won't lie. So, where are we going for lunch?'

'That's why I'm here. I have to cancel lunch. Lara needs me to help negotiate with Lord Greysteel.'

Maddie's face fell. 'Really? Are you meeting with him today?'

'Yeah. Worse, Lara wants to sail to Throscala tomorrow. I could be away for the next ten days.'

'What? But, you've only been here for three days. I wanted to take you to Seabound; Blackrose was going to fly us there.'

He sighed. 'What can I do?'

'Well, you could tell Lara to wait a few more days.'

'I tried. She says that we're running out of gold, and that we need to pay our way in Udall. She has a point.'

Maddie narrowed her eyes. 'Sea Banner ships are swarming round Throscala at the moment. Do you have to go there?'

'We can't go north – the dragons of Wyst have made that pretty clear, and there ain't any enemy ships up there. Throscala's the only option.'

'You've made me cross, Topaz. I was looking forward to the next few days.'

'So was I. Maybe we could do dinner, this evening, after the meeting's over?'

'I suppose so. I'll take what I can get, I guess.'

He nodded. 'Do you, eh, have anything small that I could take with me?'

'Like what? Why?'

'Just something of yours to remind me of you while I'm away.'

She glanced around. 'Take your pick. Except, wait – no underwear. You're not taking my smalls on board.'

He laughed, then scanned the mess in the room. Something small and silver caught his eye.

'What's that?' he said. 'A cigarette case? Did you used to smoke?'

She leaned over, removed a stray sock, and picked up the silver case. 'For a day. I didn't like it. You can have this, but it didn't originally belong to me.'

She handed it to him, and he turned it over in his hands.

'There's an engraving,' he said. 'Who's Van?'

'He was an officer in the Banner that I knew on Lostwell.'

'Old boyfriend?'

'Nope. He loaned that to me years ago, but I never got the chance to give it back.'

'You keep it,' he said, placing it back onto a heap of clothes. 'Knowing that it belonged to a Banner soldier doesn't sit right with me.'

'Fair enough.' She picked up a couple of other things. 'You can take these, if you want.'

She handed him a hair clasp and a fabric badge. He examined the badge. It had a sword emblazoned on the front, with a few words underneath.

'The Auxiliary Work Company?' he said. 'What's that?'

'That was the euphemistic name given to a unit I was attached to on my home world. Everyone called us the Rats. We used to have to sneak out beyond the Great Walls, and fix the moat, while being attacked by greenhides. I got that badge when I was promoted to sergeant, but I never got around to sewing it onto my uniform.'

She slipped her left arm out from her dressing gown, and showed him a long list of tattoos that ran down from her shoulder. She pointed at one.

'Here it is,' she said. 'The Auxiliary Work Company was the last unit I worked for in the City, so it comes at the bottom.'

He squinted at the tattoos, trying not to be distracted by her bare skin. 'They tattooed every unit onto your arm? Gods, don't be telling the Sea Banner that; they'll probably think it's a great idea.' He forced his eyes up to her face. 'And you made sergeant, eh? You told me you were no good as a soldier.'

'My commanding officer had clearly lost his mind the day he promoted me,' she said, pushing her arm back into the sleeve. 'The hair clasp is also from my home world. It's been through a lot, that clasp. I was wearing it when I arrived on Dragon Eyre.'

'Thanks,' he said. 'I'll take both. I'd better be going; you know what Lara's like.'

'I'll find out where the meeting is, and come and see you when it's over.'

They both nodded, then stood awkwardly for a moment. Topaz tried his best, but he couldn't stop imagining what lay beyond her dressing gown. He swallowed.

'I'll miss you when you go,' she said.

'I'll miss you too, Maddie.'

He turned, and walked back to the door. She closed it behind him, and he paused outside for a moment, feeling his emotions soar. He was crazy about her, but if they didn't kiss soon, then he was starting to believe that they never would. What if, at the end of her long deliberations, she decided that she didn't want to be with him? He pushed the idea from his mind, unable to bear thinking about it, and strode away.

'To summarise,' said Greysteel, 'the Realm of Ulna is offering you the following – a safe haven, in which to harbour your vessel or vessels; beach facilities, where you can clean the hulls of your vessels; unlimited access to water supplies; our protection, while your vessels are within Ulnan waters, including from any threat emanating from Olo'osso. However, we reserve the right to allow Olo'osso, and any other member of the Five Sisters consortium, to access the harbour in Udall, if they prove to be non-hostile...'

Lara yawned.

'Am I boring you, madam?' said the metal-grey dragon.

'No, no,' she said. 'Carry on summarising.'

'Tell me; is there anything else you require of us?'

'I would like to occupy a couple of derelict buildings along the waterfront,' she said. 'Somewhere to store supplies, and any goods we collect on our voyages to Throscala. Ideally, the buildings would come free of charge. They aren't currently being used.'

'We can agree to that, but I would prefer to set a nominal rental fee, to keep things above board. Shall we say one gold piece per calendar month per building?'

Lara glanced at Bosun Wyat, who nodded.

'Alright,' she said. 'The bosun and I will select a couple of buildings this evening, and we'll let you know which ones we've picked.'

'Excellent,' said Greysteel. 'Now we come to the conditions that we require from you. I shall read out a list of what the Queen, Lord Shadowblaze, and I have agreed upon. First, you must promise not to attack any Ulnan vessel or settlement. This condition is non-negotiable. You must restrict your attacks to vessels and settlements belonging to our mutual enemy.'

'Of course,' said Lara. 'No problem.'

'Second,' Greysteel went on, 'your profits will be subject to taxation, here in Udall.'

Lara groaned. 'I thought this was coming. Fine – how much?'

'Ten per cent of your profits; in coin or in kind. You shall declare your takings within twenty-four hours of your arrival, and pay the tax within seventy-two hours.'

'On profits only, yeah?'

'Naturally, madam.'

She glanced at the bosun again, who whispered something in her ear.

She nodded. 'We agree to ten per cent. What's more, we'll donate the *Patience* to Udall, right now, as an advance payment on any liable taxes. It's worth about six hundred in gold but, for you, let's call it five hundred. If you sell it, that's what you'll get.'

'The *Patience* is registered to an Ennan merchant, madam.'

'Not any more, it ain't. I confiscated it, after finding the captain of said vessel breaking maritime law by over-crowding the ship. I handed the captain over to Lord Shadowblaze's custody not long after we arrived.'

'Are you certain that he was breaking the law?'

'Oh yeah. The hold had nearly two hundred refugees crammed into it.'

'But, madam, you are a pirate. Isn't breaking maritime law one of your specialties?'

'I'm offended by such an accusation, Lord Greysteel. We are priva-teers. Pirates attack anyone, whereas we have promised only to target enemy vessels while we are at war. There's a big difference.'

Greysteel narrowed his eyes. 'Very well. We shall accept the *Patience* as an advance payment on your taxes. However, I insist upon having an independent evaluator decide the true worth of the vessel.'

Lara shrugged. 'Fair enough. Anything else?'

'Yes. Our third condition is that no one under your command attempts to impress any native of the Eastern Rim into your service. We are happy for people to volunteer to serve upon your vessels, but there shall be no pressgangs in Ulna.'

'Agreed.'

'Our final condition is that you agree to sell your goods in the marketplace in Udall, in an open and transparent manner. No smuggling, no black-market profiteering, and no hoarding will be tolerated.'

'It might be impossible to enforce that,' she said. 'Sailors like doing their little deals. What if one of them gets caught selling a bit of weed on the side? Are you going to boot us out of Ulna?'

'How about,' said Tilly, 'if we agree to publish a list of our takings – our official takings, and then the law only applies to that list? My sister is right; if we take away the opportunity for the lads to indulge in a bit of side-business, morale will plummet.'

'I will speak to Queen Blackrose about this,' said Greysteel. 'For the moment, I will strike out this condition, but I expect you to act in good faith until the wording is finalised.'

Lara smiled. 'I always act in good faith.'

Greysteel regarded her for a moment, then stretched out his wings, their tips extending to either side of the hall where they had gathered.

'I think we have a deal,' he said.

Lara and Tilly grinned.

'I shall have a scribe write up what we have agreed,' the grey dragon went on, 'and then we shall require your signatures to make it official. Until then, I am content to trust that you will keep your word. You can be assured that we shall keep ours.'

The four humans stood.

'It was a pleasure doing business, Lord Greysteel,' said Tilly.

'I shall inform the Queen that you intend to sail at first light tomorrow. Farewell.'

The humans walked from the hall, and strode back towards the palace entrance.

'I did not need to be there for any of that,' Topaz muttered.

'Shut your mouth, sailor,' said Lara. 'We might have needed you. We didn't, but we might have. We got a decent deal, I reckon. Ten per cent was pretty much what we expected. I would have taken twelve, but don't tell Greysteel. Best of all, we got rid of the bleeding *Patience*.'

Topaz eyed the way leading to Maddie's apartment. He came to a halt. 'I'll be off now. I have a dinner appointment.'

'What?' said Lara, stopping next to him. 'No chance. We're sailing at dawn; I need you on the *Gull* this evening.'

'But, I already missed lunch, Captain.'

'Tough shit, Master. We're a bleeding professional organisation; we can't just skip off for dinner with our fancy lady whenever we feel like it. There are courses to plot, and supplies to itemise; and we need to bed in some of the new crew. I want to shift Vitz into the vacant lieutenant position, which'll mean that you'll have to select a new master's mate.'

'You're making Vitz a lieutenant, Captain?'

'That is what I said. I was going to tell you all this evening, but you've dragged it out of me. Why? Do you object?'

'Well, he's a good master's mate, and I don't want to lose him.'

'You won't be losing him. He'll still be on the quarter deck. I just think he'll be more useful with a wider range of responsibilities. Tilly, back me up.'

'You know what I think about Vitz, sister.'

'Oh, come on. If he was going to run, he'd have done it by now. I used to hate the lad, but I quite like him now; he's one of the only guys on board who's ever read a book. And you, Topaz – I'd thought you'd be happy.'

'I'd be happy if I could have dinner with Maddie, Captain.'

She scowled at him. 'Yeah? Well, I'd be bleeding happy if Sable turned up, but she hasn't, has she? We can't always get what we want.' She turned, and stormed away towards the stairs. 'Move your damn asses; we've got work to do.'

The pre-dawn light was accompanied by a chill breeze, and Topaz shivered as he stood on the quarter deck, his hands on the wheel, but his eyes on the bridge palace in the distance. He had managed to get a message sent to Maddie the previous evening, to let her know that he was required on the *Giddy Gull*, but he was still unhappy about not seeing her. The hair clasp and the sergeant's badge were in his pocket, and he patted it, to make sure he hadn't lost them.

A few yards away, Lara and Tilly were speaking to Vitz, who was wearing a lieutenant's uniform. For once, he had a smile on his face, and had seemed half-shocked, half-delighted with his unexpected promotion. Topaz had gone through several of the new recruits, looking for a replacement master's mate, but he had rejected them all.

Lara nodded towards Topaz. 'Ten minutes, Master.'

He nodded back. Ten minutes? Enough time for a quick cigarette. He had just lit it when a midshipman appeared on the quarter deck.

'Captain,' he said, 'there's a woman requesting permission to come on board.'

Lara's eyes widened. 'Sable?'

'No, ma'am. Maddie Jackdaw. She wants to say goodbye to Master Topaz.'

Lara glanced at Topaz. At first, her look was a glare, but her eyes softened, and she nodded.

'Fine,' she said. 'Topaz, go down to the main deck and meet her there. If she's still on board in nine minutes, she'll be coming along with us.'

Topaz hurried from the quarter deck, the midshipman keeping pace next to him. They reached the gangway, and Topaz saw Maddie waiting on the quayside, a thick blanket wrapped round her shoulders. The midshipman beckoned for her to board, and she smiled, and walked up the gangway.

Topaz gave the midshipman a quick look, and the young lad made himself scarce.

'Hey, Topaz,' said Maddie, as she reached the deck. 'I figured that if you couldn't come to the palace, then I'd come to the *Giddy Gull*.'

'It's good to see you,' he said.

Her brow creased. 'So, ten days, yeah?'

'Give or take,' he said. 'It'll pass quickly.'

'For you, maybe. You'll be busy working, while I hang around the palace. That sounded like I was blaming you. I'm not. It's your job, I guess.'

'Maybe you need to ask Blackrose for something to do,' he said.

'Like what? I'm not particularly skilled at anything.'

'I find that hard to believe.'

'Yeah? Well, it's true. I'm good at talking too much. Do you have my clasp and badge?'

He patted his pocket again. 'Yeah. Why – do you want them back? Tough; I'm keeping them.'

She smiled. 'I don't want them back. But, it occurred to me that I don't have anything of yours.'

'Oh. What would you like? If I can give it to you, I will.'

She bit her lip. 'I, uh... I want this.'

She leaned up, and kissed him. Topaz stood frozen for a split second, his senses overloaded as her lips made contact with his. Then he pulled her close, his arms going round her back, and they kissed as if nothing else existed. They swayed, the ground feeling unsteady beneath them, and he felt her hands behind his neck.

Maddie gazed up at him. 'There,' she said. 'Now I have something to remember you by. Take care, Topaz, and please don't get killed or anything.'

She pulled away from him, smiled, then walked back down the gangway, leaving Topaz standing on the deck in a daze. He stared at her as she strode back along the quayside, then he felt a heavy slap across his back.

He turned, and saw Lara smiling at him. 'About bleeding time, Topaz. Come on; I can hear the ocean. It's calling our names.'

CHAPTER 8
EIGHT HAMMERS

N an Po Tana, Haurn, Eastern Rim – 20th Summinch 5255 (18th Gylean Year 6)

'We have been left with little choice, Sable,' said the blue and green dragon. 'Your activities will attract the attention of the enemy, sooner or later. Moving the colony to a safer location is the prudent course; do not take it as an insult.'

'I'm not insulted,' said Sable, her figure silhouetted in the last rays of sunset. 'I agree with you. We'll miss you, and the native families who have lived here for the last two years, but it's the right thing to do. I'll feel better knowing that you are all far from Nan Po Tana.'

'You have my thanks for understanding our situation. We do not blame you for the deaths of Evensward or Boldspark – they volunteered to travel with you, but we cannot remain here, not if you insist upon continuing your attacks on the gods. You should also consider moving. This temple may seem remote to you, but the gods will find it, and when they do – they will kill you.'

'I am not afraid of the gods.'

'We know this, Sable. You have courage – that is not in doubt. It is a pity, though. You are our friend, and we would rather you didn't throw your life away.'

'What will happen to the native workers and their families?' said Millen, who was standing close to Austin.

The dragon turned to him. 'We shall ensure their safety, Millen,' he said. 'The caverns that we have selected as a new colony are spacious and dry. We shall carry the humans there, and they will be welcome to stay with us for as long as they wish. We would be happy to take you and Deepblue also.'

'Thanks, but we're staying here,' he said.

The dragon tilted his head. 'So be it.' He raised a forelimb, and, at his signal, other dragons swooped down and landed in the open fields next to the courtyard. The gathered natives from Haurn scrambled up onto their shoulders, clutching their meagre possessions. The baby started to cry as he was lifted up onto a harness, then, one by one, the dragons ascended into the darkening sky.

'Farewell, Sable,' said the blue and green dragon. 'We wish you good fortune in your struggle against the gods. May your sword stream with the blood of our enemies.'

He extended his long wings and climbed into the air. He circled once over the quiet temple compound, then sped off to the south-east, following the rest of his colony to their new home.

Millen sighed. 'I'm going to miss them. Nan Po Tana will feel empty without the Haurn workers here.'

'It's for the best,' said Sable.

'Should we also move location?' said Austin. 'The dragons might be right. What if the gods find us here?'

'Then, we'll move quickly,' said Sable. 'I'm not ready to give up the temple; not yet. Millen, how are the food stocks?'

'They should last for months,' he said. 'We have stores of grain, dried fruit, and tons of olive oil; and Deepblue will carry on catching fish for us. The orange trees will be ready to harvest soon. We'll be fine.'

Sable nodded. 'And those things I asked you to make?'

'All done,' he said. 'Do you need them now? They're in the workshop.'

'After dinner,' she said. 'I've decided upon a night attack.'

'Tonight?' said Austin.

'Yes. It'll be me and you again.'

Austin felt his heart sink. Four days had passed since their attack on Yearning, and the images from that day were still imprinted into his mind.

'There will be more greenhides involved in this attack,' said Sable, 'but I've thought of something else for the main event.'

'More greenhides?' said Austin. 'Shit.'

'Come on,' said Millen. 'Our dinner will be starting to burn.'

Sable and Austin followed Millen into the courtyard. The sunset was starting to fade, and the sky was shaded in deep reds to the west, while the stars were appearing overhead. A small fire had been lit close to the temple entrance, and Ashfall and Deepblue were sitting together, the devoured remains of several fish lying in front of them. Sitting alone, on the other side of the fire from the dragons, was Dina, her arms hugging her knees.

Deepblue glanced up when she saw Millen approach. 'Have they really gone, my rider?'

Millen nodded. 'Yes. The dragons picked up every native who lived here. It's just us now.'

'It makes me sad,' said the tiny blue dragon. 'I shall miss them.'

Millen crouched by the fire, and removed several skewers from the flames, while Austin went to the cool shadows by the side of the temple, and began filling four mugs with wine.

Sable gazed at everyone. 'Thank you all for staying,' she said. 'The dragons of Haurn did what was best for them, and I'm glad that the natives are now safe. It means that we don't have to worry about them any more. Austin and I are going on another operation tonight, as soon as we've finished eating.'

She sat by the fire and lit a cigarette, her gaze on the flames that were rising up into the cool air. Millen prepared four plates of food, and handed them out, and Austin did the same with the wine. Dina glared at him as he handed her a mug.

'What about me?' she said. 'I don't want to stay here.'

Austin shrugged. 'Sorry.'

'Don't apologise to her, Austin,' said Sable. 'Dina is our hostage; our guarantee that her father will think twice before trying to attack Lara and Tilly.'

'It's not fair,' Dina cried. 'I've done nothing wrong.'

'You tried to sell one of my friends into slavery,' said Sable. 'This is your punishment. If you're unhappy, you can go back to being locked up in your room again. Is that what you want?'

Dina quietened.

'Thought not,' said Sable. 'Eat your dinner and shut up.'

'What operation will you be undertaking this evening?' said Ashfall.

'You'll find out when it's over,' said Sable. 'I may have to travel back and forward, so you might see me throughout the night, if you're still awake.'

'I shall remain awake until I know that Austin has returned safely,' said the grey dragon.

A tight smile appeared on Sable's lips. 'I'll keep your rider safe.'

Anger flitted over Ashfall's face, but she said nothing. Austin glanced at her, as he tried to quell the growing nerves that were flaring in his guts. He had been hungry while they had been saying goodbye to the dragons and natives of Haurn, but with Sable's news, his appetite had faded. He looked down into his plate of grilled fish. Deepblue had caught it for them, and she was watching to check that the humans ate what she had provided, so he picked some up and began to chew it, but it felt dry and tasteless in his mouth.

If Sable was nervous, she didn't show it. She cleared her plate in a few minutes, then drank the wine from her mug. When she had finished, she dug into a pocket and produced a weedstick.

'This is the last of the keenweed,' she said. 'I'll need to go back to Ulna soon and get some more.'

Millen narrowed his eyes. 'Should you be smoking that before an operation?'

'It's the best time to smoke it,' she said. 'I'll need to be alert. I have one stick of dreamweed left as well – that will be for when we get back.'

She lit the weedstick off her metal lighter, and took a long draw. She exhaled, and the smoke mingled with the flames from the fire. Austin forced down the last of the grilled fish, then drained his mug, partly to take away the taste; partly to fortify his nerves against what was coming. He allowed the alcohol to relax him, fighting the temptation to use his self-healing powers to clear it from his mind.

Sable nodded to Millen. 'Fetch the items I asked you to make, and bring the sack as well.'

Millen put down his plate and got to his feet. 'I'll just be a minute.'

He walked away, heading towards the wooden shack that he used as a workshop. He emerged a few moments later, pushing his new wheelbarrow. In it was a collection of leather straps, along with a bulky sack.

'I'm not going to ask what this is all for,' he said, halting the wheelbarrow by the fire.

'Good,' said Sable, 'because I wasn't going to tell you.'

'What's in the sack?' said Austin.

Millen glanced at him. 'Hammers.'

Austin frowned. 'Where did...?'

'I bought them from a store in Gyle two days ago,' said Sable. 'You'll be carrying them, and the leather straps. See if they'll all fit into the sack.'

Austin stood, and peered down into the wheelbarrow. Millen opened the sack, and Austin began stuffing the straps inside. There were eight separate sets, all identical to each other, and the sack was full by the time they had finished. Austin lifted the sack, feeling its weight.

'A backpack would be handy,' he said.

'I'll get one for next time,' said Sable. 'Will you manage to carry that alright?'

He nodded. 'It's not too heavy.'

She flicked the weedstick butt into the fire and got to her feet. She and Austin pulled on their leather cuirasses, and Sable checked that her sword was clean and securely fastened to her belt.

'Take care,' said Ashfall. 'Strike hard, but return alive.'

Sable took the Quadrant out. 'Greenhides first, Austin. Are you ready?'

He held the sack close to his chest, and nodded.

A moment later, they appeared on the dark plains of Haurn. Surrounding them were thousands of greenhides, resting in the cool evening air. A few glanced up at Sable and Austin's arrival in their midst, and several shrieked out warnings to the others. Austin watched as Sable gazed out at the beasts, and the shrieking stilled. She triggered the Quadrant again, and their surroundings changed, replaced by the interior grounds of a fortress. High stone walls lay on every side, with squat barracks lined up in the central yard. The greenhides remained motionless, as an alarm bell sounded from a tall tower. Sable stared at the greenhides, and they began to disperse, charging towards the barracks. They tore through a sentry patrol, ripping the Banner soldiers to shreds, then entered the squat buildings, pushing and shoving to get through the doors.

Sable activated the Quadrant again, and Austin found himself up on a steep ridge, his hands still grasping the sack. Ahead of them was a long coastal plain, dotted with tiny pinpricks of lights from hundreds of streetlamps.

'Where are we?' he said.

'On Ectus,' she said. 'In front of us is Sabat City. I chose this ridge because it has a good view of the coast. This shall be our base for the night. Put down the sack; we can leave it here for now.'

He lowered the heavy sack to the ground. 'And that fortress we were in?'

Sable pointed towards the city stretching out below them. 'That was the garrison of the Banner of the Swift Hawk. It's just a diversion, to keep the soldiers occupied for a while. Don't worry, Austin; that was the only time you'll see greenhides this evening.'

'Good. I hate them so much.'

'Try going into their minds. If you think they're bad on the outside, you should see what goes on inside their tiny brains.'

'No thanks. For once, I'm glad I don't have vision powers.'

'Time for stage two,' she said. 'Stand by me.'

'Where now?'

'We're going to a factory, where the explosive devices are manufactured. It'll be heavily guarded, so a frontal assault won't work. You will need to remain calm, and trust me.'

He opened his mouth to speak, but Sable brushed her fingers over the surface of the Quadrant, and they found themselves on a quiet street, lit by a few lamps. On one side were houses and shops, while a high wall ran to their left. In the distance, screams could be heard, along with the tolling of alarm bells. A few squads of Banner soldiers were rushing towards the garrison buildings where Sable had delivered the greenhides, while a few civilians were being herded indoors.

A Banner sergeant noticed Sable and Austin. 'Get off the street!' he cried. 'An attack is underway.'

'Thank you,' said Sable, her eyes focussed on the soldier.

The sergeant turned, and sped off to join his comrades.

'I thought he was going to arrest us,' said Austin.

'Humans are easy to manipulate,' she said, as they set off, 'especially when you've been practising on greenhides.'

They came to a set of large entrance gates on their left, which led into the walled compound. A squad of armoured soldiers were on duty outside, and they eyed Sable and Austin as they approached.

'Halt,' said one. 'This area is off limits.'

Sable raised a hand, and every soldier fell to the ground, their eyes closed. Sable didn't break her stride. She took one look over her shoulder, then stepped over the bodies. The gate swung open, and they entered the compound. More soldiers ran out of a guardhouse next to the gates, and Sable brought them down with another gesture, their armour and weapons clattering off the stone cobbles. One appeared from the other direction, and aimed his crossbow at Sable. Austin flicked his hand towards the soldier, and stopped his heart.

'Thanks,' said Sable. 'Now, quickly; follow me.'

He followed her as she took off, and they ran into the compound. The interior was packed with long, narrow buildings, and Sable veered towards one on the right. More soldiers were standing by the doors to the building, and Sable sent them to sleep. She kicked down the door, and they ran into the building. Austin gasped. The interior was taken up with dozens of racks that stretched down a central aisle, and each rack contained at least forty ceramic explosive devices.

'The other buildings are where these are made,' Sable said, as she slowed to a walk, 'but if we blow all this up, it should destroy their manufacturing capacity. Badblood set a building like this on flames by the dockyards, and the crater it left behind was a hundred yards wide.'

'I hear footsteps,' said Austin. 'More soldiers are coming.'

'Of course they are, Austin,' she said. 'This place is crawling with Banner soldiers. I want you to hold them off while I begin transporting some of these racks to Haurn. Can you handle it?'

'What if they send a god?'

She smiled. 'I hope Bastion himself comes, but I doubt we'll be so lucky. See you in a minute or two.'

She vanished, along with an entire rack of explosive devices. Austin stared at the empty space by the wall of the building, then turned to face the main entrance, his right hand raised. His guts began to churn. What if something happened to Sable, and she couldn't return for him? What if the soldiers decided to seal the doors and blow up the building, in an attempt to slay the Holdfast witch? What if Bastion came? Panic flitted through him, and he tried to control his breathing, which was becoming ragged.

Sable appeared next to him, and he jumped a foot in the air. She laughed.

'One down,' she said, then she vanished again, taking another full rack with her.

Two soldiers peered through the entrance doors of the building, their crossbows levelled. Austin shrank into the dark shadows, watching them. The soldiers entered the building, and another pair followed them inside, their eyes scanning the darkness for movement. Austin sent out his powers, not enough to blow their heads apart, but enough to stop their hearts. The soldiers slumped to the ground; their deaths making Austin feel wretched. The soldiers were only doing their jobs, he said to himself, as he wondered how many widows and orphans he had just created on Implacatus.

Sable appeared again. 'Still quiet?'

Austin nodded.

'This next part will be a little risky,' she said. 'Timing is everything.' She walked over to another rack of explosive devices. 'Help me move eight of them onto the ground.'

He hurried over to her, and they carefully moved eight of the ceramic pots from a rack, and placed them onto the smooth stone floor. Once they were ready, Sable brandished her lighter. She stared at the flame for a second, then reached over to the rack, and lit one of the fuse wires that dangled from the narrow end of each device. She waited until she was sure it had caught light, then she swiped the Quadrant.

In an instant, Austin found himself back on the high ridge over-looking Sabat City. Around them, were the eight devices that they had removed from the rack. Sable stared down into the coastal plain.

'Five, four, three, two...'

An enormous explosion ripped through a quarter of the city that lay before them, lighting up the sky for a moment as flames leapt into the night air, along with thick clouds of smoke and dust.

Sable sat on a rock, and lit a cigarette.

'Holy shit,' muttered Austin, as he stared at the massive fire where the munitions factory had been. A series of secondary explosions reached his ears, each one rumbling like thunder. He glanced at Sable. 'Are we done for the night?'

She shook her head. 'You're forgetting the sack. You can stay here for the next bit. Before I leave you, however, I'm going to check for a suitable target.'

Her eyes glazed over, and Austin sat down next to her. He plucked the cigarette from her hands, and took a draw, then coughed. He wondered if he would prefer to know the details of each operation before they embarked upon it. Sable kept him in the dark about most things; for instance, he had been unaware that she had been to Gyle to purchase a wheelbarrow and a sack of hammers. He decided he would rather not know; that way, he wouldn't have time to let her plans fester in his mind. He glanced at the still form of the Holdfast witch, as the flames coming from the city continued to rise over the coast of Ectus. What would Meader think of his new role – as an assistant to Sable in her insane quest to kill every Banner soldier? It would be worth it, he told himself, if it resulted in the defeat of the forces of Implacatus, and if he was then able to hunt for his mother. He had to remember why he had agreed to help the witch.

Sable broke out of her trance, then looked for her cigarette. She frowned when she saw it in Austin's fingers.

'If you want to smoke,' she said, 'take a fresh one from the packet in my tunic.'

'Sorry,' he muttered.

She stood. 'I'll be a few minutes. A brand new Banner arrived in Ectus two days ago, freshly shipped over from the Arrivals Field on Gyle. Ten thousand reinforcements, Austin, all destined to be sent to the Eastern Rim to crush the rebellion, as soon as they've been acclimatised to Dragon Eyre. They'll suffice as tonight's target. Wait here.'

She drew her sword, and vanished.

Austin stood up and stretched his legs. His eyes caught sight of the sack from before, and he walked over to it. Crouching down, he opened it, and took out one of the sets of leather straps. There were buckles and various fastenings that linked a series of thin strips, and he wondered what they were for. This time, Sable was gone for over ten minutes, and Austin began to worry. They had never discussed what he should do if he became separated from Sable, and he didn't want to think about what would happen if she had been killed or captured. He paced up and down the wide ridge, his eyes going back to the flames that were burning down in the city.

Sable re-appeared, along with the bodies of eight Banner soldiers. The edge of her sword was dripping with blood.

He frowned. 'Are they...?'

'They're sleeping. Bring the sack.'

He carried it over, and they arranged the eight men into a line along the ridge. Sable removed the leathers straps, and Austin helped her attach one to each of the soldiers. The straps went over their shoulders, and buckled round their backs, leaving a space by the fronts where something could go.

'Right,' said Sable, as they finished securing a set of straps to the last soldier. 'Now, we'll place a pisspot into each harness, with the fuses at the top. Got it? Be careful.'

Austin stared at her. 'I don't understand. How...?'

'Do as I ask, Austin,' she said. 'One device for each soldier.'

'Wait,' he said. 'You can't be considering what I think you are. This is inhumane, Sable.'

She shrugged. 'What difference does it make? I could slit their throats now, or put these soldiers to use. If you object, then our deal is off.'

She walked to where the explosive devices were lying on the ground, and picked up the first one. She brought it over to a soldier, and secured the device within the straps by the man's stomach, making sure that the fuse was at the top, by his chest. Austin watched her, then made a decision. He would help her, despite the nausea that was starting to curdle his insides. Together, they affixed the other explosives to the rest of the soldiers, then Sable picked up the sack, and placed a hammer into the right hand of each unconscious man.

'I got this idea from Lara,' she said. 'All I need to do now is imprint the correct commands into each soldier's mind. Give me a moment.'

She dropped the empty sack, and knelt down by the first soldier. She leaned over and prised open an eyelid, then sat in silence for a few moments, staring into the unconscious soldier's face, as Austin watched. She moved on to the next soldier, and repeated the process, until she had visited each of them in turn.

'You don't have to do this,' said Austin. 'We've got enough explosives to destroy the Alefian refineries.'

'You don't understand,' said Sable. 'It's not enough just to kill the Banner forces. I want them to feel terror first. I want them to lose heart.

I want them to know that they have an enemy who is as every bit as ruthless as they are, and who will stop at nothing to defeat them.'

She stood, clicked her fingers, and two of the soldiers hauled themselves to their feet. Austin looked into their eyes, but they were glazed over.

'What should I do?' he said.

'Stay here,' said Sable, 'and watch the show.' She glanced at the two standing soldiers, and repositioned the hammers in their right hands. 'Right, lads; where shall I take you two?'

'Sable,' said Austin; 'this is barbaric.'

'Is it any worse than what I forced Meader to do? This is a dirty war, Austin. Neither side has been playing by the rules, so why should I?'

She swiped the Quadrant and vanished, along with the two standing soldiers. She returned within seconds, alone, and summoned two more soldiers to their feet. Austin stared, but didn't dare to intervene, and she vanished again, taking the new pair of soldiers with her. She returned a second time, and then a third, until she had removed the last of the coerced soldiers. Austin sat on a rock, and waited. An explosion in the far distance lit up the sky, the boom coming a few moments later, followed by another explosion close by. Then, the remaining six devices exploded in quick succession, rippling across the city, the flames dancing against the horizon. Austin put his head in his hands, and closed his eyes. It was true that he had also killed that night, but transforming soldiers into walking bombs seemed an act of savagery. He tried to imagine the fear felt by the Banner personnel, as they watched their comrades striking the explosive devices with the hammers given to them by Sable.

She appeared by his side, and sat next to him.

'Those new recruits will be wishing they had stayed in Implacatus,' she said. She wiped her sword on the soft earth, and sheathed it.

'Where did you take those men?' he said.

'Are you sure you want to know?'

He nodded. 'Yes.'

'Fair enough; I warned you,' she said, lighting a cigarette. 'I took the first pair to a tavern, where the new recruits were drinking. I sent one of them into the building, while the other one waited outside to catch anybody trying to escape. I took the second pair to the officers' mess. One of them charged at a general, but I didn't stick around to see the aftermath. The third pair were dropped off at a training yard, where some of the recruits were performing night-time exercises; and I left the final pair to wander around the marketplace, where soldiers were buying supplies. Happy?'

'No, Sable. I am not happy.'

'Neither is the Banner of the Swift Hawk. This has been a bad night for them, and for the raw recruits. I thought I would be worried, coming back to Ectus, after what happened here; but I was fine. No panic; no nothing.' She glanced at Austin. 'You know, it's fine if you hate me; I couldn't give a rat's arse. But, you came close to disobeying one of my commands, and this I will not tolerate. If you want me to help you find your mother, you'll need to develop a tougher stomach for the unpleasantness of war.'

'What you did wasn't just "unpleasant", Sable. It was cruel; sadistic, even.'

'I don't take any pleasure from the pain of others. Their suffering is simply a means to an end.'

'It's wrong.'

'Who cares? The gods are just as ruthless as me. I want to win, Austin, and that's all that matters.'

'What about the civilians? The people that worked in the tavern or in the marketplace wouldn't have been soldiers.'

'Ahh, but they have chosen to work with the enemy, and that makes them a fair target – if they happen to get in the way. It was the same on Yearning – some of the dock workers there weren't members of either the Sea Banner, or the land Banners, but they were employed within the base, so, tough shit for them.'

Sable stubbed out her cigarette and stood, while Austin's gaze lingered on the flames rising from the city.

'Get up,' she said; 'we're going back to Haurn.'

He stood, then felt his stomach lurch. He vomited onto the ground, as Sable eyed him. She shook her head, then activated the Quadrant, taking them back to the courtyard by the temple of Nan Po Tana, where the others were still sitting.

'Have you finished for the night?' said Ashfall.

'We have,' said Sable, sitting down in the same place where she had eaten her dinner. Austin remained standing. He wiped his chin, but still felt used, and soiled. Sable stretched, then lit her last stick of dreamweed as she reclined next to the fire.

'Well?' said Millen. 'What were the straps and hammers for? I notice that you didn't bring any back.'

'Yes; tell us,' said Dina. 'We were discussing it while you were gone. I have a suspicion, but Millen and the dragons didn't believe me.'

Sable glanced at the Osso sister. 'Do you remember what Lara once ordered a sailor to do? It involved a hammer and a pisspot.'

'You crazy bitch,' said Dina, her face paling.

'You mean,' said Millen, 'that Dina's guess was correct?' He puffed out his cheeks, and stared into the fire. 'There were eight hammers.'

'Never mind that,' said Sable. 'We now have a barn full of explosive devices.'

Deepblue raised her head. 'Which barn?'

'Don't worry,' said Sable; 'the barn is on the far side of the temple compound, close to the houses where the natives lived. I advise you all to stay away from it. These devices are fragile, and can sometimes go off if they're knocked about. No one needs to go in there but me.'

Ashfall glanced at Austin. 'Are you well, demigod? You look ill.'

'He's fine,' said Sable. 'Just a little shocked by my depravity.' She got back to her feet, and looked around. 'I can sense that he's not the only one. You should all know that your disapproval means nothing to me. With the exception of Dina, none of you have to be here. If it's too much for you, you are free to leave.' She took out the Quadrant. 'I'm going to Ulna. With any luck, Lara will be there. Even if she isn't, I plan on picking up some more weed and booze. I'll see you all tomorrow.'

She vanished.

The others glanced at each other.

'She's out of control,' said Dina. 'If you can't see that, then you're as bad as she is. Austin, how did she manage to force eight people to blow themselves up?'

Austin looked at her, but said nothing.

'Your face is green,' she said. 'It's clear that you don't agree with her methods. That's alright; all it proves is that you have a conscience. Sable lacks one of those, and if you stay with her, she will bring us all to our deaths.'

'Be quiet,' said Millen. 'I know what you're trying to do, but it won't work.'

'I am starting to have my doubts,' said Deepblue. 'The deaths of Meader and Badblood have changed Sable. She is not the same woman whose life I rescued from the greenhides in Seabound. That woman was compassionate, and caring. The new Sable is neither of those things.'

'The old Sable will return,' said Millen. 'We just have to be patient.'

'I admire your optimism,' said Ashfall. 'I think it might be wise if we are all prepared to evacuate this place at the shortest possible notice. If Sable persists on her present course, then she will bring the wrath of the Ascendants down upon us. We must be ready to flee.'

Millen frowned. 'Am I the only one who is happy to stay loyal to Sable? We've been through so much together, and I refuse to abandon her. She won't admit it, but she needs us. Our life here in the temple might be the only thing preventing her from losing her mind with grief. You can all leave, but I'm staying.'

'Do not say such things, my rider,' said Deepblue. 'Where you go, I go. If you stay, I will also stay.'

'What are your thoughts, Austin?' said Ashfall.

The demigod lifted his eyes from the fire. 'I don't know what Sable was like before Badblood and my brother died; but I made a promise to her, and I'm going to keep it.'

CHAPTER 9
BETROTHAL

U dall, Ulna, Eastern Rim – 21st Summinch 5255 (18th Gylean Year 6)

Maddie decided that the view from her new apartment's little balcony was beautiful. She could see the town of Udall stretching out in front of her, with the broad, slow-moving river splitting the settlement in two. Where the river met the ocean, the waters of the harbour were sparkling in the sunshine. It was beautiful; it was all beautiful. Life was beautiful. She smiled as she remembered kissing Topaz on the deck of the *Giddy Gull*. She had surprised him, but she had also surprised herself. She had gone down to the harbour with the express intention of kissing him, but had doubted that her courage would be up to the task. She was glad that she hadn't been too nervous. If he had left on the ship for ten days without that kiss, then maybe he would have started to doubt if their relationship would ever work. It was strange, she thought; but if the *Giddy Gull* hadn't left Udall, then they still probably wouldn't have kissed – it was Topaz's departure that had prompted her to act. Since that moment, she had thought of little else.

Was she in love? She wasn't sure. To her knowledge, she had never properly been in love before, so had nothing with which she could compare the way she was feeling. She had harboured crushes before, and had even been slightly infatuated with Corthie Holdfast for a while, along with much of the female population of the Bulwark. But that had been different. She might have briefly fancied Corthie, but she had never seriously countenanced any kind of relationship with him. With Topaz, her expectations were wildly different. He had braved the Skerries of Luckenbay to save her. He had also killed Dax, which sat uncomfortably with her. It was taught among the Blades that to kill someone for the first time could easily break even the toughest person; and yet Topaz had seemed to have brushed it off without any ill effects. Was he suffering in secret, or was he truly unaffected by the experience? She hoped he wasn't suffering, but, at the same time, she was a little concerned that the killing had revealed a darker side to the Master of the *Giddy Gull*. He had done it to save Captain Lara, to whom he was devoted. Should Maddie worry about that? She told herself not to be silly. Lara was clearly in love with Sable, and had zero interest in boys, even boys as handsome as Topaz.

'Morning, Maddie,' said a voice from the balcony door.

Maddie turned. 'I was just thinking about you, Sable.'

Sable nodded. 'You were thinking about me? Even after you finally kissed Topaz? Sorry, Maddie, but you're not my type.'

'Ha ha,' said Maddie. 'You're very funny. What are you doing here? The *Giddy Gull* sailed a few days ago.'

'I know,' she said. 'I came to Udall to see Lara, and have just returned from the harbour.' She patted a large bag, which was slung over her shoulder. 'There was no Lara, but I did manage to buy some gin and weed.'

'And you thought you'd pay me a visit? That's nice.'

'You're the first person to call me nice for a while.'

Maddie glanced at the Holdfast woman. She seemed tired, or perhaps drunk.

'How are you feeling?' she said.

Sable lit a cigarette. 'Alright. My plan is going well. I've hit Yearning and Ectus so far; and I've added three gods to my tally.'

'I wasn't really meaning that,' Maddie said. 'I was more thinking about how you are. I'm glad you've got Millen and the others to keep you company, but I wish we were all together. I miss you, Sable.'

The Holdfast woman lowered her gaze. 'Please don't start with that. I have a hard enough time trying to hold my life together. Sometimes, I just want to scream, but what good would it do? I need to channel my anger; put it to use. Otherwise, I'll just curl up into a ball, wishing I was dead.'

'You have friends, Sable. Please remember that.'

'Look what happens to my friends, Maddie.' Her voice quietened to a whisper. 'They die, because of me. Because of my mistakes. Badblood's death was my fault, and I'll have to carry that knowledge for the rest of my life.'

'That isn't what Blackrose says. She hasn't once blamed you for what happened to Badblood. Maybe, you're being too hard on yourself. Do you want to come and speak to her? I'm sure she'd like to see you.'

Sable shook her head. 'I need to get back to Haurn.'

'Why? Haven't you just got here?'

'No. I arrived around midnight.'

'Oh. What were you doing all night?'

'I went to look for Lara, and when I realised that she and the others had already gone, I visited a few taverns; then I got invited onto the *Patience* by some crewmates from the *Gull* and the *Sneak*. You know, the ones who were selected to be left behind when Lara took the *Gull* out. It was a guy on the *Patience* who sold me the weed and gin, so I ended up smoking and drinking with them all night.' She glanced up, her eyes red. 'I did some bad things on Ectus, Maddie, and I needed to block them out of my head.'

Maddie hesitated. She wanted to ask for more details, but dreaded hearing about what Sable had done.

Sable took a breath. 'Anyway; enough of that.' She stood, and removed the Quadrant from within her clothes. 'It was good to see you, Maddie.'

'And you. Take care, Sable.'

The Holdfast woman vanished, leaving Maddie alone on the

balcony. She stared at the space Sable had occupied, then turned back to the view, as worry crept into her mind. Sable seemed fragile, as if she were made of brittle glass, and Maddie had the horrible feeling that she was seeking death, whether she was consciously aware of the fact or not. Maddie got up, and walked through the balcony doors into her apartment. She knew that Blackrose wasn't expecting her until later, but her blissful solitude had been transformed by Sable's appearance into stark loneliness, and she needed to talk to someone.

She strolled through the quiet hallways of the palace. Her new apartment was closer to the main reception hall than her previous quarters had been, and it only took a two minute walk to reach the colossal entrance doors. She walked inside, and saw Blackrose with her two trusted lieutenants – Shadowblaze and Greysteel. Ahi'edo was lurking in the shadows, keeping himself to himself as the dragons spoke.

Greysteel noticed her first. 'Good morning, Miss Jackdaw. I trust you slept well?'

'I slept very well, thank you,' said Maddie. 'I kept my windows open, and fell asleep to the sound of the river; it's very soothing. The sunrise woke me, and I had to go out onto my balcony to watch. It was very beautiful. My apartment has the most perfect view.'

'I'm glad you like your new accommodation, rider,' said Blackrose. 'You seem to be in a good mood this morning, but your eyes are telling me a different story. Is something troubling you?'

'Sable paid me a visit.'

'The Holdfast witch is here?'

'No. She's gone. She came to look for Captain Lara, and she's not here, so Sable's gone back to Haurn. She told me that she has already attacked Yearning and Ectus.'

'She went back to Ectus?' said Blackrose. 'She has courage indeed.'

'She looked emotionally drained; exhausted,' said Maddie. 'But, she had been up all night drinking, so maybe it was because of that.'

'Did she pass on any news about Ashfall, or the demigod?'

'No. I assume they must be alright; otherwise she would have mentioned it.'

'It would be most useful,' said Greysteel, 'if Sable would deign to give us a briefing whenever she visits Udall. That way, we would be kept informed of her progress. For instance, I would love to know what she did on Yearning. She might have reduced the capacity of the colonial forces to reinforce the Eastern Rim, which would be of great benefit to us, as it would isolate Throscala.'

Maddie nodded. 'I asked her to come along to speak to you, but she was too tired.'

'She seems to have prioritised drinking too much alcohol,' said Shadowblaze; 'preferring that to keeping us informed.' He hesitated. 'I did not mean for that to sound like a criticism; it was merely an observation.'

'You are free to speak your opinions, my friend,' said Blackrose; 'even when it comes to Sable. Our feud may be over, but our relationship still has room for improvement. Maddie, if Sable turns up unannounced again, please insist that she deliver an address to us. I desire to discuss Throscala with her, among other topics.'

'She also said that she killed three more gods,' Maddie went on; 'but I don't know where.'

'Three more gods?' said Greysteel. 'That pleases me immensely. If only we could coordinate our attack on Throscala with Sable, then our victory would be more certain. Without her assistance, Lady Ydril will cause us serious difficulties.'

'I agree,' said Shadowblaze. 'I would go as far as to say that any attack upon Throscala should be postponed until we can guarantee Sable's presence. We all know what Ydril is capable of – she commanded the Eastern Fleet when we attacked it off the coast of Ulna two years ago.'

'I remember,' said Blackrose. 'That was a dire day, indeed. My pride objected to accepting Sable's assistance that day, and we paid the price in dragon lives. I will not make the same mistake again. We shall not assault Throscala without her; you have my word.' She glanced at the doors. 'Where is the delegation from Wyst? They are late.'

'Are we expecting dragons from Wyst?' said Maddie.

'We are, Miss Jackdaw,' said Greysteel. 'They were due to appear at dawn.'

'Oh. Do you want me to leave? I know that the Wyst dragons don't like human riders.'

'You will stay,' said Blackrose. 'I am tired of pandering to the foolishness of Wystian traditions. If they wish to come here and speak to me, then they will have to accept the presence of my rider; and yours, Shadowblaze.'

Maddie noticed that the grey and red dragon did not turn to glance at Ahi'edo, almost as if he was ignoring his rider's presence. An uncomfortable silence descended over the hall for a moment.

'I'd like to learn how to cook fish,' said Maddie, trying to think of something to say.

Blackrose tilted her head. 'Have you given up avoiding the flesh of animals and fish, my rider?'

'No,' she said. 'I would just like to be able to cook something nice for Topaz, for when he gets back. I'm not sure that he would be happy with a plate of vegetables.'

'I'm sure he would be happy, if it were made by your hands, my rider. Has he criticised your eating habits?'

'No. He seemed a little surprised that I don't eat meat, but if he thinks it's weird, then he's been too polite to mention it. All the same, I'd like to make an effort to learn how to cook something that he'll like. He made me breakfast on the *Giddy Gull*, and it only seems fair.'

'I see. I sense that you miss him; is it so?'

'Yes. I'm a little embarrassed to say it, but I miss him tons.'

'Don't be embarrassed, Maddie. You have made your decision regarding him; yes?'

'Yes. He makes me feel... happy, and special, as if I'm the most important person in the world to him, but he doesn't treat me like I'm an accessory.' She took a breath. 'Malik's sweaty crotch; listen to me. I must sound like an idiot.'

'You sound like you are in love, Miss Jackdaw,' said Greysteel.

'Do I? Maybe I am.'

'This pleases me, rider,' said Blackrose. 'Your happiness is very important to me. However, if he betrays you, then I shall...'

'Don't say it,' said Maddie. 'I don't want to think about that. Right now, when I think of the future, it makes me excited, and I start to plan out things that I really shouldn't be considering at this stage.'

'Are you talking about children, my rider?'

Maddie's face flushed. 'Maybe. It's stupid, isn't it? It's far too early, but when I told you that I was liable to open my heart, I wasn't lying. I'm an all-or-nothing type of person, just like I said.'

Blackrose gazed at her for a moment. 'I think I shall have a private conversation with Topaz when he returns. I need to ascertain his intentions, before he breaks your heart into a thousand pieces.'

'Try not to scare him off, my Queen,' said Greysteel. 'You can be rather intimidating to mere humans.'

'I shall be calm and level-headed,' said Blackrose; 'but he needs to understand how dear Maddie is to me. I will not stand by and allow him to trample all over her feelings.'

Maddie cringed, but, at the same time, she knew Blackrose loved her. Her thoughts went to her parents, killed in the greenhide invasion of the City. Blackrose was looking out for her, just as they would have done, and the thought made her want to cry.

The huge doors of the hall opened, and two dragons strode in. Maddie recognised them. One was from Udall, and was often seen carrying out her role as a messenger and scout, while the other she remembered from when he had visited Ulna in the past.

'Earthfire of Wyst,' said Greysteel, 'thank you for coming.'

The rust-brown dragon inclined his head a fraction. He glanced around the chamber, his eyes falling upon Maddie and Ahi'edo for a moment.

'You will take a message back to your superiors in Wyst,' said Blackrose.

Earthfire gave the black dragon a look of scorn. 'I am here to dictate terms, Queen of Ulna, not to act as your message boy. The glorious legions of Wyst have now added Enna to our realm, to join Geist within the embrace of our union. I am here to tell you not to interfere in any way with our conquests. We out-number you by more than ten to one. If you try to attack Enna, we will annihilate you.'

'Do you believe that these words of aggression shall dampen my resolve?' said Blackrose. 'We are aware of your numerical superiority, but that does not mean that we are defenceless. If Wyst lands so much as one dragon upon Ulna without our permission, we shall retaliate with every force at our command. You should be aware that we are allied to a death-dealing god, and to the Holdfast witch. You shall not bully us.'

Earthfire laughed. 'To what depths have you plummeted, Queen of Ulna, that your defences have to rely upon a god of Implacatus, and a foreign witch of dubious loyalty? I recall a time when the dragons of Ulna could be counted in their thousands – where are they all now? A mere twelve thousand dragons remain upon this world, and seven thousand of them dwell in Wyst. More than half. How many do you have? A few hundred? And you have the nerve to threaten me with god powers? Have no doubt – if we wished to conquer Ulna, it would be ours in a matter of days. However, I am also here to inform you that we have no current plans to invade your pathetic island. Not yet, at any rate. We do intend to expel every human from our new territories. That process is almost complete upon Geist, and we have begun the evacuation of humans from Enna. Ulna must expect to receive more boatloads of refugees in the near future. What you do with these humans is your concern.'

'What of the dragons of Geist and Enna who wish to leave?' said Blackrose. 'Will you allow them to depart?'

'Of course,' said Earthfire. 'Why would we wish to keep those cowards? You can have them, Queen of Ulna. Do we have an agreement? You shall not interfere, and we shall not touch Ulna.'

'May I speak?' said Greysteel.

Earthfire turned to him. 'I had forgotten you were here, Lord Greysteel. How different you seem now, compared to when I knew you in Wyst. Ulna has clearly sapped your spirit.'

Greysteel tilted his head. 'I wished to inquire as to how many humans the dragons of Wyst have already slaughtered on Geist and Enna.'

'We weren't keeping count,' said Earthfire. 'Many thousands, I imagine.'

'How can you sleep at night?' said Maddie.

Earthfire pretended that he didn't know who had spoken. He glanced around the enormous chamber, before finally turning to Blackrose.

'Did an insect address me? How the standards of Ulna have fallen. What shame you must all feel.' He stared down at Maddie. 'Just as human sailors dispose of the rats that creep aboard their vessels, we shall dispose of the humans who pollute our lands.'

'This audience is at an end,' said Blackrose. 'You will depart now. If you return, we shall interpret it as an act of war.'

Earthfire tilted his head, then turned and strode from the chamber without another word.

'The insolence of the Wystians grows by the day,' said Shadowblaze. 'Perhaps we three should have ripped Earthfire to shreds. That would have sent a message they would understand.'

'He came as a peaceful delegate,' said Blackrose, 'and we are not savages. However, if he returns, then you have my permission to kill him. It would be wise to post lookouts close to the northern coast of Ulna, to act as an early warning, should the Wystians decide to break their agreement.'

'I shall see to it, your Majesty,' said Shadowblaze.

'The agreement should hold, at least for the foreseeable future,' said Greysteel. 'That leaves us free to concentrate on Throscala. Ulna cannot survive for long while its enemies exist to the north and south. Liberating Throscala from the grip of the colonial occupiers will give us a measure of security.' He glanced at Blackrose. 'There is something else, your Majesty, that should be done, in order to safeguard our future.'

'Yes? And what is that, uncle?'

'You must resolve the outstanding issues regarding the courtship, your Majesty. The deadline passed some time ago, with Lord Shadowblaze as the sole remaining suitor, and yet you have neither accepted, nor rejected his claim.'

Blackrose said nothing, and Shadowblaze glanced away.

'I realise that this is a fraught topic, your Majesty,' said Greysteel. 'However, the longer it is left unresolved, the worse it will be. The dragons in Ulna long for stable leadership. We are currently hosting refugee dragons from Geist, Enna, Throscala and Haurn, as well as our own native Ulnans. To forge this disparate group into a single entity, one that is capable of defending Ulna from Wystian aggression, the dragons need to know who is in charge. At present, the constitution is confused, as Lord Shadowblaze still has a claim to rule, as befits his status as sole suitor. Clarity is required, your Majesty.'

Blackrose seemed to sigh. She lowered her head for a moment, then turned to Shadowblaze.

'We should talk – alone; just you and I, my oldest friend.'

'I would like that, your Majesty,' said the grey and red dragon.

'Excellent,' said Greysteel. 'I shall leave you; I need to attend a meeting with a few dragons who wish to join the humans planning to resettle Plagos. I shall return later, your Majesty.'

He bowed his head, then left the chamber.

'Riders,' said Blackrose, 'remain here. Shadowblaze and I will withdraw to my private rooms for a while, to discuss the future.'

Maddie nodded. 'Good luck.'

The two dragons departed from the chamber by a different door, and the hall fell into silence. Maddie glanced at Ahi'edo, but he was keeping his gaze averted from her.

'Are humans going to resettle Plagos?' she said. 'I didn't know that.

That's the city that you were from, isn't it? It must be exciting to think that people will be living there again, after so long.'

Ahi'edo shrugged.

'Oh, come on,' she said. 'Are you still going to act like this? It's a little bit childish, don't you think?'

'Shut up,' he muttered.

'There's no need to be rude. I have never done anything to harm you, Ahi'edo.'

'No? You supported Sable, when she cooked my brain.'

'That was two years ago, and I was quite displeased with Sable for doing that. But, you recovered, and that's the important thing. Could you not just get over it? Shadowblaze seems to be getting fed up.'

Ahi'edo jumped to his feet, his eyes enraged. 'Don't you dare speak to me about Shadowblaze! My bond with him was doing fine until you turned up, and now he can barely look at me. You've ruined everything; you and that bitch Sable.'

'Would you rather still be living in a shanty town in Tunkatta? Before we arrived, the Ulnans were starving and homeless, and green-hides were roaming this island.'

'You're an idiot. You and Sable have brought this world to the edge of destruction. Was the obliteration of Lostwell not enough for you? Do you want this world to be destroyed as well?'

'Calm down. You have no idea what you're talking about, Ahi'edo. You're just unhappy because you used to be the top rider in Ulna, and now you can't handle having a woman – a foreign woman – as the Queen's rider. I wouldn't be surprised if my kidnapping made you happy.'

'I was ecstatic when the Unk Tannic carried you away. I would have given Ata'nix a medal for doing it. His only mistake was that he should have killed you, not bribed a bunch of pirates to take you away.'

Maddie raised an eyebrow. 'I see. Well, at least I know where I stand with you. I had hoped that we'd be able to forget the past, but it's clear that you still hate me. You know, I haven't punched anyone since I hit Ata'nix, but you're tempting me.'

'I heard an interesting rumour,' Ahi'edo said, his eyes tightening. 'One that I hope is true. Apparently, Ata'nix has been seen back in Ulna. He and the other Unk Tannic were forced out of Enna, and they arrived yesterday, or so I am told – I have no proof that it's true. If he has returned, then you will be at the very top of his list. Perhaps you'd better be extra careful, Maddie Jackdaw; it would be most unfortunate if Ata'nix were to stick a knife in your heart.'

'I hope he's back too,' she said; 'because then I would get to see Blackrose eat him.'

Ahi'edo opened his mouth to retort, then fell silent as the side doors of the huge chamber began to slide open. Blackrose and Shadowblaze entered the hall.

'We have an announcement to make,' said Blackrose, 'and it is appropriate that you two shall be the first to hear it.'

'Yes?' said Maddie.

Blackrose lifted her head. 'I have decided to accept Lord Shadowblaze's claim. He and I will be joined as mates.'

Maddie smiled. 'That's great news! Congratulations, to both of you.'

'Thank you, Miss Jackdaw,' said the grey and red dragon. 'And, might I say how pleased I am that you and I have overcome our previous difficulties? I admit that I was not as welcoming to you as I should have been, and for that I ask you to accept my sincere apologies.'

'Of course,' she said. 'Think no more of it. Isn't this fantastic, Ahi'edo?'

Shadowblaze's rider nodded, but the expression on his face was guarded.

'Come, rider,' said Shadowblaze; 'let us deliver the good news to the other dragons and riders within the palace. My Queen, I will see you shortly.'

Blackrose tilted her head, as Shadowblaze led Ahi'edo from the great hall. As soon as they had gone, Maddie turned to the black dragon.

'I wasn't expecting that, if I'm honest. I mean, it's wonderful news, if, you know, that's what you want. Do you want this?'

'It's complicated, my rider,' said Blackrose. 'While I respect Shad-owblaze greatly, and rank him as my oldest and best friend, I have never particularly considered him as a potential mate. However, my uncle was correct. For the good of the realm, I had to make a decision, and, when it came to it, I could not countenance rejecting him. It would have crushed his spirit, and he would have gone into exile, and I do not want to lose him. I also made a mistake. I had assumed that Shadowblaze had placed his claim due to politics, in an attempt to ensure that Splendoursun did not become the sole suitor, but I was wrong.'

Maddie frowned. 'You were?'

'Yes. Shadowblaze loves me.'

'Wow. Alright.'

'He told me just now, while we were alone. He said that he has loved me since our youth. How could I reject him? He feels... very passion-ately about me. I couldn't hurt him. So, I agreed to accept his suit.'

Maddie let out a long, slow breath. 'You were right; that is compli-cated. What happens next?'

'We now enter a formal period of betrothal. As of this moment, Shadowblaze and I are betrothed to each other. This period could last a few months, but, eventually, it will have to be consummated, or aban-doned. All I have done is buy myself some more time.'

'Did he agree that you will remain in charge of Ulna?'

'Oh yes; he was very clear about that aspect. He insisted that I will continue as the sole source of sovereignty over Ulna. He said he would be happy to retain a role as one of my chief advisors, along with you and Greysteel. Oh, Maddie, I am facing a terrible dilemma. Do I push ahead with this, and perhaps end up living a lie, or do I break my oldest friend's heart?'

'There are no easy answers, Blackrose,' she said. 'Maybe you will grow to love him in return?'

'That is my earnest hope, my dear rider. However, this is not some-thing that I can control. On the face of it, Shadowblaze is my perfect mate – he is strong, brave and loyal, and devoted to me; and he has fought for Ulna all his life. I wish I could spark a love for him inside my heart, but I fear that I never shall. What should I do?'

'We carry on for now, I guess,' she said, 'and see where it all leads. On a related topic, if you do end up as mates, would there be any expectations about how Ahi'edo and I get along?'

'Why do you ask, rider?'

'Oh, it's just that I'm not sure if Ahi'edo likes me very much.'

'That is unfortunate, but it happens sometimes. You would have to be in each other's company more often, as Shadowblaze and I would be expected to attend most gatherings together. Would that be a problem for you?'

'For me? Nope. I can handle that.'

'I sense a "but" coming, my rider.'

Maddie smiled. 'You know me well. I said I can handle it, but I'm not convinced that Ahi'edo would be able to do the same. I'm not sure why, but I get the feeling Ahi'edo would rather stick a fork in his eye than be alone in the same room as me.'

'I'm sure it's not as bad as that, Maddie.'

'You're probably right.'

'I should find my uncle, and let him know the news.'

'You do that,' Maddie said, 'and I'll head to the kitchens. There's bound to be someone there who can show me how to cook a fish.'

CHAPTER 10
COUNTING TO FOURTEEN

Alef, Western Rim – 22nd Summinch 5255 (18th Gylean Year 6)

Sable and Austin emerged from the thick forest cover, and stepped onto a long, golden beach. The sky was a deep blue overhead, with a few wisps of cloud to the south, while, ahead of them, across a short stretch of water, sat the largest island in the Alefian archipelago.

'Find somewhere to sit,' said Sable. 'Quickly; it's about to begin.'

They sat down in the shade of some trees that overhung the beach. Sable glanced up at the huge refinery on the opposite shore. Thin plumes of grey smoke were rising from several tall chimneys scattered throughout the walled refinery compound. To the west of the compound, greenhides were running amok within a fortified Banner garrison. Sable had made two trips back and forth, bringing over two hundred of the beasts to Alef, to keep the soldiers distracted while she had got on with the second stage.

'I told each "volunteer" to wait before they triggered their devices,' she said. 'I calculated that a staggered effect would cause more terror than if they all went off at once.'

Austin said nothing, his gaze on the massive refinery.

He didn't approve, and she didn't care.

'I also left each soldier in a hidden location,' she went on, 'with instructions to trigger their packages if they were discovered.' She shook her head. 'If I'd had this tactical advantage back in my home world, I would have brought the empire to its knees in a couple of thirds. Agatha did use the Quadrant, to a limited extent, to carry out a couple of assassinations, but she never utilised it to its full potential.' She glanced at Austin. 'You have no idea what I'm talking about, do you?'

'I don't think I want to know,' he said.

'Agatha's mistake was to rely upon agents to do the dirty work for her,' Sable went on. 'If she had possessed the courage to go on the operations in person, she could have easily killed the Empress, instead of merely blinding her in one eye. And, naturally, she didn't let me have the Quadrant. If I'd had it, then Karalyn would never have been able to steal it, and the history of the Star Continent would have been very different. Not better, as it turned out, but certainly different.'

Sable decided to stop talking. She knew that her present activities were stirring memories of her old life, a life she thought she had left behind, and a sense of guilt and shame threatened to overtake her. She took a breath. On her home world, she had been fighting on the wrong side; this was different. Her right hand started to shake, and she grasped it with her left, to hide the fact from Austin.

The first bomb exploded. A tremendous roar sounded from within the compound, accompanied by a flash of light, then thick, black smoke billowed up into the blue sky. She had instructed her fourteen victims to set off their devices at five second intervals, and she counted in her head.

The second bomb went off at the opposite end of the refinery complex from the first. A wooden tower collapsed into the rising flames, and debris from the explosion landed in the water among the ships that were anchored off the shore of the larger island.

'Two down, twelve to go,' said Sable.

'Why fourteen this time?' said Austin.

Sable shrugged. 'Why not? I thought that eight might not be enough...' She paused, as the third bomb went off, right in the heart of the refinery compound. 'I wanted to make sure,' she went on, as the roar from the explosion died down. 'I doubled the greenhides, and almost doubled the number of pisspots. It should be enough.'

The fourth and fifth bombs went off almost simultaneously, and she frowned, wondering if she had miscalculated. Perhaps one of her 'volunteers' had been discovered. She imagined the sense of panic that must be sweeping its way through the compound. Many native slaves were employed to work in the refinery, along with the large Banner garrison. They would be terrified, each trying to guess where the next explosion would take place. The bells in the guard towers were ringing, adding to the panic and confusion.

The sixth bomb ripped a hole in the compound's outer wall, and bricks rained down onto an oil transporter in the bay, showering the crew on the main deck as they stood staring at the destruction.

'Can we go now?' said Austin.

'No. We wait until the last explosive device goes off. I want to know the extent of the damage.'

A cluster of three bombs went off at once, and the ground rumbled beneath them as the combined explosions shook the compound. Over to the right, greenhides were starting to spill out through the garrison's main gates. They tore their way along the harbour front, their talons slashing out as they ripped through the sailors and dock workers trying to flee the explosions.

Austin put his head in his hands.

'What did you expect?' Sable said. 'We are at war.'

She watched as the unarmed dock workers tried to escape the greenhides, but others were still running out of the refinery, and were blocking their way. The tenth bomb went off at that moment, causing a huge secondary explosion as a series of oil storage tanks also ignited. Smoke was now filling the sky like a dense black cloud, while red and orange flames were whipping up from the refinery.

'It looks like the end of the world,' said Austin.

'I've seen a world end,' said Sable. 'It didn't look like this. There were earthquakes and tidal waves, and the ground opened, and lava poured out. This is nothing in comparison.'

'Is that how you justify it to yourself? It's not as bad as a world-ending cataclysm?'

'I don't need to justify anything. This was your idea.'

'I suggested it before I knew your methods.'

The eleventh and twelfth bombs went off, followed by the thirteenth in quick succession. The compound was in ruins, its walls shattered, and the buildings inside were enveloped in a huge conflagration. Smaller explosions were going off, as if they had a life of their own.

'There's nothing wrong with my methods,' she said.

'How can you say that? You forced fourteen young soldiers to trigger bombs strapped to their waists. There's nothing right about it.'

'Don't talk nonsense. Their deaths would have been swift and painless. I haven't tortured anyone. What's the difference between me doing this, and cutting their throats? I even implanted feelings of calm into them, so that they wouldn't be afraid in their final moments. I am acting in a very humane, even restrained, manner.'

Austin gestured towards the inferno on the opposite coast. 'You call this restrained?'

'I call it efficient. In a matter of minutes, we have disabled the colonial government's capacity to ship oil to their bases in Dragon Eyre. Cripple their economy – that's what you said. Is the reality different to how you imagined it?'

She frowned. The fourteenth, and final, bomb hadn't detonated. Perhaps it had, but the noise had been lost amid the roaring flames and numerous secondary explosions. The greenhides were now in control of the harbour front, she noticed. She hadn't planned that, but it was a nice touch. The beasts were clustering around the gates of the refinery, cutting down any survivors trying to escape the flames and the explosions. The quayside was littered with the bodies of the fallen, and several ships had moved further from the shore, to prevent the beasts from boarding. One of the ships was now so close, that Sable could see the people on the quarter deck, staring in dismay at the sight of the burning refinery, and the carnage on the quays of the harbour. Sable squinted. One of those standing on the quarter deck was wearing long, flowing robes, and seemed to be directing the others.

Sable stood, and drew her sword, the Quadrant in her free hand.

'Are we going now?' said Austin.

'Not yet. There's a god of some kind on that frigate in front of us. I'm going to kill her. Wait here.'

She took a guess as to the rough distance between her and the ship, then brushed her fingertips over the Quadrant. The air shimmered, and she appeared on the frigate, her feet firmly planted on the boards of the quarter deck. She smiled, then leapt towards the robed god before anyone had a moment to react. A Sea Banner lieutenant was in the way, so Sable plunged her sword into his guts, then bundled the god over. They fell to the deck, as marines stormed the rear of the ship, and a crossbow bolt whistled over Sable's head. The god beneath her tried to struggle free, her eyes lit with fear. Sable raised her right arm, and brought her sword down onto the god's neck with all her battle-vision assisted strength, severing her head. She reached for the Quadrant, and felt a crossbow bolt strike her right thigh.

Sable screamed in pain, then touched the Quadrant.

She appeared back on the beach, blood streaming from the wound in her thigh. Austin's eyes widened, and he stared at her.

'Don't just sit there,' she cried. 'Get the damn bolt out of my leg.'

He knelt by her as she lay on the sand, and placed his hands round the shaft of the bolt. He pulled, and Sable nearly lost consciousness. She closed her eyes, the pain overwhelming everything else, then she felt Austin's hands upon her skin, and a surge of healing powers rippled through her. She shuddered, and gasped.

'You need to be more careful,' Austin said.

She opened her eyes, the pain gone. She rolled onto her back and stared up at the billowing clouds of black smoke.

'The last bomb went off while you were away,' Austin went on. 'That's all fourteen, if I counted correctly. I assume you managed to kill the god on the boat?'

'I separated her head from her shoulders,' she said. 'I think she was a vision god, as she didn't try to use any death powers on me. I probably should have let her live, so that she could contact Bastion. I wonder if he knows yet. Let's wait a little longer, and see if we can persuade him to come out to play.'

'You want to wait for Bastion? Are you insane? What am I saying? Of course you're insane. How did you find fourteen more hammers?'

'I went to Gyle again yesterday evening,' she said. 'The guy in the hardware store in Port Edmond loves me. I gave him a decent tip for the hammers, and for the wheelbarrow.'

He glanced at her, as she got back into a sitting position. 'Is that where you were? You hardly seem to ever be in Haurn; at least, whenever I look for you, you're never around. I didn't see you this morning until after dawn. Were you in Gyle all night?'

'No. I made a few trips to Ectus, while you were sleeping.'

He narrowed his eyes. 'You went to Ectus? Why?'

'Well, I knew we were coming to Alef today, and I couldn't sleep. I figured it might be a good idea to create a diversion, so I transported a few loads of greenhides, and set them loose in Sabat City.'

'How many trips did you make?'

'Seven.'

'You took seven hundred greenhides to Ectus?'

'More like nine hundred. I can now transport about a hundred and twenty each time.'

'Why didn't you wake me?'

'I didn't need you, and you would only have greeted my plans with your usual look of disapproval. I made sure the greenhides were set down in the militarised districts. The Banner taverns would have been an exciting place to be last night.'

'Do you think this is funny?'

'Not particularly.'

'Nine hundred greenhides,' he said, 'rampaging through Ectus' largest city; it's obscene. They could have killed thousands of people.'

'I hope so; that's why I put them there. I filled them with a lust for blood and sent them on their way. Most are probably still on the loose as we speak.'

'I think I'm reaching my breaking point, Sable,' he said. 'I don't know if I can carry on doing this.'

'You're breaking already, Austin? We've barely begun. I had an idea when I was back on Gyle. I was thinking about killing the Eighteenth Gylean, and then using the Quadrant to take his cage into a large concentration of native slaves, so they can all see what the occupation forces did to their beloved sovereign. What do you think? I'd need to break into the Winter Palace, but I've done that before.'

'Why would you do that?'

'To spark a slave rebellion. Your brother told me all about the Gylean, and how he's treated. He showed you the dragon, didn't he?'

'I meant the killing part. Why would you need to kill him first?'

'To end his suffering, Austin. They're torturing him. Aren't they?'

'They're keeping him alive, but yes; it amounts to torture.' He put a hand to his forehead. 'Will you make it quick?'

'Of course I will. You'll be there when it happens, Austin. If, that is, you don't decide to leave me.'

'Would you let me go? I mean, if I decided that I couldn't take it any more? You said you would.'

'I might have to amend your memories first, so that you couldn't betray our plans to the enemy. If they catch you, then they'll read your mind.'

'You can alter memories?'

'Yes. I could make you forget everything you've seen me do. I'd have to go deeper, of course, and remove your memories of Ashfall, Millen, Haurn, Ulna – the lot. So much, in fact, that you'd know something was wrong – you'd be aware that a chunk of your memories were missing, but that can't be helped. I can't have you wandering around Dragon Eyre with all that information in your head.'

'You promised to take me to Implacatus. What about helping me find my mother?'

'You haven't done enough to qualify for that yet. This is only your third operation, and already you're getting cold feet. If you want me to take you back to Implacatus, you'll need to stick around a little longer. You should be grateful that I'll let you leave with your life.'

She turned back to the refinery, and watched the smoke rise from the ruins. They should go, she thought. The longer they sat on the beach, the more likely it was that someone would notice them. They were concealed by the shadows of the trees, but if a vision god was around, they would be spotted. Just a few more minutes, she thought, willing Bastion to appear. She noticed her sword lying on the beach next to her, and picked it up. She cleaned the bloody blade on the sand, and grasped the hilt, just in case.

'I'll stay,' Austin said, his voice low. 'I don't want to do this any more, but I'll stay. How many more operations do I need to go on before you'll take me to Serene?'

'Let's see. I'll need you for at least two more trips I have planned, and that doesn't include the operation involving the Eighteenth Gylean, so let's say three. The same as what you have already done. Can you manage that?'

'So, I'm halfway through? Three more trips, and you'll take me home, and help me look for my mother? Do I have your word on that?'

'No. I need to remain flexible. My schedule cannot be dictated by your needs alone, Austin. Sorry, but that's the way it is. I shall endeavour to return you after three more trips, but you're not squeezing an oath out of me.'

'That's not fair.'

'Take it or leave it.'

'I'll take it. I have no choice, do I? Not if the alternative is you wiping out months of memories from my head.'

'I'll probably have to remove the last two years, to be honest, right up to the moment when the Eastern Fleet arrived off Seabound. It'll hurt.'

'Will I think that Meader is still alive?'

'You will, but, as I said, you'll know something is wrong. You'll feel disoriented, to say the least.'

Austin glared at her, and muttered something under his breath. She wondered if he was considering fleeing. She was absent from Haurn more and more, leaving the others in the temple while she travelled to Gyle, Ectus and Ulna. What if he managed to get onto a boat and sail away? She could not allow that. She needed to be able to trust him.

She entered Austin's mind, and remained hidden there as she rooted through his thoughts. She was surprised to find that he actually liked her. He feared her, and worried about what she was doing but, at heart, he respected and admired her. She watched as he debated his options. Under no circumstances did he wish for his memories to be wiped out; he cherished his time with Ashfall, and all that he had done to assist Shadowblaze and the others in Ulna. He also feared losing the knowledge he had learned on Implacatus. That was the key. He knew why the Ascendants wanted to take over Dragon Eyre, and that was very important to him. On the other hand, he hated watching her use greenhides and bombs to slaughter so many people, and particularly loathed her method of using manipulated soldiers to trigger the explosive devices. She saw that he was tempted to flee, but his greatest desire was to find his mother. For her, he would remain loyal to Sable, at least for a while longer.

'You have been a naughty boy,' she said.

He blinked. 'What?'

'You still haven't told Ashfall that you intend to go to Implacatus, and leave her.'

'How do you know that?'

'Take a wild guess, Austin.'

'Are you inside my head?'

'I am. I was sizing out how difficult it would be to destroy your memories. Why haven't you told her? She thinks that you will be together for a long time. I think she might even love you.'

Austin gazed at the ground. 'I can't face telling her. She would leave Haurn, and I... I like her being around. Are you going to tell her?'

'No. It's none of my business what goes on between you and Ashfall.'

'Then why did you read it from my head?'

'It just leapt out at me. You must have been thinking about it. I didn't deliberately go digging for it.'

'I feel guilty about it. You don't help, either, when you refer to me as her "rider". I wish you'd stop doing that.'

'I do it to confront Ashfall with the truth, and because I think it's funny. You didn't know Ashfall in Lostwell – she detested humans there. She told me countless times that she would never form a close relationship with any human, and she mocked the entire idea of a bond. She used to say that she would never need a mere insect, and that it was a disgrace that any dragon would ever become emotionally dependent upon one; and look at her now. She fawns over you the same way that Deepblue does with Millen. That's why you need to tell her the truth.'

'I will.'

'Good. When you do, I think...' She paused, feeling another presence enter Austin's mind. She focussed her powers, and isolated the presence, sealing it off from the demigod's thoughts and memories.

'What are you doing?' said Austin. 'My head hurts.'

'Quiet,' she hissed. 'Someone else is in there with me. Someone powerful.'

She flooded Austin's mind with her powers, but didn't break the connection that the other presence had formed. Instead, she probed it, while ensuring it couldn't read any information out of the demigod. The presence tried to withdraw, but she clung onto it, forcing it to stay within Austin's mind.

She entered the presence's thoughts.

Welcome to Austin's mind, she said to the presence. *How can I help you?*

The presence didn't respond.

Is that you, Bastion? Come to pry, have you? I bet you weren't expecting to be met here by me.

Sable Holdfast?

Well done. What do you want?

To stop you, Miss Holdfast. To end your reign of terror.

Good luck with that. Where are you? Do you want to fight me?

I want to kill you. I have arrived in Alef, Miss Holdfast. You have inter-rupted my breakfast. What are your demands? What will it take for you to end this madness?

I will stop killing your soldiers and gods if you all leave Dragon Eyre, Bastion.

That will not be happening, Miss Holdfast. I have been empowered as acting governor, and I have this world's entire military might under my command. You are but one woman. Where is your red dragon?

I think you know the answer to that. Did you like what I did to Horace? I look forward to doing the same to you.

Come to the refinery gates. I shall slay the greenhides there, and then we can fight – just you and I. Is that what you want?

Yes.

I will cut you in two.

Do you remember me from Lostwell?

Vaguely. I was more interested in securing Lady Belinda. Did you know that she is going to marry the Blessed Lord Edmond?

I doubt she would do that willingly.

You would be right. It's amazing what a god-restrainer mask will do to change someone's mind. Lady Belinda resisted for a long time, but there's only so much pain even an Ascendant can take before their spirit breaks. I wish I could do the same to you, Sable Holdfast, but your mortal form is too fragile. I shall await you by the refinery gates. Now, release me from the mind of the demigod – you have made your point.

She sensed fear in Bastion's voice, and suspected that he was hiding something from her. She tried to calm her racing thoughts. She could use the Quadrant, and be by the refinery gates as soon as the last green-hides had been killed. And then she would be able to fight Bastion in person. What was she missing?

She severed the connection between Bastion and Austin, and expelled the Ancient from the demigod's mind.

'Who was in my head?' Austin said, his voice strained.

'Bastion. He wants to fight me, or so he says.'

Austin's face paled. 'Lord Bastion was reading my thoughts?'

'No. I stopped him from doing that. Shit. Now, I get it. He doesn't want to fight me; he wants to distract me, so that he can go back into your head and find out where we live.' She smiled.

'What are you talking about?' said Austin. 'We need to get out of here.'

'I agree,' said Sable, standing. 'I'm going to remain in your head until we get back to Haurn, to make sure he doesn't try to read you again. This complicates things, but I'll work something out. Come on; get up.'

She stared at the burning oil refinery as Austin stood. If anything, the flames were reaching higher into the smoke-filled sky than when the bombs had first gone off. The greenhides were still roaming the bloody waterfront, searching for survivors. The bells had gone silent, she noticed, then she realised that every guard tower along the perimeter had collapsed into the flames.

'You have murdered thousands of people,' said Austin.

'I know,' she said, brandishing the Quadrant. 'It was a good day's work.'

She flicked her fingers over the Quadrant, and they vanished.

CHAPTER 11
KILLER INSTINCT

Off Throscala, Eastern Rim – 24th Summinch 5255 (18th Gylean Year 6)

'That's it, lad,' said Topaz. 'Ease the wheel a little more to the left; yes – that's it. Remember to keep your head up. There's no point looking down at the wheel if a middie is trying to attract your attention.'

'Sorry, sir,' said the new master's mate.

Topaz noticed Vitz appear on the quarter deck, wearing his lieutenant's uniform. He spoke to Lara and Tilly, who were standing by the front railings, then Topaz beckoned him over.

'Afternoon, Vitz,' he said. 'Do you think you might have time to show the lad here how to access the ship's charts? I'll have to remain by the wheel all day.'

'Sure, Master,' said the lieutenant. 'I can do it now, if you like.' He glanced at the boy. 'What's his name?'

Topaz smiled to himself. Lara had been right about Vitz. His attitude had improved immensely since being handed his new responsibilities, and he had rarely worn his customary frown after leaving Udall.

'He's called Tommo, short for Ito'moran. He's an Olkian lad, like me.'

Vitz nodded. 'How old are you, Tommo?'

'Thirteen, sir.'

'And how long have you been a sailor?'

'Since I was eight, sir. I was up the rigging on the *Little Sneak*, sir, but I know how to read and write.'

'Course he does,' said Topaz; 'otherwise, he'd hardly be up here on the wheel, eh? He's getting a bit too tall to be scrambling round the rigging any more, so I thought I'd give him a chance.'

Vitz smiled. 'It was months before Master Topaz allowed me to even touch the wheel, lad; you must be doing well.'

The boy raised his chin. 'Thank you, sir.'

'Come on, then. I'll take you to where the charts are kept. I've got five minutes, so I'll show you how to read them at the same time.'

'Cheers, Vitz,' said Topaz, taking the wheel from Tommo. He watched the lieutenant lead the new master's mate away to the main deck, then he quickly took his bearings, checking the wind speed and direction. The southern coast of Throscala was visible as a faint line on the eastern horizon, off their port side, and he reckoned they were doing about eight knots.

'Praise the gods,' said Lara, approaching with Tilly by her side. 'It's a miracle.'

'What's that, then, Captain?'

'The fact that you've finally found a suitable master's mate. I thought the day would never come.'

'He has a new incentive,' said Tilly.

'Enlighten me, sister,' said Lara.

'It's obvious,' said Tilly. 'Before, he could afford to be extra picky, but now that he's got a sweetheart waiting for him in Ulna, it's in his interests to find his own replacement. He won't be wanting to go to sea when Maddie's pregnant.'

Lara raised an eyebrow. 'The last time I checked, you couldn't get pregnant from one kiss.'

'Ah,' said Tilly, 'but the kiss is just the start, isn't it? Next, there will be candlelit dinners and, before you know it, Maddie will have knocked out a few screaming brats.'

Lara winced. 'I'll tell you right now, Master – I ain't babysitting.'

'You're getting a little ahead of yourselves, ladies,' said Topaz.

'Did you hear what he just called us?' said Tilly. 'The bleeding cheek of it. I ain't no lady, Master.'

'My humble apologies, Captain Tilly,' he said. 'I won't do it again. Now, have you two ladies decided our next step?'

Tilly frowned. 'Sister, can I punch him?'

'Not until his new master's mate is ready,' said Lara, 'then we can both give him a good beating. In answer to your question, Master, we have decided to stay in this area for the rest of the day. Those two ships we stopped yesterday gave us a decent haul, but I want to return to Udall with the hold overflowing. One more should do it. If nothing appears today, then we'll start to head back to Ulna tomorrow.'

Topaz nodded. 'Yes, ma'am.'

Four more days, he thought, then he would be able to see Maddie again. He wondered if she had missed him as much as he had missed her. One of the merchantmen they had cleaned out on the previous day had been carrying boxes of gold and silver jewellery, and he had selected a couple of pieces that he hoped Maddie would like. He had rarely ever seen her wear jewellery, and should have asked her what she liked before the *Giddy Gull* had departed Udall, but it had slipped his mind. Maybe she didn't like jewellery, and she would accept what he gave her out of politeness, and then there would be an awkward silence. He shook such thoughts from his head. He needed to concentrate on his job, and stop day-dreaming about Maddie Jackdaw.

'Have you ever known someone who doesn't eat meat, ma'am?' he said.

Lara rolled her eyes. 'Here we go again.'

'I was convinced that Maddie would crack,' said Tilly, 'when we were on the *Sneak*, and food was starting to run low; but she stuck to it. It's weird, though. She told me that she felt sorry for the little animals.'

'I don't know how anyone could feel sorry for a fish,' said Lara. 'All they do is swim about. A little baby lamb? Now, I can sort of get that, but a bleeding fish? It makes no sense. Maybe it's cultural. On her home world, perhaps no one eats meat.'

'No, they eat meat there, ma'am,' said Topaz. 'Her people thought it was strange too.'

'Well, each to their own, I guess,' said Lara. 'We all have our foibles.'

'Yeah,' said Tilly. 'Yours is called Sable Holdfast.'

'So? I admit it. I ain't ashamed.'

'I'd wish you'd choose a nice girl,' said Tilly. 'Sable's out of her bleeding mind.'

Lara stared out to sea. 'I wonder what she's doing. I've finally found someone I want to grow old with, and she's on a mission to destroy the world.'

'You can certainly pick 'em, sister.'

'It occurs to me, ma'am,' said Topaz, 'that if Sable, Blackrose and the others are successful, then there will be no room for pirates left on Dragon Eyre. We've already restricted ourselves to only attacking ships that are declared enemies of Ulna. The dragons will want us to stop altogether if we win.'

'I was thinking the very same thing when we were talking with Greysteel,' said Lara. 'The endless wars have been good for us. It sounds harsh, but it's true. Two decades of chaos have produced the ideal conditions for people in our line of work. If peace comes, well, then I guess it's over.'

'Gods,' said Tilly; 'now I'm depressed.'

'Take us in a little closer to the coast, Master,' said Lara, 'in case any Sea Banner vessels come round the headland. I assume you know this stretch of Throscala well?'

'I know it, ma'am,' he said. 'The southern coast is a lot like Serpens – cliffs, coves, and very few inhabitants.'

'A good place to hide, Master?'

'There are several good places, ma'am.'

The captain glanced at the sun's position. 'We might shelter in one of those coves overnight, if we don't bump into anyone this evening. That way, the lads will be fresh for the morning.'

'Understood, ma'am,' he said, turning the wheel.

Topaz guided the *Giddy Gull* to within a mile of the coastline. The cliffs at the southern end of Throscala were sheer in places, with waterfalls that were sparkling in the light from the west. They cruised for an hour, as the sun began to lower off their starboard side. Topaz kept his gaze on the shore, scanning it for the numerous narrow creeks that marked the coast, when his eyes spotted something – a faint wisp of smoke, rising from a hidden cove.

'Captain,' he shouted over to Lara.

She strode over to him, and he pointed towards the thin tendril of grey smoke. She squinted at it, then nodded.

'Is there a settlement close by?' she said.

'Not that I'm aware of, ma'am. It looks like a camp fire from this distance. I think it's coming from a long, narrow creek that I've seen before. We'll be at its head in ten minutes.'

'Slow the *Gull*,' she said, 'then bring it to a halt by the entrance of the creek, but out of sight of anyone who might be lurking inside.'

'Yes, ma'am.'

Lara turned to her sister. 'Tilly! Grab the duty patrol, and bring them up here; fully-armed and ready to go. Lieutenant Vitz – get the launch prepared. We're stopping the *Gull*.'

Tilly ran off, while Vitz saluted, then began issuing orders to a group of seamen. Topaz issued his own orders, and the sails were lowered as the brigantine started to slow down. Tilly summoned a dozen men to the quarter deck, and they gathered round Lara.

'Tilly,' she said, 'I want you to lead – take the patrol in the rowing boat, and investigate the source of that smoke. If it's a ship, then stay out of sight, if you can; and report back.'

Tilly glanced in the direction of the smoke. 'It's probably just a fishing vessel, grilling their dinner.'

Lara shrugged. 'Yeah, maybe. It's worth checking out, all the same. We'll launch the boat as soon as we anchor.'

Topaz brought the *Giddy Gull* to within a hundred yards of the ragged coastline, and the two anchors were dropped, their chains grinding and rattling. Topaz stayed by the wheel as the main deck became a hive of activity. The rowing boat was swung over the side of the ship, and then lowered into the clear blue waters of the shallow bay. Tilly and her dozen men clambered down a net, and positioned themselves by the oars of the little vessel. Lara shouted down a few last orders, then the rowing boat was pushed away from the brigantine. The oars chopped through the gentle swell, and the craft headed off in the direction of the cove. Topaz locked the wheel into position, then strode to the side of the ship to watch the rowing boat. He noticed Ryan, standing with another carpenter's mate, by the railings of the main deck, and he walked down to join them.

Ryan offered him a cigarette, and they smoked as they waited.

'This is a waste of time,' said Ryan. 'We should be heading back to Ulna by now.'

Topaz smiled. 'Desperate to get back to Udall, are you?'

He nodded. 'I thought you'd feel the same, Master. Just think who's there waiting for you, eh?'

'I told Maddie that we'd be away for ten days or so, and it looks like that was a decent guess. At least I have an excuse for wanting to go back. What's yours?'

'I'm worried, mate; about Sable.'

'I don't think she's actually going to kill you, Ryan.'

'It's not that I'm worried about. What if she comes back while we're away, and finds someone else to supply her with weed?' He shook his head. 'I only sold her a small handful of smokes; she's probably run out by now, and here we are, in the middle of bleeding nowhere. I've blown my chance, mate. I should have volunteered to stay on the *Patience*.'

'The captain picked her best crew for this job; you should be flattered.'

Ryan nodded, a frown plastered onto his face. 'I know. I'm too good at my job; that's the problem. I should have been slacking off. Now, I'll be known as the guy who almost became Sable's weed dealer. Life ain't fair.'

'Master!' cried Lara from the quarter deck. 'Get your ass up here.'

Topaz flicked the half-smoked cigarette into the sea, and strode back to the quarter deck.

'Yes, ma'am?' he said.

'I'm getting the pisspots ready, Master,' she said. 'We still have three left, after dear old Dax used one to blow the *Little Sneak* to pieces. Are you able to pilot the *Gull* into the cove in a way that'll block any ship's escape route, while allowing us to loose at the bastards at the same time? Assuming, of course, that there are bastards hiding in there.'

Topaz glanced at the rocks near the base of the cliffs. The rowing boat had entered the creek, and had disappeared from sight.

'If we take it slowly, ma'am,' he said, 'it shouldn't be a problem.'

Lara nodded, her attention on the entrance to the creek. 'Good. Get ready.'

Topaz walked to the wheel, and summoned Tommo and a midshipman to stand by his side. They waited for another ten minutes, and Topaz felt his nerves rise as he ran the calculations in his head. The light was starting to fade, and he had to take reduced visibility into account, along with the vagaries of the currents that swept the southern coast of Throscala.

The rowing boat appeared again, heading back towards the *Gull*, and Lara bounded down to the main deck, and leaned over the railings. A sailor on the small craft lifted a series of flags over his head. Lara watched for a moment, then turned to the crew.

'Battle stations!' she yelled. 'Everyone to their posts.' She turned back to the rowing boat, and lifted a green flag high in the air. The small vessel stopped in the water, and began to turn, as Lara ran back onto the quarter deck.

'Take us in, Master,' she said.

'Yes, ma'am. What was the message? I didn't understand those signals.'

'Me and Tilly have our own little language for this stuff.' She grinned. 'It's our lucky day, Master. A Sea Banner vessel is anchored in the cove, and the crew are on the beach, having a bleeding party by the sounds of it. I can hardly believe it. Bleeding amateurs.'

'There have been no hostile ships in these waters for two years, ma'am,' said Topaz, as he unlocked the wheel. 'An attack by the Five Sisters is the last thing they'll be expecting.'

Lara rubbed her hands together, her eyes gleaming with excitement. Topaz rattled off a list of orders to the midshipman, then began to turn the wheel.

'Watch what I do, lad,' he said to Tommo, as the midshipman hurried away. 'I'll be taking the *Gull* in nice and slow, right behind the rowing boat. Topsails only, so that we don't get caught in a gust; and watch out for those eddies – each one marks where the current can be unpredictable. I'd die of embarrassment if we grounded the hull.'

Lara raised an eyebrow. 'You'd die, but not from embarrassment, Master.'

The brigantine began to move, its topsails filling with the breeze, and Topaz quietened as he concentrated on following the rowing boat towards the entrance to the cove. They rounded the headland, and Topaz had a clear view down into the long creek. It ended in a small beach, and he saw the source of the smoke. A group of men were gathered round a large fire, while a sleek Sea Banner frigate sat anchored in the deep water a hundred yards from shore, in the shadows of the cliff-side. The rowing boat was making directly for the enemy vessel, but there was no sign of any alarm being triggered.

'Aim the bow at the beach, Master,' said Lara, 'then get us alongside the frigate as soon as possible. Those assholes on the sand can't even see us yet – their eyesight's ruined due to their stupid fire.' She cackled. 'Let's see if they like a pisspot slamming into them, eh? Vitz! Prepare the catapult to loose on my command.'

The lieutenant saluted.

Lara watched him make his way down to the bow. 'This'll test the lad. If he can handle loosing a pisspot at his former colleagues in the damn Sea Banner, then he'll have the makings of a decent officer. Fingers crossed, eh?'

A cry rose up from the deck of the frigate, as the presence of the pirates was finally noticed. The ship's bell was rung, and a few faces on the beach turned to see what was happening.

Lara raised her hand. 'Loose!'

Moments later, a projectile was hurled from the bow of the *Gull*. It arced through the sky, then landed in the midst of the sailors on the beach. An explosion ripped through the air, along with tons of sand, and the remains of the men who had been sitting round the fire.

'Train the ballistae onto the deck of the frigate,' Lara yelled. 'Cut down anything that moves.'

The rowing boat reached the side of the anchored frigate, and Tilly led the pirates up the hanging net. One was shot in the chest by a marine from the deck, and he fell back into the waters of the creek with a splash. A ballista bolt was released from the *Gull*. It missed the marine, but he retreated out of sight, as Tilly and her men reached the deck. On the beach, dazed and wounded sailors were staggering around next to the bomb crater, while a handful of marines were trying to launch their own rowing boat.

'Another pisspot, Lieutenant!' yelled Lara. 'Aim for the marines.'

A second ceramic device was loosed from the bow of the *Gull*. It soared over the group of marines by the shoreline, and landed among the survivors from the first explosion. More sailors were blown apart, while many ran for the shelter of the nearby forest, abandoning their officers, and their ship.

Topaz brought the *Giddy Gull* alongside the frigate, and Lara ordered the pirates to storm the vessel. The crew leapt over the gap, and began fanning out through the frigate, their crossbows dealing with any resistance from the small number of Sea Banner personnel who had remained behind to guard the ship. Lara retrieved her battle axe from her cabin, and joined her men on board the frigate, as Topaz brought the *Gull* to a halt.

'Look at her go,' said Tommo, his eyes on Lara as she took command of the frigate.

'She's in her element, lad,' said Topaz.

Vitz ran onto the quarter deck. 'Where's the captain?'

Topaz pointed over to the frigate. 'She's having the time of her life over there.'

'The marines are rowing towards us,' Vitz said. 'What should I do?'

'You're the officer, lad,' said Topaz. 'What do you think?'

'We should repel them before they can board?'

'That seems the sensible thing to do. Get the ballistae trained onto the bastards. We know what marines are like; if they get aboard, they could wreak havoc.'

A flash of anxiety swept over Vitz's face. 'Right.'

'Take a deep breath, Lieutenant,' said Topaz. 'You're doing fine.'

'Am I? I just loosed two pisspots onto a group of unarmed sailors, who were sitting enjoying their dinner round a fire. What kind of man could do a thing like that?'

Topaz eyed the approaching rowing boat. It was full of marines brandishing crossbows, and was speeding towards the bow of the *Gull*, their oars cutting through the calm waters.

'They're getting closer, Lieutenant. Best act now.'

'Think about what you're asking, Master. You want me to loose ballista bolts into a rowing boat?'

'That's exactly what I'm asking you to do. If you don't, then those bastards will carve us up. Most of the crew are on the frigate.'

Vitz's face paled. 'I... I don't think I can.'

Topaz narrowed his eyes. 'Then take the wheel. I'll do it myself.'

He strode from the quarter deck, feeling Vitz's eye bore into his back. Topaz reached the main deck.

'Everyone onto the starboard side!' he yelled. 'Come on; move! Get crossbows trained onto that damn rowing boat, and cut the bastards down! Now!'

He started to shove sailors across the deck, pushing them towards the railings, and organising them into a long line.

'Don't let them board!' he yelled.

Bolts shot out from the rowing boat, and one sailor on the *Gull* was struck. This seemed to spur on the other pirates, who began loosing their own bows down into the rowing boat, as Topaz ran to the forward ballistae. The devices were unmanned, so he turned one himself, and aimed it down into the rowing boat. The marines in the small craft saw what he was doing, and crossbow bolts whistled by his head, as he loaded one of the ballista. All sympathy for the Sea Banner marines evaporated in his mind as a bolt sped by his face. He had been angry with Vitz, but he understood how the young man was feeling. The men in the rowing boat had once been their comrades-in-arms, and he knew he had to kill them, or be killed by them.

He had killed before, he said to himself, as he stared down the sights of the ballista. He had loosed a crossbow bolt into Dax. He hadn't hesitated. He had taken the bow from Maddie, to save her from having to do it, and now he was doing the same – protecting Vitz from having to add more deaths to his tally. Sending a couple of pisspots over to a distant beach was different – here, he could see the faces of the marines as they got ever closer to the side of the *Giddy Gull*. Some of them looked like boys, rather than men, and he could almost taste their fear as they saw the ballista pointing down at them.

Topaz loosed, and a yard-long steel bolt flew through the air. It went through the chest of a marine, then carried on, punching a fist-sized hole in the bottom of the rowing boat. Topaz re-loaded the ballista, keeping his head down as he did so, and trying not to think about the life of the marine that he had taken.

They would kill him if he did nothing, and he didn't want to die. His thoughts went to Maddie as he placed a second bolt into the device. He wanted to see her again, which meant he had to live. And to live, he had to kill.

He loosed the second bolt. It decapitated the marine officer, who was crouching at the front of the rowing boat, then went through the leg of a junior marine, and punctured another hole in the small craft's hull. The rowing boat began to flounder, and it slowed down, as water flooded through the two holes. The pirates on the main deck kept up their hail of crossbow boats, but the marines were now a sitting target, and they were slaughtered within a minute.

A sailor slapped Topaz on the back. 'Nice one, Master! You certainly did the business.'

Topaz looked up. The rowing boat was slowly sinking, its bottom filled with water and the corpses of the marines. Over on the beach, there was silence. The two craters had obliterated the fire, and body parts were scattered across the sand. A solitary figure stood watching from the water's edge, dressed in the uniform of a Sea Banner captain, his crew either dead, or hiding in the forest. A cheer rose up from the men on board the *Giddy Gull*, and Topaz heard them chant his name.

It took two hours to get the captured frigate ready to leave the creek. Twenty-four native members of the Sea Banner had been found on board, and had been pressed into the service of the Five Sisters; but even with their numbers, each vessel was operating with the bare minimum of crew. Tilly walked the deck of the frigate with a broad grin on her face. The vessel was fully-supplied and equipped, and was a good deal larger than the *Little Sneak* had been. She came over to the *Giddy Gull* before both ships were due to depart, and Topaz joined her and the officers in Lara's cabin. Tilly presented her sister with a large bottle of gin that had been liberated from her new ship, and Lara opened it.

'A toast,' she said to those crammed into her cabin. 'Firstly, to our new ship – the latest member of the Five Sisters – the *Sow's Revenge*.'

They all drank from their mugs.

'Although,' Lara went on, 'I hope my sister has the sense to change her new frigate's name. The *Sow's Revenge*? I mean, come on.'

'I might drop the sow part,' said Tilly, grinning from ear to ear, 'and just call it the *Revenge*, but who knows – it might grow on me.'

'Our second toast is for the hero of the hour,' said Lara, raising her mug again. 'To Master Topaz, who had the presence of mind to take command of the ballistae. If those marines had made it on board, we'd be having a wake right now, instead of a party.'

They drank again, although Topaz noticed that Vitz's eyes were downcast.

'The Master has informed me,' said Lara, 'that there is another creek less than ten miles to the east of here. We'll anchor there for the night, and sail for Ulna at dawn. Lieutenant Vitz is to temporarily take on the role of acting master for the *Revenge*, at least until we get back to Udall, then we can recruit a few more willing lads to get our numbers back up to where they should be.' She smiled. 'Well done, everyone; now piss off and get back to work. Master, you stay here.'

Tilly gave her sister a hug, then she and the officers left the cabin. Lara poured out more gin for herself and Topaz, and then gave him a cigarette.

'Thanks for the toast, ma'am,' he said.

'No problem,' she said. 'However, amid all the back-slapping and congratulations, one question kept popping into my head.'

'Ma'am?'

'Why was it you up on the bleeding ballista? You're the damn master, not a bleeding ballista-operator. If you'd been killed, then we'd all be screwed. What were you thinking?'

She stared at him, and he got the impression that she already knew the answer to her question.

'I... uh...'

'Did Vitz refuse to obey an order, Master?'

'Well, technically, ma'am, I can't give him an order. He ranks above me now.'

'Don't give me that crap. You are the master of the *Gull*. An order from you is the same as an order from me. Yes or no – did he refuse to do what you asked? I presume you told him what needed to be done?'

'Don't be too hard on the lad,' he said. 'He loosed two pisspots onto the beach. I think that pushed him to the edge. I told him to take the wheel.'

'I see. Did you tell him to take the wheel before or after you asked him to do his proper job?'

Topaz straightened his back and looked directly ahead. 'I don't remember, ma'am.'

'Why are you protecting him, Topaz?'

'He's my friend, ma'am.'

'He could have got us all killed.'

'I wouldn't have allowed that to happen, ma'am. I didn't allow it to happen.'

'Praise the gods that you were there, Topaz.' She sighed. 'Vitz is Tilly's problem now. She'll keep a close eye on the lad. I'll work out what to do with him when we get back to Udall. Now, one more question. For all the time I have known you, Topaz, you have never been a killer. How are you feeling? You look fine; calm and settled, but you looked the same after you killed Dax. What's going on inside your head?'

Topaz took a deep breath. 'I'm trying not to think about it, ma'am. I don't think it's wise to dwell on these matters.'

She frowned. 'Is that it? I've known men – tough, hard, men, who crumbled into tears when they first took another person's life. Even I threw up after I killed my first man, and I had nightmares about it for a long time afterwards. Are you one of those guys who just brushes it off? It hadn't occurred to me that you'd be like that.'

'It hadn't occurred to me, either, ma'am. Maybe I'm just a cold-hearted bastard.'

'Well, for Maddie's sake, I hope that isn't true.' She drained her mug. 'Back to work, Master, and thank you for saving the *Gull*.'

Topaz saluted, then walked back out onto the quarter deck. Lamps had been lit on the decks of both ships, and stars were shining down from the dark skies. He wondered about what Lara had said, as he took his place by the wheel. He felt sorry for the men whose lives he had taken, but, apart from that, he was untroubled by what he had done. Did that mean there was something wrong with him?

'Watch what I do,' he said to Tommo, who was standing close by.

He gestured to a midshipman and rattled out a few orders. Within a few minutes, the *Giddy Gull* was moving towards the open sea, and by the time they had left the creek, Topaz had pushed the dead marines to the furthest recesses of his mind.

Cold-hearted bastard or not, he had a job to do.

CHAPTER 12
UNINHIBITED

Nan Po Tana, Haurn, Eastern Rim – 27th Summinch 5255 (18th Gylean Year 6)

'Tomorrow,' said Dina, as she, Millen and Austin sat round the fire, 'I'll have been here, stuck on this miserable island, for a damn month.'

Millen placed the kettle onto the hot embers near the base of the fire.

'A month,' Dina went on, 'and for what? What's the purpose of me being here? I need to go home. There are no members of the Osso family left in Langbeg, except for a couple of cousins, who can't be trusted. If I don't get back, then the other families will divide up our possessions among themselves, and that includes Befallen Castle, the place I've lived since I was little.'

'Sable has a plan,' said Millen, as he wiped his hands on a rag.

Dina laughed. 'Does she? Tell me, why is she never here?'

'Don't exaggerate,' said Millen. 'Sable is here most of the time.'

'Where is she now, eh?' Dina said. 'I bet you have no idea. She tells you nothing, yet she expects you to be always here in the temple, ready for her whenever she decides to show up. Do you enjoy being her servant, Millen?'

'Look,' he said; 'it'll be light soon, and I'm busy. Can we talk about this later?'

'Yeah, right. You're always the same – "let's talk about it later"; that's what you say, but you don't mean it. If you were a real man, you'd help me escape. My family is rich; they would pay you a fortune to return me to my home, or even if you just helped me get off this damn island.'

'There's no way to get off Haurn,' said Millen. 'The boats don't stop here any more, not since the natives evacuated. Are you going to swim to Yearning?'

'You have two dragons. Neither of whom, I might add, seem particularly enamoured with Sable. We could fly away.'

Millen ignored her, so she turned to Austin. 'What do you think? Ashfall could carry us away. It's clear that Millen is besotted with Sable, but you seem to be a little bit more sensible, Austin. What are you doing here? What are you trying to achieve? I see the look on your face whenever you return from another operation – you ain't happy; it's bleeding obvious. And Ashfall ain't happy, either. She dotes on you, Austin, and I hear the things she says when Sable and you go off on another murderous expedition. She'd eat Sable if you got hurt. If you asked her to leave, then she'd jump at the chance to get out of here. All you have to do is take me with you.'

Austin gazed into the low fire. 'I'm sorry, Dina, but I'm not leaving; not until the job is done.'

'The job will never be done! There will always be more people for Sable to kill. Do you enjoy killing, Austin?'

'No.'

'Then why are you doing this? Sable is turning you into a mass murderer, but it's not too late to step back from the abyss. If Sable wants to continue on her rampage, then let her. That's her business. You know, I believe that she won't ever stop; she'll keep on doing this until she's dead. Do you long to die by her side, Austin? She's already got your brother killed – do you want the same thing to happen to you?'

Austin said nothing. The kettle whistled, and Millen removed it from the fire. He poured hot water into three mugs, then stirred each of them with a spoon. Austin watched, unwilling to turn his gaze to Dina, who was glaring at him. The Osso sister was right; Sable did seem to long for death, and Austin couldn't imagine how much slaughter would be enough for her. He had started helping her partly through idealism, with a desire to overthrow the colonial government, but he had moved beyond that. The only reason he was still on Haurn was to try to persuade Sable to help him look for his mother, but he couldn't tell Dina that. She would pass the information straight on to Ashfall, who would then leave the island in disgust.

Millen passed out the mugs, and Austin took one. The demigod lit a cigarette, unsure about when exactly he had started smoking. To the east, the sky was lightening, though a chill remained in the air. He sipped his hot coffee.

Dina shook her head. 'Why did I have to end up with you two? A more useless pair of men I have never met. Neither of you has the courage to stand up to Sable. Are you scared of her; is that it? You bleeding cowards. If my father was here, he'd kick the living shit out of both of you.'

'You should count yourself lucky,' said Millen. 'You're our prisoner, and yet we let you roam around the temple compound without any chains or shackles, and you eat the same food as the rest of us.'

'Oh yes, I'm so lucky,' she said. 'Lucky me.'

The air shimmered, and Sable appeared by the entrance to the temple. She yawned, then glanced at the fire.

'Is that coffee?' she said. 'Make me some, could you, Millen?'

'Sure,' he said, reaching for a fourth mug.

Dina muttered something under her breath. Sable eyed her, then sat down by the fire.

'Where were you?' said Austin.

'Never you mind,' said Sable. 'I was doing things that I don't want any god to be able to read out of your head.'

Millen passed the filled mug to Sable, and she took a sip. 'Yuck. It needs sugar, or whisky at the very least.' She stretched. 'Austin, we have an operation today. Are you ready?'

'I guess so.'

'Where are the dragons?'

'They're off flying somewhere,' said Millen. 'Deepblue was restless.'

Sable nodded. 'You're going to like today's operation, Austin.'

'Will I?' said the demigod. 'Where are we going?'

'You'll see. We're leaving in ten minutes.'

Austin put down his mug and stood. 'I need to go to the toilet in that case. Back in a minute.'

He walked towards the outhouse that sat at the rear of the temple, but halted as soon as he was out of sight of the fire. He took a breath, and noticed that his hands were shaking. Images of Ectus and Alef flashed through his mind, and he almost threw up his coffee. He lit another cigarette, and smoked it, feeling a knot of dread and anxiety form in the pit of his stomach. He didn't want to go with Sable, but how else was he going to get back to Implacatus? Dragon Eyre wasn't safe for him any more, not after Bastion had been inside his head. He was trapped, and he knew it. He made his way back to the fire, and sat down, his eyes lowered.

'But,' Dina was saying, 'if Lara and Tilly are now based in Ulna, couldn't you take me there? If the point of keeping me a prisoner is to deter my father from attacking my sisters, shouldn't I be with my sisters?'

'You're staying here,' said Sable, 'and that's that.'

'That doesn't make any sense,' cried Dina. 'You should...'

'Oh, shut up,' said Sable. 'I'm sick of hearing you whine all the time.' She glanced at Millen. 'Let me know if she constantly complains while Austin and I are away. If she does, then I'll lock her back inside her room.'

'You're nothing but a heartless bitch,' said Dina.

'So? Do you think I give a shit about your feelings, Dina? Where was your concern for Maddie when you were planning to sell her as a slave? This victim act that you've perfected is starting to wear thin. One more word from you, and I'll go into your mind and force you to love me. I could do that. I could make you do whatever I pleased – wipe your memories, or make you bark like a dog. I could persuade you to walk out of the temple gates, and offer yourself to the greenhides. Don't tempt me, Dina – I'm warning you.'

The Osso sister's face paled, and she lowered her head.

Sable downed the last of her coffee, and got to her feet. 'Come on, Austin. It's time.'

The demigod sat frozen for a moment, as if his legs were refusing to respond, then he slowly got to his feet. They went into the temple, and pulled on their leather armour in silence. Sable tied her hair back into a ponytail, and strapped her sword to her waist. They checked each other's straps, then Sable raised the Quadrant. She gazed at the device for a long moment, then brushed her fingers across the surface.

They appeared in a long, low barn, amid the stolen racks of explosive devices.

Austin frowned. 'We could have walked here.'

'Why walk, when you can Quadrant?' said Sable. 'Right. I think we'll need a dozen devices for today's fun-filled operation. It's hard to judge, but a dozen should suffice. Stand a bit closer to me.'

'I don't know if I can do this.'

Sable shrugged. 'Tough.'

She activated the Quadrant, and they appeared within a cave, along with a rack of explosives. One end of the cave was open to the outside, and Austin could see the ocean crashing against the cliffs below the entrance. Dozens of crates were stacked next to the walls of the cave, and several large sacks were lying piled beside them. One large crate was lying open, and was full of steel armour.

'Where are we?' he said.

'I've been working out a contingency plan,' she said; 'in the event that we have to flee Haurn in a hurry.' She gestured towards the crates and sacks. 'I've stockpiled supplies that could last us for many days. It's not as comfortable as Nan Po Tana, but it will do in an emergency.'

'Is this what you've been doing?'

'Among other things.'

'You didn't answer my question – where are we?'

'I'm not going to tell you that, Austin.'

She gazed into his eyes, and he felt a pain behind his temples.

'Ow!' he yelled. 'What did you just do to me?'

'I have sealed off some of your memories. I'll return them to you later.'

'What?'

'So, where do we live, Austin?'

He frowned. He knew where they lived, but somehow he couldn't find the name of the place, or even picture it in his mind. He felt a surge of panic.

'Where were we, five minutes ago?' Sable went on, narrowing her eyes at him.

'I... I don't know. I don't like this, Sable. I can remember you, but... but...'

'Calm yourself. It's temporary. I decided to try this approach, rather than wiping your memories permanently. It'll wear off on its own, but it will last long enough to protect us if there happens to a vision-powered god in the vicinity of where we're going next. Neat, eh?'

'We were with others,' Austin said. 'There are others where we live, but I can't remember them, Sable. I remember being on Ulna, but then...' His eyes welled up.

Sable sighed. 'Hold on a moment.'

She gazed into his eyes, and he felt a sense of calm descend over him. Everything was going to be alright. All he had to do was trust Sable, and follow her orders, and everything would work out for the best. Breathe. In and out. Relax. That's it.

'How are you feeling now?' she said.

He frowned. 'Better.'

'Good. Alright, now we're ready. We are going to Na Sun Ka, Austin, but we're not going to be targeting the Banner forces today. Bastion will be expecting that, and I like to be unpredictable.'

'Bastion?' said Austin, his eyes widening. 'Is he here?'

'I might have sealed off too much,' she said. 'Still, it's a work in progress – I can refine it when we go on our next operation.'

Austin stared at her, confusion swamping his thoughts. Did she not know who Bastion was? And what did she mean by "next operation"?

'I hope you remember how much you hate the Unk Tannic,' she said.

'Are we going to attack the Unk Tannic?'

'Yes, Austin; we are.'

'Those bastards locked me in a cage in the harbour of Udall, as if I were a monster. You're damn right I hate them.'

Sable smiled. She brandished the Quadrant, and the air shimmered. Their surroundings changed, from the damp cave to the side of a smoking volcano. The stench was the first thing Austin noticed, and he gagged from the sulphurous fumes. The sun had risen over the eastern horizon, but its rays were being blocked by the thick smoke hanging over the desolate landscape. Next to him, Sable was checking the ceramic devices. She had transported the entire rack, and it was sitting on a wide, flat ledge, overlooking a barren valley at the foot of the mountain.

She smiled. 'Now – this looks like the end of the world.'

He frowned.

'You don't remember our conversation on Alef, do you?' she said.

'I've never been to Alef, Sable.'

She rolled her eyes. 'Definitely too much. Never mind; just do exactly as I say, and we'll be fine.'

'I remember a dragon,' he said. 'A grey dragon. I think I like her.'

'Focus on the job at hand,' she said. She pointed at the slopes of the mountain on the other side of the valley from them. 'Look over there. Do you see those cave entrances? Buried beneath that mountain is the largest Unk Tannic compound on Dragon Eyre. It took me a long time to find it. They've taken every possible precaution to remain hidden from the powers of vision gods. Each cave appears to be empty for the first hundred yards or so, and there are several concealed escape routes tunnelled through the cliffs. I studied that mountain more than once before I realised that the Unk Tannic were hiding there. Crafty bastards.'

'You got the bastards part right,' he said. 'How are we going to destroy it?'

'We're going to plant explosive devices at every entrance bar one.'

'Alright. And then what?'

'Then, I shall gather up a few green friends, and send them in through the last entrance.'

'Green friends? What are you talking about?'

'You'll see. We're going to do this stage as quickly as possible. I'll take us to each entrance, and you'll plant the explosives. I'll light the fuse, then we'll come back here, and repeat the process until we've visited every escape route I've managed to find. Go on; grab one of the devices.'

Austin nodded, then walked to the rack. He took one of the heavy ceramic containers in his arms, and cradled it like a child. Sable smiled, then activated the Quadrant. They appeared in a low valley, next to a cluster of wiry, gnarled thorn bushes. Sable pointed towards a hole in the ground beneath the bushes, that was almost invisible, and Austin set the device down next to it.

'Push it all the way in,' she said, 'but leave the fuse poking out.'

He did as she asked, then she crouched down and lit a metal lighter. The flames caught the dangling fuse wire, and she triggered the Quadrant, taking them back to the wide ledge.

'Right. Next one, Austin; quickly.'

He picked up another explosive, and was gripping it against his chest when the first bomb went off. A flash of light and smoke erupted from the valley below them, then Sable took them to their next location. For ten minutes, they worked in silence, travelling back and forth between the high ledge and the sides of the opposite mountain, until all twelve explosive devices had been set off. The grey smoke from the explosions was mingling with the clouds of vapour coming from the volcano, and the sound was echoing off the cliffs on either side of the valley.

'Good work, Austin,' Sable said. 'Wait here.'

She vanished, and Austin sat down on the ledge. He had been too busy to think about what the Holdfast woman had done to his head, but he was happy that he hadn't panicked. He tried to remember when he had first met Sable, but the void in his memories made him feel sick and dizzy. He glanced across the valley at the sole cave entrance that they had left alone. Two men emerged from it, and peered out at the smoke rising from the valley. They looked tiny to Austin, but he could see their black robes, even at that distance.

Unk Tannic, he thought. Sable must have recruited him to fight the Unk Tannic. Was she working for Bastion? Meader wouldn't be happy about that. His brother hated the Unk Tannic as much as anyone, but he wouldn't like the idea of Austin working for someone like Lord Bastion. He would have to ask Sable about Meader when she returned.

A noise distracted him, then he jumped in fright as he saw a large group of greenhides on the valley slopes below the undamaged entrance. How did they get there? There were no greenhides on Na Sun Ka, as far as he knew. The disgusting beasts were charging up the hillside, and the two men at the entrance ran back inside as the greenhides approached. The beasts swarmed round the entrance, piling in as quickly as they could, almost fighting each other in their haste to enter the cave.

Sable appeared by Austin's side, and she sat down next to him.

'Are these your green friends?' he said. 'Where did you get them?'

'You know I can't tell you that, Austin. All will be revealed, once we get home.'

Austin watched as the last of the greenhides surged through the cave entrance. The valley fell into silence again.

'What do we do now?'

'We wait. I'm bound to have missed at least one escape route. Get your flow powers ready, Austin; we'll need them soon.'

Her eyes glazed over, and he remembered that Sable had vision powers, even though she was only a mortal. She had been his enemy, hadn't she? She had forced Meader to kill thousands of sailors and soldiers in Alg Bay; so why was he working by her side? He needed to go back to Gyle, and speak to his father.

'Gotcha,' Sable muttered. 'Get up, Austin.'

They stood, and she triggered the Quadrant. They appeared on a rocky slope, on the far side of the mountain. Below them, figures were streaming out of a hole in the ground. Armed men in black robes were trying to maintain order, but those running were in the midst of a panic. People were shoving and trampling each other in their desire to flee, and their screams echoed up to where Sable and Austin were standing.

'It's your turn,' Sable said. 'Kill them all.'

Austin blinked. 'What?'

'Use your powers, Austin. Blow their damned brains out.'

'But... Are you sure?'

She gazed into his eyes. 'Yes. I'm sure.'

Austin nodded, realising that she was right. She was always right. He raised his hand, and concentrated, remembering how much he hated the Unk Tannic, and everything that they had done to him. They had caged him like an animal! They had mocked and tortured him! They had to pay.

He smiled, and unleashed the full extent of his powers onto the fleeing Unk Tannic. A terrible popping sound rose up, as their heads started to explode. Austin swept his hand from left to right, making sure than none escaped his anger. Bodies tottered over, then collapsed onto the blood-slicked earth. More people were still emerging from the hole in the ground, and Austin turned his attention to them until the entrance was blocked with headless corpses. Austin's heart sang with joy, and he laughed at the sight of so much blood. He gazed around, looking for survivors, and saw a man and a woman trying to hide behind a line of thorn bushes. He pointed at the stupid mortals, and their heads disintegrated, sending blood and fragments of skull over the barren ground.

'I got the bastards!' he yelled. 'That was amazing.'

Sable glanced at him, but said nothing.

'How many of them were inside the mountain?'

'Almost a thousand,' she said. 'The greenhides will eat well today.'

A thought occurred to him. 'What if they have prisoners held in there? The Unk Tannic are always taking poor Banner soldiers hostage.'

'I saw at least a dozen Banner soldiers, when I investigated the tunnels yesterday. They were shackled together in a pit, deep inside the mountain.'

'The greenhides will eat them. Shouldn't we try to rescue them?'

'No.'

'But... why not?'

'You'll understand when I return your memories.'

'At least they won't be suffering for much longer,' he said. 'You know, I was worried before, but I really enjoyed killing those Unk Tannic bastards. Is that what we do? Do we travel around Dragon Eyre, slaughtering Unk Tannic?'

'Something like that. Come on; let's take a closer look.'

She started to walk down the slope, and he followed. They scrambled over the loose scree, until they came to the bottom of the blood-soaked valley. Austin glanced at the headless bodies, his earlier joy receding.

'Start rifling through their pockets,' said Sable; 'then pile up anything useful, and we'll take it back with us.'

'You mean, like secret documents, or plans?'

She shrugged. 'I was thinking more along the lines of cigarettes and cash.'

She stooped over a body, and pulled a small hip flask out from the inside of a set of black robes. She unscrewed the top and sniffed, then took a swig. Austin grimaced, then half-heartedly joined in the search. He crouched by a body.

'Will Meader be there when we get home?' he said.

She glanced at him.

'Well? Will he or won't he?' said Austin.

'Meader is on Ectus,' she said.

'Oh. What's he doing there?'

'Not much.' She plucked a cigarette packet out of the robes of a dead man, and offered one to Austin.

He frowned. 'I don't smoke.'

She shrugged. 'That will do, I think. Let's get out of here.'

Austin nodded, relieved to be spared the ordeal of robbing the dead. He stood by her side, then she activated the Quadrant and they appeared back in the cave where she had sealed his memories. She placed the hip flask and a few other items that she had taken from the slain Unk Tannic into a crate, then she glanced at Austin.

'Are you ready to have your memories back?'

He grinned. 'Definitely.'

'Maybe you should sit down.'

'Don't be ridiculous. I'll be fine.'

'Fair enough,' she said. She peered into his eyes, and Austin felt something wrench within his mind. His memories flooded back – of Meader, of Alef and Ectus, of Ashfall and Haurn, of Dina and Millen. His brother was dead! He fell to his knees, and threw up over the floor of the cave, shuddering. Meader was dead. His brother. And what had Austin done? He had enjoyed murdering people who were trying to escape the claws and teeth of the greenhides. He had laughed! He had blown their heads from their shoulders, and had thought it funny.

Tears spilled from his eyes, and he gripped his chest with both arms.

'You should have sat down,' said Sable.

'You are pure evil,' he said. 'Meader...'

'I'm sorry about that. I didn't entirely mean for you to forget about your brother. That was regrettable. I'll be more careful next time.'

'There won't be a next time! I can't take it any more. Stay away from me!'

'Don't you want to find your mother, Austin? Just think, she's sitting all alone in Serene – a slave. Imagine how happy she'll be when we rescue her. Remember why you're doing all this.'

'You bitch; I hate you.'

'Why? I didn't force you to enjoy killing those people. You did that all on your own. Maybe it's yourself that you hate, now that you've seen what you're capable of doing.'

'You twist everything! I feel like I'm rotting from within, as if my heart is putrid. You did this to me – you!'

'Have you finished? That was quite the tantrum.'

Austin put his head in his hands and wept bitter tears. He felt the air change around him, and when he looked out from behind his fingers, he saw that they were back on Haurn, close to the extinguished fire.

Millen peered at him. 'Holy crap, Sable. What did you do to Austin?'

Sable smiled. 'I accidentally gave him a little insight into his darkest desires, and he didn't like what he saw.'

Millen nodded. 'Are you done for the day?'

'Yes,' she said. 'Another successful operation carried out. Austin was very helpful.' She glanced up at the sun shining in the blue sky. 'What a beautiful morning. I'm going for a swim in the bay. See you later.'

She strode away, and Millen moved closer to Austin.

'Are you alright?' he said.

'Does he look alright to you?' said Dina, who was carrying fresh firewood in her arms. 'Sable's driving him insane. You called me lucky earlier, Millen, and in a way you're right. We should be thankful that Sable doesn't choose us for her little operations.'

'We don't have any powers,' he said.

'Praise the gods for that,' she said. 'If we did, then Sable would be exploiting us as well. When are you going to learn, Millen? Sable doesn't give a shit about us. She's obsessed with death and destruction, and we are just tools in her hands.'

Millen said nothing, and Dina walked away, carrying the wood over to the hut where they kept their supplies.

'She's wrong,' Millen whispered to Austin. 'Sable does care about us. I know that she's... going through a lot at the moment, but the real Sable is still in there – I'm sure of it.'

'Leave me alone,' gasped Austin.

'Can I get you anything?'

Austin glanced up. 'Yes. I need a cigarette.'

CHAPTER 13
LUNCH DATE

U dall, Ulna, Eastern Rim – 28th Summinch 5255 (18th Gylean Year 6)

The two large ships eased their way into the harbour of Udall, passing a line of small fishing vessels berthed by a long, spindly pier. On the other side of the basin were several merchant craft, lying empty after having disgorged their cargo of refugees from Enna. Among them sat the *Patience*, its deck lined with the sailors left behind by Lara and Tilly. They were cheering in the noon sunshine, glad to see the return of the *Giddy Gull*, along with its gleaming new prize. The quayside was packed with people. Some were there to welcome the arrival of the pirates, while others were part of the huge number of refugees that had doubled the population of Udall since they had begun arriving less than a month before.

Maddie stood among them, lost in the anonymity of the crowd. A dragon had reported sighting the *Giddy Gull* that morning, and she had hurried down to the harbour. She worried that she would look desperate to see Topaz again, but remaining in the palace for him to make his way there seemed too cold a welcome, and besides, she didn't care what others thought. Blackrose had asked her to take a small escort along with her, to ensure her safety, but Maddie had disregarded the dragon's advice. It was unlikely that any of the refugees would recognise her, but even if they did, why would any of them wish to harm her? She had only realised her mistake after she had been standing amid the heaving mass of people on the quayside for ten minutes, and had noticed several dark looks from a few of the men gathered there. Had some of them previously worn the black robes of the Unk Tannic? In whichever direction she turned, she seemed to catch someone staring at her, and she wished she had taken Blackrose's advice.

The *Giddy Gull* inched towards a free space along one of the short jetties that protruded out into the waters of the harbour, and a section of the crowd moved round the quayside to be closer to the brigantine. Maddie went with them, borne along by the thick crowd. Some of the group were dock workers; others were young men trying to earn a day's labour, or hoping to join the crew of the Five Sisters; while the rest were mostly young women, waiting to greet the returning sailors. The *Gull's* sails were lowered, and the vessel was tied up to the jetty, as a gangway was placed by the side of the sleek ship. Maddie gazed up onto the deck of the *Gull*, and saw Captain Lara. She was wearing the jacket of a Sea Banner officer, and was grinning from ear to ear as she looked down on the crowds lining the quayside. A dozen armed pirates strode down the gangway, and pushed the crowds back a few yards, to make space for the ship's crane to begin unloading their stolen cargo. The pirates allowed the official dock workers to pass through their cordon, and the harbourmaster walked up the gangway. Lara greeted him, her eyes turning from the crowd as Maddie tried to get her attention.

'You'll have to wait your turn,' said a young woman standing next to Maddie, as they were shoved back by the armed pirates.

'Are you waiting for someone?' she said.

'My mother owns a tavern,' said the young woman. 'She sent me down here to entice as many sailors as I can to drink there. You're here to meet a sailor, aren't you? You must be keen; they were only here for a few days. Once he's off the ship, come along to the *Dragon's Breath*; I'll make sure you're looked after, love. We do the best food in Udall.'

Maddie nodded. Over to their left, the ship that had entered the harbour with the *Giddy Gull* was berthing by another jetty, and part of the crowd moved off towards it. Maddie was nearly swept away by the mass of people, but the young woman next to her grabbed onto her sleeve, and they managed to remain in front of the *Gull*. A man stared at her as he was pushed along by the crowd, and Maddie's imagination placed him in a set of black robes. She should have stayed in the palace, she told herself. The Unk Tannic hated her, and all it would take would be for one of them to have a knife in such a crowd. They could stab her, and disappear into the noisy tumult of people before anyone would even notice.

Three armed pirates shoved their way through the crowd towards Maddie. She glanced up at the deck of the *Giddy Gull*, and saw Lara waving down at her.

'Do you know the captain?' said the young woman standing next to her, her eyes narrowing.

Maddie nodded.

'Maddie Jackdaw?' said one of the pirates, as they reached her.

'Yes,' she said.

They grabbed her arms, and pulled her through the crowd.

'Remember I helped you!' cried the young woman. 'Remember the *Dragon's Breath*!'

Maddie reached the cleared area by the side of the ship, and the pirates pushed her towards the gangway. Some of the crowd booed at the preferential treatment she had received, but she ignored their cries, and hurried up onto the deck of the *Gull*.

Lara shook her head at her. 'What are you doing down here, Maddie? The quayside ain't the place for a Queen's rider, girl. Are you trying to give my master a bleeding heart attack?'

'I didn't think it would be so busy,' Maddie said. 'Is Topaz alright?'

'Of course he is. We made it all the way to Throscala and back. Did you see Tilly's new ship? A damn Sea Banner frigate. Topaz will tell you all about it. Well, I say that, but knowing him, he'll probably miss out the part about how he saved us all.'

'Topaz saved you?'

'He took out an entire boat of marines on his own. I never even knew that he could operate a damned ballista. Listen; before you go up onto the quarter deck, I need to ask you something – have you seen Sable? Is she in Udall?'

'She was here a few days ago,' said Maddie. 'She came to see you, but, well, you weren't here, and she left again. I have no idea where she is.'

Lara nodded. 'She came to see me? That's something, I guess. Right – bugger off; I have a hundred things to do.'

Maddie smiled, then turned and made her way across the busy deck. The crane operators were loading a huge pallet with crates, and she weaved through them, then hurried up onto the quarter deck. Topaz was waiting at the top of the steps, and before she could say anything, he pulled her into his arms. The noise around them seemed to fade as he gazed down at her, his hands on her back; and they kissed, to a cheer from the sailors.

'You're back,' she said, then immediately felt stupid for stating the obvious.

'I wasn't expecting to see you down here,' he said. 'I thought Black-rose would have kept you in the palace.' He moved a hand from her back to her face, and she felt his fingers trace her cheek. 'I missed you.'

'Do you want to come up to the palace now?' she said.

'It'll be a couple of hours before I can leave the *Gull*,' he said. 'I need to finish up a few things first. You can stay on board, if you want to.'

'How was the trip?'

'Good. We cleaned out a couple of merchant vessels that were trying to re-supply Throscala, and then we captured a damn frigate.'

'Is that when you killed those marines?'

He frowned, and glanced away. 'Captain Lara tell you that, did she? I feel bad about it, but it was them or us. The crew have been acting like it was a big deal, but I feel sorry for the marines' families. It was a bad way to go, and no mistake.'

A young boy appeared by Topaz's side. 'Excuse me, sir?'

'Yes, lad?' said Topaz.

'What should I be doing, sir?'

'Get the charts and signal flags locked up, Tommo, then get all your stuff packed away and cleaned up. Maddie, this is Tommo – my new master's mate. Tommo, this is Maddie.'

'Hi, Tommo,' she said, noticing that the boy was looking at Topaz as if he were in awe of the master.

'Hello, ma'am,' he said. 'I remember you from the voyage from Olkis. I was up in the rigging back then, but Master Topaz and Captain Lara decided to move me to the quarter deck.'

'And he's done very well,' said Topaz. 'Go on, lad; off with you. Come back when you're ready to leave the ship.'

The boy saluted, then ran towards the main deck.

'He looks very young,' said Maddie.

'He's the perfect age – as old as I was when I first started assisting the master of a vessel. Did anything change while we were away?'

'A load more refugees arrived,' she said; 'from Enna this time, rather than Geist. Oh, and Blackrose is betrothed to Shadowblaze.'

The air shimmered, and Sable appeared on the quarter deck next to them. She glanced at Maddie and Topaz, who were still locked in an embrace, and she smiled.

'Gods above,' yelled Topaz.

Sable gazed into his eyes for a moment, then nodded.

'Hey!' said Maddie. 'I hope you weren't just reading his mind.'

The Holdfast woman shrugged. 'It was the quickest way to learn about their voyage, Maddie. Don't worry; I didn't pry into his deeper thoughts.'

'I don't care,' said Maddie. 'I don't like it.'

Sable turned her gaze to the main deck. She saw Lara, and started to walk towards her.

'Wait,' said Maddie. 'You will see Blackrose this time, won't you? She really wants to talk to you, Sable.'

'Maybe,' Sable muttered, then she strode from the quarter deck.

'What's been going on with her?' said Topaz.

'Who knows?' said Maddie. 'She comes and goes when she pleases, and rarely bothers to tell us what she's doing. I'm not sure that I want to know, but Blackrose insisted that I ask her to go to the palace.'

Maddie heard a shriek, then turned to see Lara run into Sable's arms.

'The captain's fallen hard for her,' said Topaz. 'I never thought I'd see anyone pierce Lara's armour, but Sable's managed it.'

Maddie frowned. 'Sable always seems to manage it. She pulls people in as if she were a magnet. I hope she doesn't break Lara's heart, but, knowing her, there's a good chance she will.'

Topaz released Maddie. 'I'd better get back to work. The sooner we're done, the sooner we can get to the palace.'

Sable transported Maddie and the senior officers to the bridge palace with her Quadrant, after stating that she had no desire to walk through the huge crowds gathered in the harbour. The unloading of the *Giddy Gull's* cargo was continuing, and the purser and bosun were interviewing prospective new recruits from among the many volunteers. Sable took Maddie and the others directly to the cavernous hallway next to the reception chamber, startling a dragon by their sudden appearance.

They entered the hall, where Blackrose, Shadowblaze and Greysteel were waiting. Lara and Tilly executed a brief bow towards the Queen of Ulna, and she regarded them with her red eyes.

'Welcome back to Udall,' said Blackrose. 'You departed with one ship, and have returned with two.'

'We captured a Sea Banner vessel,' said Lara. 'It's Tilly's now.'

'Did you travel to Throscala?' said Shadowblaze. 'How are things there?'

'We saw a few ships,' said Lara, 'but not as many as we'd expected.'

'Did you obey the rules we agreed?' said Greysteel.

Lara frowned. 'Of course we did. Not that we saw many vessels from Ulna. We're unloading everything that we took from a couple of merchantmen, and we'll have the valuation sent up as soon as it's all been counted. Did the lads we left behind behave themselves?'

'They mostly remained on the *Patience* in your absence,' said Greysteel. 'There were a few tavern brawls, but nothing too serious.'

'Any sign of our father?'

'None,' said Blackrose. 'Now, I wish to ask Sable a few questions.'

The Holdfast woman took a step forward. 'You want to know what I've been doing?'

'I do,' said the black dragon.

Sable nodded. 'I have destroyed the oil refinery on Alef, and the factory that manufactures the explosive devices on Ectus. The harbour at Yearning is out of operation, and I eliminated the largest Unk Tannic facility on Na Sun Ka. I would estimate total enemy casualties at around ten to twelve thousand. I also killed another four gods.'

The hall fell into a stunned silence.

'How is this possible?' said Greysteel.

'I told you all what I was intending to do,' she said. 'Did you doubt my resolve? It's your turn, now. When do you intend to assault Throscala?'

'That depends,' said Blackrose. 'Are you willing to lend us your support?'

'I am. Name the place and the date, and I'll be there.'

Blackrose turned to Greysteel.

'We shall be ready to begin our attack on the tenth day of Arginch, your Majesty.'

'And you want me to kill Lady Ydril?' said Sable.

'Yes,' said Blackrose, 'along with any other god on Throscala. That will clear the way for our forces to land.'

'We shall be assembling on a small island to the north of Throscala on the dawn of the tenth,' said Greysteel. 'Will you meet us there?'

'I can do that,' said Sable. 'You should know that I've had a few brushes with Lord Bastion. I had a chance to confront him in Alef, but there were unforeseen complications. I've managed to work them out, so I won't hesitate next time.'

'How are the other members of your team?' said Blackrose. 'I would be grieved to learn if anything has happened to Ashfall.'

'They're all fine,' said Sable, 'though Ashfall would probably object to being referred to as a member of my team. She's a little over-protective of Austin, but I'm not concerned about that.'

'What about Dina?' said Tilly. 'Are you still holding her hostage?'

Sable glanced at her. 'Yes.'

'Is she... is she alright?'

'She's not particularly happy about being confined to Nan Po Tana, but she's free to roam the temple complex, and we're looking after her needs. Once Olo'osso arrives in Ulna, I'll speak to him, so that he understands the situation. Dina will not be harmed, as long as your father decides to be reasonable.'

'Tell me, Sable,' said Greysteel; 'how have you achieved so much, so soon? The casualty numbers that you quoted have perplexed me. You are a good fighter, yes, but ten thousand? That doesn't seem possible.'

'I have my ways,' said Sable. 'I'm not going to tell you what they are, because you will disapprove. Leave me to get on with my job, and I'll leave you to get on with yours. Between now and the tenth of Arginch, I will continue with my tactics, wearing down the Banner garrisons on the Western Rim. I intend to target Olkis soon, and Gyle. There will be no opportunity for the colonial authorities to send another huge fleet to the Eastern Rim; I'll make sure of it.'

'You're going to target Olkis?' said Topaz.

'I am. There's an enormous prison in the city of Nankiss. I'm going to burst it open, and set off an armed uprising. Does that meet with your approval, Master Topaz?'

'I'm from Nankiss,' he said.

'I know.' She turned back to Blackrose. 'Is that all?'

'I want to see Dina,' said Tilly.

Sable frowned. 'I don't think that would be wise.'

'Why not? If she's fine, as you say she is, then why wouldn't you want me to see her? Lara, back me up on this.'

Lara chewed her lip. 'I, um... I don't know.'

Tilly glared at her sister. 'What? You don't know? Is your brain addled, Lara? Has Sable cast some sort of spell on you?'

'I have done nothing of the sort,' said Sable. 'Let's go to a tavern, Lara. I want to get drunk.'

'Try the *Dragon's Breath*,' said Maddie. 'I hear it's good.'

Sable raised an eyebrow at her, then activated the Quadrant. She and Lara vanished from the reception hall, leaving Tilly fuming.

'I hate it when she does that!' the Osso sister cried. 'Sable is out of control.'

'Sable has never been within anyone's control,' said Blackrose. 'As long as she fulfils her promises, I have learned to expect nothing more from her.'

'She appears to be doing a good job in the Western Rim,' said Shadowblaze. 'Her attack on Yearning means that Throscala is isolated, and vulnerable to our forces.'

'And what about my sisters?' yelled Tilly.

'Sable won't hurt them,' said Maddie. 'At least, not deliberately.'

'Is that supposed to make me feel better?' said Tilly. 'Dina's her prisoner, and Lara would crawl over lava if that witch asked her to.'

'And what would you recommend?' said Blackrose. 'Sable Holdfast is not a subject of Ulna, and I have no authority over her.'

'You just want her to kill gods for you.'

'That is correct. For too long, I tried to restrain the Holdfast witch, and the results were regrettable. It is time to allow Sable to act as she pleases. Her grief and rage are powering her, and it would be unwise for anyone to get in her way.'

'You mean you're absolving yourself of all responsibility for her actions? I want to know how she's managed to slaughter ten thousand people in less than a month. What happens when you re-take Throscala – will you rein her in then? What if she decides to devour the entire world?'

'Your Majesty,' said Greysteel, 'perhaps we could aim Sable at the dragons of Wyst next? She could be very useful to us in this regard.'

'Perhaps,' said Blackrose, 'though we would need to ensure that she felt she had come to the decision on her own. Sable does not take orders.'

'You're playing with fire,' said Tilly. 'Be careful that one day you're not all bowing before her. Once Sable has a taste of power, I doubt she'll relinquish it.'

'I think you overstate her abilities,' said Blackrose. 'Furthermore, we are her allies, and she has pledged not to interfere in Ulna. You, too, are our allies – you and your sister Lara. Will you help us conquer Throscala? With two ships, you could prey upon any reinforcements that make it through from the Western Rim.'

Tilly narrowed her eyes. 'Alright. I'll need to speak to Lara first, and there's no point in doing that until Sable has gone. In principle, though, I agree. Then, once Throscala has been neutralised, we'll need to sit down and discuss the future. I can't imagine that you'll be happy hosting the Five Sisters once peace has returned to the Eastern Rim.'

'That would depend upon your activities, Captain Tilly,' said Blackrose.

Tilly nodded. 'I shall take my leave, though not as dramatically as Sable and Lara. I'll return to my new ship, and start tallying up what we owe in taxes.'

The pirate captain bowed her head, then strode from the hall, taking the other ships' officers with her, until only Maddie and Topaz remained.

Blackrose glanced at the *Giddy Gull's* master. 'We need to talk.'

'Maybe later,' said Maddie, grabbing Topaz's hand. 'He only just got here.' She shoved him away from the dragons. 'See you later.'

'What was that about?' said Topaz, as they left the hall.

'Blackrose wants to interrogate you,' said Maddie. 'She's worried that you'll behave despicably towards me. It's quite endearing, I guess. Sometimes, I get the impression that she thinks she's my mother.'

They started to walk towards Maddie's apartment.

'Does she object to us seeing each other?' said Topaz.

'No. She wants me to be happy. If she threatens to eat you, don't take it too seriously. Now, what shall we do?'

He gazed at her. 'I know what I want to do.'

She returned his gaze, her mouth dry and her heart racing. She imagined ripping his clothes off in the privacy of her apartment, and feeling his hands on her skin. She swallowed. It was too soon, she thought, despite the desire growing within her.

'I thought about you every moment we were at sea,' he said. 'That reminds me; I have presents for you, but I left them on the ship.'

'You got me presents?'

'A few things.'

She smiled. 'Stolen goods?'

'Liberated goods,' he said.

'I learned how to cook fish.'

'Did you? Why?'

'So I could make you something. On second thoughts, perhaps we should get some lunch in a tavern. I don't want to poison you on your first day back.' She nodded at her apartment door. 'Also, if we go in there, I don't think we'd come back out for hours.'

'Would that be so bad?'

'I'm not ready for that, Topaz,' she said. 'I want to, but can we take it slowly?'

He stared at her as if he wanted to eat her, then he nodded. 'Alright. Lunch?'

'I know the prison that Sable was talking about,' Topaz said, as they talked over their empty plates. 'It's enormous, and is filled with hundreds of political prisoners awaiting trial. Basically, anyone who's ever crossed the Banner forces ends up inside. If Sable frees them, there will be chaos.'

'Sable thrives in chaos,' said Maddie. 'Everyone seemed shocked by what she said in the palace, but I wasn't. She's always been a little bit crazy, and now she has no one to talk her out of her mad schemes.

Badblood used to do that; he was a calming influence on her. Without him, she's liable to do anything.'

'Where will it end?'

'I don't know. Maybe Tilly was right. Maybe, Sable will end up becoming the ruler of Dragon Eyre, for all I know. Or maybe she'll be killed on her next operation. I hope not, but you saw the look in her eyes. I don't think she cares if she lives or dies.'

Topaz put down his mug of wine. 'I'm just going to nip to the toilet. Back in a minute.'

She watched him leave, and smiled. It felt good to be with him again, and she was glad that they had picked up from where they had left off. She hadn't questioned him further about the marines, but he didn't seem to be unduly affected by what he had done. It was strange, she thought; he had killed a boatload of men, despite being someone who was clearly kind and compassionate. It concerned her, but she liked that about him. He could kill, but only if he had to, not because he enjoyed it. It made her feel safe in his presence.

She was so absorbed in her thoughts that she didn't notice the three men behind her until they grabbed her by the shoulders and started to pull her out of the tavern. Several other customers glanced over in alarm, but one of the men was armed with a knife, and no one did anything to help her.

'Get your hands off me!' she yelled, as they hauled her out onto the street.

One of the men slapped her, then held the knife up to her throat. 'Shut up. Ata'nix has been looking for you, you treacherous little bitch.'

He tried to place a hood over her head, but she struggled and lashed out, her fingernails scraping down the man's cheek. He let go of her, and she kicked him in the shins, while the other two men crowded round, keeping the passers-by away from them. A crowd of sailors appeared round the street corner, and stopped to watch.

'Help!' Maddie cried.

'That's Topaz's girl,' shouted one of the sailors. 'Get stuck into the bastards!'

The sailors charged the three men. One of them ran for it, fleeing down a narrow lane, but the other two were bowled over, and the knife went flying across the cobbles of the street. Maddie crawled free, then turned, her back against a wall as the sailors kicked and punched the two men. Topaz burst through the tavern doors, his eyes wide. He ran to Maddie's side, as the two men were beaten unconscious.

'Is she alright?' cried one of the sailors.

'I think so,' said Topaz. 'Thanks, Ryan. I owe you one, mate.'

The sailor grinned. He kicked one of the prone men in the stomach, then placed a boot on his chest.

'You want to be keeping a closer eye on her, eh?' Ryan said. 'Udall's crawling with Unk Tannic assholes. They might have thrown their stupid robes away, but you can tell by the weird look on their faces.'

Topaz turned to Maddie, his arm over her shoulder. 'Is that who they were? Unk Tannic?'

'Yes,' she said. 'One of them mentioned Ata'nix to me. He must be somewhere in Udall.'

'I shouldn't have left you; I'm sorry. Did they hurt you?'

'I'm fine,' she said.

'What shall we do with these two assholes, Master?' said another sailor, gesturing at the two unconscious men.

'Take them to the *Sow's Revenge*, lads, and hand them over to Captain Tilly. She can put them in the frigate's brig until the town militia can be summoned. I'll take Maddie back to the palace.'

'Topaz, stop fussing over me,' said Maddie. 'I'm fine.'

'Are you sure?' he said, as they sat on her balcony. 'Is there anything I can get you? Do you need a blanket?'

She peered at him. 'In this weather? Listen to me – I know that you think I'm just a fragile girl, but I used to be a soldier, and, believe me, I've been in my fair share of fights.'

He raised an eyebrow. 'You've been in fights?'

'Yes. I was quite wild in my youth. Not as wild as Lara, but I had a bit of a temper when I was a Blade, and I was locked up in the barrack's holding cells more than once for causing trouble. Why do you think I have so many tattoos? I was kicked out of the Seventh Support Battalion on my first day for starting a fight. It's sweet that you want to take care of me, and I appreciate it, but please don't treat me like a child.'

Topaz gazed out over the view for a moment. 'Fair enough,' he said. 'It's just that I feel bad about what happened. I was only gone for two minutes.'

'Those guys must have been waiting for you to leave before they dragged me outside. I was scared, but, you know, I've faced worse.'

He shook his head. 'Not a single person in the tavern lifted a finger to help you.'

'I was lucky that the sailors were passing. Otherwise, you would have had to face those guys on your own – and one of them had a knife.'

He took her hand. 'I would have still fought them. There's no way I would have let them take you away without a fight.'

'They might have killed you.'

'I would have dived in without thinking about the consequences,' he said. 'For you, Maddie, I would fight a damned Ascendant.'

She smiled. 'I know.'

He touched her face with his hand, and they kissed. She had under-played how the attack had affected her, not wanting to seem weak in front of Topaz, but she could feel her wound-up nerves start to relax as they embraced on the balcony bench. No – relaxed was the wrong word to describe how Topaz made her feel. She swallowed, and took a decision.

'Let's not go out again today,' she said. 'I have some wine in my room. We can have a glass or two, and then see where things lead.'

'Are you sure?' he said.

She looked into his eyes. 'Topaz,' she said, 'I've never been more sure of anything in my life.'

CHAPTER 14
LACED WITH DESPAIR

Nan Po Tana, Haurn, Eastern Rim – 9th Arginch 5255 (18th Gylean Year 6)

Sable stood in the shadows of her room in the temple, with one foot on a chair as she laced up her leather boots. Outside, the sun was high in the sky, and she could hear the sound of birds singing in the trees of the compound. She caught sight of the walking stick that she had used for nearly two years, propped up where she had left it after being healed.

That was when it had all gone wrong. Before Blackrose had arrived, she had been happy. She had endured near constant pain from her injuries, but she had experienced peace and a simple joy in life. Her wounds had forced her to reconsider her entire outlook, and she had managed to come to terms with the limits they had placed upon her without bitterness or regret.

Now, she knew nothing but regret. Blackrose had forced her body to undergo a healing and, physically, she was in better shape than ever before; but mentally, she felt her wounds run deep. She remembered being welcomed by the sight of Badblood sleeping in the sunshine every morning when she had risen from her bed; and the sights and sounds of the native workers who had farmed the land within the temple walls. She remembered the joy of the baby's arrival, and how they had gathered at the home of the new mother to celebrate; and how she had sat most evenings on the little bench overlooking the bay, under the shadows of the old olive tree, content just to watch the days pass. Badblood had been the rock upon which she had constructed her new life of peace and acceptance; it was he who had borne her broken body all the way back from Ulna, and he who had provided the love that she had needed to overcome her initial frustration at her injuries. He had remained patient with her, and had calmed her by his mere presence. She had loved him like she had loved no other. Without him, did she care if she returned home after another day of slaughter? She had done things that would have horrified Badblood; things that she would never have been able to do if he was still alive. His silent disapproval had kept her from breaking the bounds of morality that she was now flagrantly transgressing. The others who remained – Austin, Ashfall and the rest – they also disapproved, but their censure meant nothing to her. Badblood was gone, taking with him a large piece of her soul, and leaving a void that she was filling with blood and death. He would loathe what she had become, and the knowledge of that made her hate herself. In his absence, she had slipped back to her old persona, one that she thought she had abandoned forever.

Where would it all lead? At what stage would she be able to say – enough?

She finished lacing up her boots and sat on the chair, feeling as though a weight was pushing her down. She lit a cigarette and tried to compose herself. The others were waiting for her, but she couldn't bear to face them. Her thoughts went to Lara, and the time they had spent together in Udall, after she and her sister had returned from Throscala. Lara's embrace could make her forget everything, and she had been drawn to her like a moth to a candle, taking what she needed from the pirate captain without any thought for the future. It had been a mistake, she knew that. The longer she spent with Lara, the more she was allowing her feelings to distract her from what she needed to do. Was she falling in love with her? No, not yet; but if she continued to see Lara, then it was only a matter of time. She needed to cut her out of her life before it reached that stage, despite the fact that she was her only source of joy in an otherwise bleak existence. Lara would be hurt, but life was full of hurt. Besides, Sable didn't deserve her love. If Lara knew what she had been doing, she would be revolted; disgusted, just as Sable was disgusted with herself.

She glanced out of the open doorway, and saw Austin sitting hunched by the extinguished fire. Next to him, Millen and Dina were talking while they prepared coffee, but the demigod was sitting in silence, his face downcast as he stared into space. Sable felt a surge of guilt flow through her. Austin was tormented, his mind filled with anguish and self-loathing. She had made him do things that ran counter to the person he thought he was. She had pushed him, cajoled him, manipulated him; moulded him into a weapon, and the nervous wreckage that remained was plain for all to see. She should let him go – take him back to Implacatus and help him search for his mother, but she needed him. His healing and flow powers were essential to the success of her mission. Just one or two more operations, she told herself; but she had been telling herself that since they had started. When would it be enough? Austin was at risk of a full breakdown, one that not even her powers would be able to fix. Was he strong enough to carry on a little longer? Would his mother even recognise the man she had raised after Sable had finished with him?

A tear rolled down her cheek, but she felt as if it were happening to someone else, as if she was incapable of feeling anything other than grief and anger. She thought of her family, scattered across different worlds. She had longed for Daphne's approval when she had been trying to live a better life; but she sensed that she had lost it forever by her recent actions. The Empress had been right – she couldn't be redeemed. Karalyn had been delusional to have thought so. The Empress would be nodding along grimly if she could see her, vindi-cated at last. Sable had tried to be a good Holdfast, but she had failed. She was an evil, twisted version of Daphne, who should have been hanged for her crimes as she had deserved. If Daphne hadn't interceded to save her life, then she would have been spared the pain of Badblood's death; and spared the misery of Dragon Eyre.

She thought about giving up. What if she went back to bed, and never got up again? What if she walked outside, and announced that she was ending her campaign of terror and destruction? What if she used her Quadrant to find Lara, and disappeared with her. Together, they could hide in a cave on a remote island, never to be found by anyone. The temptation to run away with Lara built in her mind, a shining light compared to the grinding darkness of the path she had chosen.

She stood. She couldn't afford to be weak. She pushed all other thoughts from her head and took a long breath. She had to carry on, blindly hurtling into the abyss. It was too late to run away, and unfair on Lara. If the feelings she was developing for the pirate captain were genuine, then the best thing she could do for her would be to stay away; otherwise the poison that infected her mind would spread to her, and no one deserved that, least of all Lara. She hardened her will. She had made her choice, and there was no going back.

Sable strode out into the bright sunshine, her eyes dazzled by the glare. The conversation around the cold hearth fell away, as Millen and Dina turned to look at her. Austin remained unmoving, his eyes still gazing towards the ground. Across the courtyard, the two dragons also turned to stare at her, and Sable could see the accusation in their eyes.

Sable sat on the ground, and Millen passed her a mug of black coffee. She lit another cigarette, and collected her thoughts.

'We're going on another operation today,' she said.

Austin glanced up at her, his eyes heavy and bloodshot. 'Where?'

'Gyle,' she said. 'Over the last few days, I have been busy. I've been transporting greenhides to garrisons and bases on Ectus and Na Sun Ka, but they have been mere distractions for the main event.'

'How many trips have you made?' said Millen.

'Since the last operation?' she said. 'Six to Na Sun Ka, and four to Ectus. I have hit a limit of around a hundred and twenty greenhides that can be transported at any one time, and the beasts are starting to scatter as soon as I appear on the plains of Haurn. Still, the supply here is inexhaustible.'

Millen puffed out his cheeks. 'That's a lot of greenhides you've moved about. They must be causing terrible damage.'

'I don't ever hang around to see what they do,' she said. 'Sometimes, I'm in and out after only a second or two. Yesterday, when I dropped off a load of greenhides at a Sea Banner base on Ectus, there were still a few roaming the streets from the last time, and I caught a brief glimpse of the carnage they had caused. I told Blackrose that I had killed around ten thousand enemy personnel, but that was a guess; the total could be far higher. I may have killed ten thousand just on Ectus alone.' She paused for a moment. She was rambling, and the effect of her words was obvious on the faces on those listening to her. Ashfall in particular was staring at her with intense anger. 'Anyway,' she went on, 'as I said, the next operation will be on Gyle, not Ectus or Na Sun Ka. I've been stockpiling weapons and supplies, close to several large slave compounds. It's time to ignite a native rebellion. Any earlier, and I would have risked a rebellion being crushed by the occupying forces, but the Banner garrisons are suffering all over the Western Rim, and a rebellion would now have a better chance of success. There are nearly eight hundred thousand slaves on Gyle, and the majority are corralled within enormous walled compounds in the farming districts, guarded by a mixture of Banner soldiers and local settler militia. A full-scale slave rebellion will tie down the entire garrison of Gyle, leaving me free to attack Port Edmond.'

'Port Edmond?' said Austin, a glimmer of hope in his tired eyes. 'You mean, our campaign is reaching its final stages?'

'Removing the upper levels of the colonial government is a signifi-cant step,' she said, 'but the campaign will not be over until every last Banner soldier is dead or gone. We need to encourage an evacuation. We need Implacatus to realise that their occupation here is unsus-tainable.'

'That's never going to happen,' Austin cried, his cheeks flushing. 'To stop Implacatus, you would need to go there, and kill every last Ascendant and Ancient. Not even you could do that, Sable.' He put his head into his hands. 'This nightmare will never end.'

Sable ignored his outburst. 'Tomorrow, we have a different task altogether. We shall be going to Ulna, to...'

'We're going to Ulna?' said Dina, her eyes widening.

'Not you, Dina,' said Sable. 'Austin and I will be going, to offer our assistance to Blackrose. We shall be god-killing on Throscala. Don't interrupt me again.'

'You mean,' said Austin, 'that I have an operation today, and another one tomorrow? It's too much, Sable. I can't do it.'

'Yes, you can,' said Sable.

'Stop this!' cried Ashfall. 'You need to start listening to us, Holdfast.'

'I listen to you,' she said.

'No, you don't,' said the grey dragon. 'You issue orders and sweep our concerns away as if we mean nothing to you. Austin has just stated that two operations on consecutive days is too much, and I agree. You are pushing him too hard, and I can see the strain that afflicts his every waking moment. I came here to ensure that you did not mistreat him, and I have failed miserably. You have brought him nothing but sorrow and misery, and to what end? To fulfil your unattainable objectives? Whatever he does, it will never suffice; it will never be enough for you.'

Sable flicked ash onto the cold hearth. 'Finished?'

'Damn you, Sable,' said Ashfall. 'You are acting like the gods you profess to hate.'

'I'm going to take that as a compliment,' she said. 'I need to be ruthless. My heart is full of hate, and if I can use that to destroy our enemies, then I will do so. Do not force me into hating you, Ashfall.'

'Sable,' said Deepblue, 'I fear what you have become. Please listen to us. Please take a moment to remember that we are your friends. Our lives have been entangled since Lostwell, but you have changed. It is not too late to step back.'

'You're wrong,' said Sable. 'It's far too late. Do none of you understand? We are in a fight to the death, and I will not be swayed from my course. If you don't like it, you can leave.'

'But we can't, can we?' said Ashfall. 'For you will not allow all of us to depart. Tell me; what would you do if you awoke one morning to find us all gone?'

'I would hunt you down and take Austin from you.'

Ashfall's eyes burned. 'Need I say more? You tell us that we are free to leave, but that is a lie. Blackrose was right – you lie as easily as breathing. I used to believe that you had honour, but I was mistaken. You are shameless.'

'Yes, probably,' Sable said. 'And? One day soon, Blackrose will realise that I have done the dirty work for her, and that she owes the freedom of her realm to the actions that I have taken. Will she care about the methods I employed to bring this about? You all seem to forget that I was not the first person to commit atrocities on Dragon Eyre. The gods, the Banner forces, and the Unk Tannic – they all have blood on their hands; the blood of children and innocents. I target the military. Have I killed a single child? Have I set greenhides loose among peaceful civilians? You know the answers to these questions, and you still see me as evil incarnate. Luckily, I couldn't give a rat's arse for your opinion of me. I will carry on, alone, if I have to.' She stood. 'Austin, you can stay here today. I'll manage Gyle on my own. But, you will be ready for tomorrow's operation; understand?'

He glanced up at her, and nodded.

'Thank you,' said Ashfall.

Sable strode back into the temple and closed the door behind her. She had no reason to venture back into the shadows of her quarters, but she needed to calm down. She could feel her temper rising to boiling point, and had almost told Ashfall that Austin intended to abandon her and return to Implacatus. She couldn't go to Gyle in such a state of nervous rage. She raised her right hand, to check it wasn't shaking, then closed her eyes.

Just breathe, she told herself. Take it one breath at a time.

She wondered how many slaves would die in a rebellion. The garrisons on Gyle were mostly intact, as she had never sent greenhides to that island. A few regiments had been transferred to cover the losses on Ectus and Na Sun Ka, but the units that remained on Gyle were still formidable. A rebellion would keep them occupied, but at the cost of potentially thousands of dead natives. Could she bear their blood on her conscience? In the old days, she had been able to justify her actions by appealing to her faith in the Creator; no matter what she had done, she had believed that she was serving a higher purpose. What cause had she to rely on now? Revenge? She had already killed the Ancient that had taken Badblood from her. She realised that she had no answer worth giving.

She grabbed a bag, and withdrew the Quadrant from beneath her clothes. She activated the device, but not to take her to Gyle.

The air shimmered and she appeared on the mountainside on Ectus where she had built the cairn to cover Meader's body. A cold wind was howling across the barren landscape, and she sat down next to the tall pile of stones. She wouldn't be going to Gyle that day. All she wanted was to be alone. She reached into the bag, and took out a bundle of weedsticks. She selected one, and lit it with Meader's lighter. The flame flickered in the wind but didn't go out, and she wished she had a spirit that was as resistant as the flame. She took a draw of the weedstick, then yawned, as exhaustion seeped through her body.

She awoke with a start, and shivered in the chill air. She glanced around, dizzy and confused; and it took her a few moments to remember where she was. The others would assume that she had gone to Gyle, when all she had done was fall asleep by Meader's cairn. The sleep hadn't refreshed her, and she felt as drained as she had before. She pulled herself to her feet, and almost stumbled. Next to the cairn was a sheer drop into a narrow ravine, and she gazed down into the shadows at its bottom. If she took another step forward, then the ache in her heart would cease forever. What did she have to live for? Badblood was gone, and Millen and the others would be better off without her. Blackrose was depending upon her assistance the following day, but was that a good enough reason to carry on? Perhaps she should allow the dragons and gods to fight it out among themselves; after all, the conflict on Dragon Eyre was none of her business. The idea of oblivion tempted her. No more cares; no more responsibilities; no more pain – just an endless nothing.

Part of her mind tried frantically to think of a reason to stay alive. There was Lara, she thought; but Lara would be happier in the long run without Sable. The same went for Millen and Maddie; she had brought them nothing but anguish. She fell to her knees and wept, then raised her head and screamed into the wind. Why did Badblood have to die? She missed him so much that everything in her life had lost its meaning since his death; all was colourless, worthless ash and dust. Her campaign of blood and slaughter had sustained her; if she lost the will to carry on doing that, then what else was there? Revenge was not enough – there had to be more. She realised that what she wanted more than anything was the chance to tell Karalyn how sorry she was for what she had done to Lennox. It was a slim chance indeed, but she clung onto it as if it were the key to the rest of her life. If she lived, then she could, somehow, maybe, seek forgiveness for the most sadistic act of her life, the one she regretted more than any other. It was pathetic, but it was enough for her to turn away from the darkness of the deep ravine. She activated the Quadrant before she could change her mind, and found herself back in her rooms in the temple.

She sat down and rested her head onto the surface of the table. She glanced up, sniffing. Smoke. Without hesitating, she sent her vision out through the keyhole of the front door, and saw flames. The orchards and groves of Nan Po Tana were burning. Banner soldiers were crowded into the small courtyard in front of the temple, while Millen, Austin and Dina were kneeling with their hands clasped behind their heads by the cold hearth. By the edge of the courtyard, the two dragons were lying unconscious, as soldiers wrapped chains round their wings, and affixed muzzles to their jaws. Standing directly in front of the three human prisoners were two men in steel armour. Lord Bastion was one of them; but Sable did not recognise the other. They were speaking, but Sable's vision could hear nothing, so she slipped into Austin's mind, and looked out from his eyes.

'We've told you,' Millen was saying, 'we don't know when Sable will be back.'

'He's telling the truth,' said Bastion. 'It appears that the Holdfast witch has been keeping her friends in the dark about the specifics of her operations. It is as I told you, Lord Ascendant; Sable Holdfast is cleverer that we imagined.'

'So you keep saying, Lord Bastion,' said the other man. 'In that case, we should kill these mortals now; they are of no further use to us.'

'On the contrary, Lord Ascendant,' said Bastion, 'these three humans, and the two dragons, are the witch's only friends. They will be far better employed as hostages, to tempt the witch into coming to us. We should, I suggest, take them back with us to Port Edmond, and set a trap for Sable there.'

Sable delved into Austin's thoughts as she gazed at the man she did not recognise. He was tall and handsome, with dark skin, and hair that fell past his broad shoulders. In his right hand was a sword too large and heavy for a mere mortal to wield.

She found a name in Austin's head – Lord Kolai – the Fifth Ascendant, and she nearly laughed out loud. So, Implacatus had sent an Ascendant to assist Bastion? Or perhaps not assist – perhaps the Ascendants were displeased with Bastion's lack of progress on Dragon Eyre, and had sent Kolai to take charge. She kept a thin thread of her powers lodged in Austin's head, and got to her feet, only then noticing that her room had been thoroughly ransacked. The two gods were continuing their conversation outside, but she blocked it out of her thoughts, and drew her sword. Her heart was still in turmoil over her glimpse into the abyss of the ravine, but she knew that her chance had come, and she tried to prepare herself. The gods were facing the entrance to the temple building, and she dismissed the idea of a frontal assault. Hadn't Corthie tried to fight two Ascendants at the same time? Her nephew was the greatest mortal warrior in existence, and yet he had been defeated, because he had attempted to take on both Arete and Leksandr simultaneously. But, if she did nothing, then they would take her friends to Gyle.

She would have to risk it. She pushed the Quadrant into her clothing, but kept her left thumb poised over it, as she gripped the sword in her right hand. She moved her thumb, the air shimmered, and she appeared in the courtyard behind Bastion. She swung her sword with all her strength, and the blade slammed into the thick armour protecting the Ancient's neck, then deflected upwards, slicing through Bastion's right ear. Behind them, a dozen voices cried out as the Banner soldiers aimed their crossbows at her, but she was too close to Bastion and Kolai, and no bolts were loosed. Kolai moved faster than Sable's eyes could follow, and he swept his mighty sword at her. She ducked and rolled, and the blade passed over her head. She surged out her powers, but the Fifth Ascendant was wearing the slender eye-coverings that Lord Maisk had worn on Lostwell, and her vision couldn't penetrate his mind. Bastion attacked her from the other side as Kolai lashed out again, and Sable felt the blade of the Ancient's sword cut through her leather armour and bite into the flesh by her waist. She cried out in pain, and fell to one knee.

'Stand back, Bastion,' shouted Kolai; 'she is mine.'

Austin raised his hand, and Kolai staggered from the blast of flow powers that hit him. He fell forward onto Sable, nearly crushing her with the weight of his steel armour. Austin stretched out his hand, and his fingertips grazed Sable's arm. She felt a burst of healing powers enter her, then saw Bastion kick Austin in the face. The Ancient drove his sword into Austin's chest, pinning him to the ground, as Dina screamed. Kolai reached out with his hands for Sable's throat, and her fingers swept over the Quadrant.

Sable gasped, and found herself on a grassy hillside on a small island in the Riggan archipelago. Dina was still screaming, while Millen was shaking in fear. Sable turned her head, and saw the two shackled dragons lying a few dozen yards away, and she panted in relief.

She remembered Austin. She pushed herself to her feet, and stared around the hillside. The demigod wasn't there. Sable felt something break within her, and she fell back to her knees, her eyes clenched shut.

'It's alright; it's alright,' she could hear Millen saying over and over, as he tried to calm Dina.

The dragons stirred. Ashfall raised her head, then struggled against the chains.

'Holdfast!' she cried. 'Where are we? Where is Austin?'

Sable said nothing. She felt Millen place a hand on her shoulder, and she pushed him away.

'You saved us, Sable,' he said; 'but where is Austin? Did you leave him behind?'

Ashfall roared and strained her limbs, trying to break free from the shackles, as next to her, Deepblue sobbed in despair.

Sable got back to her feet.

'We are on a small island close to Rigga,' she said. 'I built a camp here, in case we had to flee. Austin...' She paused, and a tear fell down her cheek. 'Austin is still on Haurn.'

'You left him behind!' cried Ashfall. 'I will kill you for this, Holdfast!'

'I didn't mean to leave him,' she said. 'Bastion drove a sword through his chest, fixing him to the ground, and I only had a split second to work out the calculations for the Quadrant. I reached out to bring the dragons, but I didn't take Austin's position into account, and... I failed. I made a mistake.'

Millen ran over to Deepblue, and began loosening the chains that bound her.

'This is unacceptable,' said Ashfall. 'You are the only reason that Bastion and the Ascendant came to Haurn. They tracked us down, and Austin has paid the price. This is your fault, Holdfast; you are to blame for our misfortunes. Nan Po Tana is a smoking ruin, and Austin is in the hands of our enemies, because of you. Were it not for these chains, I would rip your head from your shoulders.'

'I would probably deserve it,' Sable said. 'You're right. It's me that they want. I am the enemy they fear the most. I am the reason they sent an Ascendant to Dragon Eyre.'

'How will you make this right?' said Ashfall. 'You know what honour demands of you.'

'Yes, I know,' said Sable. 'Bastion and Kolai will already be on their way back to Gyle, to set a trap for me. They think that I'll come for Austin, and they're right.'

Millen stared at her. 'You're going to walk into their trap?'

'That's exactly what I'm going to do.'

Sable glanced at the others. Dina was a quivering wreck, and was still on her knees, while Millen was next to Deepblue, pulling the chains from her wings. Only Ashfall was motionless, as she stared at the Holdfast woman.

'My father killed an Ascendant, Sable,' said the slender grey dragon. 'To save Austin, you might have to do the same.'

'I might,' she said. 'I need to put on some better armour, and get ready. There's food in the caves below us.' She glanced at Ashfall. 'Will you let me take those chains off you?'

'I will,' she said. 'Holdfast, save Austin, and I will forget our old arguments.'

Sable reached for the chains. 'Don't worry,' she said; 'I'll bring back your rider.'

CHAPTER 15
SKULDUGGERY

North of Throscala, Eastern Rim – 9th Arginch 5255 (18th Gylean Year 6)

The *Giddy Gull* lay anchored within the narrow bay, its crane lifting the barrels of fresh water onto the main deck, where sailors were waiting to lower them into the hold. Above the ship, the blue sky was studded with white clouds, and Topaz watched them pass for a moment, keeping an eye on the wind's speed and direction.

Ryan was sitting cross-legged on the deck next to where Topaz was standing by the railings, his guitar cradled in his arms. The carpenter's mate was adjusting the strings: loosening some, and tightening others, as a cigarette dangled from his lips.

'Are you ever going to answer me, mate?' he said, looking up at Topaz.

'I thought my silence was answer enough.'

'Fair enough, mate,' said Ryan, 'but you should be aware that I'm going to interpret your silence as a "yes". If you hadn't done the business with Maddie, then you would tell me, just like you told me when you hadn't kissed her. If you're going to keep quiet about what you've been up to, then you need to be consistent.'

Topaz glanced at the crane. 'Another ten minutes, and we'll be done here.'

'Don't change the bleeding subject, mate. This is a big deal. If it was me who had been sneaking in and out of the palace every night, then no one would care. Folk expect me to have a girl in every harbour, but this is you we're talking about. I'm not saying you're a prude, but you kept your pants on in some of the best brothels in Pangba; so you'll have to forgive me if I take an interest in your love life, now that you finally have one.'

'You're not going to squeeze any details out of me, mate.'

Ryan grinned. 'Ahh! So, there are details to be squeezed out, eh? I bleeding knew it. Good for you, mate; I'm happy for you. Tell me; was it all awkward fumbles, or did you go at it like wild animals?'

'This is exactly why I didn't want to have this conversation.'

Ryan laughed. 'Only teasing you, mate. You owe me a few details, though.'

'Yeah? How's that?'

''Cause I saved her bleeding life, mate – twice over. Once on Wyst, when that dragon tried to carry her off, and then in Udall. If it weren't for me... well, you probably don't want to think about that.'

'Ryan, you had a dozen other sailors with you in Udall.'

'Aye, but it was me who led the damn charge. I could've been stabbed. Now, if you're needing any tips about how to keep Maddie satisfied, I'm your man. Don't be shy.'

Topaz rolled his eyes. 'I'll bear that in mind.'

'You do that, mate. I'm a bleeding expert when it comes to women. I could charge for my advice, but you can have it for free.'

'You're an expert, eh? Then how come none of your relationships ever last?'

'Because life is short, and it would be unfair to restrict my talents to just the one bird.'

'How noble of you.'

'That's what I thought. I'm on a mission – to bring joy to as many women as possible, before I get all old and wrinkled. You'll probably end up marrying Maddie, and having a family and settling down; and that's great, for you. But it ain't the life I want. I'm a free spirit.'

The last of the water barrels was lowered onto the main deck, and the crane was turned into position to lift the *Giddy Gull's* rowing boat. No new orders were given, but the crew sensed that they were close to departing, and started to drift back into their positions.

'I'd better get back onto the quarter deck,' said Topaz.

Ryan frowned. 'Any excuse to get out of telling me what you got up to with Maddie, eh? You're a poor friend.'

'See you later, mate.'

He left Ryan sitting by the ship's railings, and strode up onto the quarter deck. Lara was there, along with Tommo and a few others, keeping an eye on the crew's activity.

Lara nodded to him. 'Get ready to take us south, Master. We need to time our approach with care; ideally, we'll be nearing the main harbour of Throscala Town at dawn tomorrow.'

'That's achievable, Captain,' he said.

'Then achieve it. With any luck, the *Sow's Revenge* will meet us there; as long as Vitz hasn't got lost.' She narrowed her eyes. 'Or, as long as Tilly hasn't murdered him.'

'Let's just hope the lad behaves himself, ma'am.'

'This is his last chance, Master. If he does a good job for Tilly, he'll be fine; but if he messes up again...' She made a slitting motion across her throat. 'I've done all I can for the lad; you know that, Master. I couldn't have been fairer with him.'

'Yes, ma'am.'

They watched as the rowing boat was dropped onto the main deck. Several sailors scrambled over it, securing it to the *Gull*, then a midshipman turned to the quarter deck and signalled that they were ready.

'Raise the anchors,' said Lara, her hands clasped behind her back. 'Guide us out to sea, Master.'

Topaz issued a series of commands, and turned the wheel. The narrow bay was flanked by high cliffs, and it took some time to turn the

Giddy Gull so that it faced the ocean. Sails were adjusted and trimmed, and the breeze started to push them away from the uninhabited island where they had stopped for water. Tommo stood by Topaz's side as he piloted the ship, watching the master's every move, and listening to the orders he imparted to the midshipmen.

Topaz found his attention drifting away as the *Gull* edged towards the open sea. He had performed such manoeuvres countless times in the past, and they had almost become second nature. He made a conscious effort not to dwell on the nights he had spent with Maddie in Udall; he couldn't afford to lose himself completely, but it was hard not to remember being alone with her, and he longed to be back in her untidy bed, feeling her arms wrapped round him.

'Steady, Master,' said Lara. 'We're getting a little close to the cliffs off the port side.'

Topaz nodded, and made a few corrections to his course. Concentrate, he told himself, annoyed that his focus had slipped.

Lara frowned. 'You'd better be giving this your full attention, Master. If you're day-dreaming about Maddie again, I'll take the back of my hand to you.'

'Sorry, ma'am.'

'Imagine having to tell Blackrose that we were unable to assist in the conquest of Throscala, because the ship's master was distracted by the thought of her rider's nether regions.'

'It won't happen again, ma'am.'

'So you say. Tommo, keep a close eye on lover boy. If he grounds the hull, you'll be the new master of the *Giddy Gull*.'

The young lad laughed, then looked uncertain, unable to tell if Lara had been joking.

The ship cleared the rocks at the entrance to the bay, and Topaz sighed in relief. He had ridiculed sailors in the past for being distracted by the thought of their girlfriends ashore, and had never imagined it could happen to him. He was the best master in the Eastern Rim, and the crew looked up to him; but all that would be lost in an instant if he steered them into the rocks.

The wind picked up as they left the bay. The small island's ragged coastline stretched away to the north and south, and was pock-marked with inlets and coves, and small beaches overhung with palm trees. Topaz turned the wheel, and aimed the bow of the ship towards the south. The northern shore of Throscala was barely a hundred miles over the horizon, but it would be night by the time they reached it. From there, it was another fifty miles down the western coast to Throscala Town. He had made the voyage there many times in the past, while in the Sea Banner, and the shore of Throscala was the one he probably knew best. He planned the route out in his mind, pushing Maddie from his thoughts as he calculated the numbers. To reach Throscala Town at dawn, when Sable and the dragons were due to attack, he would need to steer out into the Inner Ocean, in order to waste some time; otherwise they would arrive too early.

'Vessel off the starboard bow!' cried the lookout from atop the main mast.

Lara squinted into the distance.

'Two miles and closing,' yelled the voice from the mast. 'No sails.'

'No sails?' said Lara. 'That'll be why I can't see the damn thing. Tommo, fetch me the eye-glass, there's a good lad.'

The master's mate ran to the rear of the quarter deck, and rummaged in the locker where the signal flags were stored. He retrieved the long eye-glass, then hurried back to Lara. She took it, and held it up to her eye.

She frowned. 'I see it. It's a rowing boat, and it's heading towards us. What's a damn rowing boat doing out here?'

'Is there anyone aboard, ma'am?' said Topaz.

'It's packed full,' she said. 'Slow us down, Master. Let's take a closer look.' She nodded to a midshipman. 'Prepare the forward ballistae, just in case.'

The young man ran off, while Topaz had the sails lowered. He nudged the *Gull* towards the position of the rowing boat, as the brigantine began to slow. Up on the bow, sailors hauled the waterproof coverings from the two ballistae that sat there, and prepared the machines, turning them to face the small craft that was fast approaching. Topaz brought the *Gull's* speed down further, until he could see into the little boat. At least twelve men were sitting in the craft, along with chests and a few sacks. Four of the men were handling the oars, while the others were crammed onto the narrow benches.

'This could be our lucky day,' said Lara. 'We're still under-crewed. If these lads are experienced seamen, we could be back up to a full complement.'

'As long as they ain't Sea Banner, ma'am.'

She nodded. 'Naturally.'

Lara walked to the side of the quarter deck, and looked down into the vessel, as the *Gull* came to a halt alongside it.

'Thank you!' yelled one of the men from the rowing boat. 'Our ship went down on the rocks four days ago, and we've been stuck on that damn island ever since.'

'I wouldn't thank us just yet,' shouted Lara. 'Are you all Olkians?'

'We are, ma'am. Are you one of the Five Sisters?'

'My name is Captain Lara, and this is my vessel, the *Giddy Gull*. What ship were you on?'

'A merchant caravel from Na Sun Ka, ma'am. We were on a supply trip to Throscala, but were blown off course.'

'You don't seem particularly upset to have been found by pirates.'

'We're hungry and exhausted, ma'am. Better you than the damn Sea Banner.'

'If we let you on board, you'll have to join the crew,' said Lara. 'Are you willing to do that?'

The men in the rowing boat glanced at each other.

'What if we say no?' said one of them.

'Then I'll give you some food and water, and leave you here,' she said. 'It's up to you.'

The men debated for a few moments. Topaz glanced down at them. For having spent four days marooned on the small island, all of them looked fit and strong. He scanned their faces, but didn't recognise any.

As Olkian sailors were scattered all over Dragon Eyre, that wasn't too surprising.

One of the men hailed Lara. 'If we promise to serve for one year, will you honour that?'

'I will,' she said. 'But trust me; once you've served under me, you won't want to leave.'

The man nodded. 'We accept.'

Lara grinned, then gestured to some sailors to lower the net down the starboard flank of the brigantine. The men in the rowing boat clambered up, hauling their chests and sacks with them, until the small craft was empty.

'Take them below,' said Lara, 'and make sure they have plenty of food and drink. I'll take their oaths later. Bosun, write down their names and occupations. Let me know if there are any petty officers or skilled tradesmen among them, and we'll work out where to place them.'

The bosun saluted. 'Yes, ma'am.'

A group of sailors herded the new arrivals down the forward hatch, and Lara smiled.

'Our crew shortage – resolved in two minutes,' she said.

'We don't know anything about these lads, ma'am,' said Topaz.

'They're Olkians, Master,' she said. 'If any are duds, we'll drop them off in Udall when we get back. Some of our new Ulnan recruits are still wet behind the ears, and if these guys are all experienced seamen, they should fit right in with a minimum of training. Get the *Gull* back up to full speed, Master.'

He nodded. 'Yes, ma'am.'

———

They sailed onwards for an hour, clearing the southern headland of the small island. It was the only landmass in sight, and the ocean stretched out in front of them, empty in the afternoon sunshine. Topaz allowed Tommo to take the wheel, and watched the lad as he maintained their speed and direction. They were tacking into the wind, and Topaz was looking forward to showing the master's mate how to make quick course adjustments. He was about to suggest a few changes, when an explosion from the lower deck knocked him off his feet. The windows in the captain's cabin blew out, showering the quarter deck in glass, and an awful sound of rending timber echoed up from the stern of the ship.

Lara had also been knocked over, but she leapt to her feet. 'Is some asshole playing with the bleeding pisspots?' she cried. 'Tommo, get down there, and tell me what in the name of the gods is going on. Move!'

Topaz took the wheel, and instantly felt that something was wrong.

'We've lost rudder control, Captain,' he yelled. 'The wheel is inoperable.'

'Shit,' said Lara. 'Bring us to a halt, Master, before the wind turns us round.' She gestured to a group of sailors. 'Action stations. Get to your posts. Bring down the sails and get the anchors ready.'

A dazed sailor, his uniform ripped and bloody, stumbled up the stairs of the aft hatch. Another sailor caught him as he toppled over. Topaz locked the useless wheel into position, and ran down the steps to the main deck, Lara by his side.

'Relax, sailor,' Lara said to the wounded man. 'Take your time. What happened?'

'A pisspot went off, ma'am,' he gasped.

'I'd bleeding well guessed that,' she said. 'What caused it to go off?'

A scream echoed through the main deck from somewhere below.

'It was the new lads, ma'am,' said the wounded sailor. 'They had weapons hidden in their chests, and they stormed the hold by the rudder, where the pisspots are kept.'

Lara's eyes darkened. 'Those bastards!' She glanced up. 'I want every man on this deck armed and ready to go below. Tommo, fetch my axe. I'm going to carve those assholes into pieces.'

The sailors scrambled for their crossbows and swords, and within a few minutes, thirty of them ready to brave the aft hatch. Lara paced up and down the deck, her fingers swinging her axe back and forth as she waited for her crew to get organised. She had ordered Topaz back onto the quarter deck, and had placed him in charge while she led the crew below to deal with the men from the rowing boat. When they were about to rush down the stairs, another sailor emerged from the darkness, his hands raised.

'Don't shoot!' he yelled. 'I have a message for the captain.'

'He's one of ours,' Lara shouted. 'Let him approach.'

The crew parted, and the sailor staggered over to Lara.

'They've got hostages, ma'am,' he said, his voice edged with panic. 'They have the bosun, and the carpenters, and they have the last pisspot. They sent me up here to tell you that if there is any attack, the next pisspot will put a hole in the ship's hull as large as a bleeding wagon, ma'am.'

Lara stared at him. 'What do they want?'

'They said you'll find out soon enough, ma'am.'

One of the midshipman glanced at the aft hatch. 'What are your orders, ma'am? Should we storm the lower deck?'

'Shut up,' said Lara. 'Give me a second to think.' She turned back to the sailor and grabbed his collar. 'Were they serious? Will they really send the *Gull* to the bottom of the ocean if we attack them?'

'That's what they said, ma'am. They've taken the last pisspot down into the lower hold, along with the bosun and the others, and they were barricading the doors when they sent me up here.'

'And they've taken the carpenters,' Lara said, 'which means we can't repair the damage to the rudder caused by the first explosion.' She put a hand to her face. 'Holy crap; we've been stitched up good and proper. I don't understand – are they Sea Banner in disguise? But I heard their accents; they're definitely Olkians. Some bastard is behind this; someone sent those assholes to do us in.'

'Ship off the stern!' yelled the lookout from the main mast.

Every pair of eyes turned towards the rear of the *Giddy Gull*. Less than a mile away in the distance, a vessel was sailing towards them from the southern headland of the small island.

Lara's face froze into an expression of horrified realisation. 'The *Flight of Fancy*. Oh no.'

'What should we do, ma'am?' said the midshipman.

Lara sat down on the steps leading to the quarter deck, and lit a cigarette.

'Ma'am?' said the midshipman.

She glanced up, her eyes red. 'Signal our surrender to my father.'

Olo'osso walked onto the quarter deck of the *Giddy Gull* with a subdued smile on his face, as if he were trying to appear delighted with his day's work. The crew of the *Gull* had been lined up along the starboard side of the brigantine, while the *Flight of Fancy* was secured to its port side. The twelve men that had been in the rowing boat were laughing and slapping each other on the back; a grim contrast to the dispirited expressions on the faces of the *Gull's* crew.

Topaz was standing with his hands on his head, a crossbow pointed at his back, as Olo'osso glanced around. He spotted his errant daughter, and nodded.

'Alara,' he said. 'We meet again, my little princess. Did you truly believe that I would not hunt you down?'

'I knew you'd try it, father,' said Lara, 'but I reckoned Ann's crappy boat would never make it this far.'

'The *Flight of Fancy* might not be as fast as this brigantine, but we got here in the end.' He shook his head, and sighed loudly. 'Why? Why, Alara? I trusted you, and yet you stole my ship. Worse, you murdered your own cousin. Do you understand that I cannot forgive such a crime against the family?'

'It wasn't Lara who killed Dax,' said Topaz.

Olo'osso turned to him, fury blazing in his eyes. 'Did I ask you to speak, Oto of the Sea Banner? You will keep your mouth shut, unless I directly address you.' He turned back to his daughter, and his features softened. 'Is that true, my little flower?'

'I ain't saying a thing,' Lara said.

'Did you kill Udaxa'osso?'

'Is that what Dina told you?'

'Never mind what your sister said. Did you kill your cousin?'

Lara glanced at Topaz, her eyes unsure.

'I killed him,' said Topaz. 'He had a knife to Captain Lara's throat, so I shot him down; and I would do it again.'

Olo'osso gestured to a burly sailor from the *Fancy*, who struck Topaz's leg from behind with a crossbow butt, forcing him down to his knees. Another sailor then punched Topaz in the face, bursting his nose open. Blood streamed down Topaz's chin, as his eyes watered.

'I will deal with you shortly, Oto of the Sea Banner,' said Olo'osso. 'First, I want to know where my other daughter might be found. Why is Atili not on board the *Giddy Gull*?'

Lara kept her eyes on Topaz, her anger building.

'Answer me, Alara.'

'Tilly has her own ship now,' she said. 'I don't know where she is, and that's the truth. We left Udall together, but we don't live in each other's shadows.'

'I see. What type of vessel has Atili commandeered?'

'A Sea Banner frigate that we captured fifteen days ago,' said Lara.

'You captured a frigate? Well done. We shall take it back to Olkis with us. We shall be leaving as soon as the necessary repairs to the *Gull* are carried out.' He smiled. 'Did you like my little ruse? Admit it, Alara, you are a little bit impressed at how easily I managed to prise the *Giddy Gull* out of your hands.'

'It was a dirty trick, father,' she said. 'Your thugs could have killed half my crew, or put a hole in my ship's hull. Where did you find those assholes?'

'I bought them at a slave market in Pangba,' he said. 'Then I freed them, on the condition that they served me on this voyage to the Eastern Rim. Ironically, it was the same slave market where Maddie Jackdaw should have been sold. I assume the girl is back with her dragon?'

'She is.'

'I also assume, therefore, that Queen Blackrose has not sought to punish our family for her rider's abduction.'

'The Queen forgave us, father, because we returned her rider to her home; just as I said she would. If you had been successful in selling her as a slave, she would have killed us all.'

'Perhaps,' he said. 'However, I acted upon the information I had at the time; and I have no regrets.' He glanced at Topaz. 'Your master will have to die, of course, Alara. The murder of Udaxa cannot go unpunished.'

Lara smirked. 'Oh, father, I don't think that would be a good idea.'

'And why not?'

'You have no idea, do you?' she said. 'Blackrose and Sable Holdfast made it to Olkis, in the end. Sable has Dina in her custody. If you harm me, or Tilly, or Topaz, then Sable will kill Dina.'

Olo'osso hesitated for a moment, his eyes narrowing. 'You're lying.'

'No, father, I'm not.'

'But, how is it possible that you could know this? If Blackrose was in Olkis, she would not have returned by now.'

'Sable killed Governor Horace on Ectus, and took his Quadrant, father. She has a base on Haurn, and she placed Dina there. She hasn't been harmed, or so Sable tells me. She's keeping her as a hostage, to make sure you don't do anything stupid; like killing Topaz, for instance. You should also be aware that Topaz is in a relationship with Maddie Jackdaw, so he has the might of Blackrose and her Ulnan dragons at his back as well. If you kill him, then Dina won't be the only member of our family to die.'

'You little traitor,' Olo'osso growled. 'You sold out our family to curry favour with a dragon? Next, you'll be telling me that you have entered into an alliance with Ulna, or some such nonsense.'

'We are in an alliance with Ulna, father. We protect and support each other. Right now, we are assisting Queen Blackrose, and you are hindering us. She is expecting us to be outside the harbour of Throscala Town by dawn tomorrow. If we aren't there, then she will send out dragons to search for us. But, I'd be more worried about Sable, if I were you. She's relentless, father, and she loves me.'

Olo'osso remained calm. He nodded slowly, then turned to a group of the *Fancy's* crew.

'Start the transfer. I want half of the *Gull's* people put onto the *Fancy*, and I want every available carpenter working through the night to repair the *Gull's* rudder. As soon as it's fixed, we shall hunt for Atili's vessel, and then set sail for Rigga.'

'Rigga?' said Lara.

'That's right, my little petal,' he said. 'We cannot sail back to Olkis via Na Sun Ka and Gyle, and the way north is now closed to us.'

'Why?' said Lara. 'Why can't we go north?'

'We encountered some... difficulties with the dragons of Wyst,' he said, 'and it wouldn't be safe for us to return that way. Rigga is the best option. If Atili was able to shake off her dragon pursuers when she stole Maddie Jackdaw, then we shall be able to do the same.'

He walked across to the port side of the quarter deck, and waved over to Captain Ann, who was standing at the rear of the *Flight of Fancy*.

'Ani, my dear,' he said. 'Prepare a holding cell for two, with shackles. I'm transferring Alara and Oto'pazzi over to your vessel. The *Fancy* shall then tow us back to the cove where we anchored last night. I will be remaining on the *Gull*.'

Ann nodded. 'Yes, father.'

Olo'osso glanced down at Topaz. 'It appears that your execution has been postponed, Oto of the Sea Banner; but fear not – I will kill you myself as soon as we pass out of the range of the Ulnan dragons. Black-rose cannot save you; no one can.'

Lara shook her head. 'Were you not listening to me, father? Sable will bring death and destruction down upon you if you follow this course.'

Olo'osso snorted. 'She is but one woman. What can she do against us?' He gestured to his men. 'Take these two over to the *Fancy*, and make sure that they are chained up, and confined to the holding cell.

Oh, and ensure you give Oto of the Sea Banner a thorough beating; but do not kill him.'

The burly sailors nodded. Two took hold of Lara's arms, while another pair lifted Topaz up by the shoulders, as the crews from the *Gull* and the *Fancy* watched in silence.

'You're making a mistake, father!' Lara cried, as she and Topaz were led down to the main deck. 'If Sable comes, I won't be able to save you.'

Olo'osso laughed. 'Am I supposed to be scared of one, solitary foreign girl? Let her come. She will feel the taste of my sword, and then I will pluck her Quadrant from her dead hands.'

The sailors pushed Lara and Topaz across the gap and onto the deck of the *Flight of Fancy*, where Ann was waiting for them. She half-smiled at Lara, then led them down into the shadows of the hold. She stopped in the depths of the bow, in front of an open door.

'Put them in here,' she said to the sailors.

Lara and Topaz were shoved inside the tiny cabin, then the sailors began to attach shackles to their ankles.

'You have to speak to father, sister,' said Lara, as her leg was gripped. 'You have to make him understand what Sable is capable of doing.'

'I've tried,' said Ann. 'He doesn't listen to me. He's fixated on getting you and Tilly back to Olkis, along with the *Giddy Gull*. Is it true, though – does Sable have Dina?'

'It's true,' Lara said.

Topaz was pushed to the deck as a set of shackles was fixed to his leg. One of the sailors kicked him in the stomach, then the others joined in. Topaz raised his arms to protect his head as the sailors rained blows down upon him.

'Leave him alone, you assholes!' Lara yelled.

One of the sailors winked at her. 'Just following orders, ma'am.'

'That's enough,' said Ann. 'This is my ship, and you'll obey my orders while on board. The shackles have been attached. You are dismissed.'

The sailors pulled back from Topaz, leaving him groaning on the deck.

'You have to get us out of here,' said Lara. 'Ann, please.'

'I've done what I can, sister,' said Ann. 'You brought this on yourself.'

She nodded to a sailor, and the door was closed, and locked. Topaz sensed Lara crouch down next to him in the darkness of the tiny cabin, then he felt her hand wipe some of the blood from his face.

'Topaz,' she whispered; 'can you hear me? Are you conscious?'

He rolled onto his back, his ribs and torso in agony. 'I'm conscious,' he said. 'Unfortunately.'

'I tried to warn them,' she said. 'I tried.'

'I know, ma'am.'

'Sable's going to go crazy when she finds out; and Blackrose too. My father has no idea what he's just done. He's pissed off the most powerful beings on Dragon Eyre.'

'He must believe you, ma'am; otherwise, I'd already be dead.'

'Why did you have to take the blame for Dax? I was prepared to say that I killed him. Father wouldn't execute me, not even for killing my cousin. But you? He'll cut your throat as soon as we get to Rigga.'

Topaz pulled himself up into a sitting position, and leaned back against the wooden bulkhead.

'I don't regret killing Dax, ma'am. If I hadn't, then he would have killed you. And don't worry about me; Sable will find us long before we reach Rigga.'

'And then what? What if she kills my father? What if she wipes out the crew of the *Fancy*? I want her to come for me, but I dread it at the same time.'

He felt Lara take his hand.

'She scares me, Topaz,' she whispered. 'I love her, but she scares me.'

CHAPTER 16
BAIT

Port Edmond, Gyle, Western Rim – 10th Arginch 5255 (18th Gylean Year 6)

'Don't exaggerate, Lord Bastion. Sable Holdfast may be in possession of a few meagre powers, but she is a mortal – and mortals die.'

The voice drifted through to Austin, as the demigod slowly regained consciousness.

'I see it now,' the voice continued. 'Your caution and hesitancy is at the root of what has gone wrong here in recent days. A bold new approach is required on Dragon Eyre, and I am the fellow to see it through. As soon as we have dealt with the Holdfast freak, I intend to push ahead with the extermination of the entire stock of superfluous sub-created humans. Orders will be sent to every Banner garrison on this benighted world, instructing them to begin the cleansing operation. While the Western Rim is being cleared, I will expect you to strike at the heart of the so-called rebellion in the Eastern rim. Are you listening to me, Lord Bastion?'

'I am,' said a second voice, one that filled Austin's heart with fear.

The demigod opened his eyes and saw a ballista positioned in front of him, the razor-sharp point of its loaded bolt just two yards from his face. Around it were dozens of Banner soldiers, and several gods in long robes. Shadows flickered off the walls of the large, windowless chamber, its illumination provided by a series of wall-mounted oil lamps. More soldiers were standing to Austin's left and right, but he couldn't see behind him, as his head wouldn't turn. He glanced down, and saw that he had been shackled to an upright metal rack, his wrists and ankles chained to the solid structure, with his hands ensconced in thick gauntlets, while his head had been fixed in place with straps that dug into his forehead and chin.

'The Blessed Lord Edmond is most disappointed in your performance, Lord Bastion,' the first voice said.

Austin looked up again, and saw Lord Kolai standing next to Bastion. Unlike the others, they were wearing thick steel armour from head to toe. The Ancient's face was expressionless, but a simmering anger was shining from his eyes as the Ascendant reprimanded him.

'In order to restore your reputation, Lord Bastion,' Kolai went on, 'it is imperative that you obey my every command, without question. You shall destroy the dragons of Ulna, and relieve the siege of Throscala; and then await my further orders. The Blessed Lord Edmond placed me in charge; you must not forget this.'

Lord Bastion said nothing. He turned from Kolai and looked into Austin's open eyes, then glanced away again, as if the demigod was beneath his attention. A side door of the chamber opened, and two robed gods entered. They bowed low before the Ascendant and the Ancient.

'Well? What is it?' said Kolai.

'Forgive the interruption, your Grace,' said one of the gods. 'There is news from the city harbour. Several hundred greenhides have been released by the quayside warehouses and depots, and are currently rampaging through the harbour district. Should we send gods to deal with them?'

'No,' said Kolai. 'This move by the Holdfast witch was expected. She wants us to divide our strength, to enable her to rescue her friend. Every god and demigod with death powers must remain here, until the freak falls into our trap. Go back to your posts, and continue to scan the area with your vision abilities.'

The two gods bowed again, then backed out of the chamber.

'I sense your disapproval, Bastion,' said Kolai, his eyes tight; 'but the lives of a few Banner soldiers and dock workers mean nothing compared to the elimination of the Holdfast mortal. Moreover, the blood of those who are slain in the harbour is on your hands. If you had done your job properly when you were first sent here, then none of this would be necessary.'

'I know why you want Dragon Eyre,' said Austin, his voice rasping.

Kolai and Bastion ignored him.

'Implacatus is dying,' Austin went on, but it was as if he hadn't spoken. 'You destroyed it – you!' he cried, raising his voice.

Bastion pointed at him, and he felt the muscles in his jaw constrict. Austin choked for a moment, then felt the pressure lessen. Why weren't they listening to him? Then, he realised. He meant absolutely nothing to them – he was the bait to lure Sable into their trap, nothing more. To Kolai and Bastion, he was as worthless as any mortal, and the sole reason he was still alive would expire as soon as they had killed Sable. He wondered if they had even bothered to read his mind. He closed his eyes. His life was over. If Sable came, they would execute her, then him; if she didn't, then they would kill him without a second thought.

A stab of guilt went through him. They were treating him in the same way that most gods treated mortals; the way that he had once treated mortals. The way that his father had treated his mother. Like her, Austin was expendable.

'Keep alert,' said Kolai to the group of robed gods in the chamber. 'She might appear at any moment. As soon as she does, strike with everything at your disposal. I want that freak obliterated. I want...'

His voice edged away as the air crackled. Austin opened his eyes as a cacophony of noise erupted within the chamber. Dozens of greenhides appeared, shrieking and howling. In their midst, Sable also appeared, dressed in full steel armour, but was gone in the blink of an eye, as the greenhides tore into the assembled ranks of Banner soldiers. Austin cried out in terror, as talons ripped through mortal flesh. Bastion had his hand raised, and greenhides were falling along with the soldiers. Three green-hides turned to the chained demigod, but their eyes passed over him as if he were invisible. Crossbows were thrumming, and the bodies were starting to pile up around the metal rack in the centre of the chamber.

'Kill them all!' cried Bastion.

Kolai stood aloof from the slaughter, a bemused expression on his face. A greenhide charged at him, but one of the robed gods raised his hand, and the beast's head exploded, showering the vicinity in green blood.

The air crackled again and Sable appeared in the air, a foot above Kolai. She drove a long knife down, ramming it into Kolai's right eye as she fell, then the air shimmered and she disappeared, along with the Ascendant. Bastion swept his hand from left to right, killing everything mortal that stood, greenhides and Banner soldiers alike. The chamber fell into silence. One of the demigods struggled to his feet, his robes smeared in blood, as Bastion stared into the space where the Fifth Ascendant had been. The doors to the chamber burst open, and more soldiers piled in, then they stopped as they came face to face with the scene of carnage. More than two hundred bodies littered the stone floor, with greenhides entangled with Banner soldiers.

'My Lord Bastion,' said a newly arrived Banner officer, 'where is the Fifth Ascendant?'

Bastion smoothed down the front of his robes. 'Gone. The Holdfast witch took him.'

The officer staggered back in shock. 'Taken? But, my lord, where?'

Bastion glanced at the officer then strode across the blood-slicked floor towards Austin.

'She allowed you to be captured, didn't she, demigod?'

'I don't know what you're talking about,' said Austin.

'No, you probably don't. I hardly imagine that Sable Holdfast includes you in her plans. I'm going to scour your memories now; something Lord Kolai should have permitted me to do when we first took you into custody. In a few moments, your mind will cease to function. If you know where Sable has taken the Fifth Ascendant, speak up now.'

'Do your worst,' said Austin; 'you'll get nothing from me willingly.'

A tiny smile crossed Bastion's lips. 'Oh, how I would love to do my worst. However, we have no time for the long, drawn-out torture that I would like to inflict upon you.'

On the other side of the chamber, the same two gods from before pushed their way through the crowds of Banner soldiers.

'My lord!' cried one. 'Greenhides are in the Winter Palace! Hundreds of the beasts have appeared, on different floors. We need your assistance.'

Bastion glanced at the two gods, as screams filtered through the open door. They were in the subterranean levels of the Winter Palace in Port Edmond, Austin realised – close to where the Eighteenth Gylean was held.

'Please, my lord,' said one of the two gods. 'The settlers working within the palace are being slaughtered.'

Bastion frowned, then gestured to the death-powered gods who had survived the greenhide assault.

'Remain here,' he said. 'Kill the Holdfast witch if she appears; I will deal with the palace.'

He strode from the chamber, leaving seven gods and the Banner reinforcements, who were still staring at the heaped-up corpses filling the chamber.

'How can this be happening?' wailed one of the gods. 'Sable Holdfast is a demon; she killed Lord Horace, and now she's taken the Fifth Ascendant. We can't fight her!'

'Shut your mouth,' said another god. 'Do you want Lord Bastion to hear you saying such things?'

'I don't care any more! Sable has slaughtered thousands, and we'll be next!' He pointed at Austin. 'The greenhides didn't touch him – do you understand what that means? Sable can control them. Sable can...'

Another god slapped him across the face. The god whimpered, and tears spilled down his cheeks. The air shimmered again, and another hundred greenhides were transported into the midst of the soldiers and gods. Pandemonium erupted within the chamber, and the screams and shrieks nearly deafened Austin as the blood flowed again. A thick wall of greenhides surrounded the shackled demigod, forming a barrier of solid flesh between him and the ballista, then Sable appeared next to the metal rack, dressed in full armour. She laid a hand onto Austin's arm, winked at him, and slid her fingers over the Quadrant.

The air crackled.

Freed from the chains and straps, Austin fell onto a cold stone floor. He glanced around. He was in a small cave, along with Sable, but they weren't alone. A few yards away, a figure was lying on the ground, and Austin almost vomited at the sight. It was Kolai. He had a knife driven into each of his eye sockets, up to their hilts, while his severed hands lay bloody by his sides. His steel breastplate had been removed, and a sword was sticking out of his chest, as he groaned and writhed in agony, bloody foam coming from his lips.

'I didn't have a god-restrainer mask handy,' Sable said, as she lit a cigarette; 'so I improvised.'

Austin stared up at her. Her face was calm as she glanced down at the Fifth Ascendant.

'All I have to do now,' she said, 'is decide what to do with him. I could use him as a hostage. We could barter his life, and hand him back if the occupation forces evacuate Dragon Eyre; or I could kill him, to teach Implacatus a lesson. The bastard's only been on Dragon Eyre for a few days, so it would be quite a lesson.' She glanced at Austin. 'Well? What do you think?'

Austin tried to speak, but he was shaking all over, his body trembling.

'To be honest,' she said, 'it doesn't matter what you think, Austin, as I've already decided what to do. I'm going to kill him.'

'He's... he's an Ascendant,' Austin gasped.

'Eh, yes. I'm aware of that. So? Two of them were killed on Lostwell, as I'm sure you know. Deathfang got one, and Belinda got the other one.

Of course, that's simplifying matters. Frostback and Halfclaw were also present at the death of Leksandr, and none of the dragons would have been able to kill him without my niece's assistance. I want to be the first Holdfast to do it unaided. Is that childish of me? I don't care. Do you want a cigarette?'

He stared at her. She shrugged, lit a cigarette for him, and pushed it into his hands. She sat down next to him on the stone floor of the cave, and gazed at the writhing body of Kolai.

'Each knife blade is at least three inches into his brain,' she said, 'and he's still alive. I have to admit; it's quite impressive.' She grunted. 'I hate wearing all this metal armour; it really slows me down. You know, Ashfall will be pleased to see you.'

'How can you be so nonchalant?' he said. 'Lord Kolai has conquered entire worlds.'

'Do I look nonchalant? Good. There's a crate over to your right with a saw in it. Pass it to me.'

'A saw?'

'That's what I said, Austin. I'm not going to risk removing the sword from his chest, or either of the two knives. You don't need to watch if you don't want to.'

He felt a strange sensation behind his temples. 'Are you in my head?'

'Yes,' she said. 'I want to see if anyone else is in there. You can relax; there's no one rooting about your thoughts; well, except for me. Did they read your mind?'

'Bastion was going to, then you appeared. Before that, it was like I was nothing to them. But, what does it matter? I have no idea where we are; Bastion won't be able to find us through me.'

'I wasn't worried about that, Austin; I was thinking of your mother. The time to take you back to Implacatus is approaching, and I want to know if they'll be waiting for us.' She glanced away. 'As far as I can tell, they haven't been in your head. Your mother is very fortunate, but I'm not going to take any more chances. I'm going to seal the memories of your mother up, somewhere deep within your mind. You'll still be able to remember her, but anyone who comes looking will see nothing.'

A flash of pain tore through Austin's head, and he cried out.

'There,' she said. 'All done. It'll wear off after a month or so, by which time I'll have taken you back to find her.'

'A month?'

She nodded. 'The saw, please, Austin.'

'You can't.'

'Why not?'

'Do you understand who the Ascendants are? They've been alive for over thirty millennia; they were there at the very beginning.'

'I doubt that, Austin. You know, I'm tempted to rip out one of the knives, so I can read Kolai's mind. The secrets that lie in there would be very enlightening. For example, how did the Ascendants get their powers? Who constructed the first Quadrants and Sextants? What came before?' She sighed. 'I want to know the answers to these questions, but I think that Karalyn is the only Holdfast powerful enough to tame an Ascendant's mind. Yes, you heard me correctly. My niece can do things that are beyond my powers. Still, she's never killed an Ascendant, and neither has Daphne. I will show them. They will never be able to look down on me again, not after I do this.'

'Is that what this is truly about, Sable? Please tell me that your sole motivation isn't family rivalry. I thought revenge was bad enough, but are you only doing this to prove yourself to the other Holdfasts?'

Sable stubbed out her cigarette. 'I don't know what I want, Austin. I came to Dragon Eyre to help Blackrose, and for a fresh start, but nothing makes sense without Badblood. I had dreams of saving the natives of this world, of trying to fix everything, but I can't. This world is too broken for me to fix on my own. The rage that took me after Badblood's death is starting to fade, and all I feel is emptiness and loss. I realise now that I have to crawl back to my family. I need Karalyn's forgiveness. Therefore, if I have to face them again, then I want to do so with an Ascendant to my name. Pass me the saw.'

Austin remained motionless. Sable shook her head at him, then leaned over and dragged the crate towards her. She rummaged in it for a moment, then pulled out a metal-toothed saw with a wooden handle.

'Do you think he can hear us?' said Austin.

Kolai's head turned an inch. 'I can hear every word you say,' the Ascendant hissed. 'I can give you the answers to your questions – I was there, at the dawn of the Ascendants, when Theodora and Edmond stood side by side, the world in their hands. I witnessed the creation of the first Sextant, and saw the new world that it created bloom and grow. I fought in the War of Dominance, when the Ascendants took control – I remember it all. Free me, and I will tell you everything. Free me, and the Holdfasts will be elevated to the highest station; I promise. You are not like other mortals – that is clear to me now. Nathaniel may have created you, but you and your kin have risen above the dregs. Save me, and you shall have palaces and slaves; gold and riches. I beg you; do not kill me.'

Sable narrowed her eyes. 'Where is Belinda?'

'She is in Cumulus, with Lord Edmond,' gasped Kolai. 'They are to be wed.'

'How did you make her agree to that?'

'Lord Edmond chastised her with a restrainer mask, until her will buckled. In time, she will realise that it was done out of love.'

'Love?' said Sable. 'In your mind, does torture equate to love?'

'Lord Edmond has loved Lady Belinda for many millennia. The coward Nathaniel stole her from him, and his corpse now hangs, withered and ugly, from the front doors of the Second Ascendant's palace.'

Sable snapped her fingers. 'Of course. I forgot about him.' She laughed. 'How could I forget the Creator himself? Karalyn assisted in his death, but it was Keira who actually killed him, so I'll still be the first Holdfast to do it unaided.'

She gripped the handle of the saw, and moved it over Kolai's neck.

'No!' he cried. 'Wait! What do you want? I can give you anything you desire.'

'No, you can't,' she said. 'You can't bring back Badblood; therefore, you have nothing to offer me that I want. Except your head.'

She drove her hand forward, and the saw ripped through the skin on Kolai's neck. Blood gurgled from his lips as her hand settled into a rhythm, the teeth of the saw tearing through the Ascendant's throat. Austin tried to look away, but he was transfixed by the sight. Sable got onto her knees, her right forearm moving back and forward, as the saw bit ever deeper through Kolai's flesh. Blood sprayed out from the wound, covering her steel breastplate. Kolai's body spasmed, so she gripped the hilt of one of the knives to keep his head steady. The noise of the saw changed as the teeth chewed through his spinal cord, then she sped up, until the saw was scraping off the stone floor of the cave. Sable dropped the bloody saw, then lifted Kolai's head by his long black hair.

'I am an Ascendant killer,' she said, her eyes shining. 'Never again will I think of myself as being worth less than my sister. Oh, Daphne – I wish you could see me now.'

Austin gripped his chest and vomited onto the ground. The situation seemed unreal to him, as if everything he had ever known had come tumbling down. The Ascendants were the greatest beings in existence, and yet the mortal woman kneeling two yards to his left had disposed of one with two knives, a sword, and a saw. Sable plucked a rag from the crate and mopped up the blood from her armour, then she pulled the knives from Kolai's dead eyes, while his head swung from her left hand.

She stood. 'I'm going back to Gyle.'

Austin wiped the sick from his chin. 'Why?'

She shrugged. 'There's not much point in killing him, if no one knows about it. I'll deliver his head as a nice little present for Bastion. You coming?'

Austin said nothing. What could he say? He had told Sable that she was insane many times, yet she went her own way, regardless of the opinions of others.

'Thank you for rescuing me,' he said. 'Did you let them capture me so that you could kill Kolai?'

Sable smiled. 'Did Bastion tell you that? Honestly, I wish I'd thought of it; but no. I made a mistake with the Quadrant; I didn't mean to leave you behind on Haurn. Get up, and stay very close to my side.'

She took out the Quadrant as Austin scrambled to his feet, then she swiped her fingers across the copper-coloured surface. The air shimmered, and they appeared back in the Winter Palace in Port Edmond. The marble-lined hallway was covered in the dismembered bodies of greenhides, and the human staff who had worked in the palace. Ten yards away, Bastion was standing with a group of soldiers. They glanced up at Sable and Austin, and Bastion raised his hand, his eyes dark.

'Surprise!' Sable shouted, then she threw the head of Kolai at Bastion. It struck him on the shoulder, then Sable activated the Quadrant as the soldiers loosed their crossbows at her. Sable and Austin reappeared back in the cave, and Austin watched as Sable started to laugh.

'Stop it,' he said.

Sable leaned over, as manic laughter came from her. She seemed almost hysterical for a moment, as if she had witnessed the funniest thing imaginable, and tears spilled down her cheeks. Her laughter faded, but the tears continued, and she fell to her knees, sobbing. Austin stared at her, fear gripping his heart. She was so close to him, that, if he wished, he could reach out with his hand, and end her life, as easily as she had ended that of the Fifth Ascendant. Maybe he should do it. Maybe she had lost all semblance of self-control, and needed to be stopped.

'Maybe I do need to be stopped,' she said, wiping her eyes. 'But even if you managed it, I've still killed an Ascendant, and nothing you can do will ever change that, Austin.' She glanced at him. 'No? Do you lack the guts to kill me?'

Austin took a step back. 'I want to find my mother.'

'Of course you do,' she said. 'Two more missions, Austin, and I will take you home.' She hung her head, then slowly got back to her feet. 'I'm sorry for what this has done to you. You probably don't believe it, but I am. Whenever I read your thoughts, I can see the conflict in your mind. You regret making a deal with me, but you're clinging on to the hope that everything will turn out all right in the end. It probably won't, Austin; you should know that. Nothing turns out the way you want it to. I'm just grateful that you can't see what goes on inside my head. The pain, the guilt, the shame; the endless dark, twisted thoughts that have corrupted my heart in Dragon Eyre. I used to think that I would never again be able to do the things that I'd done on my home world, but I was wrong.' She looked him in the eye. 'It's going to get worse, Austin. I shall wade in blood before I'm finished with this world.'

Sable took a breath, then she leaned over the headless body of Lord Kolai, and pulled the sword from his chest. She sheathed it, and gripped the Quadrant.

She glanced at Austin, and smiled, as if nothing had happened.

'Come on,' she said; 'we're late, and Blackrose will be starting to wonder where we are.'

She swiped her fingers across the Quadrant, and they vanished.

CHAPTER 17
FEARFUL ALLIES

North of Throscala, Eastern Rim – 10th Arginch 5255 (18th Gylean Year 6)

North of Throscala, Eastern Rim – 10th Arginch 5255 (18th Gylean Year 6)

The sky to the east was so red that it reminded Maddie of the City. The small clouds that had gathered above the horizon were pink, reflecting the light of the sun that had yet to appear, and if she squinted her eyes, and ignored the beach in front of her, she imagined that she could almost be back in the Bulwark.

Behind her, the birds in the forest that spread from the beach up into high cliffs were chattering and singing, preparing themselves for the dawn. The sixty dragons that Blackrose had brought to the small island from Ulna were quiet, resting after the long flight through the hours of darkness. They, too, were preparing themselves for dawn, for the attack on Throscala Town. All they needed was Sable to appear, but so far there had been no sign of the Holdfast witch.

'She has betrayed us again,' said Ahi'edo.

Maddie glanced at him. The two riders were sitting together on the beach, with no one else close by. Ahi'edo had wanted to sit with the other riders, but Shadowblaze had insisted that he keep Maddie company, and so he had been following her like a shadow since they had arrived on the tiny island.

'She hasn't betrayed us a first time,' Maddie said, 'so I don't know what your "again" is supposed to mean. I'm going to say something to you, Ahi'edo; and you're probably not going to like it, but you need to stop obsessing about Sable. You act as if you have this big rivalry with her, but she couldn't give a damn about you, which means that the only person you're hurting with all this is yourself.'

Ahi'edo frowned. 'I'm not obsessed with her.'

'Oh, come on.'

'No. Listen to me, Maddie – Sable has bewitched you; and not just you. She has cast her spell on Queen Blackrose too, and on my master Shadowblaze. I'm the only one who can see through her tricks, because I'm the only one who has been affected by them and has then recovered. I still have nightmares about what she did to me; sometimes I awake in the middle of the night in a cold sweat, shaking and weeping like a child. Don't roll your eyes at me, Maddie. I know it's been two years, but the fear she implanted into my head has never completely gone. She used me, then discarded me; and now she's using all of you.'

Maddie turned back to gaze at the eastern horizon. At any moment, the sun would appear, and Sable would be officially late. Ahi'edo had got it the wrong way round. As far as Maddie was concerned, it was Blackrose who was using Sable; taking advantage of the opportunities brought about by the Holdfast woman's rage, and her overwhelming grief for Badblood. It left a sour taste in Maddie's mouth, and she felt sorry for Sable.

'How long should we wait for her, do you think?' said Ahi'edo. 'The Queen is going to feel a little embarrassed if Sable doesn't turn up. I mean, the entire invasion will have to be called off. We should never have trusted her. When all this is over, and I'm proved right, I'm not going to gloat.'

'You were wrong about me,' she said. 'Or, do you still think I'm unworthy to be the Queen's rider?'

Ahi'edo closed his mouth and looked away. 'My master has forbidden me from voicing my opinion about you. He told me that I was in danger of breaking our bond.' He sighed. 'He loves the Queen, and I have to accept that you are her rider. Maybe I was wrong about you, Maddie. You are certainly nothing like Sable. Perhaps, once this is all over, you will let me teach you about our traditions.'

Maddie raised an eyebrow. Was Ahi'edo trying to be friendly?

'I'm not sure,' she said. 'Don't your traditions say that riders shouldn't have romantic relationships? What about me and Topaz?'

Ahi'edo shrugged. 'I think it's a mistake.'

Maddie laughed. 'I knew you'd say that.'

'Let me put into simple terms – what would you do if Topaz decided to sail back to Olkis? Imagine for a moment that he asked you to go along with him – what would you do?'

'I don't know.'

'Exactly. A dragon rider can't allow their loyalties to be split; especially if you are the Queen's rider. You owe her all of your loyalty, not half of it. The best thing you could do is break off your relationship with the pirate. If you have to sleep around, then select another rider, or one of the palace staff; someone casual.'

'But I don't want that. I want Topaz and Blackrose.'

'It'll end in tears and pain. I'm not saying this to hurt you; it's the truth. If you fall pregnant, then it'll be the beginning of the end for you and the Queen. You won't be able to ride on her shoulders with a newborn baby in your arms.'

'Blackrose thinks it'll be fine.'

'The Queen loves you – that's obvious. She wants you to be happy; but deep down, she'll be worried about where it'll lead. Our traditions are there for a reason.'

'Don't place your own fears onto me,' she said. 'I know that you're worried about the future. If Shadowblaze thinks that you hate me, then you're worried that he might break the bond, and discard you as his rider.'

Ahi'edo said nothing, his eyes downcast.

'I can tell you're trying,' she said; 'and I appreciate it. You have my word that I won't do anything to split up you and Shadowblaze.'

'Thank you,' he said, his voice a whisper. 'It might already be too late; but thank you.'

The sun lifted above the horizon, and the sky began to revert to its usual shade of deep blue. The clouds turned white, and the chorus of birds in the forest grew louder. A dragon circled overhead, then started to descend onto the long stretch of golden beach. Several dragons appeared at the edge of the forest, along with a smattering of riders. Blackrose and Shadowblaze were at the centre of the group, side by side, as they always were. Maddie and Ahi'edo got to their feet, and walked along the sand towards them.

The newly-arrived dragon was bowing his head towards the royal couple as the two riders approached.

'I have seen one of the pirate vessels, your Majesties,' he said to Blackrose and Shadowblaze; 'the one that used to be a Sea Banner frigate. It was sailing to the west of Throscala Town, about ten miles from the coast, as agreed. There was no sign of Lara's ship.'

'Did you search the area for her?' said Blackrose.

'I did, your Majesty,' said the scout. 'There were no other vessels in the vicinity.'

A streak of alarm rippled through Maddie at the scout's words. Where was the *Giddy Gull*? The ocean looked calm and peaceful, but she remembered the storm the *Little Sneak* had endured off Rigga. There were shipwrecks all over the Eastern Rim – underwater grave-yards for drowned sailors. Every time she saw the ruins of a ship she was reminded of the fragility of life, and how easy it would be for the *Giddy Gull* to strike a reef and sink.

'This news does not affect our plans,' said Shadowblaze. 'The pirates' role in the assault is marginal compared to the aid we are expecting from Sable Holdfast.' The red and grey dragon glanced at the rising sun. 'She is late.'

'She is,' said Blackrose. 'However, we shall wait a little longer before ordering the return to Ulna. There are a number of ways in which Sable could have been delayed; we shall not give up hope just yet.'

A few of the riders glanced at each other, but none of them spoke.

Blackrose's red eyes scanned the watching crowd. 'Rest, for now. We shall wait one more hour for the Holdfast witch. If she does not appear by then, we...'

The air shimmered on the beach, and Sable appeared, along with Austin. Maddie smiled in relief, then she noticed that the demigod was shaking. His eyes were staring about, as if he were in the grip of some unseen terror.

'Good morning,' said Sable, her voice as bright as the smile on her face. 'Apologies for being a little late. I had some business to attend to.'

Blackrose eyed her. 'You seem unusually cheerful, Sable. How goes your campaign?'

Sable shrugged as she eyed the dragons lined up on the beach. 'Fine.'

'Fine?' cried Austin, his hands trembling. 'I can't take this any more.' He started to weep, as the others stared at him. 'Please take me back to Ashfall and the others; I can't do this today.'

Sable gave him a sideways glance. 'Don't mind him,' she said to the dragons. 'He has a weak constitution. Still, maybe he has a point. I've just rescued him from Lord Bastion's clutches. That's why we were late.'

'I see,' said Blackrose. 'Why didn't you take him to safety before coming here?'

'I didn't want to be even later than I already am,' said Sable. 'Are you all ready to go? Say the word, and I'll pop over to Throscala to kill some gods for you.'

'You make it sound easy,' said Shadowblaze. 'Lady Ydril is a mighty opponent. Over-confidence often presages defeat.'

Sable laughed, the sound echoing along the beach.

'Tell them what you did!' cried Austin, his eyes red.

'I don't like to boast,' said Sable.

Blackrose tilted her head. 'Perhaps you should tell us, demigod.'

'Implacatus sent an Ascendant to Dragon Eyre,' Austin said, as tears spilled down his cheeks. 'A real Ascendant, in person.'

The dragons reared up, as fear passed over their faces.

'There is an Ascendant upon our world?' said Shadowblaze.

Sable grinned. 'Not any more.'

'I don't understand,' said Blackrose. 'Has the Ascendant left already?'

Austin raised a finger, and pointed at Sable. 'She hacked his head off with a saw.'

The beach fell into silence, and Maddie heard nothing but the sound of the birds, and the lapping of the ocean against the sand.

'Sable,' said Blackrose; 'is this true? Did you slay an Ascendant?'

The Holdfast witch placed a hand on her hip. 'I did. You are looking at an Ascendant-killer. The bastard might have been alive for thirty thousand years, but he only lasted a few days on Dragon Eyre. I was tempted to kill Bastion as well, but someone needs to be in command to order the withdrawal. Are you impressed?'

'I am bewildered,' said Blackrose. 'What else have you been doing?'

'The Western Rim is devastated,' cried Austin. 'Alef, Ectus, Na Sun Ka, Yearning, and now Gyle. The blood... everywhere you look. Sable is insane. She is doing to the occupation forces what Lord Sabat once did to the natives of this world when he was governor. The carnage...'

'I am merely being efficient,' said Sable. 'I told you, Queen Blackrose, that I was going to bring this world to its knees. Did you doubt me?'

'I didn't doubt your motives,' the black dragon said, 'but I had concerns about whether or not you would be successful.'

'Doubt no more,' said Sable. 'I am not just a Holdfast; I am the greatest Holdfast. Once we've dealt with Throscala, I will turn my attention back to Gyle. I will unleash a whirlwind of death and destruction among the Banner forces and the settlers they protect. If they don't evacuate this world, I will kill them all.' She glanced at Austin. 'Stay here, and get a grip of yourself. I can handle today on my own.'

The demigod stared at her, then turned away.

'Launch your attack as soon as I've gone,' Sable said to the Queen. 'When you approach Throscala Town, cast your gaze towards the top of the Citadel that overlooks the harbour. If you see me on the roof, you'll know that I've been successful, and that the way is clear for you to begin your assault.' She winked at the black dragon. 'See you soon.'

Sable vanished from the beach.

'I cannot fathom how this is possible,' said Shadowblaze. 'How could a mere mortal end the life of an Ascendant? Demigod – did you see it happen?'

'I watched it,' Austin said, a hand on his face. 'I wish I'd looked away, but I couldn't. Lord Kolai was begging for his life; promising Sable whatever she wanted. I'll never forget the sound the saw made as it tore through his throat. Then... then, she threw the head at Bastion.'

'You are from Implacatus,' said Blackrose; 'how do you think they will respond to this news?'

Austin shook his head. 'I have no idea. The gods are terrified of Sable; I heard them panicking when I was being held captive. They might decide to withdraw, or... or... I don't know.'

'Two Ascendants were slain on Lostwell,' said Blackrose, 'and Edmond destroyed that world in its entirety. All the same, I admit to being in awe of what Sable has achieved. The death of this Lord Kolai will surely give the gods pause. I cannot imagine that Edmond will find other volunteers willing to come here, not after this.'

'May I speak?' said Maddie.

'Of course, my rider.'

'Lord Edmond had already decided to destroy Lostwell before the two Ascendants were killed there. I think that if we're ever going to win here, and by win, I mean live out our lives in peace, free from the soldiers and gods of Implacatus, then Sable did what needed to be done. That Ascendant could have changed everything, but, instead, he's dead.'

'Sable Holdfast has become too powerful,' said Shadowblaze. 'If she is ultimately successful, what will she then do, if there are no more Banner forces for her to slaughter?' He glanced at Blackrose. 'Perhaps, it might be wise to point her at Wyst, your Majesty, as Lord Greysteel suggested? She could redress the balance that exists to the north of Ulna.'

'I don't see how,' said Blackrose, 'and I'm not sure I want Sable to turn her powers towards the dragons of this world. The Wystians are arrogant and aggressive, but they remain our kinfolk.' She glanced at the dragons crowding onto the beach. 'Riders, dragons; it is time to go. Throscala Town is only two hours flight from here – to your positions.'

Maddie glanced at Ahi'edo, then began walking towards Blackrose, as the assembled riders climbed up into their dragons' harnesses. Austin sat down onto the sand, watching them.

'Do you want to come along?' Maddie said to him. 'You can sit next to me on Blackrose's shoulders.'

The demigod shook his head. 'I've seen enough death. I want to go home.'

'You mean, back to where Ashfall and Millen are hiding?'

He gazed at her. 'Yes. Yes; that's what I meant.'

She got the feeling he was keeping something from her, but she could also sense Blackrose's impatience, so she ran across the sand, then clambered up onto the harness and strapped herself in. The black dragon ascended, her great wings lifting them into the sky. All around her, the other dragons were also climbing into the air.

'Poor Austin,' said Maddie, as she glanced down at the small figure left alone on the beach below them.

'It was his decision to help Sable, rider,' said Blackrose.

'I know, but you can see the effect it's having on him.'

'Perhaps he will ponder his choices more carefully from now on.'

The massed dragons sped off towards the south, the sun on their left as they soared low over the ocean. Maddie gazed ahead of them, but could see nothing but water and sky.

'Could you keep an eye out for the *Giddy Gull*?' said Maddie.

'Of course. Are you concerned about your friend?'

'Yes.' She frowned. 'I need to ask you something. What if, hypothetically, in the distant future, I got pregnant? I wouldn't be able to ride on your harness before or after giving birth, and then I would have a little baby to look after. How will it work?'

'The same applies to me, rider. If I agree to consummate my

betrothal to Shadowblaze, then I too shall have new responsibilities. Do you imagine that I will be flying when I have a brood of eggs to guard?'

'I never thought of that.'

'Has Ahi'edo been filling your head with doubts again?'

'Um... well...'

'I shall speak to my betrothed about this. Ahi'edo must cease trying to undermine our bond.'

'No; don't, please. Shadowblaze is ready to throw Ahi'edo away, and I don't want to be the cause of that.'

'Very well. I shall hold my tongue for now, unless Shadowblaze asks me directly.'

'Thanks. Are you in love with him yet?'

'No.'

'Oh. That's a shame, I guess.'

'I cannot force myself to feel something that isn't there. However, I might still take him as my mate. There is no other dragon I feel closer to than him, and he would be a loyal and loving mate. I could do far worse. I also have Ulna to consider. My realm would be more secure were he and I to remain united.'

'That seems a little cold.'

'It is the truth. It is also true that I do love Shadowblaze, although I am not in love with him. The days of our youth were spent in each other's company, and they were happy times. Perhaps that is the problem – I see him almost as a brother, rather than a mate. If I were to meet him afresh, having never known him, I might well be attracted to him. Still, such musings are without worth. Let us deal with Throscala, and see how matters lie.'

The coastline of northern Throscala appeared after forty minutes – a shimmering grey line on the horizon in front of them. The dragons continued onwards, then veered to the west as the ragged cliffs approached. Throscala Town was on the western side of the island, and

Blackrose led the dragons to the cape on the far north-western shore, then turned south.

'I can see the *Sow's Revenge*,' said Blackrose; 'precisely where the scout said it would be. There is no sign of Topaz's vessel, however.'

Maddie felt her heart sink. There was no way that Lara and Topaz would have decided to run away, which could only mean that something bad had happened.

'The ocean looks so big from up here,' she said.

'Try not to worry,' said the black dragon. 'We can ask Sable to use her powers to look for your friend. I imagine that she will be concerned for the safety of Captain Lara, if she still has space in her heart for such feelings.'

'Do you agree with Shadowblaze? Is Sable too powerful?'

'That is yet to be seen, my rider. Her fury may burn itself out, or perhaps the death of the Ascendant has given her notions of invulnerability. I am unable to see how this will end.'

Behind her, the dragons began to wheel and circle over the calm ocean, while Blackrose pressed onwards, Shadowblaze by her side. The two dragons soared towards the main town on Throscala, until Maddie could see the masts sticking up from the large harbour. Above them, the town's citadel loomed over the rest of the settlement. Maddie strained her eyes, but could see nothing up on the roof of the highest tower.

Blackrose glided closer to Shadowblaze.

'I see the Holdfast witch,' she said. 'Her attack must have been successful.'

'I see her too, my beloved,' said Shadowblaze. 'I also see who is standing by her side. Greenhides? Is this how the witch has been carrying out her massacres?'

'It appears so.'

'What?' said Maddie. 'Are there greenhides on top of the citadel?'

'Yes,' said Blackrose; 'two of the creatures. They are standing next to Sable, as if guarding her. Wait; I can feel the witch's presence in my mind.' Blackrose fell silent for a few moments, then turned her neck to face Shadowblaze. 'Go back and inform the others that the attack is to commence immediately. The gods of Throscala are dead.'

Shadowblaze tilted his head, but before he could turn, Maddie caught the expression on Ahi'edo's face. The face of the red and grey dragon's rider had paled at the news of the greenhides, and he looked queasy. Shadowblaze soared away, leaving Blackrose alone as she scanned the harbour in the distance.

'I don't understand,' said Maddie. 'How could Sable get greenhides to protect her? And, why don't you seem surprised?'

'I learned on Haurn that Sable has the ability to control the beasts.'

'She can control them?' Maddie cried. 'But, how? This is amazing; and awful. Do you think she's been using greenhides to fight the Banner soldiers?'

'I suspect that this may be the truth.'

'No wonder Austin is a nervous wreck. Malik's hairy ass; why did it have to be greenhides? I hate those things; they make my flesh crawl.'

'They are the means to her end.'

Maddie smothered her response. How could Sable have stooped so low? Memories of the greenhides breaching the Great Walls of her home flooded her. They were vermin; disgusting beasts who understood nothing but violence, and Sable was using them to kill humans. How could she? Maddie felt sick. Was this what Austin had been hinting at, when he had stated that Sable was behaving in the same way as Lord Sabat? The Ancient had used greenhides to slaughter untold thousands of Dragon Eyre's inhabitants; and now Sable was treating the occupation forces in the same manner.

Behind them, the other dragons caught up, and Blackrose led the way towards Throscala Town. Two wings peeled off to either side, each composed of a dozen dragons, while the central strike force aimed directly for the harbour. The sound of bells ringing reached Maddie's ears as the dragons sped through the air. Ballistae were positioned along the tall breakwaters that guarded the entrance to the harbour, and they began to loose as the dragons passed within range. Blackrose banked, and descended to a few feet above the ocean, as a bolt ripped through the air to her left. She opened her jaws, and incinerated a wooden platform jutting up above the left breakwater, and the two ballistae posted there burst into flames. To their right, a dragon cried out in pain, then crashed into the blue waters of the ocean, two bolts protruding from his abdomen. Other dragons were weaving as they darted back and forth, spewing out flames all over the breakwaters. As soon as the last ballista had been burned, they surged over the packed harbour. Lines of Sea Banner frigates were berthed by the main jetties, and the dragons soared over them, flames enveloping the helpless vessels. A few ballista bolts were loosed up at them, but the destruction of the vessels took mere moments, and the entire harbour seemed aflame. Smoke rose like a thick cloud over the burning ships, as sailors jumped overboard, or tried to flee down gangways. Half a mile to the south, the Banner fort was under attack from the right wing of the assault force. Maddie saw two more dragons hit by ballista bolts, but without gods to protect the soldiers, the outcome was inevitable. Flames were belching from the high barrack blocks, while dragons were sweeping up the main routes of the town between the fort and the harbour, incinerating anything that moved. The palm trees by the quay-side were all burning, while settlers fled in panic, stampeding through the streets. On the northern side of the town, the left wing was destroying the large warehouses that supplied the Sea Banner, and an enormous explosion rang out, the flash from it dazzling Maddie's eyes. The dragons in the air were pushed aside by the blast, and it took a few moments for Blackrose to regain her balance and composure. A huge cloud of light grey smoke billowed up from the source of the explosion, and the roar of tumbling masonry drowned out the screams from the settlers and soldiers caught by the harbour.

Blackrose glanced around for Shadowblaze, and flew up to meet him.

'My love,' he said, his amber eyes glowing, 'the town is ours. Resistance is at an end – should we call off the slaughter, to spare the natives?'

'There are other Banner garrisons on Throscala,' the black dragon said. 'Send the left and right wings to destroy each of them in turn; and then join me at the citadel after you have delivered their orders. I wish to speak to Sable before she decides to disappear.'

Shadowblaze tilted his head. 'The other dragons, and their riders, took the news of the greenhides badly.'

'Perhaps you shouldn't have mentioned it to them.'

'Perhaps I shouldn't have. However; I did. I do not think it wise if I attend the citadel. I am unsure if I will be able to stop myself from killing the two beasts that stand by the witch's side.'

'Very well,' said Blackrose. 'I shall go alone. I doubt that Sable will remain long.'

'Take great care, my Queen,' he said. 'There is no knowing what the witch might do next. I fear that her ambitions have grown in tandem with her powers. What if she turns her gaze to Ulna next?'

'She will not; she gave her word.'

Shadowblaze bowed his head. 'So be it.'

He turned and soared away, calling for the other dragons to join him above the burning ships in the harbour. Maddie watched as the dragons pulled up from their pursuit of the remaining soldiers and sailors, then her eyes were drawn to the heaps of smouldering corpses that littered the ground all around the harbour. Did it matter if Sable used greenhides, when dragons were even more deadly? The entire battle had taken less than fifteen minutes, and the town was in smoking ruins, the survivors staggering around in a wide-eyed daze.

'Come,' said Blackrose; 'it is time to visit the famed Ascendant-killer.'

CHAPTER 18
A FAIR CONCEIT

Throscala, Eastern Rim – 10th Arginch 5255 (18th Gylean Year 6)
Sable leaned on the stone parapet, watching as the dragons burned the ships and Banner fort of Throscala Town. The explosion that had torn through the northern district had answered the question about where the explosive devices had been stored; the crater left behind was still clouded with dust and smoke, while the buildings around it were ruined shells, their roofs and windows gone.

Behind her, the two greenhides were so silent that she could almost forget that they were there. Austin's reluctance to assist her had forced Sable to return to Haurn to gather a hundred greenhides for the assault, and the two standing by her shoulders were the sole survivors – Lady Ydril had indeed been a formidable opponent, and had wiped out swathes of the beasts before Sable could get close enough to remove the god's head from her shoulders. Compared to her, the other two gods resident in the citadel had been easy to kill – they had wailed at the sight of her approach, fear paralysing them. All three heads were gathered by Sable's feet, in case anyone needed any proof of what she had done.

Thirteen-and-a-half, she thought to herself.

She glanced up, and lit a cigarette. Blackrose was approaching through the clouds of dark smoke that were streaming up from the ships burning in the harbour. The attack had been impressive, and had gone exactly as Blackrose had planned. One dragon was easily worth a hundred greenhides in combat, Sable reckoned. She stopped herself. Badblood had been worth more than every greenhide in existence. That was different. He had been her soulmate, not a tool in her hands designed to kill her enemies. At the thought of Badblood, her calm smile evaporated. She was an Ascendant-killer, but that meant nothing next to her beautiful dragon's death. She felt her will start to crumble, and it took a great effort to remain still as she waited for Blackrose to arrive. She must not break. The route she had chosen ran in only one direction, and there was no going back.

The black dragon hovered above the wide roof, then she slowly set herself down, her bulk squeezing between the sides of the parapets. She glanced at the greenhides for a moment, then turned to Sable.

'Greetings, Ascendant-killer,' the black dragon said, 'and thank you for your aid today.'

'It was nothing,' said Sable.

Maddie clambered down from the harness, then hesitated, her eyes on the two greenhides.

'Don't worry about them,' Sable said, 'they are under my control.'

'Yes; I heard,' said Maddie, her eyes tight. 'It doesn't mean I like it, though.'

Sable shrugged. 'I don't like it either, Maddie. One must use whatever tools are to hand, and Haurn has an inexhaustible supply of the beasts.'

Blackrose's eyes burned red. 'Have you transported any queens?'

'Of course not,' said Sable. 'Do you think I'm crazy? Don't answer that. No; it's just the humble foot-soldiers that I've been taking around Dragon Eyre – a hundred here, a hundred there. These two are all that's left of a hundred that I brought to the citadel. Ydril killed the rest.'

Blackrose moved her face closer to Sable, and the two greenhides growled and raised their claws.

Sable laughed. 'Don't come too close,' she said; 'these lads have been instructed to protect me, and they will attack you if they think I'm being threatened.'

'Oh, Sable,' said Maddie. 'Can't you see how wrong this is? How is this any different from what the gods did to Dragon Eyre in the first place? They used greenhides to slaughter thousands of natives, and now you're doing the same.'

'Yeah.'

'Does this not concern you?' said Blackrose.

'No. Within the course of a few short months, I have dismantled the entire security apparatus of the colonial occupation, as well as killing the governor, and that Ascendant.' She glanced down at the heads by her feet. 'And Lady Ydril, of course. There are still several gods on Gyle, though; they're my next target.'

'And after that?' said Blackrose. 'What will you do then?'

'That's none of your concern, Blackrose.'

'Your arrogance is getting tiresome, witch. Your actions upon this world also affect me.'

'I said I would leave Ulna alone, and I shall. I will decide what to do with the rest of this world.'

'The power has corrupted your mind, Sable,' said the dragon. 'You are not immortal. If I so wished, I could strike you down now. Your two greenhides would hardly be able to stop me.'

Sable laughed. 'You can't hurt me, Blackrose. When I was on the beach with you this morning, did you feel a light tingling in your head?'

The black dragon said nothing.

'You didn't?' said Sable. 'Excellent; I must be getting better at manipulating dragons.'

Blackrose opened her jaws, her eyes tight. 'What did you do to me, witch?'

'The same thing that I did to every other dragon who was on the beach. I went into your minds, and placed blocks there, to stop any of you from harming me. I figured that you'd soon realise how I had achieved so much, and I knew that you would disapprove of my methods. Call it an insurance policy; it wasn't personal.'

'You have gone too far, witch!'

'How many times have you said that to me? And yet, here I am, prepared to go even further – right into the abyss, if need be.'

'I am deeply insulted by this. We worked together as close allies, from Haurn to Ectus, and yet you felt it necessary to tamper with my mind?'

'Yes. I have garnered a lot of enemies in recent days. I need to be careful.'

'This conversation is over,' said Blackrose. 'Maddie, climb onto my shoulders – being in the presence of this vile witch is making me feel ill.'

'Wait,' said Maddie. 'What about the *Giddy Gull*?'

'What about it?' said Sable.

'It's missing,' said Maddie. 'Tilly's ship was where it was supposed to be, but the dragon scouts couldn't locate Lara and Topaz.'

Sable's eyes narrowed. 'I see.'

'Will you look for them? Please?'

'Alright. I need to deal with the official surrender of the occupying forces first – I've summoned every senior commander in Throscala to meet me in the citadel. Then, I need to collect Austin. After that, I'll search for the *Gull*.'

'Thank you,' said Maddie. 'I mean; I'm sure everything's fine, but you know – I worry.'

'It's no problem,' said Sable. She glanced at Blackrose. 'See? I'm not completely unreasonable. I can see that you also wish to ask me something.'

Blackrose reared up. 'Get out of my head, witch.'

'I'm waiting. Ask me.'

'I don't think I should. You are clearly out of control, and...'

'You want me to help you with the dragons from Wyst?' said Sable. 'They are threatening your northern borders, and you fear that they might launch an invasion of Ulna?' She shrugged. 'It sounds like your problem.'

Blackrose stared at her. 'Shadowblaze was right – you have grown too powerful.'

'Shadowblaze is also unable to harm me,' said Sable. 'His mind was easy to manipulate, as I've done it to him before. Do you recall?'

'Why are you taunting me?' cried Blackrose. 'I came here as your friend, and you are forcing me to depart as your enemy. Where will this end, Sable?'

'In blood, Blackrose; waves of it. I'll think about helping you with the Wyst dragons, but I'm not going to promise anything.'

'I don't want your help, witch; not any more. Maddie, climb up onto the harness; now.'

Maddie glanced from Sable to Blackrose, then ran to the dragon's side, and clambered up.

'I will issue this warning to you only once, witch,' said Blackrose, as she extended her wings. 'Stay away from Ulna.'

'Your warnings mean nothing to me,' said Sable. 'I shall do as I please.'

Blackrose beat her wings, and soared into the sky. Sable glanced down, as a wash of warm air passed over her from the dragon's wings. Why had she acted like that? It had taken Blackrose a long time to accept her, and yet she had thrown it all away in a matter of moments. She was pushing everyone away, she realised; Austin, Ashfall and Millen, and now Blackrose and Maddie. She didn't deserve their friendship – that was it. She had soiled her soul with the cruellest deeds, and had to make them understand that she was beyond redemption. Her composure cracked, and the two greenhides behind her grew restless.

Beyond redemption? Truly? How had it come to this? Freed from her control, one of the greenhides raised its claws, its jaws clacking. She stared at it.

Jump off the tower.

It cried out, shrieking, then clambered up onto the parapet and hurled itself over the edge. The other greenhide snapped back under her control, obedient to her will once more. She had to stop doubting herself. The time to think about redemption was when she was face to face with the other Holdfasts, and not a moment before. She glanced over the parapet, and saw the green smear on the ground a hundred feet below her – all that remained of the greenhide. She tossed the cigarette butt after it, turned, and walked down the steps leading to the interior of the citadel.

The bottom of the stairs resembled a charnel house. Body parts of greenhides and Banner soldiers lay scattered next to blood-spattered walls. Lying amid them was the headless body of one of the gods she had killed, and Sable stepped over it, then continued on her way. The steel armour was weighing her down, so she boosted her battle-vision to compensate, then held her head high as she entered a great hall, the surviving greenhide trotting along behind her.

Inside the vast chamber, a group of around three dozen people had gathered. They turned to face Sable as she walked towards them, their eyes betraying their terror and despair. She scanned them. There was a mixture of senior Banner officers, Sea Banner officers, and the top mortal officials who had served in the colonial government of Throscala.

'Thank you for gathering here,' Sable said to them, a hand resting on the hilt of her sword. 'Did you all get a good look at what the dragons of Ulna have done to your town? Yes? Good. Who is in charge?'

A Banner officer stepped forward. 'I am the senior officer left, ma'am. I am the commander of the Banner forces stationed in the Eastern Rim.'

Sable nodded. 'I want to hear your surrender.'

The commander pursed his lips for a moment. 'What about the ordinary soldiers and sailors, ma'am? If we surrender, what will become of them?'

Sable sat on a chair, and put her feet up onto the long table. 'I want them disarmed, and confined to their barracks. Other than that, I have no interest in their well-being.'

'Will the dragons slaughter them, ma'am?'

She shrugged. 'Maybe. You'd have to speak to them about it. The same goes for the settlers. As of this moment, slavery no longer exists on Throscala. I want orders sent out to that effect. No compensation, and no right of appeal. Your reign is over. Now, your surrender, if you please, Commander.'

The officer bowed his head. 'All armed forces loyal to the colonial government in Throscala hereby surrender to you, Lady Holdfast.'

She nodded, then glanced at an official. 'Send word of my orders down into the town.'

The official trembled. 'Your orders, ma'am?'

'Weren't you listening?' said Sable. 'All Banner soldiers are to hand over their weapons to the natives and return to their barracks. All Sea Banner personnel are to remain in their base, pending the dissolution of the Eastern Fleet. And, all slave-owners on Throscala are to immediately free their slaves. You have my permission to utilise any sea-worthy vessel that remains on the island to evacuate. Get your arses off Throscala and sail back to the Home Islands.'

'But, ma'am,' said the official; 'there are close to eighty thousand settlers living on Throscala. Even if every available ship is used, there will be room for only a small fraction of the total populace.'

Sable shrugged. 'You should have thought about that before colonising someone else's land. Go.'

The official glanced around for a moment, then ran for the door.

A Sea Banner officer slammed his fist down onto the table. 'This is an outrage. You will pay for what you have done here.' He smiled. 'You don't know it yet, but your killing spree will soon be at an end.'

'Really?' said Sable. 'Why is that?'

The officer puffed out his chest. 'Because, my dear lady, we received word two days ago that a blessed Ascendant has arrived on Dragon Eyre.'

'Who; Kolai?' she said. 'Should I be scared of him?'

'How did you know it was him?' said the officer.

'Never mind that,' said another officer. 'When Lord Kolai gets here, he will destroy you, and your dragons. You may have the upper hand now, but your death is inevitable.'

Sable laughed. She stretched her arms, then glanced at the greenhide, imprinting some orders that would persist in her absence for a few minutes.

'Wait here a moment,' she said to the group.

She activated the Quadrant, and appeared inside the rough cave near Rigga where she had killed Lord Kolai. His decapitated body was still lying where she had left it. She glanced down at the two hands she had severed, and noticed that one had a large ring on a finger. She picked up the hand, and gazed at the ring for a moment, then transported herself back to Throscala Town. She smiled at the assembled officers and officials, and threw the hand onto the table.

'Here's what's left of Lord Kolai,' she said, as her prisoners gazed at the severed hand. 'I would have brought his head, but I've already given that to Bastion.'

Most of the officers and officials stared at her in disbelief, but the Banner commander picked up the hand. He examined the ring for a moment.

'She speaks the truth,' he said. 'I have seen this ring before, in Cumulus.'

Some of the officials broke down in tears, while the Sea Banner officers fell silent. The Banner commander placed the severed hand back onto the table.

'What do you intend to do with us now, ma'am?' he said.

'I'm going to take you to a place where you will no longer be a threat to the people of Dragon Eyre,' she said. 'Are you ready?'

She swiped her fingers across the Quadrant, and everyone who had been in the chamber appeared on a gentle slope, with a view of the ocean ahead of them. She turned, and saw a vast horde of greenhides at the bottom of the slope.

'Welcome to Haurn,' she said to the assembled officers and officials. 'In a matter of moments, those greenhides will be here. You can face them, or throw yourself off the cliff; whatever you think best. Farewell.'

She activated the Quadrant, and appeared back in the empty chamber. She frowned. She had left her last surviving greenhide in Haurn with the others. Freed from her dominating mind, it was probably ripping its way through the senior officers of Throscala before the main horde had a chance to reach them. She shrugged. Did it matter? Her thoughts turned to Austin, but before she triggered the Quadrant again, she walked over to a window, and gazed out over the town. Dragons were still circling over the harbour, while others were on the ground, herding disarmed soldiers back towards their barracks. Lines of settlers were making their way towards the quayside, while crowds of jubilant natives yelled abuse and mocked them from either side. A few settlers were assaulted as they trudged along, but the dragons paid no attention, and none intervened. She wondered for a moment what the future held for the eighty thousand settlers on the island, then pushed the thought from her head. It was none of her concern. Let Blackrose and Shadowblaze decide what to do with them. She saw a settler family with small children being jeered and spat at by a group of natives, and she felt dizzy, and sick. Part of her wanted to go down to the quayside, in order to protect them from the wrath of the natives, but it would be pointless, as well as hypocritical. The road she was travelling went in one direction, and she had no choice but to keep going.

She flicked her fingers over the Quadrant, and appeared on the long stretch of golden sand where she had left Austin. She glanced around, but there was no sign of the demigod. She realised that she was thirsty, and began walking towards a waterfall that tumbled down the face of the cliffs a hundred yards from where she stood. At the base of the waterfall was a deep pool, with water so clear that she could see the rocks and sand at the bottom. Tiny silver fish were darting around, while birds with bright plumage were flying down from the branches of the nearby trees to take a drink. Sable knelt on the grass by the side of the pool, cupped her hands, and raised some water to her lips.

'I wasn't sure if you'd come back for me,' said Austin.

She glanced up, and saw the demigod sitting on a rock, with his bare feet in the water.

'You thought I'd leave you here,' she said, 'after all the trouble I endured to rescue you?'

'Killing Kolai didn't seem to cause you much trouble.'

'No; that was simple.' She sat on the grass. 'How are you feeling?'

He shrugged, and glanced away. 'Conflicted. Sorry about earlier.'

'There's no need to apologise. I've put you through quite a lot in recent days.'

He nodded. 'How did it go in Throscala?'

'A complete success. The gods are dead, and the dragons are in control of the town. Listen; even though you didn't come along, I'm not going to hold that against you. In other words, it still counts as an operation. That means there's only one more operation for you to complete.'

He glanced back at her, an eyebrow raised. 'This feels strange. Why are you being nice to me?'

'Aren't I usually nice?'

'No, Sable. Your mood swings are becoming more extreme with every operation. You veer from depressed to enraged, then cold and calculating, but rarely nice.'

She lay back on the grass and closed her eyes. 'I was lying about Throscala. Not everything went well.'

'Oh?'

'I... I rather foolishly attempted to drive Blackrose and Maddie away. I couldn't help myself, and, unfortunately, I think my attempt worked. Blackrose is back to being disgusted and furious with me. I think it might have been due to the death of Kolai. My success went to my head, and I was simultaneously both cocky and cruel.'

'And now?'

She pictured the settler family who had been mocked and spat at in her mind.

'Now?' she said. 'I'm veering back towards depression. It's impossible to save everyone. If the settlers win, then the natives will continue to suffer; but if the dragons and natives win, then what will happen to the million settlers already in Dragon Eyre?'

'Are you thinking of giving up?'

She half opened an eye and glanced at him. 'Don't be ridiculous. I can't give up. Where would I go? Who would welcome me?'

'Sable, you have a damn Quadrant.'

'But I don't know how to make it take me home.'

Austin remained quiet for a while. 'Are you homesick?'

'I don't know. I don't think I belong anywhere.'

'Back in the cave,' said Austin, 'where you killed the Ascendant, you told me that you wanted to seek forgiveness from your family.'

'I remember saying that. It was only last night, but it feels like months ago. The problem, Austin, is that I can't go home. I can travel all around Dragon Eyre, and I can go to Implacatus, but that's it. I have no idea where I need to touch the Quadrant to make it take me back to the Star Continent.'

'Maybe someone on Implacatus knows.'

She laughed. 'That's highly unlikely. If the Ascendants knew how to get to my world, then they would have invaded.'

'Maybe they have. Who knows? You've been here for two years, and you were in Lostwell before that. Who's to say that the Ascendants aren't already there?'

'When you were in Serene, did you ever hear of any talk about my world?'

'No, but I'm just a young demigod, whose only claim to any renown was through my father. There were lots of secrets on Implacatus that no one would ever dream of telling me about. Like the reason they invaded Dragon Eyre, for instance. Has it occurred to you, that if you are successful, and you manage to drive out the occupation forces from this world, then Implacatus might select another one to invade?'

'When I was on Lostwell, they were hunting for the location of the salve world – you know, the place Maddie is from.'

'Yes, I knew all about that. Lord Renko's mission, and then the two Ascendants that were sent after he returned. They failed. As a consequence of that, Implacatus must be running low on salve about now.'

'That wasn't the point I was trying to make. If the Ascendants couldn't find the salve world, then how could they possibly find my world? Wouldn't they need a Quadrant that had been there?'

'I guess so. But that means you're stuck here, unless you can find a

Quadrant that's been there; and, to be honest, the chances of that are nil.'

'My only hope is Karalyn.'

'How would she be able to help?'

'She has the Sextant, or at least I presume she does. As far as I know, Belinda was going to send it back to the Star Continent with Corthie and Aila. If that happened, then Karalyn would have taken possession of it. She has the ability to travel without a Quadrant, so imagine what she could do with a Sextant.'

'Wait a moment. Did you say that she can move around without a Quadrant? Sorry, Sable, but that's impossible.'

'So are mortals with powers, apparently. Look; I know she can do it, because she took me and Belinda to Lostwell without a Quadrant. There was a slight mix up with the time it took, but we got there in one piece. In theory, that means she could travel to any world the Sextant can see, once she's learned how to operate it. And that means she can come here. She won't, though – why would she? To rescue me? Yeah, right. She abandoned me in Lostwell; she'd never go out of her way to come to my assistance.' She sighed. 'We'd better go. As much as I love it here – the waterfall, the pool, the flowers; we have things to do.'

She got to her feet, and watched as Austin pulled his boots on.

'Thank you,' she said.

'For what?'

'For listening. For making me feel normal again. For not being angry with me, or terrified. Meader was right about you – you're too good for Dragon Eyre.'

He glanced up at her. 'One more operation?'

She nodded. 'But not today.'

She waited until he was standing, then swiped her fingers over the Quadrant. They appeared on a desolate hillside, with a blustery wind coming off the ocean to their left. A dragon cried out to their right, and they turned.

Austin smiled. 'Ashfall!'

He ran to her, and wrapped his arms round the slender grey dragon's face. Sable watched in silence for a moment, then saw Deepblue, Millen and Dina appear over the crest of the hill.

'Sable,' said Ashfall, 'thank you; thank you.'

'You did it!' cried Deepblue. 'Well done, Sable.'

'Are you both alright?' said Millen. 'Are you hungry? Thirsty?'

'Yes to both,' said Sable, as she pulled at the straps holding her heavy steel armour on. 'Can someone give me a hand?'

Millen hurried over to her, and helped her out of the armour.

'How did you get away from the Ascendant?' he said.

Sable smiled. 'Oh, I think the Ascendant had some trouble getting away from me.' She stretched her tired limbs. 'I need to bathe, then eat and drink; and then it's back to work.'

'Already?' said Millen. 'You only just got here.'

Austin frowned. 'I thought you said I didn't have another operation today?'

Sable raised her hands, as Ashfall and Deepblue glared at her. 'Steady on. This isn't an official operation; it's just something that I have to do. I won't be needing you, Austin.' She turned to Dina. 'I will, however, be requiring you, Miss Osso.'

Dina blinked. 'Me? What do you need me for?'

Sable smiled. 'I think it's time we reunited you with your sisters.'

CHAPTER 19
LEGEND

North of Throscala, Eastern Rim – 11th Arginch 5255 (18th Gylean Year 6)

The air in the small compartment was stifling, and Topaz could feel the sweat roll down his back. Next to him, the sound of Lara breathing drifted over to him, but in the darkness, he had only a vague idea of where she was. The cabin was too restricted for him to stretch out in, and he had been experiencing sharp cramps in his legs that had kept him awake throughout the two nights they had spent confined there. He scratched his ankle. The shackles were rubbing against his skin, and he could feel a couple of blisters developing.

'Don't do that, Topaz,' said Lara. 'Scratching ain't going to make it better, and, more importantly, the sound of you doing it annoys the crap out of me.'

'Now you know how I feel when you whistle, ma'am.'

'Shut up. I am an excellent whistler.'

'You're off-key, ma'am. It's like listening to Ryan tune his damn guitar.'

'If I could see your face, I'd slap it.'

Topaz re-arranged himself for the tenth time that morning, unable to get comfortable. The bruises on his back and sides were almost as painful as the cramp, and he grimaced as he got up into a sitting position.

'Stop moving around,' Lara muttered. 'It makes me nervous. This cabin's so small that I'm expecting a knee in the face every time you get into a new position.' She groaned. 'How long does it take to fix a bleeding rudder?'

'I hope it takes them a lot longer, ma'am' said Topaz. 'We'll be leaving as soon as the Gull's been repaired, and it'll be worse down here once we're on the move. And we'll be harder to find.'

'Stop being bleeding right all the time. Gods, I need a piss.' She thumped on the cabin door. 'Hey! I need a bleeding piss, you assholes! Let me out.'

They listened at the door, but no sounds came from the other side.

'This is humiliating,' Lara said. 'Am I supposed to pee on the damn deck? There ain't no way I'll be able to hold it in until Rigga.'

'Rigga might be a month away, ma'am. Your father still has to track down and capture Captain Tilly and her ship first. He wouldn't leave her behind in the Eastern Rim, would he?'

'I don't know, Topaz; he might. It was the *Gull* he was after, and he's got it. Tilly could be heading back to Udall by now, and if she's there, then my father wouldn't dare to go after her. He's a crafty bastard, but he ain't reckless.'

They quietened as more footsteps sounded from outside the cabin. A key was thrust into the lock, and turned, and the door swung open, blinding Topaz and Lara with light.

Topaz squinted, and saw a figure in the doorway.

'Good morning, you two,' said Ann.

'If you ain't here to let us out,' said Lara, 'you can piss right off.'

'Your shouting's been disturbing my crew,' Ann said.

Lara snorted. 'Am I meant to be sad about that?'

Ann gestured to a sailor behind her. 'Take my sister to the heads; she needs to relieve herself.'

The sailor stepped forwards. 'Yes, ma'am.'

Lara pushed herself to her feet, and shuffled forward, the shackles round her ankles making it difficult to walk. The sailor reached out with a hand to assist her, but she slapped it away with a scowl. Ann moved to the side to let them pass, then she leaned over and picked up a basket. She placed it into the small compartment next to Topaz.

'Breakfast,' she said. 'Leave half for my sister.'

'Thanks,' Topaz muttered.

He picked up a water skin from the basket, pulled out the stopper, and drank. The water was tepid, but felt like the best thing he had ever tasted.

Ann smiled. 'Better?'

He nodded. 'When are we leaving, ma'am?'

She shrugged. 'The carpenters are still working on the *Giddy Gull's* steering mechanism. That pisspot wrecked the control rod, and split the rudder itself. It'll be at least another full day.'

'How are the crew?'

'Why? Are you hoping that the lads on the *Gull* will mount a rescue attempt?'

He shrugged.

'No Five Sisters crew would mutiny against my father, Topaz,' she said. 'You should know that. No matter the... mistakes he makes.'

'And what mistakes has he made, ma'am?'

Ann smiled down at him, but said nothing.

'You got a cigarette, ma'am?'

She nodded, then reached into her tunic, and produced a tobacco pouch.

'You'll have to roll your own,' she said, handing it to him. 'The papers are inside.'

'Thanks,' he said, opening the pouch. He made a small cigarette from the contents, then Ann lit it for him with a match.

He inhaled, and leaned back against the bulkhead. Lara appeared in the doorway, and was shoved back into the compartment by the sailor who had been escorting her. She sat, then glanced at the basket, then at Topaz.

'Roll me one of those,' she said. She looked up at Ann. 'Why are you still here? Are you bleeding enjoying the sight of us like this?'

'Not particularly,' Ann said. She nodded to the sailor, and he hurried away.

'Do you have any news for us, ma'am?' said Topaz, as he prepared a cigarette for Lara.

'Aside from what I told you about the repairs, no,' Ann said. 'There's been no sighting of any other ship since we anchored in the creek, and the lads have been swimming about and lazing on the beach; waiting until the *Gull* is ready to sail again. Then, we'll be moving out, and hunting for Tilly. Once we have her ship, we'll be sailing for Rigga.'

'We bleeding well knew all this,' said Lara.

'Why Rigga, ma'am?' said Topaz. 'It would make a lot more sense to go via Wyst, even if the dragons there aren't allowing any stops for water.'

Ann glanced over her shoulder, to check that the passageway was empty, then she crouched down by the two prisoners.

'We can't go by Wyst,' she said in a low voice, 'not after what happened when we passed it on the way south.'

Lara frowned. 'Why not?'

'We stopped off for water in the usual place; you probably know it – and then a couple of dragons appeared, and told us to leave.'

'So?' said Lara. 'The same thing happened to us.'

Ann regarded her sister. 'Did you leave, as they requested?'

'Of course we bleeding did.'

'Well, father refused. He seemed to take it as a personal insult, and thought that the dragons were trying to mess with him. He ordered the crew to carry on with filling the water barrels, and then the dragons killed one of the lads – tore him in half. So father, in his wisdom, loaded the pisspots and ballistae, and loosed the lot at the two dragons. One was brought down and killed by ballista bolts, and the other was injured, but managed to fly away. Father thought it was all very exciting; he was acting like he'd won a great battle. It was only when we were departing that he realised that things ain't that simple. About a dozen dragons soared over from the mountains, and we had to scarper. We loosed nearly every damn bolt we had at them, but they were too quick for us. We were damn lucky to get away. We steered into a fog bank, and drifted west for a while, until we had lost them.'

'Holy crap,' said Lara.

'Exactly,' said Ann. 'The Wystians got a good look at the *Flight of Fancy*, and they know father's name, mainly because he kept shouting it at them. You can imagine – "I am the great Olo'osso", and all that crap. Anyway, he's shit-scared of heading up that way again, and I don't blame him. The Wystians will mince us if they see us. Hence Rigga.'

'The old bastard should have stayed in Langbeg,' said Lara. 'He's out of touch with what's been going on in the world.'

'Yeah? Well, the capture of the *Gull* has cheered him up again. To be honest, I didn't think you'd fall for it. Why didn't you search those guys he sent over in the rowing boat?'

Lara narrowed her eyes. 'I've been asking myself the same bleeding question. We were under-crewed, eh? It never occurred to me that father would risk sinking my ship to get it back. What kind of maniac does that?'

'After Wyst, father had a lot to prove to the crew. They were starting to doubt his leadership, and he needed a victory. You were dumb enough to hand it to him on a plate.'

'Screw you, Ann.'

The two sisters glared at each other.

'Ma'am,' said Topaz, 'will you be letting us up on to the deck when we sail?'

The captain of the *Flight of Fancy* glanced at him. 'That's up to father.'

'No,' said Lara, 'it's up to you. Father will be on the *Gull*, and the *Fancy* is your ship. Anyway, who's going to pilot the *Gull*, eh? We're short of decent masters, and the best one is stuck in here.'

'There's no way that Topaz will be master of the *Gull* again,' said Ann. 'Father...' She puffed out her cheeks. 'I guess you might as well know. Father is going to have Topaz executed, as soon as we're out of range of the dragons of Ulna. He says it's a matter of family pride. Topaz killed Dax, so Topaz has to pay. I've tried to talk him out of it, but he's a stubborn old goat.'

Lara's eyes brimmed with anger.

'What about Lara, ma'am?' said Topaz.

'She'll probably end up with a slap on the wrist,' said Ann. 'Father's decided that the easiest course of action is to blame everything on you, Topaz. Still, all this might be a while away. Tilly could be anywhere by now, and father doesn't know how he's going to find her.'

'You have to let Topaz escape, sister,' said Lara. 'Let him slip past the guards and swim to shore. You could blame it on me. If father kills him... I will never speak to him again; I bleeding swear it.'

Ann said nothing, then she stood.

'Don't go,' said Lara. 'You have to do something to help us.'

'I'm doing what I can, sister,' she said, then she closed and locked the cabin door.

'Bitch!' Lara cried, as the compartment was plunged back into darkness.

'That's good news about you,' said Topaz.

'Stop being so bleeding cheerful,' Lara said. 'This is bullshit of the highest order. How can he make you shoulder the entire blame? Every sailor on board the *Gull* will know the truth of it. Dax blew up the bleeding *Little Sneak*, and killed two dozen of Tilly's lads, and father's acting as if you were the bad guy?' She sighed. 'Come on, Sable; where are you?'

An hour passed. The temperature inside the cabin rose in the heat of the morning, until Topaz's tunic was sticking to his back. They ate everything that was in the basket, then tried to get comfortable, as sounds of yelling, and boots thumping, filtered through to their ears. They remained quiet, listening to every noise, and trying to work out what was happening on the decks above them.

The door was pushed open, and four armed sailors gestured for them to get to their feet. Topaz blinked in the light, and pulled himself up, his back and legs aching.

'Come on,' said one of the sailors. 'You're wanted on the quarter deck.'

Lara and Topaz shuffled out of the small cabin, and were shoved up the steep steps and through the forward hatch. Outside, the sun was shining down on the little creek, and Topaz savoured the fresh breeze as it hit his face. Fifty yards away, the *Giddy Gull* was anchored. Men were dangling from ropes over the stern, as they continued to repair the rudder, while most of the crew were up on the deck, staring at the entrance to the creek, where it met the ocean. The same was true on the deck of the *Flight of Fancy*, and both Topaz and Lara turned to gaze in the same direction. Blocking the creek's entrance was a ship. At first, Topaz thought it was a Sea Banner frigate, then he realised his mistake.

'Tilly,' gasped Lara. 'What's she doing here?'

'That's exactly what I want to know, my disobedient little princess.'

They turned again, and saw Olo'osso striding towards them, with Ann and a few armed sailors behind him. He carried on walking until he reached the quarter deck, and the two prisoners were shoved up the steps after him.

'Well?' said Olo'osso. 'What manner of trick is this? How did Atili know that we were here? Someone must have sent a signal or message to her, and I want names.'

Lara squinted at him. 'Eh? Have you been smoking dreamweed again, father?'

Olo'osso's eyes darkened. 'Do not treat me like a fool, errant daughter. There are a hundred coves and creeks within fifty miles of here. Are you telling me that Atili chose this one at random?' He pointed at the *Sow's Revenge*. 'Do you see the ballistae and catapults pointed at us? Atili knew what to expect when she arrived here. So, how did you do it?'

Lara and Topaz glanced at each other.

'Keep your eyes on me,' said Olo'osso. 'I don't believe in coincidences; therefore someone must have told Atili our location – who was it?'

Lara smirked. 'You got me, father – it was me. I used my godlike vision powers to communicate with Tilly.'

Ann sniggered.

'Move the prisoners to the edge of the railings,' said Olo'osso. 'If Atili has an eye-glass, I want her to see that we have hostages.'

The sailors shoved Topaz and Lara to the side of the quarter deck and pushed them up against the railings.

'Ow!' yelled Lara.

'Hush, my dear,' said her father, as his eyes scanned the frigate in the distance. 'Now, if Atili decides to loose against us, I will have Oto of the Sea Banner's limbs slowly cut off.'

'Should we launch the rowing boat, father?' said Ann. 'Maybe Tilly wants to talk.'

'No,' said Olo'osso. 'She can come here, if a reasonable discussion is what she's after. I admit, that's a nice ship she's got herself.'

'And why did she need a new ship, sir?' said Topaz.

Olo'osso ignored him.

'That's a good question, Master,' said Lara. 'Hmm. Let me think. Was it because that asshole Dax loosed a pisspot at the *Little Sneak*? Is that the right answer?'

'Quiet; both of you,' Olo'osso cried. 'I want none of that – understand? Udaxa is dead, thanks to Oto of the Sea Banner, and can no longer speak for himself.'

'That little bastard tried to kill me and Tilly,' said Lara, 'and you're acting as if he's the damn victim. As far as I'm concerned, Topaz did the family a favour, getting rid of him.'

Olo'osso slapped Lara across the cheek. He raised his hand again, then the air shimmered behind him, and Sable Holdfast was holding a sword to the old pirate's throat.

'Lower your hand,' said the Holdfast woman, her eyes glinting, 'or I'll slice your head off.' Sable glanced at the sailors on the quarter deck.

'Take a step back, all of you, or the old guy will be dead before you can blink.'

Olo'osso froze, as a line of blood trickled slowly down his neck. One of the sailors whipped his crossbow up to aim at Sable. She shot him a glance, and he toppled over onto the deck, his eyes closed, the crossbow skittering across the planks. Lara stooped down and picked it up, then pointed it at Ann.

Sable drew her arm back, then clubbed Olo'osso on the back of his head with the hilt of the sword. The pirate captain fell to his knees, groaning in pain.

'That's for slapping Lara,' Sable said, her expression fierce. 'How dare you touch her? I should kill you now.'

'No!' cried Ann. 'Please, Sable – I surrender.' She turned to her crew. 'Do you hear me? We surrender. Drop your weapons and get back to your posts.'

'A little late to change your tune, sister,' said Lara.

'Do you think I wanted any of this to happen?' said Ann, her eyes on the crossbow in her sister's hands. 'I tried to reason with father; I tried to warn him what could happen.' She beckoned towards a small group of sailors. 'Get the shackles removed from Lara and Topaz. Now.'

Sable watched as the sailors ran up onto the quarter deck. One of them fetched a hammer, and they removed the pins keeping the shackles in place from Lara and Topaz's ankles. Sable then turned to Ann, and stared into her eyes.

'Alright,' said the Holdfast woman; 'here's what we're going to do. Ann, I'm going to allow you to remain in charge of the *Flight of Fancy*. Lara, you can stop pointing the bow at your sister.'

Lara frowned. 'How can we trust her?'

'Because I've read her mind,' said Sable. 'She wishes she had stood up to her father more; she thinks his decisions had been stupid and spiteful, and she regrets following his orders.'

Olo'osso raised his bruised face. 'Is that true, my little Ani?'

Ann lowered her gaze. 'Sorry, father.'

'I am surrounded by traitors!' he yelled. 'My own daughters, conspiring against me. How the other families in Langbeg will laugh when they find out.'

He sprang up at Sable, his hands reaching for her throat, and she punched him in the nose. Blood erupted from his face, and he howled as he writhed about on the deck. Topaz glanced over at the *Giddy Gull*. The railings on the port side were crammed with sailors, all staring at the quarter deck of the *Flight of Fancy*, while even the men dangling from ropes over the stern had stopped work to watch. Up by the bow, a group of sailors was pulling the covers off the pair of ballistae mounted there.

'Miss Holdfast,' he said. 'There might be trouble on the *Gull*.'

'It's the same bastards that blew up my rudder,' said Lara, staring at the bow of the neighbouring ship.

'Get down!' cried Ann, as a ballista bolt spat through the gap between the two ships. Topaz threw himself to the deck, as the bolt passed overhead, then he glanced around to check that everyone was unhurt. He saw Lara, Ann, and Olo'osso, who was still clutching his bloody face, but there was no sign of Sable. His eyes went to the *Gull*, and he peered through the railings. Sable was up on the bow, the sword in her hands. She swung it, and the man operating the ballista fell, his neck half-severed. She dodged a crossbow bolt, then sliced through the other men, until four corpses were lying across the bow of the *Gull*. Topaz then saw Ryan, a carpenter's tool bag over his shoulder, run up to her. He turned, and pointed around the ship, his words to the Holdfast witch too quiet for Topaz to make out. Sable listened to Ryan, nodded, then set off. She killed two more men by the front mast, then disappeared down the forward hatch.

Topaz, Lara and Ann slowly got back to their feet. A scream rose up from the lower deck of the *Gull*, and they glanced at each other.

'Praise the gods that she's on our side,' said Topaz.

'Is she?' said Ann. 'Sable only cares about herself.'

'Shut your face,' said Lara.

Ann narrowed her eyes at her sister. 'Are you and her...?'

'Yes,' said Lara, 'so keep your stupid opinions to yourself.'

Olo'osso staggered to his feet. 'This is our chance, girls, while that bitch is on the *Gull*. Get the ballistae ready, and order the...'

'No, father,' said Ann. 'Your time as captain is over. I am in charge of the *Fancy* again, whether you like it or not. If you keep complaining, there are two sets of shackles on the deck that might fit you.'

Olo'osso glanced from daughter to daughter, and Lara turned her crossbow to point it at his chest.

'You heard the captain, father,' said Lara. 'I'd keep my mouth shut, if I were you.'

Another scream tore out from the bowels of the *Gull*, then Sable appeared at the top of the aft hatch. Ryan was there waiting for her, and they spoke again. Ryan nodded, and Sable slapped him on the back and flashed a smile at him.

Lara passed the crossbow to Topaz. 'Keep it trained on the old goat,' she said. 'If he moves, shoot him in the leg.'

'Yes, ma'am.'

Lara clambered up onto the poop deck, and raised her arms towards the crew of the *Giddy Gull*. The sailors roared out in joy at the sight of their captain. Moments later, Sable appeared by her side, and they kissed, while the crews of both boats cheered.

'What has the world come to?' said Olo'osso, shaking his head. 'Beaten by a damn girl.'

An hour later, Topaz was sitting in the captain's cabin on the *Giddy Gull*. Ann and Lara were there, with Sable, while Tilly had been rowed over from her own ship, along with Dina, whose unexpected appearance had been the cause of a mixture of both joy and savage recriminations among the four sisters. Lara was glaring at her from over her mug of wine, while Dina was keeping her head down. A few other senior officers from the three ships were also present, and the cabin was packed out. Ryan was also there, after Sable had insisted. His advice on locating the remainder of the thugs who had disabled the

Giddy Gull had earned him his place, she had said, and no one had disagreed.

Sable seemed full of the joys of life, and was smoking a stick of dreamweed, while she listened to the sisters retell the story of what had happened.

Ryan nudged Topaz in the ribs. The carpenter's mate was grinning from ear to ear.

'The boys back in Udall are going to lose their shit over this,' he said. 'This is the best day ever, mate.'

'Speak for yourself,' said Dina, who was sitting to Ryan's left. 'The way Lara's staring at me, I think I was safer back on... um, the place we were hiding.'

'Have you been with Sable this entire time?' said Topaz.

'Unfortunately,' said Dina. 'Though, to be honest, she was hardly around. She was too busy slaughtering Banner soldiers and gods to pay much attention to her friends, let alone me.'

'And no gods came looking for you?'

'No, they did,' said Dina. 'An Ancient and a damn Ascendant invaded our refuge, and nearly killed us.'

Ann turned her head, her eyes sharp. 'What did you say? There's an Ascendant on Dragon Eyre?'

The cabin stilled.

Sable got to her feet. 'Listen to me,' she said, then she waited until every eye was on her. 'There was an Ascendant on Dragon Eyre. I killed him.'

Gasps came from most of those present, along with a sceptical mutterings.

'The Western Rim is in chaos,' Sable went on. 'I've hit Alef, and Ectus, and Gyle is next. The Banner forces are in full retreat all over this world. Yesterday, the Ulnan dragons and I destroyed the forces occupying Throscala. Lady Ydril is also dead. Right now, there are no gods left in the Eastern Rim, and precious few in the west.' She waited a moment for her words to sink in. 'I want you to start thinking about what comes next,' she went on. 'If you take my advice, you'll sail north as soon as the *Gull* has been repaired, and berth at Udall. Speak to Queen Blackrose, and make a deal with her.'

'You mean,' said Lara; 'the war is nearly over?'

Sable gazed down at her. 'Maybe. I still have much to do. I'm not going to rest until the last gods are dead, and the Banner forces have either evacuated or surrendered.'

'What about Olkis?' said Topaz. 'You didn't mention that.'

Sable nodded. 'I had plans for Olkis, but I can't use my normal tactics there. Too many innocent lives would be lost in the confusion. However, I have hit Ectus so hard, that more than a dozen Banner regiments have already been shipped out from Olkis, to defend the bases on Ectus and Gyle.'

'A dozen?' said Tilly. 'Holy shit. Nankiss will be in flames by now, with that number of soldiers gone.'

'It is my intention to drive every Banner soldier back to the Home Islands,' said Sable. 'In that way, I hope that Olkis can be spared further destruction. Then, once the Banner regiments are regrouping on Gyle, Ectus and Na Sun Ka, I intend to hit them with everything I've got, until Bastion has no choice but to open a portal and order a full evacuation.'

'I don't understand,' said Topaz. 'Do you have an army under your control?'

'Of sorts,' she said, 'though I'm not going to elaborate.' She reached into her leather armour and pulled out her Quadrant.

Lara's face fell. 'Are you leaving?'

'Yes,' said Sable. 'I'm going to take Olo'osso back to Udall ahead of you, and hand him over to Lord Greysteel. I'll make sure he's treated fairly.'

'So, I'll see you in Udall?' said Lara.

'I don't know,' said Sable. 'I'm not sure I'm welcome there any more. It's safe for me to go there right now, as Blackrose won't be back in Ulna yet, and Lord Greysteel has no idea that his Queen and I are not seeing eye to eye at the moment.'

'Why not?' said Ann. 'Have you and Queen Blackrose broken your alliance?'

'We shall see. Perhaps my words to Lord Greysteel will help smooth things out between us. Blackrose does not approve of my methods, even though those methods are winning the war for us. As for now, you have three ships, and three captains.' She smiled. 'I'll let you fight over who gets to look after Dina.'

'I ain't taking her,' cried Lara.

'She is welcome on the *Fancy*,' said Ann.

Dina looked up, her cheeks flushing. 'Thank you, sister.'

Sable slipped the Quadrant back under her armour, then turned to Lara. 'Come with me for a moment.'

Lara got to her feet, and the two women squeezed through the packed cabin, and out of the door onto the quarter deck.

'She killed an Ascendant?' said Tilly.

Ann crinkled her brow. 'It seems beyond belief.'

'Not to me,' said Dina. 'I've seen what Sable is capable of. I watched as she nearly killed the Ascendant when he first attacked us. She managed to fight off Bastion and Lord Kolai for long enough for us to make our escape, and I've listened each evening as Austin and Sable told us what they've been doing.' She lowered her voice. 'The Western Rim is drenched in blood. Sable is more powerful than any god.'

'Then,' said Ann, 'you know about her methods?'

Dina nodded.

'Well?' said Tilly.

Dina snorted. 'As if I'm going to tell you. Sable would gut me if I revealed her secrets.'

The cabin door opened, and Lara walked back in alone, her eyes red.

'Sable's gone,' she said, her voice almost breaking.

Tilly and Ann glanced at each other, then the eldest sister got to her feet.

'Right, then,' she said; 'Everyone back to their posts. Let's give Captain Lara a little privacy.'

The senior officers started to file out of the door, while Ryan snatched a bottle of wine and slipped it into his tool bag. Lara sat down at the table. Tilly patted her shoulder, then she, Ann and Dina left the cabin. Topaz lingered, until he was alone with Lara.

'I'm sure everything will work out fine, Captain,' he said, his heart breaking at the sight of the tears rolling down Lara's cheeks.

She nodded, and he strode from the cabin, closing the door behind him. Ryan was waiting for him on the quarter deck, a cigarette hanging from his lips.

'That was something, eh, mate?' he grinned.

Topaz frowned. 'Haven't you got a rudder to repair?'

'Did you see the way Sable tore through those lads, eh? I ain't never seen anything like it in all my years. Did you see her slap me on the back? One day, I'll be telling my grandchildren all about it.'

'I saw her. She was impressive.'

Ryan laughed. 'Impressive? Mate, she's a bleeding legend.'

CHAPTER 20
LIGHTING THE FUSE

Riggan Archipelago – 13th Arginch 5255 (18th Gylean Year 6)

Austin and Ashfall watched the sunrise from the Riggan cliffs. The dragon had a forelimb curled round the demigod, as if protecting him, and he leaned back into her soft grey scales.

'One last operation,' said Ashfall, 'and then you are free of your obligations to Sable?'

'Yes,' said Austin. 'At least, that's what she told me. I do believe her, and yet, I find it hard to imagine that it'll be that simple.'

'What do you intend to do then?'

Austin hesitated. He still hadn't told the grey dragon anything about his mother, nor his plans to find her on Implacatus.

'Are you keeping something from me, Austin?' said Ashfall. 'We are friends, are we not? I have tried to do my best to shield you from danger, although I admit my efforts have not been successful. All I want is to see you safe and happy, and out of the Holdfast witch's clutches. We could be happy on Ulna, could we not?'

'Ashfall,' he said; 'you know that I love you.'

'I know,' she said; 'and yet I dread your next words, my beloved friend.'

Austin gazed at the horizon, as the sun slipped away. 'My mother is a slave.'

Ashfall said nothing.

'She's on Implacatus,' Austin went on, 'and I have a duty to rescue her, if I can find her.'

'I see. How long will it take, do you think?'

Austin blinked. 'What do you mean?'

'I mean, how long do you think it will be before you return to Dragon Eyre? I assume that you shall return, bringing your mother with you?'

Austin suppressed a groan. Why hadn't it occurred to him that he could come back? The more he thought about it, the more it made sense. After all, it would be difficult to remain undetected upon Implacatus indefinitely and, in Ashfall, he had a friend and protector waiting for him on Dragon Eyre.

'I'm not sure,' he said.

'You're not sure about what, Austin? How long it will take, or whether you shall return? Do you intend to leave me forever?'

He turned to face her. 'I'll come back.'

'Do you promise?'

'Yes,' he said, without hesitation. He felt a strange warm glow pass through him, as if this were the answer to all of his problems. If Sable could take him to Implacatus, then she could come back, and collect him and his mother, and take them both to Ulna, where they could live in peace, and where he could be with Ashfall.

'I assume that Sable will use her Quadrant to take you away from me?' Ashfall said.

'Yes. The truth is that I don't know how long it might take to free my mother, or exactly how I am going to do it.'

'You will be hunted upon Implacatus, Austin,' she said. 'Lord Bastion knows who you are, and your father was once a famous man. It will be very dangerous. Be as quick as you can.'

'I will,' he said. 'And then, we can move back to Ulna, and everything will be perfect.'

Ashfall tilted her head as she gazed at him. 'Perfect? Nothing is ever perfect, Austin. We must strive to make things better, but perfection is nothing but an ideal. It does not exist in reality. Come back from Implacatus, safe and sound, with your mother, and that will be enough. We have our whole lives to seek perfection.'

Austin nodded.

'When did you last see your mother?' said Ashfall.

'Not since I was a child. I was born in my father's harem, and then sent to school. I have been a bad son. I was unaware that my mother was sold into slavery after I went to school, but that was because I didn't even try to find out what happened to her. I hope that she can forgive me.'

'I'm sure she will, Austin.'

'My greatest fear is that she's dead,' he said; 'that she died alone, without her only child even sending her a note, to show her that he cared. Sorry. I didn't want to get maudlin. I have to try to stay positive.'

There was a noise to their right, and Ashfall turned.

'Holdfast,' she said.

Sable nodded to the slender grey dragon as she approached, and Austin felt Ashfall's protective forelimb curl round him a little tighter.

'Here you are, Austin,' said Sable. 'Are you ready to go?'

'May I ask,' said Ashfall; 'where are you taking him?'

'Gyle. Are you going to release him from your grip?'

Ashfall moved her forelimb, and Austin got to his feet. Sable pulled a large bag from over her shoulder, and threw it at the demigod.

'There's leather armour inside,' she said; 'put it on. Things might get rather interesting right from the start. Kill anything that looks threatening – yeah?'

'Are we going back to Haurn first,' he said, 'to get... you know?'

'Not today,' she said. 'It'll be just you and me for the first stage.'

She took out the Quadrant as Austin pulled on the leather breastplate. Sable examined the copper-coloured surface of the device closely, then hovered her thumb over a certain section, and unsheathed her sword with her free hand.

'We'll stand back to back,' said Sable, once he was ready. 'Remember – no mercy. Kill everything.'

She pressed her thumb against the Quadrant, and the air shimmered around them. They appeared in a dimly-lit passageway, the wall sconces illuminating a series of large paintings that hung on either side of the wide corridor. Austin glanced around, but saw no one.

'I've been here before,' he said.

'I know; you told me.'

His heart pounded in anticipation and dread, as he glanced at a nearby set of double doors. He knew what lay on the other side. Sable noticed where he was looking.

'It's through there, isn't it?'

'You mean "he" is through there?'

She nodded, then glanced along the corridor. 'I was expecting guards.'

'The last time I was here,' Austin said, 'there were eight or so through those doors.'

Sable smiled. 'Shall we?'

She walked over to the set of doors, and kicked them open. She ran through, and Austin chased after her. He ignored what was in the centre of the room, and turned towards the group of soldiers, who were rising from a table where they had been playing cards.

'Hey!' one cried. 'You can't come in...'

Austin raised his hand, and stopped their hearts. The soldiers slid to the ground, their eyes still open. A few groaned and choked, then there was silence.

'Good job,' said Sable, but she wasn't looking at Austin. Instead, her eyes were focussed on the huge cage that sat in the middle of the chamber's floor. Austin walked over to stand next to her, and gazed through the thick bars at the golden dragon. If anything, the Eighteenth Gylean was in a worse condition than when Austin had last visited, when Meader had taken him down into the basement of the Winter Palace in Port Edmond to show him what, or who, was imprisoned there. The sores seemed more widespread, and were oozing pus, which sat in globules running down the thick chains that enclosed the small dragon. The Gylean turned his face towards them, but his eyes were empty.

'I feel a little sick,' said Sable. 'Austin, shut the door, while I take a closer look.'

Austin ran back to the double doors, and pulled them shut. There was a bar leaning against the wall, and he placed it into position, sealing the chamber from the passageway outside. When he returned to the cage, Sable was standing next to the bars, her face revealing a mixture of pity and anger.

'You know,' Sable said, 'I'm tempted to take him to the slave compound in this condition, so that the natives can see exactly how the gods have been treating him, but that would be wrong.'

Austin glanced at her. 'Slave compound?'

'Yes. Do you not remember the plan I had a while back, about fomenting a rebellion among the slaves of Gyle? I stockpiled supplies, and then didn't use them. They're still there, ready. The Gylean is going to be the spark that lights the fuse.'

She walked over to the dead soldiers, and rifled through their pockets, as the dragon stared with his vacant eyes at Austin. A few moments later, Sable returned with a set of keys. She searched for the correct one, then unlocked the barred gate at the front of the cage. She swung it open, but the golden dragon inside remained motionless.

Sable stepped up into the cage, and reached out with a hand to stroke the dragon's nose. The dragon flinched back, then opened its jaws in fright.

'He has no teeth,' Sable said.

'The soldiers removed them,' said Austin, 'along with his claws.'

Revulsion passed over Sable's face. 'I didn't think I was capable of hating the gods any more than I already did. I was wrong.'

Austin nodded.

'Does no teeth mean no fire?'

'I'm not sure,' he said. 'You're more of an expert on dragons than I am.'

'Get in here, and heal him. Give him whatever you can spare, while I work some of the chains loose.'

Austin stepped into the cage. It stank. He fought an urge to throw up as he approached the small golden dragon. His powers worked fine through the air, but were more concentrated if delivered via physical contact, and so he placed his palm on the side of the dragon's head, and closed his eyes. He found his healing powers, and sent a surge into the Gylean – slowly at first, and then building. The dragon shuddered and spasmed, and Austin had to move in order to keep his hand pressed flat against his golden scales. He sensed the Gylean's wounds close and heal; along with the open sores that had plagued the creature for his entire life. There was also a mass of infections, and parasites that lived off the dragon, and Austin eradicated them all, clearing his gut. He turned his attention to the dragon's wasted muscles, then stopped, as he felt the Gylean's heart start to strain.

Austin removed his hand. The dragon spasmed again, then slumped to the floor of the cage, unconscious.

'All done?' said Sable, glancing at him.

'Not quite,' he said, 'but I've given him as much healing as his body can take right now. He's too weak for any more. Once he's rested and eaten, I can heal him some more.'

Sable pulled a whole section of chains from over the Gylean's wings. 'Did you ever find the salve that I left behind in Ulna?'

'Yes. I used it to help Ashfall escape from Splendoursun. That reminds me, Sable; there's something I need to ask you.'

Sable nodded, though she was examining more chains.

'When you take me to Implacatus; and we find my mother...'

'Yes?'

'Will you bring me back to Dragon Eyre?'

Sable nearly choked. 'What? You're joking, I assume?'

'No.'

'You hate it here; why would you want to come back?' She shook her head. 'Let me guess. Ashfall?'

He nodded.

'You'd give up your life to please Ashfall? Now I've heard it all.'

'It's not just Ashfall,' he said, 'though she's the main reason. Lord Bastion knows my face, and my name, and my family. Where exactly on Implacatus am I supposed to hide? I might get away with it for a while, but not forever. Sooner or later, someone will find me. Remember, I'll be hiding with my mother. I'll need to find us both a place to live, and then I'll have to earn money to survive. I'd already reconciled myself to pretending to be a mortal, but it's risky. What would be the point of freeing my mother if we got caught? She'd be in a worse position than if I never went back at all.'

Sable pulled another chain loose. 'I see.'

'So? Will you bring me back or not?'

'And where would you live on Dragon Eyre?'

He shrugged. 'Ulna?'

'Remember, Austin – you would be the only god left on this entire world. With no salve around, your healing abilities would be in great demand. You could have power here, and wealth.'

'I'm not interested in that. I just want to live in peace, with Ashfall and my mother. Plus, it would be nice to see you now and again, as well as Millen and Deepblue. I consider you all my friends.'

'I'm not sure what Blackrose would say about it.'

'Come on, Sable; don't pretend that you care what Blackrose thinks.'

'I don't, but I promised her I would leave Ulna alone. I'll ask her. That would be a good excuse for me to go back there. Lara will be on her way to Udall right now, and I want to reach a compromise with the big black dragon; one that allows me to visit now and again without setting off another war.'

Austin smiled. 'You're thinking of the future, Sable. A peaceful future. That's the first time I've ever heard you talk about what might come after this.'

Sable raised an eyebrow, then smiled back at him. 'You're right. I should cast it out of my mind immediately. Nothing is more likely to wreck my plans than hope.'

'You don't mean that.'

'I do. I need to be fully committed to my task; anything else is a distraction. As soon as I start day-dreaming about a peaceful future, as you call it, I'll be finished.'

Austin's eyes widened. 'Dear gods – you're in love with Lara, aren't you?'

Sable glared at him. 'Don't say that; don't even think it. I can't afford to be in love. How am I supposed to bring myself to do the terrible things that need to be done, if I'm pining after someone? I need my heart to be made of stone; do you understand? If I weaken now, then all that I have achieved will have been for nothing.' She closed her eyes and took a breath. 'Alright. I'll bring you back from Implacatus. Now, please, don't bring any of this up again.'

Austin stood in silence as Sable removed another long set of chains from the dragon's back. He reached out with his powers, and checked on the Gylean. The golden dragon was still unconscious, but he wasn't in any pain, possibly for the first time in his short life.

Sable took a step back. 'That will do, I think.'

'Aren't we going to remove all of the chains?'

'No. We need the natives to see them, to prove that he was a captive, not a guest.' She pulled the Quadrant from under her armour. 'Remember, where we're going next, your accent might provoke anger. The slaves, quite understandably, detest gods from Implacatus. They might run from you in panic, or they might assault you. Be careful.'

He nodded, and she activated the Quadrant. They appeared out in the open air, in the middle of a large, flat courtyard surrounded by long lines of low wooden huts. In the far distance, Austin could see a high wall, with watchtowers, while a few groups of slaves were standing by the entrances to their huts.

Sable raised her arms in the air.

'Gather round!' she cried. 'Tell everyone – the Eighteenth Gylean has been freed from the prison under the Winter Palace. Come and see for yourself. The Eighteenth Gylean is free, and among his people once again!'

Not much happened at first. A few slaves glanced over to see who was shouting in the middle of the square, then some others began to warily walk closer, peering into the lamplit gloom of the evening. Someone cried out, a hand to their mouth, then a few hut doors opened, and slaves began to spill out, attracted by the noise. More and more emerged from the squat huts, while the ring of people around the golden dragon slowly contracted.

A man fell to his knees, sobbing openly at the sight of the chained dragon, then a group began to pray aloud. An edge of hysteria swept through the crowd as more joined the growing mass of people in the square. Sable made a show of removing the last chains, and threw them to the ground.

'Come closer!' she cried. 'Behold the Eighteenth Gylean with your own eyes. We have liberated him from his chains!'

'Who are you?' someone shouted.

She placed her hands on her hips. 'I am Sable Holdfast – Ascendant-killer, and liberator of Dragon Eyre. You know my name.'

At these words, the last restraint of the crowd dissolved, and they surged forward, shouting, cheering and weeping. Hands reached out to touch not only the Gylean, but Sable too, as if she were as sacred to them as the golden dragon. Grown men fell prostrate in front of the Holdfast woman, their faces wet with tears, as they pledged their undying loyalty to the saviour who had freed their living god. Austin retreated, but he was soon surrounded by the massed crowd. He managed to place himself behind Sable, who was smiling benevolently at the people trying to get near enough to touch her. Over to their left, an angry voice cried out, and a group of armed slaves shoved their way through the crowd towards its centre.

'What is the meaning of this?' shouted an older man, wearing a badge on his cloak to denote his rank in the slave militia. 'Everyone, get back to your huts before the Banner soldiers arrive!'

He broke through the crowd, then halted as he caught a glimpse of the golden dragon. His eyes widened, and a tear rolled down his cheek. His militia comrades appeared next to him, but none spoke, and they lowered their weapons.

Sable turned back to the crowd. 'As I have cast off the chains of the Eighteenth Gylean, so, tonight, every slave in Gyle shall cast off their own chains. Are you with me?'

The crowd roared as one, raising their arms into the air as their voices thundered across the compound.

'Wait!' cried the militia officer over the tumult. 'Without weapons, we would be slaughtered. An entire Banner regiment lies only two miles from this compound. Already, the soldiers up on the watchtowers will have seen this commotion. The Banner will be on their way soon. How do we...?'

Sable smiled. 'Do you want weapons?'

The crowd roared in approval.

'Then clear a space,' she yelled. 'Go on; move back ten paces. I shall return in a moment.'

Sable flicked her fingers over the Quadrant, then she and Austin appeared inside a ramshackle old building, with wooden walls that looked as though they were about to collapse. Sable ran to a heap of mouldy old straw, and pulled on a rope that had lain hidden on the ground. A tarpaulin sheet slid away, taking the straw with it, and revealing a mass of crates. Without even turning to Austin, she swiped the Quadrant again, and they re-appeared in the midst of the huge crowd in the slave compound, to gasps from the closest onlookers. Sable ripped the lid from a crate, and held up a crossbow.

'Here are weapons!' she cried. 'Take them, and fight for your freedom.'

Austin turned to look at the Gylean while Sable began handing out weapons to the crowd. A cordon had been set up around the unconscious golden dragon, consisting of a ring of men and women linking arms, to keep the crowds from accidentally harming him in their enthusiasm. In front of the cordon, a multitude of slaves were on their knees with their arms in the air, giving thanks to the dragon spirits for the return of their living god. Austin frowned. The atmosphere in the huge square seemed tinged with a kind of madness, as thousands of slaves wept, chanted, prayed and sang.

The militia officer ran up to Sable, his arms out-stretched.

'Please, madam,' he said; 'we must talk at once; somewhere quieter than out here.'

Sable glanced at the man. 'And why should I speak with you?'

'Because, madam, I am in charge of an entire wing of this compound. I know where the gates are, and where the Banner soldiers gather when they are about to conduct one of their searches.' He lowered his voice. 'I also need to warn you.'

Sable nodded, then she gestured for Austin to follow her. They set off through the packed crowd. Everywhere Sable went, hordes of native slaves reached out to touch her clothes, begging her to lead them to freedom. Sable smiled at them as she passed. The militia officer led them to a squat hut, which was surrounded by armed slaves under the officer's command, and they entered.

The officer lit a lamp, and gestured for Sable to sit.

'No, thanks,' she said. 'I'll stand. Make this quick; we need to keep the initiative.'

'Is it true?' the officer said, as a bead of sweat rolled down his forehead. 'Are you Sable Holdfast?'

'I am.'

'Part of me wants to sing with joy at your arrival here, madam. We have long awaited a sign from the dragon spirits that the time for our freedom has come.'

Sable smiled. 'What does the other part of you want?'

'The other part wants you to leave – now. You are unleashing forces beyond your control. Even with a few crates of weapons, the people here are no match for well-trained Banner soldiers. This compound sits upon a major thoroughfare that links Port Edmond to the main agricultural areas of central Gyle. We are practically surrounded by Banner fortresses. I understand that your intentions might well be good, but the outcome will be a vast slaughter of our people. Yesterday, orders arrived from Port Edmond, issued by Lord Bastion himself. In the wake of Lord Kolai's murder, he has ordered the occupation forces to begin the complete destruction of every native on the Home Islands.'

Sable frowned. 'It sounds as though I have arrived just in time.'

'You don't understand. In order to be successful, we require far more than a few crates of crossbows. We need explosives, and ballistae. There are twenty thousand slaves of working age living here. Do you have twenty thousand crossbows?'

'You said that you wanted to warn me. About what?'

The officer rubbed his chin. 'The Unk Tannic, madam. Their agents have been infiltrating this compound for years. I even suspect that some of my own militia guards might be secret members. They've been causing me trouble for a long time, sowing discord and urging the people to revolt.'

'So?'

'The Unk Tannic despise you, madam. They claim that you destroyed their command centre on Na Sun Ka. Is it true?'

'Yes. The Unk Tannic will have to go. Dragon Eyre will not be going back to the old days.'

'Then why did you bring the Eighteenth Gylean with you? That poor creature looks close to death, but his mere presence here will inspire all kinds of religious fervour – the good, and the bad. The Unk Tannic will use the return of the Gylean as an excuse to increase their hold over the people here.'

'That is of little concern to me. I will bring the Unk Tannic down, in my own time.'

'They want you dead, madam. They have named you as a false prophet; an imposter, a fake. They have also claimed that you are working side-by-side with a god from Implacatus.' He glanced at Austin. 'It's you, isn't it? Are you the son of the old governor?'

'Yes,' said Austin, 'but how did the Unk Tannic know I was working with Sable?'

'Spies in Ulna reported this to the Unk Tannic leadership here on Gyle, and I have my own agents implanted within their ranks. For your own safety, you should both leave, at once.'

Sable lit a cigarette. 'I was intending to lead the people in storming the compound gates.'

'If you do so, then someone will stab you in the back. There will be many Unk Tannic agents hiding among the massed crowds, waiting for an opportunity to take your life in revenge for what you did on Na Sun Ka. Many may treat you as if you are a god, but I know that you are mortal.'

Sable stared into the man's eyes, then frowned and looked away.

'Why are you helping us?' said Austin.

'Because I loathe the Unk Tannic, almost as much as I loathe the occupation.' He sat, and put his head in his hands. 'Unfortunately, most of the people here loathe me, and the militia. The Banner forces allow us to police ourselves, and many here see us as collaborators, when all we are trying to do is keep the peace. I imagine, that before this night is through, the Unk Tannic shall come for me. Your coming here, Sable Holdfast, will unleash a torrent of violence and savagery not seen since Lord Sabat was governor. I lived through those terrible times, but I fear I will not live through this.'

Sable looked stunned. She opened her mouth to speak, but closed it again. She gazed at the officer, then took out the Quadrant, and swiped her fingers across the surface.

Austin found himself back on the rocky islet off Rigga. He and Sable were standing near the top of a cliff, with the ocean crashing into the rocks beneath them.

'What now?' said Austin.

'Let me think,' said Sable. She still had her cigarette clutched in her left hand, and she took a long draw.

'I guess it was a success, of a kind,' Austin said. 'We got out alive, didn't we? The Gylean is free, and the slaves are rising up.'

'Yes, to be slaughtered,' said Sable. 'I need... something that will tip the balance.'

'Not more greenhides; please, Sable.'

'No, not greenhides. Damn it. I thought I'd covered every possible angle, but I underestimated the strength of the locals' faith in the dragon spirits, and how that might bind them to the lies of the Unk Tannic. I meant what I said back there; I'm not going to allow a bunch of religious fanatics to dictate the future of Dragon Eyre. I need something that will destroy the Banner forces, and the Unk Tannic – something that hates them both. Something powerful.'

Her eyes shone in the gloom.

'Are you ready for stage two, Austin?' she said.

'I guess. Tonight?'

'Yes. Tonight; otherwise the rebellion will be throttled before it even gets started.'

'Where are we going?'

Sable turned to him. 'Wyst.'

CHAPTER 21
RETALIATION

Udall, Ulna, Eastern Rim – 14th Arginch 5255 (18th Gylean Year 6)

The two dragons circled over the river and landed by an old stone bridge. On either bank of the wide stream, empty fields stretched out in both directions, but the landscape had changed following the destruction of the majority of Ulna's greenhides. Grass, flowers and shrubs were now growing, where once there had been only mud, and the sight of new life made the derelict farmhouses seem less desolate, at least to Maddie's eyes.

'Where are we?' she said to Blackrose.

'About ten miles north of Udall, rider,' said the black dragon. 'That ancient bridge carries the main road from Plagos on the west coast, to Gliden on the eastern flank of the island. This area used to be the most fertile farming region of central Ulna, and the land supported a multitude of farms and small villages.'

'And it shall once more,' said Shadowblaze, who was standing next to her with Ahi'edo on his shoulders.

'Indeed,' said Blackrose. 'The reason for our visit today is that we plan to send new settlers here, to rebuild the farms. Udall is growing, and its need for food grows with it.' She scanned the area with her red eyes. 'A dozen human families could do well here, with a dragon to protect them from any stray greenhides.'

'I haven't seen a greenhide here for ages,' said Maddie.

'That is true,' said Shadowblaze, 'but any resettlement might attract the few remaining in the mountains to the north of here.' He glanced down at the banks of the river. 'There used to be wooden piers here, if my memory serves me well, to allow barges to travel down to Udall.'

Ahi'edo pointed to the far side of the bridge. 'Over there, master. I think I can see what remains of the piers.'

'Well spotted, rider,' said the red and grey dragon. 'The piers shall need to be rebuilt, along with the farmhouses, and perhaps a tall watchtower.'

'This is exciting,' said Maddie, as she glanced at the dozen or so ruined structures that clustered by either end of the bridge. 'I can almost picture what it will look like. Houses, and gardens, and boats on the river. Maybe even a tavern, for travellers. It'll be beautiful.'

'I will begin compiling a list of the necessary materials,' said Shadowblaze. 'Timber will be the priority, along with stone for rebuilding, and slate to tile the roofs.'

Maddie unbuckled the straps on the harness and slipped down to the ground, as Blackrose and Shadowblaze discussed the various quantities of each material that would be required. She walked up onto the paved road that led to the bridge, passing through knee-high wild grasses and flowers in bloom. A few stunted trees lined the road, some of which were starting to recover from the greenhides, their green shoots emerging from the gnarled branches. She walked onto the bridge, and noticed that Ahi'edo had joined her. She smiled at him, more from the joy of seeing the potential in the area, than through friendship, but he didn't scowl or look away.

They strode to the side of the bridge and gazed down at the slow-moving river. It was the same waterway that went under the bridge palace in Udall, but was a little narrower than down in the city.

'I don't think Blackrose will have any problems finding volunteers to come here,' Maddie said. 'Not now that it's safe.'

Ahi'edo nodded. 'I remember passing through this village when I was a child.'

'Was that before you became Shadowblaze's rider?'

'Yes.'

'It must be nice for you see the land recover.'

'Maddie, you're acting as if the war is already over. It's not. Things could fall apart at any moment.'

'But things are much better now – you must see that?'

'I've lived through false dawns before. I've learned not to expect too much as a consequence. Have you forgotten that the Wyst dragons are currently ravaging Enna? If they decide to turn their attention to Ulna, then nothing will be able to stop them.'

'And what about Throscala? Just a few days ago, we were all worried about Lady Ydril, and the thousands of Banner soldiers at her disposal. We got rid of them, didn't we? Well, with Sable's help.'

'Sable used greenhides to win that battle; is that what you want?'

Maddie frowned. Once again, Ahi'edo had brought her hopeful spirits crashing down.

'The battle in Throscala has made Ulna weaker, not stronger,' Ahi'edo went on. 'Udall's lost every dragon that comes from that island – they've all gone back home, along with a few others from Haurn and Geist. If Wyst does invade, we'll have fewer dragons here to protect us. We'll be out-numbered twenty-to-one.'

Maddie glared at him. 'Do you always have to take the negative point of view?'

'I'm just being realistic. I haven't even got started on what Lord Bastion might do next. Do you really think he's going to give up Dragon Eyre? Sable might have caused them some pain, but there are still tens of thousands of Banner soldiers in the Western Rim. They aren't going to just pack up and leave.'

'That's why Sable is going to deal with Gyle next. She has a plan – remember? And it's been working so far.' She paused. 'I don't like the thought of her using greenhides either; it disgusts me, to be honest, but she hasn't transported any queens.'

Ahi'edo rolled his eyes. 'And that makes it all right?'

'No, but it's a lot better than it could be.'

'Maddie, Throscala is in chaos, with settlers fighting natives, and thousands of hungry and angry Banner soldiers hemmed into their garrison fortresses. It has no government, beyond the say-so of a few dragons who have taken charge. Throscala needs imports of food to feed everyone there, and there's no sea trade. What happens when they start to starve?'

'That's why Ulna needs to step up its food production, so we can send supplies there.'

'By the time this area is growing food again, it'll be too late.'

Maddie glared down into the river. 'I'm not going to argue with you.'

'Why not – because you know I'm right?'

Maddie said nothing. She had been trying her best with Ahi'edo, but his incessant pessimism was wearing her down. She wondered if what Sable had done to his mind was partly responsible. She had seared fear into his brain, making him terrified of everything for a while; perhaps the effects were lingering. She tried to remember what he had been like before that.

'Sorry,' he muttered.

'Are you,' she said; 'or are you just worried that I'll tell Blackrose?'

'Tell her if you want,' he said. 'I'm on the verge of giving up being Shadowblaze's rider. If Queen Blackrose finally agrees to be his mate, I think that might be it. He doesn't trust me any more, and it's been a long time since we shared the same opinions. We used to see eye-to-eye on everything, and now I can't think of a single subject that we agree on. He's even dropped his objections to your relationship with the pirate.'

Maddie smiled as she thought of Topaz. As soon as she and Black-rose had returned from Throscala, Lord Greysteel had told them what had happened to the *Giddy Gull*. Blackrose had been angry that Sable had returned to Udall, after expressly forbidding her from setting foot upon Ulna, but she had been happy to keep Olo'osso in the prison cell where Greysteel had placed him. Maddie had been happy too, knowing that the man who had tried to sell her into slavery was securely confined, and that his attempt to seize the *Gull* had been thwarted by Sable; and she was looking forward to seeing Topaz as soon as he arrived back in Udall. It had been eight days since she had waved goodbye to him at the quayside, and her bed had felt empty without him.

'You have that faraway look in your eyes again,' said Ahi'edo. 'Here I am, pondering the end of my bond with Shadowblaze, and you're dreaming about a sailor.'

'I often disagree with Blackrose,' she said. 'Having disagreements is no reason to break the bond.'

'That's not what I was taught. Our traditions state that the opinions of a dragon and their rider should always align, and, on the rare occasions where they don't, the rider should remain silent.'

'Maybe some of your traditions are sensible, but that one is plain stupid. Dragons and humans are different, and that's alright. Dragons let pride and honour rule them, and sometimes they need to be told that they are wrong. Shadowblaze might respect you more if you stuck to your opinions, in a polite way, of course; I'm not advising you to be rude.'

'That's a novel way to look at it, I suppose.'

Blackrose called over to them, and they turned. The black dragon and Shadowblaze were striding along the wide road towards the bridge.

'I think it is time to move on,' said Blackrose. 'There are still a few potential resettlement sites that I would like to visit, and we have yet to check on the progress being made in Plagos. We...'

Blackrose fell silent as a low rumble sounded in the distance.

'That felt like an earthquake,' said Maddie; 'like on Lostwell. The bridge shook a little.'

For a moment, Blackrose didn't respond, her red eyes staring off to the south, then she glanced down at Maddie.

'It was no earthquake,' she said. 'It was an explosion.'

'Come, Ahi'edo,' said Shadowblaze; 'mount the harness. My beloved, I think we should return to Udall.'

'I concur,' said Blackrose. 'Maddie – let us depart at once.'

The two riders ran off the bridge, and scrambled up onto their dragons. Blackrose swept out her wings and ascended into the air, with Shadowblaze to her left. They soared away to the south, following the wide, sluggish river as it flowed towards the ocean. After a few minutes had passed, Maddie caught sight of a thin plume of grey smoke rising into the blue sky.

'Do you see that?' she said.

'I do,' said the black dragon. 'It is coming from Udall. There is also a dragon approaching, though I doubt that your human eyes would be able to discern it from here.'

Maddie glanced around, until she finally saw a small speck in the distance. It grew rapidly in size, as the two dragons sped south to meet it, and then Maddie recognised him as one of Udall's scouts. The three dragons began to circle together.

'Your Majesties,' said the scout; 'Udall is under attack.'

'From whom?' said Blackrose. 'Has Wyst invaded?'

'No, your Majesty; a fearsome god has arrived in the city, bringing greenhides and soldiers with him. The soldiers have blown up several buildings along the harbour front, and the god is preventing anyone from stopping them.'

'Which god?' said Shadowblaze.

'It must be Bastion,' said Blackrose, her eyes burning. 'No one else would be so bold. Come; we must make haste.'

The black dragon broke away, and surged her speed southwards, as Maddie clung on to the harness.

'Blackrose,' she said, 'if it is Bastion, then his powers are too strong for us.'

'I am aware of that, rider. However, I shall not abandon my people, no matter the cost.'

Maddie began to make out the edge of Udall as the three dragons soared through the sky. The sun was starting its descent to the west, but there was enough light to see the faint outlines of the buildings as they approached. The plume of smoke grew taller and wider, and flames became visible, rising above the roofs of the building along the quayside. The dragons crossed the farmed area that encircled the landward side of the city, and then the derelict housing districts. The bridge palace in the city centre loomed up. Several dragons were hovering or circling above its high towers, and Blackrose made straight for them. Lord Greysteel was among them, and he turned to see Blackrose approach.

'My Queen!' he cried, flying up towards them. 'Lord Bastion is devastating the harbour district. He has killed four dragons already – those I sent to investigate the initial disturbance. Should we evacuate?'

'No,' said Blackrose, her voice firm. 'We shall fight.' She stared at the dragons above the palace. 'Follow me.'

She turned towards the harbour, and Maddie glanced down. Flames were tearing through a line of harbour warehouses, and the housing blocks next to them, while the streets were filled with rubble and the dead. She saw the bodies of three of the dead dragons sprawled out where they had fallen. Greenhides were crouching by one of the dragon corpses, feasting upon its flesh, but there was no sign of any god or soldiers.

Blackrose raced down towards the harbour, and Maddie tried to make herself as small as possible, expecting a blast of death powers to hit them at any moment. Shadowblaze and Greysteel were close behind the black dragon, along with the others from the palace. Several peeled away, swooping down to deal with the greenhides roaming the streets. Blackrose made it to the harbour walls, but no powers had risen up from the city.

'The soldiers have gone, your Majesty,' said Greysteel. 'Your presence has scared them away.'

'Don't flatter me,' said Blackrose. 'If they have left, it was part of their plan, and had nothing to do with me. Where is Bastion?'

'He was last seen by the harbour market, my Queen. Do you think he has also departed?'

'If he were still here, we would all be dead,' said the black dragon. 'Ensure that the last of the greenhides have been annihilated, and then have the human militia sweep through the harbour.'

'At once, my Queen,' said Greysteel.

Shadowblaze hovered next to Blackrose, his amber eyes scanning the ground. 'Why would he leave? I don't understand.'

'Neither do I,' said Blackrose.

'I think I know,' said Ahi'edo.

Shadowblaze turned his long neck to gaze at his rider. 'Yes?'

'Lord Bastion is doing to us,' said Ahi'edo, 'exactly what Sable Hold-fast has done countless times to the occupation forces. He's sending us a message. He's telling us that whatever she can do to them, he can do to us.'

———

'Almost a thousand humans perished in the attack,' said Lord Greysteel, from the comfort of the large reception hall, 'although there may still be bodies buried in the rubble by the quayside. And, of course, four dragons – all killed by Bastion himself.'

Blackrose lowered her head. 'And the casualties among the invading forces?'

'Some hundred or so greenhide bodies have been found, your Majesty,' Greysteel went on, 'but only a small handful of Banner soldiers – five, at the latest count. We must assume that the soldiers were using the greenhides as a shield, behind which they were free to place their explosive devices. As soon as the last bomb went off, Bastion and the soldiers disappeared.'

'It appears my rider was correct,' said Shadowblaze. 'These tactics seem to mirror those employed by the Holdfast witch.'

'I agree,' said Lord Greysteel. 'Greenhides, explosives, and a Quadrant – a formidable combination.'

'And one that we seem powerless to oppose,' said Blackrose. 'One thousand humans, in an attack that barely lasted a few minutes. Do we know the names of those who died?'

'A list is being put together, my Queen,' said Greysteel. 'Due to the location of the attack, it is safe to say that most of those who died were recent arrivals: refugees from Enna and Geist, in the main, along with those working by the docks. None of the ships in the harbour were targeted, which seems strange.'

'The purpose of this assault was to sow fear,' said Blackrose, 'and to keep us on edge. We must be prepared for further attacks, of a similar nature. It would be wise to disperse the human population. We should relocate people from the city centre to the out-lying suburbs, so that they are spread more thinly.'

'I shall speak to the local officials in the town,' said Greysteel, 'and see that it is done, my Queen.'

At that moment, the tall doors of the hall were pushed open, and a squad of human militia entered. In their midst was a man in Banner uniform, crossbows aimed at his back. The man seemed unperturbed, and was holding his head high.

'We have located one of the soldiers, your Majesties,' said one of the militia. 'He surrendered to us willingly, and made no attempt to resist.'

'Where did you find him?' said Shadowblaze.

'In the harbour district, your Majesty.'

'May I speak?' said the man.

The dragons stared at him, then Blackrose tilted her head slightly. 'You may.'

'Thank you, Queen of Ulna,' he said. 'My name is Captain Tallius of the Banner of the Silver Wolf, and I was instructed to remain behind, in order to pass on a message from the most noble Ancient, Lord Bastion of Implacatus. I am here as an emissary, and kindly request that you treat me as such.'

'You will not be harmed, messenger,' said Blackrose. 'What does Lord Bastion wish us to know?'

The officer bowed his head a little. 'Thank you. Lord Bastion imprinted the message into my mind. Shall I recite it for you?'

'Please do.'

The officer cleared his throat. 'To Queen Blackrose of Ulna, greetings. As you are no doubt aware, the rogue witch known as Sable Holdfast has been rampaging across Dragon Eyre these recent days, slaughtering innocents, and throwing this world into chaos and turmoil. Due to her nefarious activities, the colonial government of Dragon Eyre has been left with no choice but to begin the removal of all natives from the Home Islands, in order to restore the peace and tranquillity that used to exist there. Any deaths caused by this decision are the responsibility of Sable Holdfast, and none other. Furthermore, as the rebel administration of Ulna has clearly allied itself with the Holdfast war criminal, it is my solemn duty to proclaim that your subjects are now considered to be suitable targets for appropriate retaliatory action. Today was just a taste of what lies in store for the citizens of Ulna. The sole way to protect your subjects is to offer conclusive proof to the colonial government that you hold Sable Holdfast to be an outlaw and enemy. In short, surrender Sable to the legitimate authorities upon Dragon Eyre, or see your people annihilated. Yours, cordially, Lord Bastion of Port Edmond.'

The officer bowed his head. 'So ends the message.'

Blackrose kept her eyes on the Banner captain. 'Was your attack launched from Gyle?'

'It was.'

'And these "removal" plans – what exactly do they entail?'

'I am not at liberty to discuss these matters, Queen of Ulna. However, I am sure you are aware that Lord Sabat used the same term to describe the slaughter of half a million natives of Dragon Eyre while he was governor.'

'So, Lord Bastion intends to massacre the native inhabitants of the so-called Home Islands?' said Shadowblaze. 'This is a grim day, indeed. It was spurious of him to expect us to blame Sable Holdfast for a slaughter that will be carried out by Banner forces.'

'Those were the Ancient's words, my lord,' said the captain. 'I have no personal comment to add.'

'You vile creature,' said Greysteel. 'The Banner forces are savage killers, and nothing more.'

'I humbly disagree, my lord. The Banner of the Silver Wolf is a highly professional organisation. We are well-trained, disciplined, and obey the orders given to us. We are merely following the guidelines of the contract established between ourselves and the gods of Implacatus.'

'How many Banner soldiers has Sable killed?' said Blackrose.

'My best estimate would be in the region of thirty thousand, Queen of Ulna. However, if we were to include Sea Banner personnel, settlers, and impressed native labourers, the combined total would exceed fifty thousand.'

'Fifty thousand?' cried Maddie. 'Malik's ass.'

'Quite,' said the officer. 'Sable Holdfast is a formidable opponent. Might I ask if I am free to go?'

'You may not leave,' said Blackrose.

'Might I remind you, Queen of Ulna, that you stated that I would be treated as an emissary?'

'I remember what I said, soldier. However, things are not so simple. Where would you go? Do you have a Quadrant, or a ship ready to bear you back to the Western Rim?'

'No, ma'am; I do not.'

'Has Lord Bastion made arrangements to collect you?'

'Not to my knowledge, Queen of Ulna.'

'Then, it appears that you are stranded here. I see that you have been disarmed. Do you swear to refrain from any hostile activity, if I allow you the freedom of Udall?'

'But, my Queen,' said Greysteel; 'we cannot let this piece of Banner filth walk the streets of our city. He is an enemy. At the very least, he should be cast into a prison cell.'

'Come, uncle; we are a civilised realm,' said Blackrose; 'and I have dealt with Banner officers before. They are men of their word. Our fight is not with them, it is with those who issue their orders. If this captain swears to remain peaceful, and to cause no trouble, then we should take the opportunity to prove that we are honourable, unlike the master he serves.'

The officer bowed his head. 'I swear, on the honour of my Banner, that I shall continue to behave as an emissary while in Udall. I shall not instigate any acts of violence or agitation, unless in self defence. If I am still here after fifty days, then my contract will expire, and I will no longer consider myself bound by its strictures.'

'He will spy upon us!' Lord Greysteel cried.

The officer smiled. 'Lord Bastion's vision powers can already reach as far as Udall, my lord. He has no need of me as a spy. In fact, he is likely listening to this exchange right now. He would want to ensure that I delivered his message correctly.'

Greysteel turned to Shadowblaze. 'How do you feel about this?'

The red and grey dragon shifted uncomfortably on his limbs.

'Speak out,' said Blackrose. 'Reveal your thoughts to us.'

'Very well, my Queen,' said Shadowblaze. 'In my opinion, this man is sheltering under the guise of an emissary, when the simple truth is that, a matter of hours ago, he was planting explosives in the harbour of this city, while the greenhides he brought along slaughtered a thousand of our subjects.' His amber eyes burned. 'He should die.'

Blackrose and Shadowblaze's eyes met, and Maddie could sense the tension between them. She glanced over at the Banner officer, but he seemed unconcerned. He reminded her a little of Van Logos, in the way that he carried himself. If things had turned out a little differently, it could have been Captain Van of the Banner of the Golden Fist standing before them.

'Maddie,' said Blackrose; 'your opinion, if you please.'

Maddie puffed out her cheeks. 'I don't know. If Sable were here, he'd already be dead, but do we have to act in the same way? The militia said he surrendered willingly; it's not like he tried to escape or anything. I guess, if I had to choose, then I'd keep him under house arrest within the palace. He could walk around, but he'd also be guarded at the same time.'

'That seems like a sensible compromise,' said Ahi'edo.

Maddie blinked in surprise. Was Ahi'edo agreeing with her? Not only that, but was he disagreeing in public with his own dragon, without being asked to speak?

'I tend to agree,' said Blackrose. 'Very well, I rescind my earlier statement. The officer will not be permitted the freedom of the town;

instead, he will remain within the boundaries of the bridge palace, and will have a troop of militia on hand to ensure his safety.'

'You have my thanks, Queen of Ulna,' said Captain Tallius.

'Dismissed,' said Blackrose. 'Guards, take him to the lower levels and find him a small apartment. Wherever he goes, I expect at least four guards to accompany him at all times.'

The militia soldiers bowed, then they escorted the Banner officer out of the hall.

'This is a mistake,' said Shadowblaze. 'It will be interpreted as weakness on our part.'

'Not so,' said Blackrose. 'It would be weakness if we had acted out of fear. We simply chose the more honourable path.'

'Do you believe that Bastion would treat one of our emissaries in the same manner?'

'No, because we possess more honour than he does. If you do not understand that, my old friend, then perhaps you do not understand me.'

Shadowblaze glared at her, then strode from the chamber. Ahi'edo glanced at Maddie, then ran after him.

'Oh, my dearest niece,' said Greysteel. 'Was that necessary?'

'I believe it was, dear uncle.'

'If Lord Bastion is indeed listening to us, then he will be laughing at our needless divisions. A show of strength and unity would have been better.'

'If by that, you mean I should have ripped the Banner officer's head off, then I am forced to disagree. We are at war uncle, but that does not make us savages.'

'And what about Bastion's threat, my Queen? Is our alliance with the Holdfast witch at an end?'

Blackrose pondered for a moment. 'Before today's attack, I would have said yes to that question. Now, I am not so sure. Sable Holdfast is probably the only being on this world with the power to defeat Bastion. He knows this, and is trying to drive a wedge between us. Despite Sable's recent insolence, I am inclined to forgive her. Whether or not she wishes anything to do with us is, however, a different question.' She glanced at Maddie. 'Perhaps my rider has an opinion on the subject.'

'Unfortunately,' said Maddie, 'as far as I can see, we need Sable more than she needs us. What can we offer her that she can't do without?'

'One day,' said Blackrose, 'her burning rage will turn to cold ash, and she will be alone, surrounded by a world she has tried her best to burn to the ground. On that day, we can offer her exactly what she needs.'

Maddie frowned. 'What's that?'

'Friends,' said Blackrose, 'and a home.'

CHAPTER 22
DISCRIMINATING

Wyst, Eastern Rim – 14th Arginch 5255 (18th Gylean Year 6)

Sable snapped her vision back to her head, and closed her eyes. The area behind her temples was throbbing, and she took a moment for the worst of the pain to pass. For hours, she had been scanning the dark mountains and forests of Wyst, hunting for wherever dragons were concentrated. Small groups of one or two were no good to her – she needed more if her plan was going to have a chance.

She rummaged in her pocket, and withdrew a stick of keenweed. She flicked Meader's metal lighter, and touched the end of the weed-stick to the small flame. In the dim light, she saw Austin close by, sleeping on the floor of the cave with a blanket wrapped round him. She would wake him soon, but she would enjoy a quiet smoke first. She took a draw, and leaned back against a wall of the narrow cavern. It had been a long time since the use of her powers had caused her so much pain. Back in her teens, it had been a regular occurrence, but the aches had lessened with practice. She must be close to over-doing it, she guessed. No more four-hour stints, she told herself. The keenweed was heightening her senses, and the pain lifted. She stretched her neck muscles, and gazed out of the cave entrance. It was close to dawn, and they had been in the cave all night; deep in the heart of Wyst. The dragons on the large island lived in scattered communities, in conditions that Sable would have described as primitive, at best. With no humans to clean up after them, or to build them comfortable structures where they could dwell, their caverns were little more than filthy holes in the ground, damp and reeking.

She finished the weedstick, and nudged Austin. His eyes opened, and he rolled onto his back.

'Is it morning already?' he said.

'Almost. Did you sleep well?'

'I think so. Is that keenweed I can smell?'

'Unlike you, I've been up all night,' she said. 'I needed something to keep me alert.'

He sat up, and stretched his arms. 'Have you never heard of coffee?'

She smiled. 'There don't appear to be many cafés on Wyst.'

'Yeah; I heard they were a little uncivilised up here. So, what's the plan? Why are we here?'

'You'll see. Your role is to watch my back. I'm going to try an experiment first, before we go all-out. My biggest difficulty has been tracking down large groups of dragons – they seem to live in tiny, isolated family units, with usually only two or three adults and their children in any one location; but I did manage to find a few larger groups, The younger males and females seem to congregate together, then once they find mates, they head off to start families. There are also a few groups of elderly dragons, but they're no good for what I want to do.' She glanced at the growing light in the sky. 'It took me longer than I'd hoped. There's a small chance the slave rebellion on Gyle has already been crushed.'

'After one night?'

'Yes, if Bastion was able to respond immediately. I wish I knew what he was doing, but I can't reach Gyle with my vision from here.'

'Well, I'm ready to go.'

She nodded. Austin seemed to be in a good mood, and she didn't need to read his thoughts to know why. This was his last operation, and he was looking forward to it being over, so that she could fulfil her promise to him.

They stood, and Sable took out the Quadrant.

'We're going to a large cavern,' she said. 'It'll probably be dark, and dragon eyes are sharper than ours, so stay alert. If in doubt, use your flow powers, and we'll run for it. As I said, this first attempt is an experiment, and if it goes wrong then we'll have to learn from our mistakes.'

She swiped her fingers across the Quadrant, and the air shimmered around them. They appeared in a large space, lit by openings in the cavern ceiling, where shafts of grey light competed with thick shadows. The next thing Sable noticed was the smell – a rancid, sour tang of unwashed dragon.

A pair of yellow eyes blinked open from amid the darkness. 'Who is there?'

'Dragons!' Sable cried. 'Look at me!'

More eyes opened, and a few growls reverberated around the cavern.

'Intruders!' called out a voice. 'Human insects!'

Sable turned in a circle, her eyes piercing every corner of the cavern.

You cannot harm us. You will not try to escape. Stay calm, and relaxed.

A dragon groaned, as if in pain. 'Something is in my head!'

Sable stared at where the voice had originated.

Be quiet.

The cavern fell into silence.

'Stay very close to me, Austin,' Sable whispered, then she swept her fingers over the Quadrant.

The air shimmered again, and their surroundings changed – from the dark confines of the Wystian cavern, to the half-ruined harbour district of Sabat City on Ectus. Around them, the eight dragons she had brought with her cried out in panic and alarm. One of them arrived in mid-air, and fell from the sky, crashing through the roof of a burned-out warehouse. Banner soldiers started shouting, and a bell pealed out its warning.

Sable stared at the dragons.

Fight. Kill.

She swiped the Quadrant again, and she and Austin appeared on the side of a tall mountain, overlooking the north coast of Ectus.

Austin stared at her. 'What have you done?'

'You were there, Austin; do I really need to spell it out for you?'

'You've brought dragons all the way to Ectus?'

'Hush,' she said, sitting on the stony ground. 'I want to see what they're doing. Get a cigarette ready for me.'

She sent out her vision, and raced it down onto the coastal plain. She surged over the farms and fields, then crossed the outer suburbs of Sabat City. The huge settlement looked like a warzone. She had sent over two thousand greenhides into its streets over the previous month, as well as blowing up much of its infrastructure. Craters pock-marked the entire harbour front, and the harbours were full of burnt-out and wrecked vessels. She reached the area where she had deposited the eight dragons, and saw flames rising over the rooftops. Two of the dragons were already dead, but the others had recovered from the shock of arriving in a strange place, and were sweeping over the roads, incinerating every human in sight. Soldiers were piling out of a fortress, as more bells rang, and ballistae were loosing yard-long steel bolts at the dragons darting above the city. A watchtower exploded in flames, along with the pair of catapults that had been sitting on the platform at the top. The soldiers began to retreat, but the dragons went after them, splitting off into pairs as they hunted the humans like prey.

Sable brought her vision back to her body, and Austin handed her a lit cigarette.

'Well?' he said.

She smiled. 'I think it might just work. It'll certainly keep the occupation forces on Ectus busy for a while. Still, that was only eight; I'll need more to make a real difference.'

As the sun rose to their right, she began to see wisps of smoke rise from the horizon to the north. Sabat City was burning again. With any luck, the news of the attack would reach Bastion's ears, and he would rush off to Ectus to deal with it, leaving Gyle practically undefended. Her biggest concern was her own strength. Manipulating dragons was far harder than doing the same to a group of senseless greenhides, but it was worth the risk.

Austin frowned. 'Sable, won't the Wystian dragons kill indiscriminately? They hate all humans – Banner soldiers, settlers and natives alike. They won't make any distinction between the groups.'

'That's why I chose Ectus for the experiment,' she said. 'The dragons are surrounded by military personnel. They'd have to kill thousands before they even reached the districts where the civilians live.'

'Unless they decide to fly away. Can you control them in the same way you control greenhides?'

'I can put blocks into their minds – that's pretty straightforward. I did that in the cavern – I ordered them not to harm us. That kind of thing should last a while. However, trying to give them detailed instructions – kill those humans, but not these humans – is a lot harder. On Gyle, I'll have to remain connected to their minds, to keep reinforcing the message.' She stubbed out the cigarette. 'Right; let's head back to Wyst.'

They got to their feet, and she activated the Quadrant. They appeared in a narrow space underground, and were plunged back into darkness. Sable allowed her eyes to adjust to the gloom, and headed for a faint patch of light. The tunnel they were in opened out into a huge cavern, ten times larger than the one that had contained the eight dragons from before. Sable crouched down by the tunnel entrance, and stared into the open space. At least forty dragons were resting inside the enormous cavern. Most were juveniles, about the same size and age that Frostback and Halfclaw had been on Lostwell – too old to live with their parents, but too young to have yet mated. If anything, the smell was even worse than it had been in the first cave, and Sable's eyes watered.

Austin crouched down next to her, his eyes wide. She glanced at him, took a breath, then got up and walked into the cavern.

'Hey!' she cried, waving her arms above her head.

Three dozen dragons turned to stare at her.

You cannot harm me.

Her knees almost buckled from the strain of trying to dominate so many dragons at the same time. A few dragons by the periphery roared out in defiance, her powers unable to reach them. Next to her. Austin raised his right hand, ready to defend them from attack, as Sable clutched the Quadrant.

'Kill them!' cried a young dragon, as flames leapt from her jaws.

Sable swiped the Quadrant, and they appeared in the middle of a vast field, where wheat was growing. Sable grunted, her powers stretched to their limit as she tried to calm the dragons she had forced to accompany them. The Quadrant had transported twenty-three from the cavern, and they were staring around in confusion and anger. Screams rose up from a line of slaves who were being marched along a track next to the field, and their armed escorts fled in panic at the sight of the dragons.

Sable focussed, and imprinted an image of a Banner soldier into the minds of the dragons.

Kill all who look like this. Spare the others.

She flicked her fingers over the Quadrant, withdrawing to a safer location that was a few miles away, but still close to the massive slave compound. A farmhouse was lying deserted, its front door swinging open in the morning breeze. There was a wooden bench by the gate, and Sable sat down onto it, panting with the effort it had taken to control the dragons.

'Sable,' said Austin, his voice low. 'Look at this.'

She turned. Austin was gazing out over the low wall that surrounded the farmhouse. Irritated, she got back to her feet, and walked over.

'Shit,' she muttered.

'It has begun,' he said.

On the other side of the wall, dozens of bodies were lying on the ground, their corpses riddled with crossbow bolts. From their clothes, it was obvious that they were all natives.

'None are armed,' said Austin. 'They weren't part of the uprising, and they weren't killed in a fight. This is exactly what that militia officer was talking about. The colonial authorities are going to slaughter them all.'

'Not if I can help it,' she said. 'Keep watch. I'm going to guide the battle from here. If anyone comes, kill them.'

She returned to the bench, and calmed her breathing. She patted her pocket. There were still a few sticks of keenweed left. If she smoked them all, then she would soon pay for it, but what choice did she have? She had brought nearly two dozen dragons to the fields of Gyle; without her guidance, they would scatter, and kill anyone they saw, slave and settler alike.

She sent out her powers again, and located the group of young dragons. Most of them were gathered together, and she glanced around for the few who were missing; but they had already fled. There was nothing she could do about that, so she concentrated on the nineteen who remained.

Fly. Rise into the sky, and fly west.

The dragons obeyed. Without a word passing between them, they arose into the lightening sky, and soared away from the rising sun, towards the slave compound. Sable nestled her powers within a green dragon, who was leading the others, and looked out from his eyes. The walls of the compound were soon visible. Smoke was rising from several locations and more than a dozen of the squat huts where the slaves lived were burning. Companies of Banner soldiers were moving through the compound, slaughtering anyone who got in their way. A few slaves were fighting back, using the weapons that Sable had brought them, but they were no match for the disciplined ranks of Banner soldiers. Other slaves had built barricades blocking the lanes that led onto the huge central square, and hundreds of natives were surrounding the figure of the Eighteenth Gylean, forming a human barrier between their living god and the advancing Banner soldiers.

Observe the difference between the two groups of humans, Sable said to the dragons. *Soldiers, and natives of Dragon Eyre. Leave the natives unharmed. Kill the soldiers. Kill them all.*

The dragons responded immediately. They formed into a long line, and soared down over the compound. Their jaws opened, and a massive wall of flame erupted from the nineteen dragons, tearing through the ranks of Banner soldiers who were massing along the western side of the compound. The soldiers had no time to look up or scream; they were incinerated where they stood, their bodies rendered to smouldering ash as the flames lit up the dawn sky. The dragons pushed on, traversing the compound, and getting closer to the huddled and panicking natives with every second.

At the last moment, the dragons pulled up from the compound, and the natives in the central square gasped in amazement, then let out a loud roar of joy. They surged forward through the smoking ruins of the camp, running between the piles of dead soldiers in the direction of the gates.

Now, said Sable to the young dragons, *do the same thing to the Banner soldiers outside the compound. Hunt them; kill them; drive them back to Implacatus. You are the heroes who will free this world.*

The dragons banked and circled, then split off into groups, each one heading in a different direction. Several moved out of Sable's range, and were lost to her influence, but she had no time to worry about that. She concentrated on the small group led by the green dragon in whose mind she was hiding, and directed them to the main road leading to a Banner fortress. The road was filled with soldiers, and carts bearing ballistae, and the dragons unleashed flames down upon them. They swept above the road, burning everything that lay in their path.

Leave the others to finish the job, Sable said to the green dragon. *Fly back to the compound.*

The green dragon pulled away from his comrades, and headed back the way he had come. Armed natives were streaming through the open gates of the compound onto the main road, while the Banner forces were in full retreat. Dragons circled, then swooped down, raining fire onto the fleeing soldiers. Down by the compound gates, Sable noticed a large group of men in back robes, who were trying to exert control over the mass of natives.

Do you see those black-clad humans? They are also your enemies. Kill them, but be careful to spare the others.

The green dragon plummeted from the sky in a steep dive. The Unk Tannic agents were mingled within the crowds of ordinary slaves, and any blast of flame would destroy equal numbers of both. The green dragon landed heavily next to the gates, and the masses of people cheered, their hands in the air, while several Unk Tannic agents fell to their knees, singing the praises of the dragons in loud voices. The green dragon stared at them for a moment, then strode forward, and began ripping them to shreds with his long talons. The natives screamed and started to scatter, but the dragon was targeting only those who were wearing the long black robes. The Unk Tannic agents stared at the green dragon in dismay as he tore through their ranks.

Sable ordered the green dragon to convey her words to the crowd.

'Death to the occupiers!' the dragon roared. 'And death to the Unk Tannic! Sable Holdfast has sent us this day, to cleanse the land of its enemies. Death to all who oppress the people of this world!'

Many in the massed crowd had heard the words of the dragon, and their eyes were wide as they watched the last of the Unk Tannic agents being torn apart. No doubt there were many more, hidden among the crowds, but Sable hoped her demonstration would have the desired effect. She ordered the green dragon back into the air, and he banked to the east, flying over the compound walls. The entire area was in chaos. Dragons were hunting soldiers along every road, and chasing them through the wheat fields, while thousands of slaves were loose in the countryside. A company of Banner soldiers attempted to surrender to a dragon, but were incinerated where they stood, their cries adding to the terrible cacophony of destruction. The green dragon wheeled about in the sky, then he cried out in agony, and began to fall, his life extinguished. Sable pulled her vision back, and watched the dragon crash into a wide ditch by a road's edge. She scanned the area, and saw a god standing on the back of a wagon, his arms in the air. He was surrounded by dozens of Banner soldiers, who had their shields up in a wall around him, and he was staring up at the skies, waiting for more dragons to enter the range of his death powers.

Sable blinked, and came back to her own body. She glanced at Austin, whose gaze was on the fires in the distance.

'Ready your flow powers,' she said. 'We have a god to kill.'

She examined the Quadrant, performed a quick calculation in her mind, then triggered the device. She and Austin appeared in the air twenty feet above the wagon. Austin yelled out in fright, as Sable yanked her sword from its scabbard. The god saw them, his eyes widening as they plunged down towards him. Austin recovered his composure, and sent a blast of flow powers into the soldiers surrounding the wagon, knocking a dozen off their feet. Sable landed on top of the god, then wriggled free before he could touch her skin. She brought the sword down in a powerful lunge, just as the god tried to get up. The blade hit the middle of his face, cleaving through muscle and bone, and shearing the top of his head off. She activated the Quadrant again, and she, Austin, and the mutilated god appeared back next to the abandoned farmhouse.

Austin placed his hands on his knees, and panted. Sable got to her feet, and examined the body of the god. Was taking the top of his head off enough? She imagined it was, but there was no point in risking it. She chopped the rest of his head off, then drop-kicked it over the low wall.

She noticed Austin eyeing her.

She shrugged. 'I'm not taking any chances; not today.'

He looked away, his face pale, and she sat back down on the bench, and sheathed her bloody sword.

'Back to work,' she said. 'Stay alert.'

She sent her vision back out, despite the grinding exhaustion she was beginning to feel. She could rest later. The dragons had scattered. Most were still pursuing bands of Banner soldiers, but a few had soared away in the direction of the high mountains on the western horizon, seeking refuge and safety. She decided to go into each remaining dragon one at a time, to imprint her instruction more effectively, and selected a light blue female. She took over the dragon's mind, and led her back to the road leading to the fortress.

Carry on up this road. Kill every soldier you see.

She pulled out of the dragon's mind, and looked around for another. For the next two hours, she continued in a similar fashion, leaping from dragon to dragon, and reinforcing her hold over them. She had them fan out away from the slave compound, attacking the columns of retreating Banner soldiers, and pushing them back towards Port Edmond. She manoeuvred four of them into a pincer movement, blocking a narrow bridge that led north with two dragons, while the other pair herded a full company of soldiers towards their waiting flames. When the last of them had fallen to the ground, she turned her attention to a nearby fortress. She was about to summon some of the dragons to attack it, when she felt something hit the side of her body.

She fell to the ground, her vision springing back to her head. She blinked, and saw a dragon right in front of her, his eyes staring down at where she lay. A few yards from her, Austin was sprawled on the ground, his back torn and bloody.

'Holdfast!' cried the dragon. 'We know who you are. You will pay for bringing us here.'

Sable raised her hand. *Sleep.*

Nothing happened. Perhaps it was her exhaustion, or perhaps that particular dragon was too strong for her to control.

'Now, you shall die, witch.' The dragon opened his jaws, then he shuddered, his eyes rolling up into his head. He made a gargled choking noise, then he collapsed to the ground, flattening half of the farmhouse with his weight.

Sable glanced at Austin. The demigod was up on one knee, his hand raised.

'Thank you,' she said.

Austin groaned, and pulled himself to his feet. 'Just doing my job.'

Sable scrambled back up onto the bench, her side aching. She noticed blood on her right arm.

'The dragon almost got you with his claws,' said Austin. 'I managed to get myself between you and him, and took the brunt of it for you.' He walked over, and placed a hand on the side of her face. She felt a jolt of healing powers ripple through her, and the pain in her side and arm receded.

'Did you hear what he said?' Austin went on. 'Even the dragons of Wyst know who you are. You know they'll be after you.'

She shrugged. 'Just another enemy to add to the list.' She lit a stick of keenweed, and felt her exhaustion start to dissipate.

'How's the battle going?'

'The Banner forces have been routed,' she said. 'Around half of the dragons are still obeying my orders. Of the other half, a quarter are dead, and the rest have fled.'

'Fled? Where have they gone?'

'Towards the mountains in western Gyle. To be honest, I'm not even sure they know that they're on Gyle, but I guess the mountains looked inviting. More inviting than down here, at any rate.'

'Once they realise where they are,' he said, 'some of them might try to fly back to Wyst.'

'Then they have a long journey ahead of them,' said Sable, drawing on the weedstick. 'They'll have to go via Haurn; that's if they have any idea about how to make it home. I half hope that some of them decide to settle on Gyle.'

'Are you mad?' said Austin. 'Sorry; stupid question. Let me rephrase – why would you want wild Wystian dragons to settle on Gyle? They loathe humans.'

'They have no experience of humans. You saw the disgusting squalor in which they live. Perhaps, once they've seen the dragon palaces on the western coast, they might realise that they would benefit if they cooperated with humans.'

'Or, they'll use the palaces as bases from which to raid the country-side for decades to come.'

'They might.' She took another long draw, and tossed the butt away. She rolled her shoulders, stood, and activated the Quadrant.

Sable and Austin appeared back on the small islet in the Riggan archipelago. The sky was cloudy, and a fresh wind was gusting in from the west. Sable tucked the Quadrant back under her leather armour, and they walked down the rough track to the caves where they had been living. Ashfall's head was protruding from one, and her eyes burned with joy as she saw Austin returning.

'How was it?' said the slender grey dragon.

Austin raised an eyebrow. 'Interesting.'

'You're toughening up,' said Sable, as they reached the entrance to the cave. 'Not so long ago, you would be on your knees throwing up by now.'

'I guess I have you to thank for my transformation into a heartless monster.'

Sable narrowed her eyes, then squeezed past Ashfall and entered the cave. Beyond the grey dragon, Millen and Deepblue were sitting by another, smaller entrance to the network of caves. Sable sat down next to them without a word, and unbuckled her armour. Her head was spinning from the keenweed, but her body was exhausted. Millen handed her a mug of water, and she drank.

'Is it over?' said Deepblue.

Sable glanced at the small blue dragon.

'You said that this was Austin's last operation,' Deepblue went on. 'Does that mean that we can return to Ulna?'

Sable said nothing. It had been a good day, but it still wasn't enough. Just one more push; one more, and then she could rest. She turned, and saw Austin enter the cave, a satisfied smile on his lips. He took a mug of water from Millen, glugged it down, then lit a cigarette.

'Austin,' said Sable.

'Yes?'

'Will you give me one more day?'

The demigod's face fell. 'But you said...'

'I know what I said. But, really, the operation isn't over. The first part is over, but I'll need you tomorrow, so that we can finish it.'

Austin's eyes glimmered with fury. 'You made a promise.'

'And I intend to keep it. Don't make me go into your head and persuade you. I want you to agree willingly, so that we don't fall out. Come on; just one more day, then it will be over.'

Austin rubbed his face and sighed. 'Fine. One day, though – no more.'

She smiled at him. 'Thank you. You know, I couldn't have done this without you. You saved my life today, and I'm grateful.'

'You don't need to flatter me; I've already said yes. So, one more day? What are we going to do? What urgent task do you need me for?'

She looked him in the eye. 'We're going to burn the Winter Palace to the ground.'

CHAPTER 23
WITHIN THE LAW

Udall, Ulna, Eastern Rim – 15th Arginch 5255 (18th Gylean Year 6)
As the sun rose over the eastern horizon, Topaz knew something was wrong. There was no smoke rising from Udall, but several buildings along the quayside were scorched and blackened, while others had collapsed into heaps of rubble.

'Holy crap,' said Lara, as Topaz guided the *Giddy Gull* past the breakwaters. 'What have we missed?'

A few sailors were up on the deck of the *Patience*, and they waved over at the *Gull*, and to the other two ships that were entering the harbour behind them. Along the quayside, only a handful of dock workers were present, compared to the usual crowds that gathered there, and the market square was deserted. A few refugees were sitting by the side of the main street, looking dirty and exhausted.

Lara pointed. 'Greenhides.'

Topaz glanced over, and saw a large pile of greenhide bodies by the edge of the quay. Workers were labouring to drag more bodies towards the pile, while drums of oil were close by, ready to assist in the burning of the corpses.

Lara put a hand to her mouth. 'If this was Sable...'

'If Sable had done this, ma'am,' said Topaz, 'then the dragons would already be attacking us. Anyway, why would Sable do such a thing?'

'You heard her – she said that she'd fallen out with Blackrose.' The captain shook her head. 'No. I can't believe it was her. She would have warned us not to return here.'

Topaz piloted the vessel towards one of the long piers. Unlike the buildings by the quayside, the piers and ships in the harbour seemed untouched by the violence that had taken place. A few workers were there to meet Lara's brigantine, and ropes were secured forward and aft. The *Flight of Fancy* was small enough to berth at the same pier, while the *Sow's Revenge*, with Vitz on the wheel, found space by the main quay.

Lara gestured to a midshipman. 'Lad,' she said, once he had bounded up onto the quarter deck, 'announce the following to the crew – no shore leave until sunset. I want everyone who isn't busy on board lending a hand with the clear-up on the quayside. Have them report to the local militia to offer their services. Shore leave starts as soon as the sun goes down. Got it?'

The middie saluted. 'Yes, ma'am.'

Topaz locked the wheel into position, and ordered Tommo to tidy away the charts and empty coffee mugs. He and Lara walked to the side of the quarter deck, and gazed down at the town. A group of militia soldiers were striding up the pier towards them, and Topaz noticed Maddie in their midst. He smiled down at her, and she waved back.

A gangway was put in place between the ship and the pier, and Topaz accompanied the captain as she walked down to the main deck. The sailors had gathered round the midshipman, who was relaying Lara's orders. A few were grumbling, but the majority simply nodded and got on with it.

'It feels odd,' said Lara, 'not having any stolen cargo to unload. I wonder if it's a sign of things to come.'

A militia officer asked for permission to come aboard, and Lara nodded. The officer ascended the gangway, with Maddie and a couple of soldiers.

'Welcome back to Udall, ma'am,' said the officer. 'As you can see, the harbour facilities have taken a beating.'

'What happened?' said Lara.

'It was Bastion,' said Maddie. 'He was trying to teach us a lesson about who we should be friends with.'

Lara puffed out her cheeks. It was from relief, Topaz guessed – relief that the destruction hadn't been caused by Sable.

'Hi, Topaz,' Maddie went on. 'How are you?'

'I'm fine,' he said. 'Still a little bruised from what happened.'

She narrowed her eyes. 'Olo'osso has been put into a small, dark cell under the palace. He won't be bruising you again.'

'Have you gone to visit him?' said Lara.

'No,' said Maddie. 'The last time I saw your father, he was sending me off with Dax to be sold in Pangba. Why would I want to visit him?'

'Madam,' said the militia officer; 'if I may?'

'Oh, sorry,' said Maddie. 'Carry on.'

The officer cleared his throat. 'Captain Lara, Queen Blackrose requests that you attend the bridge palace, along with the captains of the other two Five Sisters vessels. You may bring your senior officers, if you see fit to do so.'

Lara nodded. 'Alright. I'll bring Topaz. I've already ordered the rest of the crew to help out in the harbour.'

The officer bowed his head. 'I'm sure the workers clearing away the debris will be grateful for the assistance, ma'am. Now, if you will excuse me, I need to pass on the same message to the *Flight of Fancy*.'

The militia about-turned, and strode back down the gangway, leaving Maddie on the deck of the *Gull* with Topaz and Lara.

'When did the attack take place?' said Lara.

'Yesterday,' said Maddie. 'It was over in minutes. Don't worry about Blackrose, though – her resolve is as strong as ever.'

'And Sable?'

'Um, what about her?'

'Has she been back to Udall?'

'Well, she dropped off Olo'osso, but that was before Blackrose and all of the other dragons got back from Throscala. It was a little sneaky of her, as Greysteel had no clue that she and Blackrose had been arguing again.'

'Would she be welcome here if she came back?'

'I'm not sure, Lara,' said Maddie. 'I guess it depends on her attitude. Blackrose is prepared to reconcile, but if Sable turns up and insults her again, then...' She shrugged. 'Dragons are stubborn, and Sable is just as bad.'

'Will I see you after the meeting in the palace?' said Topaz.

Maddie smiled. 'I'm coming to the meeting, along with my shadow.'

'Your shadow?'

'Yes. Ahi'edo's been following me everywhere I go; I'm surprised he didn't insist on coming down to the quayside this morning.'

Topaz narrowed his eyes, as a surge of jealousy ran through him. He wanted Maddie to have friends, but didn't like the idea of another man spending so much time alone with her while he was at sea.

Lara laughed. 'Look at his face. I don't think Topaz wants to share you, Maddie.'

'Are you jealous?' said Maddie.

'No,' said Topaz, a little too quickly. 'It's just, you know... I hope he hasn't been getting over-friendly.'

'There's nothing for you to worry about,' she said. 'Shadowblaze is adamant that he and I have to at least try to get along, and Ahi'edo is only doing what he's told. Should we go? It looks like the militia have finished speaking to Ann on the *Flight of Fancy*. They've already been to the *Sow's Revenge*.'

Lara nodded, and they strode down the gangway and onto the wooden pier. They joined Ann, Dina and the militia, who had left the *Flight of Fancy*, and walked onto the solid ground of the long quay, where Tilly was waiting for them, along with a couple of her officers. They turned left and, accompanied by the militia, made their way through the debris and destruction along the harbour front. Red and green blood was being scrubbed from the large flagstones by workers, and craters were being filled with gravel taken from a row of wheelbarrows by the water's edge.

The militia led them along the banks of the river to the bridge palace. They entered, and ascended to the upper, dragon levels. The halls and wide passageways were as quiet as ever, with only a handful of guards on duty, but a larger group was waiting for them in the huge reception chamber. Blackrose, Shadowblaze and Greysteel were there, along with Ahi'edo, while a squad of militia were guarding the shackled figure of Olo'osso, who was standing proud despite the four nights he had spent in the dungeons beneath the palace.

'Ah, my disobedient daughters,' he exclaimed; 'have you come to knife me in the back again?'

Greysteel directed a stare towards the old pirate. 'You will speak when addressed, Captain Osso.'

'Of course,' said Olo'osso; 'my mistake. You may proceed, Lord Greysteel.'

The four sisters assembled into a line, and each bowed their heads a little before the Queen of Ulna, to the sound of coarse chuckling from their father. Lord Greysteel gestured to a row of seats, and they sat, while Maddie went to stand with Ahi'edo next to the dragons.

'Thank you for coming,' said Blackrose.

'I think I can guess what this is about,' said Lara. 'You want us to give up our current means of employment, now that Throscala has been neutralised. Am I right?'

'You are,' said Blackrose.

'I knew it!' cried Olo'osso. 'You want my girls to transform themselves into nice little law-abiding servants of Ulna. You're deluding yourselves, dragons. My family has more pride than that; you'll see.'

'Be quiet, father,' said Ann. 'Let's listen to what the Queen of Ulna has to say first, before condemning it out of hand.'

Olo'osso glowered at his eldest daughter, then folded his arms across his broad chest.

'All piracy in the Eastern Rim must cease,' said Blackrose. 'This is a natural consequence of our victory over the forces that occupied Throscala. There is no enemy shipping left to raid, apart from a few isolated Sea Banner vessels that remain at large. The liberated islands are facing serious shortages, and any vessel that preys upon merchant shipping will be severely punished. You must understand this. However, in light of our recent alliance, we are prepared to offer you a new contract. If you agree to protect these ships, instead of robbing them, we would reward you and your crews well. As I mentioned, there are still a few Sea Banner vessels lurking throughout the Eastern Rim. Cut off from their masters, and without any safe harbours in which to dock, they will be desperate and hungry. I want you to hunt them down, and eliminate the threat they present. In return, you will have free access to any port from Ulna to Throscala.'

Tilly frowned. 'It almost sounds as though you want us to form an Ulnan navy.'

'In essence, yes,' said Blackrose. 'Do you agree?'

The four sisters shared a glance.

'We should vote on it,' said Tilly.

'Yes,' said Ann, 'but only after we have each discussed our opinions. As eldest, I should go first.'

Lara rolled her eyes. 'Meaning I have to go last? Typical.'

'And father's here,' said Tilly. 'Should he get a vote? If he does, then he's the eldest, not you, Ann.'

Lara smirked. 'Maybe we should vote on whether father gets to vote. I say no.'

'I say yes,' said Dina.

'I don't think he should be allowed to vote,' said Tilly.

'Then why did you bring it up?' said Ann. 'Personally, I think he should be allowed a vote.'

'But that's two votes each,' said Lara. 'What do we do now?'

'Isn't it wonderful to see my daughters so united?' said Olo'osso. 'At times like these, I doubt if they'd be able to agree that water is wet. Therefore, I shall go first. I vote against any such contract. The Osso family are free spirits, and are not bound to any island government. If we are not able to carry out our age-old traditions, then we should sail back to Olkis, immediately.'

'I agree,' said Dina.

'Shut up, you dozy cow,' said Lara. 'It ain't your turn.'

They all turned to Ann, who was pursing her lips.

'Well?' said Tilly.

'I would need to study the contract in detail,' Ann said, 'before signing anything. But, in principle, I would be happy to stay in Ulna for one year. I'd always planned on being in the Eastern Rim for that length of time, and I see no need to change my plans. Dina, you're next.'

'She's already told us what she thinks,' said Lara.

'I want to hear her reasoning,' said Ann.

Lara lit a cigarette. 'Fine.'

'It's alright for you three,' snapped Dina. 'You all have ships here in Ulna; but what about me? Am I expected to play lieutenant to one of you?'

'You're dreaming if you think I'll ever let you on board the *Gull*,' said Lara. 'I wouldn't let you serve as a middie, never mind a bleeding lieutenant.'

'I will never work for you, Lara,' said Dina. 'I'd rather throw myself to the greenhides. I want to go back to Langbeg. My ship's still berthed there, though my crew have probably all run off and joined other ships by now; which is another reason to get back as soon as possible. I vote with father.'

'I don't,' said Tilly. 'The *Revenge* is a great ship, and...'

'*Sow's Revenge*,' muttered Lara. 'Don't forget the pig.'

'Shut up,' said Tilly. 'Anyway, I'm with Ann on this. I'll give it a year.'

The others glanced at Lara.

'Oh,' she said, 'is it finally my turn?' She glanced at Blackrose. 'I have a question, before I answer.'

Blackrose gazed down at her. 'Then ask it, Captain Lara.'

'Alright. Is Sable Holdfast welcome in Ulna?'

'That renegade is not up for discussion,' said Greysteel, his eyes burning.

'Wait a moment, uncle,' said Blackrose. 'Let me answer Captain Lara.' She turned her attention back to the youngest Osso sister. 'I am unable to make any promises on that account. Would it satisfy you to hear that I remain open to the possibility? Sable and I parted badly in Throscala, and I feel that she owes me an apology for the insults she cast in my direction. However, if she apologises to me, then I would be prepared to declare a truce. You have some influence over her, I think. It would benefit us all if you were to nudge her towards a reconciliation.'

Lara nodded. 'You might be over-estimating any influence I have on Sable, but I'll try, if I see her again.'

'Are you satisfied with my response?'

'You've left the door open, so, yes.' She glanced at her sisters. 'I want to stay here, for at least a year, maybe more.'

Dina groaned aloud, while Tilly slapped her younger sister on the back.

'There we have it,' said Ann. 'Stay wins by three votes to two.'

'What about Elli?' said Olo'osso. 'The fifth sister is not here, and I know for a fact that she would vote to have us return to Olkis. Think – she will be alone in Langbeg, unaware of where we are, or what is happening to us. She will be worried, and scared.'

'Oh, shut up, father,' said Lara. 'You lost, and that's that. We can ask Sable to send a message to Ellie, and then she can stay there, or come here; whatever she fancies.'

'You have turned into a most truculent young lady, Alara'osso,' her father cried. 'If you intend to captain the *Giddy Gull*, then I demand that you give me back the sum that I paid to clear your debts. Two thousand, wasn't it? Where's my money?'

'This meeting is at an end,' said Blackrose, her voice booming out over those in the chamber. 'The Osso family can argue about money later. Lord Greysteel will oversee the preparation of a written contract for you to sign...'

'I shall never sign such a document!' cried Olo'osso, a finger pointed in the air.

Blackrose stared at him. 'That is irrelevant. I only require signatures from the captains of the three vessels currently sitting in the harbour. Furthermore, you are my prisoner, under arrest for the illegal seizure of the *Giddy Gull*.'

Olo'osso laughed. 'I'm being charged with stealing my own ship?'

'The *Gull* is mine, father,' said Lara, jumping to her feet. 'It will always be mine. You'll get your damn money, as that's all you seem to care about.'

'How dare you?' cried Olo'osso. 'After everything I've done for you? You ungrateful, spoilt little princess. I should...' His voice tailed away, as his eyes went to the back of the huge chamber. 'Hold on; is that a bleeding Banner officer by the doorway?'

Topaz and the sisters turned. Leaning against the doorframe was a man, dressed in the uniform of a Banner captain.

'What's he doing here?' cried Tilly.

'I was listening, ma'am,' said the officer. 'It was amusing to hear you all squabble. You're quite different from how I imagined you to be. The tales of the notorious Five Sisters speak of ruthless cunning, and, frankly, I wasn't expecting all the bickering.'

'This is Captain Tallius,' said Maddie. 'He's an emissary from Lord Bastion, and...'

'I don't care who he is,' spat Olo'osso. 'He shouldn't be here.'

'Perhaps he should return to his quarters,' said Greysteel.

'Actually,' said the officer, striding forward into the chamber, 'I came here to tell you that the palace has been infiltrated by Unk Tannic agents. As they are mutual enemies of both Ulna and the colonial government, I thought you might find the information useful.'

Olo'osso's hand moved in a blur. He plucked a knife from the belt of one of those guarding him, drew his hand back, and flung the blade at the officer. It struck him in the left eye, and the captain cried out, then fell to the floor of the chamber, blood pooling around his head. A guard ran towards the body, and rolled the Banner captain onto his back.

The guard glanced at the dragons. 'Tallius is dead, your Majesties.'

'Ha!' yelled Olo'osso. 'The old man's still got it, eh?'

'Restrain him,' cried Blackrose.

The soldiers around Olo'osso gripped his arms and shoulders, and one shoved the tip of a crossbow into his back.

'That man was being treated as a peaceful emissary,' Blackrose went on, her eyes glowing with rage. 'For that, you shall be placed back into your cell immediately. Take him away, before I kill him.'

'I regret nothing!' Olo'osso shouted, as the guards hauled him out of the chamber.

'Sorry about that,' said Ann, her eyes on the body of the dead officer. 'Father can be a little impulsive at times.'

'You are not responsible for his actions,' said Blackrose. 'You are all dismissed.'

'Me too?' said Maddie.

'Yes, you too, my rider. I will see you later.'

'It sounds like being back in the bleeding Sea Banner, mate,' said Ryan, a mug of ale in his hand.

'I know,' said Topaz, 'but it's better than nothing.' He glanced at Maddie, who was deep in conversation with Tilly as they all sat by the long tavern table. 'Much better than nothing.'

'I wish I'd seen Olo'osso kill that bleeding Banner officer,' Ryan went on. 'I miss all the fun.'

Maddie turned. 'He shouldn't have done it.'

'Why not, lass?' Ryan said. 'Banner is Banner, eh?'

'He was just a soldier, and he was unarmed. Also, I wanted to hear what he had to say about the Unk Tannic. It makes my skin crawl to think that there might be agents in the palace.'

'There's no "might" about it,' said Lara, sitting opposite them. 'There are definitely Unk Tannic agents in the palace. When Sable gets back, she'll root the bastards out; wait and see.'

'You have too much faith in that woman,' said Tilly.

'Don't you bleeding well call her "that woman" again, sister. She has a name – one that every bastard on Dragon Eyre will have heard by now. Gods, I wonder where she is.'

'She'll be blowing the shit out of something or other, ma'am,' said Ryan, a faraway expression in his eyes. 'She's amazing.'

'Hoi,' said Lara. 'She's mine, and don't you forget it.'

A waitress came over to the long table, and unloaded a large tray. The four sisters were paying for the evening's food and drink, and half of the *Giddy Gull's* crew were packing out the tavern, along with sailors from the other two ships. They had all listened to Ann and Lara tell them about their new contract, and had been alarmed at first; but they had settled down when they had been told that their pay and conditions would be unaffected.

Topaz glanced at Tilly. 'How is Vitz doing, ma'am?'

Tilly shrugged. 'I've had worse masters. He's still a little green around the edges, but I reckon I can mould him into something useful.'

'Has he obeyed orders?' said Lara.

'He has. He's been quiet, though; keeps himself to himself.' She took a drink. 'I left him in charge of the *Sow's Revenge* tonight; I just hope he's still there in the morning.'

'We should cut him loose once the war's over,' said Lara. 'Let him go back to his father's big estate on Gyle.'

Tilly frowned.

'That's if the estate is still there,' said Ann, from Lara's left. 'Sable told us she was going to hit Gyle with everything she had – remember?'

'Yeah, but what does that mean, exactly?' said Tilly. 'Dina knows how Sable's been doing it, and I'll bet Maddie does too.'

'I don't want to talk about it,' said Maddie.

'Dear gods,' said Tilly, 'are you scared of Sable too?'

'No,' said Maddie, 'but if I tell you, then you'll think less of her.'

'Nothing you say will make me think less of Sable,' said Ryan.

Maddie glanced at him. 'In your case, that's probably true. No. Sable can tell you herself.'

'I have my suspicions,' said Lara.

'Whatever they are,' said Dina, 'the truth is far worse.'

The table fell into silence.

'I don't care what you all think of her,' said Lara. 'You might think she's over-confidant, cruel, or even evil, but I know what she's really like.'

'So do I,' said Maddie. 'I've known her since she helped me escape from prison on Lostwell. I've seen her good side, and her bad; but you have to understand something, Lara – Badblood's death has changed her. No offence, but that dragon was her best friend; their bond ran deep.'

Lara held Maddie's gaze for a moment, then lowered her eyes.

'That's enough about Sable,' said Ann. 'What are we going to do about father?'

'Nothing,' said Lara. 'Let him rot in jail.'

Ann ignored her youngest sibling. 'Maddie,' she said, 'could you speak to the dragons about him? See if they'll release him?'

'I don't think that's a good idea, not after he killed that officer. Blackrose had to argue with the others to get them to agree not to kill him in the first place. She'll be angry for a while that Olo'osso ruined all that for her. I'd give it a few days before bringing it up.' She glanced at Topaz. 'Did you notice that Shadowblaze said absolutely nothing during the meeting? They disagreed over how the officer should be treated. He probably thinks Olo'osso should be given a medal for killing him.'

'I'm with Shadowblaze,' said Ryan. 'I've seen enough of Banner soldiers to know that they're all bastards.'

'That's not true,' said Maddie.

The Olkians at the table stared at her.

Ann raised an eyebrow. 'Would you care to clarify that comment, Miss Jackdaw?'

Maddie's eyes flashed with defiance. 'I knew a Banner officer on Lostwell. He was one of the good guys.'

'Yeah?' said Lara, laughing. 'How well did you know him? And be careful, we don't want Topaz getting jealous again.'

'He fancied Sable's niece – a slightly annoying girl called Kelsey Holdfast.'

'Was he the owner of that silver cigarette case?' said Topaz.

'Yeah. He loaned it to me. He didn't like the gods much, but he obeyed orders. Anyway, what I'm trying to say is that, under different circumstances, there are men in the Banner armies that you might like. They're just ordinary guys.'

'I know what you mean,' said Topaz.

Lara peered at him. 'You what?'

'It was the same with the settlers in the Sea Banner. Sure, there were assholes, but there were decent ones too; like the old master of the *Tranquillity*.'

'Right enough,' said Ryan.

'We have to think of the future,' Maddie went on. 'Sable can't possibly kill every single last member of the Banners, or the Sea Banner, for that matter. Many will survive, even if we drive the gods out of Dragon Eyre. And what about the million settlers who live here? Implacatus will abandon them if the gods withdraw, and both sides will have to live with each other. Somehow, the natives and the settlers have to find a way to get along; otherwise, this world will fall back into conflict.'

'She's right,' said Topaz.

'I knew you'd agree with her,' said Tilly.

'What's the alternative?' he said. 'That we keep killing each other, over and over, until the end of time? If, and it's still a big if, Sable manages to force the gods to leave Dragon Eyre, then we'll have to confront the situation on the Home Islands. Gyle, Ectus and Na Sun Ka are filled with settlers, and Alef and Throscala have plenty as well. Who's going to govern them? What laws will each island follow? The colonial constitution will have to be ripped up and thrown away, and about bleeding time. But, what will replace it?'

'Who cares?' muttered Dina.

'I do,' said Topaz. 'We have an opportunity to change this world for the better; to get rid of slavery, and to ensure that land is fairly apportioned among natives and settlers alike. These opportunities rarely come along, and future generations will curse us if we squander it.'

'Leave it to the dragons,' said Tilly. 'That's the traditional Dragon Eyre way.'

'And look at the trouble tradition has brought us,' said Topaz. 'We have Unk Tannic agents infiltrating Ulna, as well as several thousand Wystians who would love to occupy the entire Eastern Rim. This time, the humans have to be involved in the big decisions.'

Ryan grinned. 'It's been a while since I heard Topaz give one of his political rants; it's like being back on the bleeding *Tranquillity*.'

'Play a tune on your guitar to drown him out,' said Tilly, as she laughed.

'Pay no attention to these savages, Master,' said Lara.

'I haven't before,' he said, 'and I ain't going to start now.'

Maddie caught his glance. 'Walk?'

'Sure,' he said.

They stood, and squeezed past the people lining the long table. They passed through the tavern and stepped outside into the warm evening air. The tavern was a few streets back from the harbour, and the building had survived Lord Bastion's attack intact.

'Sorry about that,' he said, as they started walking. 'I get a bit carried away when I start talking about politics.'

'It's fine,' she said; 'I do, too. It's funny; I never used to care about that sort of thing when I was on my own world. I guess that being the Queen's rider has made me think about it a lot more. And I'm glad we agreed about the settlers. Now, I just have to work out how to steer Blackrose to the same opinion.'

He took her hand.

'We don't need to go back to the tavern,' she said.

'No? What did you have in mind?'

She stopped, and looked up at him. 'It's been nine days since I had you all to myself. What do you think I have in mind?'

The rest of the world seemed to vanish as he gazed down at her beautiful face.

'Come back to my apartment,' she said, 'and you can tell me how much you missed me.'

CHAPTER 24
OUT OF CONTROL

Riggan Archipelago – 15th Arginch 5255 (18th Gylean Year 6)

Austin felt someone shake his shoulder, and his eyes opened.

'Sable,' he groaned. 'What time is it?'

'Forget the time,' she said. 'Heal me.'

Austin sat up. The air inside the cave was cool, and he could barely see Sable crouching in front of him through the shadows. He reached out with a hand, and touched her arm. As soon as his skin made contact with hers, he sensed the wound on her right shoulder. Something sharp had torn through the woman's leather armour, and slashed a deep gouge just inches from her neck. He sent a burst of healing powers into her, and the wound closed.

Sable shuddered, then leaned back against the wall of the cavern, her breath slowing.

'Thanks,' she gasped.

'Dragon injury?'

'Yes.'

'Have you been up all night?'

Next to them, Ashfall stirred. She opened her eyes and glanced around the inside of the cave.

'It is not yet dawn,' said the dragon. 'Are you starting early today, Holdfast, on this, the last day of Austin's service to you?'

Sable lit a cigarette.

'Answer me,' said Ashfall.

'Stop nagging,' said Sable. 'I was going to wake up Austin when the sun rose, but I needed him to fix a minor injury I picked up on Wyst.'

'You were on Wyst without me?' said Austin.

'I was,' she said. 'I didn't need your help to transport dragons from one side of Dragon Eyre to the other. Well, not until I got injured.'

'That's two nights in a row you haven't slept,' said Austin. 'You must be exhausted. Is that why you got injured?'

'No. I was just a little sloppy on my last trip,' she said.

Ashfall raised her head. 'How many trips have you made, Holdfast?'

'Eight,' said Sable. 'I have deposited thirty-five dragons on Ectus, thirty-one on Na Sun Ka, and fifty-nine on Gyle. I was going to do one more run, when a small red dragon took exception to being awoken from its slumber on Wyst.' She laughed. 'He was so small that I hadn't noticed him, but his claws were sharp enough. That will have to do for Wyst, for now, at any rate. The island is in an uproar.'

'I'm not surprised,' said Ashfall. 'You have stolen nearly two hundred dragons from their homes in less than two days. How many have died?'

Sable shrugged. 'I have no idea. There are no gods currently on Ectus, but there are still a couple on Na Sun Ka capable of killing a dragon or two. Does it matter? The Home Islands are burning.'

'It sounds as though you don't need Austin any more.'

'I won't, after today.'

Ashfall eyed her with suspicion.

'I mean it,' said Sable. 'This is his last day. If I wanted to, I could go into your minds, and scrub out every memory of me promising to take Austin back to Implacatus. I could make you believe that Austin had pledged to serve me forever. I haven't done any such thing, and you still don't trust me.'

'That doesn't change the fact that you broke your word,' said the dragon. 'Austin should be beginning the search for his mother today.'

'I will take him back tomorrow,' said Sable.

'Be sure that you do so.'

'Don't argue,' said Austin. 'Let's just get it over with.' He yawned, and stretched his arms. 'I'm up now; should we get started?'

Sable nodded, then rummaged around in a pack that sat on the stone floor of the cave.

'Are you looking for food?' said Austin.

'Not quite,' she said, her fingers grasping a leather pouch. She opened it, and took out a weedstick. 'This is the last of the damn keen-weed,' she said; 'at least until I can go back to Udall and buy some more.' She stubbed out the cigarette, and lit the weedstick.

Austin frowned. 'Is this how you've managed to stay awake for so long?'

'Yup,' said Sable.

'You'll pay for it,' he said. 'You'll sleep for days when the effects wear off.'

'I'm a big girl, Austin. I know what I'm doing.'

A faint glimmer of dawn light entered the cave through the narrow entrance, and Austin could see the Holdfast woman more clearly. Her eyes were heavy, and she looked as though she was carrying the weight of the world on her shoulders. He reached into a corner of the cave, and pulled out the bag containing their food supplies.

'I'll make some breakfast,' he said. 'Do you want some?'

Sable shook her head.

'When did you last eat?'

'I can't remember.'

'You need to eat something,' he said. 'Even an apple would do.'

'The thought of food makes me want to throw up,' she said. 'Have your breakfast, and then we'll go.'

Austin prepared a small bowl of fruit, nuts and dried olives, as Sable smoked. He was partly to blame for her condition, he thought. She had been racing to do as much as possible, in order to make the best use of his last day working for her, and the strain was showing.

He began to eat. 'What's the plan?'

'We're going to shift our focus away from Wyst,' she said.

'Praise the gods for that,' he said. 'We're playing a risky game with the dragons.'

'Oh, there will be dragons involved,' she said; 'but this time, we're going to intervene directly in the conflict threatening Ulna's northern borders.'

'Are you striving to restore your reputation with Queen Blackrose?' said Ashfall.

'Not particularly,' said Sable. 'Helping her is just a side effect. Still, it will be a useful side effect, if it means that I can safely return to Udall.'

'Are you going to change your armour?' said Austin, glancing at the gouge ripped through the leather on her right shoulder.

'This is the only set I have,' she said, 'apart from the steel armour, which just weighs me down. It'll do.'

Austin filled two mugs with wine, and passed one to Sable. Within a couple of days, he could be drinking wine on Implacatus, he thought, trying to imagine what that would be like. He would have to learn all about Serene, a city that he only knew vaguely, having spent most of his youth up in Cumulus with the majority of the gods. Now that he was so close to going home, he was starting to feel nervous about it. It was only for a few days, he told himself, then he would be back in Dragon Eyre, his mother by his side, as they prepared to start a new life on Ulna.

They drained the contents of the two mugs, and Austin pulled his boots on. The daylight from outside was growing stronger, and Sable sat by the entrance, gazing down at the ocean.

'Take great care, Austin,' said Ashfall.

'I will,' he said, standing. 'I'm ready, Sable.'

She turned and nodded. She stood next to him, and activated the Quadrant. Their surroundings shimmered, and they found themselves standing on a thickly-forested hillside, as the sun rose to their right.

'Where are we?' said Austin.

'We are on the eastern tip of Enna,' she said. She pointed into a deep ravine. 'The last Ennan dragons have been chased all the way here, out-numbered and out-fought by the Wystians. If we don't do something, then Wyst will have won, and Enna will be theirs. Come on; let's go and introduce ourselves.'

They set off down the slope, following a rough track that wound its way down towards the ravine. A river ran through the middle of the steep valley, and they waded through it to reach a line of caves on the far bank.

'Go no further!' cried a voice from the shadows. 'One more step, and you will die.'

Austin raised his arms, to show that he was unarmed. The bushes by the entrance to the caves rustled, and he saw a group of humans with crossbows.

'We are here to help,' said Sable. 'We have come to fight the Wystians, on your behalf.'

A dragon's long neck poked out of a cave. 'What do you want, strangers?'

'I want to speak to the Ennan leadership,' said Sable. 'The Wystians are camped only a few miles west of here.'

'We are aware of that,' said the dragon. 'Who are you?'

'My name is Sable Holdfast.'

The dragon and humans stared at her.

'You know what I can do,' Sable said. 'And today is your lucky day. By nightfall, Enna will be yours once more. May I come in and speak to you?'

The dragon said nothing for a moment, then he tilted his head. 'Enter.'

Sable and Austin walked up the steep bank of the river, and passed through the humans guarding the entrance. The dragon led them into a network of wide tunnels, until they reached an enormous cavern, packed with dragons and hungry, desperate-looking humans. The cavern fell into silence as soon as Sable and Austin walked in.

'Behold,' said the dragon who had met them at the entrance; 'Sable Holdfast, and her immortal companion.'

Austin felt a hundred pairs of eyes bore into him. An elderly green dragon strode forwards. He sniffed Sable, his black eyes wide and glowing.

'What business do you have here, humans?' he said.

'I have come to tell you my plans,' said Sable, 'as a courtesy. For over a month, the dragons of Wyst have been ravaging and conquering your territory. That ends today. I shall remove a hundred of the Wystians from Enna by nightfall; you should be prepared.'

The dragons glanced at each other.

'You are going to kill one hundred Wystians, human?' said the old green dragon.

'I didn't say anything about killing them,' said Sable, 'though some will likely die.' She brandished the Quadrant. 'I am going to transport the dragons, far from Enna, and use them to fight the last of the Banner forces in the Western Rim.'

'Did Queen Blackrose send you? We appealed for her aid when the Wystians first arrived, after they had subjugated Geist. She did nothing to help us. Port Talbot is in ruins, and thousands of humans have already perished in the conflict, incinerated or torn to pieces by the Wystians – and now you decide to help us? It is a little late.'

'I can only be in one place at a time, dragons of Enna,' said Sable, 'and I have been fighting all over Dragon Eyre. The hour is late, but Enna is not yet defeated. With my aid, you will be able to retake your island realm, and hold it. The Wystians shall not trouble you again; I'll make sure of it.'

'The rumours of your arrogance are not unfounded, it seems,' said the old green dragon. 'However, such are our troubles that I accept your offer, Holdfast witch. There are sixty Wystian dragons advancing towards this position, with further reserves based upon the mountains in the centre of Enna.'

'I know,' said Sable. 'I have undertaken a detailed survey of this island. I will deal with the closest sixty first, before turning to the mountains. Send a messenger to Ulna; many Ennan refugees there will soon be able to return to their homes.' She glanced at Austin. 'Let's go.'

She triggered the Quadrant, and Austin found himself on another hillside, surrounded by pine trees. The day was starting to warm up as they walked along a high ridge, then Sable signalled for silence, and they crept forwards another few yards. Sable crouched down, and peered over the crest of the ridge. Austin joined her, and saw a large group of dragons resting at the bottom of the hill, by the banks of a wide stream. Austin's eyes widened. Each dragon was huge, and battle-scarred. A pile of scorched human bones lay heaped amid the trees next to the clearing where the dragons lay. Austin counted the skulls that he could see, then realised that at least a hundred humans had been consumed by the Wystians.

'These are the veterans,' Sable whispered; 'Wyst's frontline soldiers in the war. They'll be more effective than the juveniles and others I've been taking before now. Keep your flow powers ready; I somehow doubt that they'll enjoy being abducted.'

She gestured to him, and they crept down the side of the ridge, keeping to the thick undergrowth. Austin's arm brushed past a thorn bush, and every dragon turned their heads at the noise.

Sable sprang to her feet, her eyes staring at the dragons. A few remained motionless, but several of the larger ones cried out in alarm, as Sable tried to control their thoughts. She swiped her fingers over the Quadrant, and pulled twenty-three of the Wystians with her, along with Austin. They appeared among the smoking ruins of a large city. Austin had no idea where they were, but then he noticed a row of enormous temples, and realised that they were in Sun Ta, on the island of Na Sun Ka.

Three seconds later, they were back on the forested hillside on Enna.

Sable sat down, looking worn out.

'Some of those bastards were too strong to manipulate,' she muttered. 'One at a time would be no problem, but together? Shit.'

A tumult arose from over the edge of the ridge, of angry dragons, outraged by what had happened. One of them flew up over the side of the mountain, calling out curses upon the name of Sable Holdfast. Her head glanced down, and she saw the two humans sheltering among the undergrowth.

'The witch is here!' the dragon cried. 'She's here!'

The dragon opened her jaws, and Austin sent a blast of flow powers in her direction. The dragon's scream cut off short, as blood exploded from her eyes. Sable grabbed his arm, and they ran to the side as the dragon crashed into the thick undergrowth. The huge body ploughed through the ground, felling trees on either side. Sable leapt over the crest of the ridge, as Austin stumbled after her.

When he fell, he landed on solid paving slabs, skinning his knee. He glanced up, and realised he was in Sabat City on Ectus, along with a further twenty-six Wystian dragons, all transported in the blink of an eye. Most were still airborne, and all were angry. Flames roared down at the two humans from the sky, and Sable triggered the Quadrant again, taking her and Austin back to Enna.

She panted, and leaned against a tree.

Austin pulled himself up, his eyes staring in every direction.

'We're a few miles from the dragon camp,' said Sable. 'The dozen or so left behind will be scattering by now. You know, it's a lot easier when they're sleeping.'

'You've broken your oath,' he said.

She frowned at him.

'You said that you would leave the settlers alone,' he went on. 'Those huge Wystian dragons won't care who they kill, Sable. Right now, both cities will be under attack – Sun Ta and Sabat City.'

Sable nodded, her eyes heavy. 'It was unavoidable. I can't control that many dragons at the same time, especially ones so strong. As long as they slaughter the Banner forces, then the price is worth paying.'

'Tell that to the families on Na Sun Ka and Ectus.'

'Don't take that tone with me; I'm doing what has to be done.'

'You're exhausted, and you're making mistakes.'

Sable looked away. 'The caves where the majority of the Wystians are gathered lie thirty miles to the west of here. We should hurry, to make sure we get there before the others arrive in time to warn them.'

'Are you joking?' said Austin. 'Haven't we done enough?'

'No. Nowhere near enough.'

She triggered the Quadrant before Austin could say anything else, and they found themselves in a dark tunnel that stank of dragon. Austin opened his mouth, but Sable placed a finger on his lips, and shook her head. They stole forwards, heading in the direction of a dim glow, and came to a vast cavern, its ceiling supported by thick pillars of stone. Inside, dozens of massive dragons were sleeping, or resting. A few were grooming each other, or rooting through piles of bones for any leftover meat. Sable crouched down on the ground, and stared out into the cavern for several minutes, her eyes going from dragon to dragon. When she had finished, every dragon in the cavern was slumbering.

'Stay here,' she whispered, then she vanished, along with thirty of the sleeping beasts.

Austin stared into the cavern. Despite losing so many of their number, the other dragons continued to sleep. Then, in the far corner, a large brown dragon cracked open an eye, and raised his head. He gazed around the cavern for a moment, then stood, his eyes burning.

Sable re-appeared by Austin's side, and he jumped.

'Intruders!' cried the large brown dragon. 'Insects in our home!'

Sable's eyes widened, then she activated the Quadrant again, taking a further two dozen dragons with her, including the large brown one. Austin threw himself to the tunnel floor, trying to remain unseen as the rest of the dragons awoke.

'The Holdfast witch was here!' shouted a massive brute of a dragon, with scars down his face and flanks. 'We are betrayed!'

A purple dragon sniffed the ground, then looked up, and saw Austin lying in the tunnel.

'Here is her god helper!' she cried. 'The witch has abandoned him.'

Several huge dragons charged towards Austin. He raised his right hand, and brought down the closest one. Momentum carried it forward, and the enormous dragon crashed into the side of the cavern, battering into the tunnel entrance. Rocks rained down onto Austin, and he wriggled backwards. A burst of flames lit up the entrance to the tunnel, and the rocks glowed red hot as the dragons tried to get to him. Austin got to his feet, and sprinted down the tunnel, as the dead dragon was hauled away. A torrent of flames filled the tunnel, catching Austin as he ran. Heat overwhelmed him, and he stumbled, the flames enveloping his body. He crawled on a few paces, then collapsed, his self-healing soothing his scorched skin. One more blast of flames, and it would be over, and he waited for the end.

Nothing happened. He listened, but no sounds were coming from the cavern. With time to heal himself, Austin remained still for a few more minutes, as the pain eased, and his skin reformed over the patches that had been burnt. He slowly got to his knees, and turned his head. The tunnel entrance was clear, and silent. He crept towards the cavern, using a hand against a wall to guide his steps, then gazed through the entrance. The cavern was empty.

Sable appeared by his side. She glanced at his scorched clothes, then at the body of the huge dragon he had killed.

'Where did you take them all?' Austin said.

'Gyle.'

'How many?'

'Almost ninety. Added to the fifty I took from the forward camp, I've more than fulfilled the pledge I made to the Ennan dragons. With just a few scattered outposts of Wystians left on Enna, they should be able to retake their island.'

'Are we done?'

Sable sat on a rock and lit a cigarette. 'No. We're going to Gyle, to coordinate the Wystians' attack. I just need to smoke this first.'

'You look like you're about to collapse.'

'Are you saying that I shouldn't try to control the ninety dragons currently in Port Edmond?'

'You took them to Port Edmond?'

She nodded. 'Right to the heart of the colonial government. I estimate that there are still sixty or seventy dragons in the farmlands of Gyle. With an extra ninety in Port Edmond, the defences will be overwhelmed. It's been a bad couple of days for the Banners.'

'And for everyone else on Gyle.'

'I know what you think of me, Austin. It's impossible to destroy the Banners and government without a few civilian casualties. But, that is what I am about to try. If I can direct the Wystians onto military targets, then the civilians will have a chance to evacuate the city.'

'And go where? As you said, there are still plenty of dragons roaming the countryside, hunting at will.'

'I'm doing my best.'

'You are a whirlwind, Sable. You have scoured this world from east to west. Is that how you want history to remember you – as a mass murderer, in the same league as someone like Lord Sabat?'

'Who cares about Lord Sabat? I want to be in the same league as the other Holdfasts. No, I want to be better than them. I'm already better than them; I killed an Ascendant. We're nearing the end of the road, Austin. Come with me to Port Edmond, and then your part will be over; and I can finally sleep.'

She stubbed out her cigarette, and stood. She gazed at the Quadrant in her hands, and swayed, as if about to collapse; then she swept her fingers across its surface, and the air shimmered.

They appeared on the roof of a high building, with the Winter Palace less than half a mile away. Dozens of dragons were swooping over Port Edmond, sending flames down into the streets and houses, and a large portion of the city was burning. Thick columns of black smoke were rising into the blue skies above Port Edmond, and the noise of people screaming competed with the sound of the raging conflagrations ripping through the city's buildings. In the distance, the ships in the enormous harbour were also burning, as dragons soared down again and again.

Sable walked to the edge of the building, and gazed out at the destruction.

'What have I done?' she said.

Austin joined her, but remained silent.

Sable pointed towards a small plaza to their right. The buildings surrounding it were on fire, and the fountain in the centre was scorched and blackened.

'My little café,' she said. 'I drank wine and ate cakes there with Millen, back when I thought I was going to be the saviour of this world. Now, I am its destroyer.'

A dragon swooped low over the roof where they were standing, and banked.

'That one saw us,' said Austin.

Sable stared up, and the dragon pulled away from the roof, and turned back towards the Winter Palace. Sable staggered from the effort.

'I... I'm too tired to control them all,' she gasped.

Austin said nothing, his eyes on the Winter Palace in the distance. Flames were coming from one level, the windows on that floor blown out, and over a dozen dragons were circling overhead, attacking at will. Austin squinted. A figure had appeared on the roof of the palace.

'Sable,' he said, pointing, 'is that Bastion?'

She glanced up. 'Yes.'

A dragon above the palace cried out in agony, and fell, its death wail echoing off the burning buildings of the city. The dragon crashed into the gardens behind the palace, just as another one screamed in pain.

'Stay here,' said Sable, drawing her sword.

'Don't be a fool,' said Austin. 'You're exhausted; Bastion will kill you.'

'So?' Sable cried, her eyes wild. 'Look what I've done! Thousands are already dead, and thousands more will die before this day is over – because of me! I have brought this world to its knees, as I promised I would, but doing so has turned me into a monster. Listen to the people scream, Austin; do you hear the children among them? They're dying, and it's my fault. I deserve to die with them.'

'No,' said Austin, raising his palms towards her. 'You're not thinking straight.'

'You just want to go back to Implacatus; you don't care about me.'

'That's not true. I need you to take me to Serene, but I don't want you to throw your life away.'

Sable turned her face, and stared at the roof of the Winter Palace. 'The bastard's laughing at me. He knows I'm here; he wants me to see him. I can't stop now. Don't you get it, Austin? This is where it all leads; this is where it ends.'

Austin lunged forwards, knocking the Quadrant from Sable's grip. The copper-coloured device skittered across the roof tiles, as Sable clenched her fist and punched Austin. Her blow struck the side of his head, but he was heavier than she was, and they fell to the roof. He closed his eyes, to prevent her from invading his mind, and she punched him again, in the stomach. He groaned, and she wriggled free. He opened his eyes as Sable leapt for the Quadrant, and he grabbed hold of her leg, and pulled her away from the device.

'Don't make me kill you,' Sable cried.

'If you want to die at Bastion's hands,' he grunted, 'then you'll have to kill me. I'm not going to let you do it, Sable.'

He dived over her, and clutched the Quadrant in his hands, then sat with his eyes closed, waiting for her to attack him. He heard nothing for a moment, then the sound of sobbing reached his ears. He glanced at Sable. She was sitting on the roof, weeping, her face a mixture of exhaustion and regret.

'Let's go home,' he said. 'Back to Ashfall and the others. There's nothing we can do for Port Edmond.'

'He's gone,' she said.

'What?'

'Lord Bastion – he's gone.'

Austin glanced back at the roof of the Winter Palace, but no figure was standing there.

'I missed my chance,' Sable went on.

'Your chance to die? Do you really want to die? What about Lara, and Maddie? There are people on this world who love you, Sable.'

'I don't deserve their love.'

'Then remember forgiveness. You want Karalyn to forgive you, yes?

You'll have to stay alive for that to happen. Don't give up, Sable; not now.'

She bowed her head. An explosion ripped through a building fifty yards behind them, and the ground shook. More smoke was rising from the city and, without Bastion to defend the palace, the dragons were renewing their massed attack.

Sable held out her hand, and Austin passed her the Quadrant. She swiped her fingers over the surface, and they appeared back in the Riggan archipelago, where a warm wind was blowing off the ocean.

'Austin!' cried Ashfall. 'What happened to your clothes?'

'A Wystian dragon burnt them,' he said.

Ashfall's eyes darkened. 'Holdfast; tell me that Austin's role in this madness is finally over.'

Sable nodded. 'He's free. I'll take him back to Implacatus tomorrow.'

Austin got to his feet, and gazed around. Millen and Deepblue were also on the hillside, and both were glancing at Sable.

'What did you do?' said Millen.

'We saved Enna,' said Austin, 'and then we destroyed Port Edmond. The capital of the Home Islands is burning, along with its inhabitants.'

The Holdfast woman turned and stared out to sea, then she toppled over, hitting the grass by the side of the track. Austin ran to her side and crouched by her.

'What's wrong with her?' said Deepblue. 'Is she injured?'

'She needs to sleep,' Austin said. 'Her body has reached its limit.'

'It is not her body that concerns me, Austin,' said Ashfall. 'Sable Holdfast looks close to insanity. Will her mind recover?'

'Give her some space,' said Austin. 'Millen, help me carry her to the caves.'

'I notice that you did not answer my question,' said Ashfall, as Millen hurried over.

Austin glanced up into the slender grey dragon's eyes. 'I don't have an answer, Ashfall.'

'Can you heal her mind?' said Millen, as they lifted Sable from the grass.

'I can only heal physical wounds,' said Austin. 'I cannot remove guilt or regret. I cannot make her happy.'

'Only Badblood made her happy,' said Deepblue.

'If she has lost her mind, then we are all at risk,' said Ashfall. 'I dread what will happen when she wakes up.'

'I will remain with her until then,' said Austin.

'And afterwards?' said Deepblue.

Austin said nothing. He and Millen carried Sable across the side of the hill, as the two dragons watched in silence, their eyes never leaving the Ascendant-killer.

CHAPTER 25
WORDS AND ACTIONS

U dall, Ulna, Eastern Rim – 16th Arginch 5255 (18th Gylean Year 6)
Maddie stretched as sunlight flooded her bedroom. Topaz was going from window to window, flinging open the shutters, while he whistled a nautical tune.

'Is it time to get up?' she said.

'It's an hour past sunrise, if that's what you mean,' he said.

'You need to learn how to enjoy a good lie-in,' she said. 'You're not on a ship.'

'No, I'm not,' he said, 'and I have no idea when I'll next be heading out to sea. All the same, I can't sleep once the sun is up; not unless I've been on the night watch.' He glanced at the small table next to the main windows. 'I made you breakfast.'

She smiled. 'Bring it over.'

'I just cleaned the bed sheets yesterday,' he said; 'you're not messing them up with breakfast. Sit at the table.'

Maddie groaned. 'It's just my luck to find a man who's obsessed with everything being neat and tidy. I hardly even recognise my room.'

'I cleaned up while you were sleeping,' he said. 'I can't handle mess; sorry. Too many years at sea.'

She sat up in bed, and rubbed her face. 'Is there coffee?'

He smiled. 'Freshly brewed.'

'And what about the food? Did you remember that I don't eat meat?'

'Of course I remembered. You're the only person I've met who doesn't eat meat.'

She got out of bed, and pulled on a dressing gown. She felt a little self-conscious about him seeing her naked in broad daylight. She hadn't cared the previous evening, not after a few bottles of wine, but it seemed different in the daytime. She wandered over to the table, yawned, then sat. Topaz sat down opposite her, and filled her mug with black coffee.

'Eggs, beans and toast,' he said. 'It's quite hard to think of a meatless breakfast, and the food here is different from Olkis, which you probably remember. If there had been oats, I would have made you porridge, but I don't think they grow them here.'

'This looks great,' she said, picking up her mug of coffee. 'My head hurts.'

'That's probably from the gin.'

'We had gin?'

'Yeah, after we ran out of wine.'

She sipped her coffee. 'Is this apartment big enough for both of us, do you think?'

'I'm used to tiny cabins, or no cabin at all. This seems enormous in comparison. And the view is amazing.' He glanced out of the window. 'You can see the top of the *Gull's* masts from here.'

She nodded. 'Do you ever, um... consider what else you could do? I mean something that doesn't involve going to sea?'

'Not really. Why would I?'

'For me?' she said. 'Imagine it was the other way around. Would you be happy to stay in the palace while I went off sailing two or three times a month?'

'No, but I'm not the Queen's rider. You're needed here; I wouldn't be.'

'Fine; but you know what I mean.'

'I've never tried to hide the fact that I love what I do,' he said. 'If you made me choose between being with you, and being a sailor, then I would choose you. But, that kind of ultimatum seems a little drastic, especially now that I'm no longer a pirate, and my job is a bit safer than before. After a few dull patrols, I might decide that I prefer it on land.'

'Really?'

He shrugged. 'Maybe.'

She sighed. 'I doubt it, Topaz. I reckon that you would be happy in a rowing boat.'

'Am I that transparent?' he said, laughing. 'You know, I had a read of the contract that Lord Greysteel negotiated. As a master, I'm in line to receive a hefty wage. Even better, I get paid whether the *Gull* is at sea or not; in fact, I'm getting paid for sitting here eating breakfast with you. I'll probably end up saving a lot of it, to tide me over once I do decide to quit sailing.'

'What if Lara decides to go back to Olkis after a year?'

'If we're still together, then I'll stay here, and get a place on another local ship.'

'What do you mean *if* we're still together? Do you think we're going to split up?'

'No, but the future is impossible to predict. I think, and hope, that we'll be together forever, Maddie. That's what I want.'

Maddie put down her fork and pushed the empty plate away from her. She glanced at Topaz, and knew that she wanted the same thing.

'What are your thoughts on children?' she said.

'What, right now?' he said.

'In a few years, say.'

'I'd like a couple. As long as I was a better parent than my own mother and father. I've never had a secure, happy family life, and I worry that I might not be up to the job.'

'You'd be fine,' she said; 'better than fine.'

'What was it like, growing up with a mum and a dad who cared about you?'

'It was great, but I didn't appreciate it enough at the time, and I never got to say goodbye to my parents before they were killed. The last time we met, we argued, over Blackrose, mostly, and we parted in anger. I regret that now. I wish I'd told them about Blackrose, but I was sworn to secrecy, and so I didn't. They couldn't understand why I didn't want to go home with them. If I could change one thing, it would be that. I also wish I could see my brother and sister again. We squabbled constantly while I was living with my parents, but I miss them, especially Rosie. She'll be eighteen by now – a young woman, and I'd love to know what she was doing.'

Topaz opened his mouth, but before he could speak, someone knocked on the front door of the apartment.

'Are you expecting visitors?' he said.

'No,' she said. 'Maybe if we ignore it, they'll go away.'

The door was rapped again.

Maddie sighed and got to her feet. She walked out of the bedroom and into the main chamber of the apartment. She slid the lock free, and opened the door.

Ahi'edo glanced at her dressing gown.

'Yes?' said Maddie.

'Shadowblaze sent me,' Ahi'edo said. 'He wants me to spend more time with you.'

'It's a little early, don't you think?'

'Shadowblaze and I were out flying, and we saw that your shutters were open. He wanted to be alone with the Queen, so he suggested that I visit you. And by "suggested", I mean he ordered me to come round. Do you want to go for a walk, or something?'

'I have company.'

'You mean the sailor?'

'Yes, Ahi'edo, the sailor. He has a name, you know.'

'He can come for a walk too.'

Maddie thought about sending him away. It was what she wanted to do, but she worried that Ahi'edo would get in trouble.

She opened the door more fully. 'Come in, then. You can have some coffee while I get dressed.'

She led Ahi'edo into the main chamber, and gestured to a seat, then she walked back into her bedroom. Topaz glanced at her.

'Could you talk to Ahi'edo for a bit,' she said, 'while I get some clothes on?'

Topaz frowned. 'Ahi'edo's here?'

'Yes. He was ordered to be my friend by Shadowblaze, apparently. Take him some coffee, and try not to argue with him. I'll just be a few minutes.'

Topaz got to his feet, the expression on his face betraying how he felt about having to speak to a man who hated him. He loaded a tray with mugs and the coffee pot, then strode through to the main room of the apartment. Maddie listened for a moment, then dressed as quickly as possible. Ahi'edo had mentioned a walk, so she put on clothes that would be suitable for a stroll around Udall, then sat by her dresser and brushed the tangles out of her hair. She wondered why Shadowblaze was adamant that they become friends. Blackrose rarely brought up Ahi'edo with her, and never suggested that they spend more time together. Either Shadowblaze disapproved of Topaz, and was trying to edge him out, or the dragon was so sick of Ahi'edo's company that he was using Maddie as an excuse to get rid of him for long periods of time.

She gazed at her reflection for a moment, then got to her feet and walked into the main room. It was empty. She frowned, then noticed that Topaz and Ahi'edo were out on the balcony. She opened the door and walked out into the warm sunshine. The two men were sitting by a table in an uneasy silence, while Topaz smoked a cigarette, and they glanced up as Maddie approached.

She raised an eyebrow, then took a seat at the table. 'I suppose silence is better than fighting each other. So, what shall we do?'

'I'm happy here,' said Topaz, 'but we could go for a walk down to the harbour if you want. I have a couple of messages I could pass on to the crew of the *Patience* while we're there.'

'The harbour's a mess,' said Ahi'edo. 'Had you not noticed?'

'The Five Sisters have lent out over three hundred men to assist in the clear up,' said Topaz. 'We noticed.'

'And who's keeping an eye on the crews while they clean up?' said Ahi'edo. 'We all know pirates are thieves. I mean, that's what pirates do – they steal from people.'

Maddie glanced at Topaz, half-expecting him to explode with anger, but the sailor just smiled.

'They have a new contract,' she said to Ahi'edo.

'I know,' he said. 'At a stroke, the Queen has forgiven decades of murder, plundering and robbery, but people don't change. The first chance they get, they'll go back to their old ways. Just wait and see.'

'I'm not sure you understand how ships operate,' said Topaz. 'If the captain of a vessel gives an order, the crew obey; and it's the captains who have signed the contract.'

'There are two problems with that,' said Ahi'edo. 'First, I'll bet at least half of the crews disagree with the new contract. Olkians are born thieves; everyone knows it. And second, what's to stop one of the captains from pretending to honour the contract while they'll in Udall, only to rob the first ship that they come across in open waters?'

A flash of anger passed over Topaz's face, but instead of responding, he took a draw on his cigarette, and gazed out at the view.

'You've never even been to Olkis, Ahi'edo,' said Maddie. 'They're not all thieves.'

'That's right,' he said; 'you were there, weren't you? And why were you there? Let me see... Oh, yes, it was because an Olkian stole you from this very palace. And then, one of them tried to sell you into slavery. The Olkians care about money, and not much else.'

'I'm not going to defend Olo'osso,' said Topaz. 'What he did was wrong, and we stopped him. And there are plenty of problems on Olkis that need fixing; but the people there are just like any other folk. There are idiots on every island on Dragon Eyre, as well as kind and generous people; but two decades of occupation by Banner soldiers has been hard to live with. The Olkians have suffered a lot.'

Ahi'edo snorted. 'You had soldiers – we had greenhides. Ulna lost four out of every five of its population; don't lecture me on suffering.'

'This is exactly what the colonial authorities want,' said Topaz, 'for folk from the different realms to fight each other, instead of uniting. For too long, the Western and Eastern Rims have been rivals, but we shouldn't let the gods and Banner soldiers divide us.'

'The Western Rim has always thought that they're better than us,' said Ahi'edo. 'To you, we are all simple, rustic peasants, who need to be guided by our betters.'

'The people on Gyle used to think the same about Olkians,' said Topaz. 'Alright, many Olkians are noisy and brash, while folk here are more reserved, but deep down, we're all the same.'

Ahi'edo eyes bulged. 'We are not the same! Ulnans have honour, and respect, while Olkians would cut your throat for a few coins.'

'Fair enough,' said Topaz. 'I don't want to sit here and bicker with you, Ahi'edo. I'm sorry that you feel the way you do about Olkis, but you should know that I don't harbour any ill will towards the Eastern Rim.'

'You're only saying that because Maddie's here,' said Ahi'edo.

Topaz glanced at Maddie and shrugged, as if to say – I tried.

'Everyone hates the settlers,' Ahi'edo went on, 'because they enslaved so many natives on Dragon Eyre. But slavery also exists in Olkis, doesn't it?'

'Yes,' said Topaz.

'And, you have to admit, piracy has greatly contributed to the trade in slaves?'

'Yes.'

'And the Five Sisters have also been involved in abducting and selling natives as slaves?'

'Not any more,' said Topaz.

'Do you expect me to believe that?' said Ahi'edo. 'Slavery is deeply ingrained in Olkian culture. I heard that some people are so cruel and savage, that they even sell their own children into slavery. What kind of animals could do that?'

'That's enough,' said Maddie. 'Ahi'edo, I think you should leave.'

Ahi'edo glared at her. 'Why? I'm telling the truth; it's not my fault if your sailor friend can't deal with it.'

'My mother sold me into slavery when I was seven,' said Topaz.

For a brief moment, the glare on Ahi'edo's face almost cracked, then he sneered at Topaz. 'And you think you're worthy to be Maddie's partner? She's the Queen's rider, and you were a slave?'

Maddie stood, and pointed at the door. 'Out.'

'Oh, I'm going,' said Ahi'edo, getting to his feet. 'In time, Maddie, you'll come to your senses and realise what a mistake you're making by getting involved with an Olkian. They're thieves, and thieves cannot be trusted.'

He stormed out from the balcony, and the sound of the front door of the apartment slamming came a moment later.

'Sorry about that,' said Maddie.

Topaz glanced at her. 'It's not your fault. A lot of what he said was right, unfortunately. The Olkians have a bad reputation on Dragon Eyre, for slavery, violence and piracy. I'm not surprised that he has doubts.'

'I thought you were going to lose your temper with him.'

'What's the point? I've heard it all before, especially when I was in the Sea Banner. A lot of the settlers serving in the Eastern Fleet said the same things to me over the years. Some Olkians like to think of themselves as loveable rogues; while the rest of the world sees us as devious and shifty. Just like how we see the Ulnans as uptight and unfriendly, while they see themselves as honourable. If we had stuck together at the time of the invasion, then we might not have been so easily conquered, but then, as now, we're hopelessly divided.'

There was a loud knock on the front door.

Maddie sighed. 'Is Ahi'edo back already?'

Topaz stood. 'He didn't knock like that the last time he was here. Should I answer it?'

'If you want,' she said. 'I could do with another coffee out here. If it's Ahi'edo, send him away, unless he's here to apologise.'

Topaz disappeared through the balcony doors, and Maddie poured a fresh mug of coffee from the pot on the table. She heard a few words being exchanged from within the apartment, then turned to look out over the view of the town.

'Maddie,' yelled Topaz; 'it's the palace militia for you.'

She frowned, and got to her feet. She walked through to the main room, and saw three men standing by the entrance to the apartment.

'This won't take a moment, ma'am,' said one of the men, who was wearing an officer's badge. 'May we come in?'

'Sure,' said Maddie. 'What is it?'

The three men entered the room, and one of them closed the door behind them.

'We have been asked to root out any possible Unk Tannic agents that might have infiltrated the palace,' said the militia officer. 'We have a few questions, about any suspicious activity that you may have seen.'

'Would you like some coffee?' said Topaz.

'That would be wonderful, thank you,' said the officer.

Topaz nodded, and turned towards the balcony. The officer raised his crossbow, and drove it down, striking the back of Topaz's head with the wooden stock of the weapon. Topaz's knees buckled, and he went down, knocking over a small table.

'Don't scream,' said the officer, as the other two militia guards pointed their crossbows at Maddie. 'Don't make any sound.' He gestured to one of the men. 'Send the signal.'

'Yes, sir,' said the man. He ran out onto the balcony, and began waving down to someone in the street outside.

Maddie crouched by Topaz. He was still conscious, but his head was bleeding, and he was groaning in pain next to the broken table.

'What do you want?' she said.

The officer struck her with the back of his hand. 'I told you to be quiet.'

Topaz rolled onto his front and sprang up at the militia guards. His left hand grabbed the crossbow of the guard standing next to the officer, and he punched the man in the face with his right fist. The guard cried out, and Topaz wrestled him to the ground. He gripped the man's throat, and rammed his head off the marble flooring, knocking him out. The officer placed his bow next to Maddie's throat.

'Back off,' he cried, 'or I'll kill her.'

Topaz released the guard's throat, and raised his hands, his eyes on the officer's bow.

The other guard came back in from the balcony. He glanced at his unconscious comrade on the floor, then pointed his bow at Topaz.

'Should I kill him, sir?' he said. 'It's the girl that we want.'

'Not yet,' said the officer. 'The boss might want to interrogate him first.'

'What boss?' said Maddie. 'Who are you working for?'

The officer smiled. 'Surely, you can guess? Even that half-witted Banner captain could tell we were Unk Tannic. He was about to expose us when that fool Olo'osso killed him.' He snapped his fingers. 'Move them all into the bedroom. We wouldn't want any dragon flying past to glance through the window, now, would we?'

The officer herded Topaz and Maddie into the bedroom at the point of his crossbow, while the other guard dragged his comrade through and set him down on the floor.

'Close the shutters,' said the officer.

The room fell into shadows as the guard went round the room, sealing up every window. A sound came from the front door, and then a man walked into the bedroom, wearing a long cloak with a hood.

'Maddie Jackdaw,' he said. 'We meet again.'

He pulled back the hood, but Maddie had already recognised the man's voice.

'You dare return to Udall, Ata'nix?' she said. 'You'll never make it out alive.'

The Unk Tannic leader laughed. 'As long as Sable Holdfast isn't here, we're safe enough. The dragons suspect nothing, and the militia was frighteningly easy to infiltrate.' He glanced at Topaz. 'You? I'd heard that Miss Jackdaw had fallen for a sailor, but I didn't know it was you, Oto'pazzi.'

'You should run, while you still have the chance,' said Topaz. 'No one in Ulna wants you here.'

'They shall,' said Ata'nix, 'once the established order on this world has utterly collapsed. Sable Holdfast's deranged campaign of destruction has driven the occupation forces to the brink of annihilation, and the Unk Tannic are ready to step into the chaos that will follow. Queen Blackrose remains our chief obstacle, but, as we cannot reach her, her rider will have to suffice. We all know what happened the last time Maddie was torn from her dragon. Blackrose's mind will crack when she sees her beloved rider lying dead; betrayed and murdered by her lover.'

Ata'nix pulled a long knife from his robes. 'An Olkian sailor wouldn't use a crossbow. He'd stab her to death, I think; and then use the same weapon to cut his own throat, out of despair.' He glanced at the two militia guards. 'That's how we'll make it look, and then we'll slip back into the shadows. Did anyone see you enter this apartment?'

'No, sir,' said the officer.

'Good.' Ata'nix smiled. 'The Unk Tannic shall inherit this world, Maddie Jackdaw. It is inevitable. Without the colonial government, the people will cry out for leadership, and for a return to the old ways. Our agents are on the move, all over Dragon Eyre. It is a pity that you will not live to see our moment of triumph, but I will be thinking of you, when the Ulnans bow to our authority.' He glanced at the knife in his hand. 'Crossbows are so impersonal. When you feel this blade cut into your flesh, you will sense the hatred I have for you; and you will know it is deeply personal.'

'You're delusional,' said Maddie. 'You've already tried to govern Ulna, and the people detested you.'

'As long as they obey,' he said, 'I can live with their loathing. They'll learn, soon enough, especially when they discover that the Eighteenth Gylean has been freed, and is under our protection on Gyle. Our living god is back among us, and his presence shall inspire the people to worship the dragon spirits once again. I really must thank Sable Holdfast for releasing the Gylean from his long years of captivity, though I doubt that she understood the forces that she was unleashing. She might well be insane, but she has been of great assistance to the Unk Tannic.'

'Sable will kill you all,' said Topaz. 'There will be nowhere to hide.'

'What a disappointment you turned out to be, Oto'pazzi,' said Ata'nix. 'You could have been one of us; a respected and admired member of the Unk Tannic. Instead, you will have to watch as I butcher Maddie in front of you.'

Topaz jumped to his feet, and the two militia guards restrained him, each grabbing hold of an arm. Topaz continued to struggle, and they pulled him to the floor.

'Don't shoot him,' said Ata'nix. 'We need this to look like a murder-suicide.'

He took a step forward, and Maddie backed into the corner of the bedroom.

'Maddie?' came a voice from the main room of the apartment. 'Maddie, are you in there?'

Ata'nix froze.

'Maddie,' the voice continued; 'I want to apologise; so, if you're in the bedroom, I'm sorry about before. I shouldn't have said those things about Topaz. Can you hear me?'

'Say nothing,' hissed Ata'nix.

'Maddie,' the voice came again. 'Please don't tell Shadowblaze what happened. I really am sorry. If you're in there, say something, even if it's just "piss off".' There was a long pause. 'Fine. I understand if you don't want to speak to me.'

Topaz struggled on the floor, but one of the guards had his hands over the sailor's mouth. The voice from the main room went quiet for a few moments, and Ata'nix puffed out his cheeks in relief.

'Right,' he said, glancing at Maddie; 'where were we?'

The bedroom door burst open, and Ahi'edo charged through. Ata'nix's eyes widened, then Ahi'edo clubbed him over the head with a table leg. One of the guards restraining Topaz raised his crossbow, but Topaz lunged at him, and the bolt sped past Ahi'edo, and struck the wall. Ahi'edo hit Ata'nix again, then did the same to the guard with the crossbow, striking him in the face with the table leg and breaking his nose. Topaz wrestled the crossbow out of his hands, and the two guards backed away, their hands raised. Ahi'edo picked up the other crossbow, and stood by Topaz, aiming it at the two guards.

'Don't move, you bastards!' Ahi'edo cried.

Topaz crossed the floor to where Ata'nix was lying, as Maddie watched. He kicked the knife out of Ata'nix's hand, and pressed the tip of the bow against the back of the Unk Tannic leader's head.

'Time to say goodbye, Ata'nix,' he muttered.

Ata'nix whimpered in terror.

'No, Topaz,' said Maddie. 'Don't kill him.'

'Why not? He was going to kill us.'

'I don't care about him,' she said. 'It's what it'll do to you that worries me.'

'Let the dragons deal with them,' said Ahi'edo.

Maddie turned to him. 'Thank you,' she said. 'How did you know?'

'I saw the broken table when I was leaving, and I figured that something must be wrong.' He smiled. 'You can tell Shadowblaze about this, if you like.'

Topaz remained motionless, his eyes on the back of Ata'nix's head as he pointed the crossbow down at him. Slowly, he began to step back. One of the guards tried to run towards the bedroom door, and Topaz shot him in the leg. The man went flying, and crashed to the floor, howling in pain as he clutched his leg.

Topaz calmly reloaded the crossbow, then placed a boot onto Ata'nix's back. 'Alright,' he said; 'let's take them to the dragons.'

Fifteen minutes later, the four Unk Tannic prisoners were standing in front of Blackrose, Shadowblaze and Greysteel, their wrists bound with strips of Maddie's bed sheets. Two of the guards were supporting a third, who had a bandage on his leg. Topaz was standing with his arm round Maddie's waist, his eyes never leaving Ata'nix.

'Well done, Ahi'edo,' said Blackrose.

'Yes, my rider,' said Shadowblaze; 'you did well. Ata'nix – do you have anything you wish to say?'

'Oh, mighty dragons!' Ata'nix cried. 'It is not too late for you to turn to the path of righteousness. Forgive what I did, and believe that I acted in the best interests of Dragon Eyre, and on behalf of every dragon. Evil-doers, such as Sable Holdfast, are conspiring to seize power from the dragons. All I want is to bring back the old days, when everyone knew their place, and everyone was happy.'

'Have you finished?' said Shadowblaze.

'I have, my lord; I...'

Shadowblaze lunged forward, raised a huge forelimb, and tore Ata'nix's head from his shoulders. Blood sprayed across the floor of the cavernous hall, then the body of the Unk Tannic leader slid to the ground. The Unk Tannic guards trembled and wept, then Shadowblaze opened his jaws and devoured them all with one bite. His teeth ground together, then he swallowed, leaving no trace of the three men.

'Justice has been done,' said Lord Greysteel.

'I concur,' said Blackrose. 'Thank you for dealing with them so swiftly, my betrothed.'

Ahi'edo turned to Topaz and Maddie. 'I still owe you both an apology.'

'You owe me nothing,' said Topaz. 'Your actions carried more weight than any words you might have spoken to me in anger.'

He held out his hand, and Ahi'edo shook it.

'And you, Maddie?' said Ahi'edo. 'For too long I have nursed a grievance against you. I'm ashamed to say it, but I cheered when you were abducted by the Five Sisters. All this time, you've tried to be my friend, and I have behaved like a child. I am sorry.'

'Let's start over,' she said. 'I'm not the kind of person who holds grudges, and I accept your apology.'

He smiled. 'Thank you.'

'This pleases me,' said Blackrose. 'Despite the Unk Tannic's attack, I feel reassured, knowing that Maddie has friends willing to risk their lives for her. Uncle, we shall need to purge the entire palace militia, and root out any more agents who may be hiding within their ranks. Set up an investigation, and...'

'Your Majesty,' cried a dragon, entering the huge hall; 'I bring tidings.'

'Then speak,' said Blackrose.

'Several Sea Banner frigates have been seen by scouts, your Majesty. They are sailing north along the eastern coast of Ulna. They loosed a barrage of ballista bolts at the scout, and he was driven away.'

'What are Sea Banner vessels doing in our waters?' said Greysteel.

'There can't be many of them left in the Eastern Rim,' said Blackrose. 'We must intercept and destroy them. Topaz, the time has come for the new contract to prove its worth. Will the Five Sisters answer my call?'

Topaz straightened his back. 'Yes, your Majesty. I shall go down to the harbour, and we shall be on the seas within the hour.'

'Thank you,' said Blackrose. 'You are dismissed.'

Maddie turned to face Topaz. 'So much for boring patrols. This sounds dangerous.'

'It'll be fine,' he said, the excitement in his voice unmistakeable. 'I'll be back in a day or so.'

She kissed him, then frowned. 'You'd better be.'

CHAPTER 26
HOMELESS

Eastern Ectus, Western Rim – 16th Arginch 5255 (18th Gylean Year 6)

Sable lit another cigarette and leaned back against the pile of rocks marking Meader's grave. On the stony ground next to her were a dozen cigarette butts, a testament to how long she had been sitting on the lonely mountainside. Ahead of her, on the northern horizon, a cloud of thick smoke lay above Sabat City.

'I've made a mess of everything, Meader,' she said. 'I started off by wanting to change this world for the better, but my rage got in the way, and now Dragon Eyre is burning. Alef is a wasteland, Ectus a slaughterhouse, and civil war has broken out on Gyle and Na Sun Ka; and I'm responsible. My rage has gone, leaving nothing behind but emptiness. I've damaged every person I've met, especially those who tried to be my friend; I've hurt them all.'

Far to her left, she saw two dragons circling over a distant mountain peak. She waited for a moment, until she was sure that they hadn't seen her, then turned her glance back to the northern horizon. Down in Sabat City, the slaughter was continuing. With no gods to shield them, the Wyst dragons had gone on a rampage, burning everything in sight, and massacring the human inhabitants. It was the same on Na Sun Ka, and on Gyle. Just as Austin had predicted, the Wystians had no interest in discriminating between settler and native, or soldier and civilian – to them, every human was a target. Earlier that day, she had watched as four dragons had departed Ectus, heading south towards Gyle. Were they attempting to fly back all the way to Wyst? She didn't care any more. What was done was done. The news of her criminal acts would soon make its way round to the Eastern Rim, and then she would be welcome nowhere; an outcast, damned by her own actions.

She had assumed that being close to Meader's tomb would make her cry, but she felt hollow instead; her only emotion one of over-whelming guilt. Why hadn't she stopped before it was too late? She could have tried to negotiate while she had Lord Kolai under her control, but she had hacked his head off instead. Implacatus might have offered a peace treaty to save the life of the Fifth Ascendant, but she hadn't been interested in that; all she had wanted was to prove to herself that she was worthy of the Holdfast name. Sable, the famed Ascendant-killer. A grim laugh escaped her lips. Sable, the mass murderer, was closer to the mark. Sable, the killer of children. Her thoughts went back to the tiny café in Port Edmond, where she and Millen had enjoyed a glass of wine in the sunshine. At the time, she had been outraged by the thought that Blackrose's victory might mean the deaths of a few settlers. In trying to prevent that outcome, she had destroyed the very thing she had wanted to preserve.

Badblood would be ashamed of what she had become, and so would Meader. For once, she didn't care what Daphne would think. The chances of ever seeing any of the other Holdfasts again were so slim as to be negligible. Why had she tried to impress people who would never discover what she had done? It was vanity, she thought – vanity, pride, and a feeling of inferiority. That, married to the grief she had felt over Badblood's death, had produced a toxic brew that had resulted in the deaths of tens of thousands of people.

Once she had ferried Austin to and from Implacatus, she would go back to Haurn, she decided. On Haurn, she would live like a hermit, hiding from the rest of Dragon Eyre, and never using her powers again.

She would bury the Quadrant, or throw it down a well, and pretend to be someone else; someone who wasn't feared and hated by the entire population of a world she had brought to the brink of destruction.

She pulled the Quadrant out from the folds of her clothes, and stared at the strange engravings marking its surface. If only she knew how to make it take her back to the Star Continent, but such dreams were pointless. She was never going home.

She noticed the steep ravine a few yards to her right. No. All thoughts of ending her own life had passed. It would be too quick; too easy, and she deserved to live with the guilt of what she had done.

Sable glanced up at the position of the sun. She had been away from their hideout in the Riggan archipelago for longer than she had promised, and she had yet to visit the location she had told Austin she needed to see before taking him back to Implacatus. She stood, wondering if she should bother, and dreading what she would witness.

Her fingers brushed over the Quadrant, and she appeared on the roof of the highest tower in Nankiss, the largest city on Olkis. Like Sabat City, smoke hung over the settlement like a shroud, and fires were raging through several districts. Shops had been looted, their produce trampled and scattered over the roads, and the central marketplace was on fire. Sable turned to glance down at the harbour. A small flotilla of Sea Banner vessels was anchored a hundred yards from shore, their decks crammed with evacuating Banner soldiers. More soldiers were trying to board the last of the ships still in the harbour, but were under heavy attack from the natives of Nankiss. Several bombs exploded by the quayside, one after the other, blowing a column of retreating soldiers to pieces, as the massed crowds cheered. It was the first time Sable had been in Olkis since she and Blackrose had visited Langbeg in their search for Maddie, and she had wondered if the locals had required her assistance. Gazing down into the storm of violence spreading through the city, she knew that her services were not required. The fuse she had lit had done its job, and the natives were exacting every ounce of revenge upon the fleeing occupation forces. Several soldiers were being dragged through the streets by wagons, their ankles attached to long ropes, as the crowds on either side spat and jeered at them. Down by the quayside, a surging mass of people broke through the shieldwall defending the gangway leading to the last ship, and half a dozen objects were hurled onto the overcrowded deck. Moments later, the ship exploded in a crescendo of noise, then the screams of the survivors ripped through the air, as mutilated and bloody sailors and soldiers staggered across the burning deck. The ship began to list to the side, then it sank into the dark, bloody waters of Nankiss harbour, to howls of delight from the watching crowds. At this, the small flotilla weighed anchor, unfurled their sails, and began to speed away from Olkis as quickly as possible. The few remaining soldiers on the quayside were cut down by the mob in seconds.

It was over. After twenty-six years of bloodshed, the long occupation of Olkis was at an end. Sable broke down and wept at the sight. She had achieved what she had sought to achieve, and yet her heart felt scarred and rotten.

She triggered the Quadrant, and appeared in the Riggan archipelago, on the windy hillside next to the caves where they had hidden after fleeing Haurn. She wiped her eyes, trying to conceal the tears, then turned, and walked down the track. The others were waiting for her. Austin was hugging Ashfall round her long neck, while Millen and Deepblue were close by, ready to say their farewells to the demigod.

Ashfall noticed Sable's approach. 'Holdfast,' she cried; 'if you have come to request "one more day" from Austin, then my wrath shall know no bounds.'

'Relax,' Sable said. 'I do have a change of plan, but it's not that.'

'What change of plan?' said Millen.

Sable looked at the small group, wondering if she was doing the right thing.

'Well, Holdfast?' said Ashfall.

'I'm going to take everyone back to Ulna first,' she said.

Millen grinned. 'This is great news! Back to civilisation, at last.'

Ashfall tilted her head. 'I suspect that the witch is not giving us the full story.'

'Your suspicions are well-founded,' said Sable. 'Once I've fulfilled my promise to Austin, and brought him and his mother back from Implacatus, I will be leaving you all.'

'What do you mean?' said Millen. 'Where are you going?'

'To live alone,' she said. 'To live as far away from other people as it's possible to do on this world.'

'Why?' said Deepblue. 'Are we not your friends?'

'No,' said Sable. 'I know perfectly well what you all think of me. You first came to Haurn as friends, and I'll always be grateful for that. You saved me from the greenhides at Seabound, Deepblue, and you too, Millen, and you, Ashfall. The time we spent together at the temple in Nan Po Tana will always be special to me, at least, until Blackrose arrived and made Austin heal me. That's where it all started to go wrong.' She lowered her gaze. 'You all know what I have done. You are filled with revulsion and disgust at my actions, and I don't blame you for that. This is for the best. I need to live alone.'

'If you read my mind, Sable,' said Millen, 'then you would see how wrong you are. I'm not revolted, or disgusted – do you think that's how I've been feeling every day, waiting for you to return? You know, I often think back to the Bloodflies stadium in Alea Tanton, and the decision I made that day, to follow you. Sometime, I admit, I've regretted it. You changed my life, Sable; and not always for the better. But you're my best friend, and I love you.'

'I don't deserve your love, Millen.'

'I don't care; that's not your decision to make. I stuck by you through the Catacombs, and on Haurn; so what makes you think I'd be happy to see you alone? And Deepblue loves you too. Do you think she was unaware of your faults when she saved your life from the greenhides? Each one of us is flawed in our own way, and yet we stick together; because that's what friends do.'

'I have made too many enemies, Millen. If we stick together, then I will be putting you all in danger. I don't want to be alone just for my own sake; I'm doing it for all of you, so that you can be safe.'

Austin shook his head. 'I admire your sentiments, but don't you think it's a little late for that? Your enemies are now my enemies, Sable. Haven't I stood by your side throughout every operation? The gods of Implacatus, the dragons of Wyst, and the Unk Tannic – they all know my face, and my name. It will be dangerous for me in Serene, but I'm under no illusions that Dragon Eyre will be much better. That's why we need to stay together, to protect each other. Frankly, I'd feel a lot safer if you were around.'

'I agree,' said Deepblue. 'Each one of us made a choice, to stay here and support you.'

'Don't speak for me,' said Ashfall. 'I agreed to join this band to protect Austin. However, I concur with the words the demigod spoke. If you left us now, Sable, it would feel as though you were abandoning us.'

Sable said nothing. It didn't matter what arguments they employed, she knew they would be better off without her.

She took out the Quadrant. 'Are you ready?'

'This conversation isn't over,' said Millen. 'Once we're in Ulna, we need to sit down, have a few drinks and a decent meal, and talk it through.'

Sable smiled. Did Millen really believe that a pleasant dinner and a glass of wine would resolve everything? She swiped her fingers over the surface of the Quadrant, and the air shimmered on the hillside. A moment later, they appeared in an open area of Udall, close to the harbour. Sable had been expecting to see lots of people, but the square was deserted, and there were signs of fire damage on the nearby buildings.

Her glance caught on a large crater by the side of the road, then four sailors walked past, carrying shovels.

'Hey!' Sable shouted.

The sailors turned.

'What happened here?'

'Just arrived, have you?' said one of the sailors.

'Yes,' said Sable.

The sailors stopped, and leaned on their shovels.

'It was Lord Bastion, ma'am,' said one. 'He brought a load of green-hides, and a few Banner soldiers, and they went on a little rampage.'

'When was this?' said Ashfall.

'Two days ago, madam dragon,' said the sailor.

'Are the Five Sisters in town?' said Sable.

'Nah. The *Gull*, the *Fancy*, and the *Sow* all left an hour ago. Reports of Sea Banner vessels, apparently. Us lads are part of the reserve crew, stationed on the *Patience*. We're just lending a hand with the clean up.'

'The damage ain't too bad,' said another sailor. 'It's just in this little area, next to the harbour. The rest of the town's fine.'

'Yeah,' said the first. 'The attack was over and done with in ten minutes. Boom, boom, boom, and then it was over.'

'It was a warning, or so I heard, ma'am. Hand over Sable Holdfast, or else.'

Sable narrowed her eyes. 'I see.'

'It ain't going to work, though,' the sailor went on. 'Sable's a bleeding legend. That Bastion has another thing coming if he thinks anyone in this town would betray Sable. She's more popular than the bleeding Queen.'

'And is the Queen at home?' said Ashfall.

The sailors shrugged. 'Probably,' said one. 'You'll want to check the palace for that.'

'Thank you,' said Millen.

The sailors set off again, and the group turned to Sable.

'Take us to the palace,' said Ashfall.

'You can fly, can't you?' she said. 'You go ahead of me. I want to walk.'

'Very well,' said the grey dragon. 'Austin; climb up.'

The two men went to their respective dragons, and clambered up onto the harnesses.

'We shall see you soon, Sable,' said Deepblue, then the dragons extended their wings and took to the air. Sable watched them rise into the blue sky, then strode towards the harbour. She squeezed past a pile of rubble, and emerged between two blackened buildings. The quayside was busy with workers, all toiling to clear up the mess left by the attack, while gulls shrieked and circled overhead. The harbour itself was undamaged, and the small fleet of fishing boats was tied up in their usual places. She saw the old *Patience* berthed by a pier, but there was no sign of the Five Sisters' vessels. Her heart sank. She had believed the sailor, but had needed to check for herself that Lara wasn't there.

She turned for the palace, and walked through the deserted market-place. Beyond the harbour district, the rest of the town seemed normal, and the streets were bustling with people. She tried to get Lara out of her mind, and focussed on Bastion instead. Unable to find Sable, he had lashed out at her friends, punishing them for her actions. The population of the town should hate her, and yet, if the sailors had been correct, they didn't.

She approached the ground level of the palace, where its right flank sat on the eastern bank of the wide river. Two militia soldiers were guarding the entrance, and they eyed her as she got closer.

'What do you want?' asked one.

'To speak to the Queen.'

'You got an appointment?'

'My name is Sable Holdfast; will that do?'

The two guards stared at her, then moved aside.

'Be careful, miss,' said one, as she passed.

'Why?' she said.

'A couple of guards turned out to be working for the Unk Tannic, miss,' he said. 'They were discovered in the palace just a couple of hours ago. There might be others.'

'Is that why you're here, miss?' said the other guard. 'Are you going to root the bastards out?'

'Maybe,' she said, as she entered the building.

She climbed up a long flight of stairs, then saw a woman running towards her.

'Sable!' the woman cried.

'Maddie.'

'I just saw Millen, and Ashfall, and Deepblue. They're upstairs,'

Maddie said. 'They told me that they're going to be staying here again; is it true? Are you all moving back to Ulna?'

'They are,' said Sable, 'if Blackrose approves.'

'Of course she'll approve. She's missed Ashfall, especially. And what did you mean by "they"? What about you?'

Sable resumed climbing the stairs, and Maddie kept pace by her side.

'Well?' said Maddie.

'I know I'm not welcome here,' Sable said. 'Blackrose made that quite clear in Throscala.'

'Speak to her. Say you're sorry for insulting her, and who knows? Blackrose isn't as stubborn as you think.'

'I'm not really in the mood to beg.'

'Did I say beg? Don't be stupid, Sable. You and Blackrose have a long history of squabbling, but her opinion of you has changed a lot since the old days. After all you went through together, trying to get to Olkis – you earned her respect. She'll forgive you if you apologise.'

'What if I don't want her forgiveness?'

Maddie groaned. 'Why do you have to be like this?'

'You wouldn't be asking questions like that, if you knew everything that I'd done.'

'I know about the greenhides. I don't like it, but it doesn't mean that I never want to speak to you again. Without you, we would never have been able to force the Banner out of Throscala. You've won the war, Sable.'

'Really? Tell me; does Bastion agree with you on that? I saw what he did to the harbour.'

'But, if you're here, then you can stop him if he comes back.'

'I see. Is that why Blackrose would be willing to forgive me?'

'Stop twisting my words, Sable. I'm going to tell Blackrose that you're here, and I strongly advise you to come with me.'

'Where's Lara?'

'With Topaz on the *Giddy Gull*. They just left. Topaz said that he thinks they might be back tomorrow. Will you stay until then, at least?'

'I made a promise to Austin that I'll have to take care of first.'

They came to the top of the stairs, and Maddie raised an eyebrow.

'Fine,' said Sable. 'I'll come with you to see Blackrose, and then I want to speak to her alone.'

'I can arrange that. Come on.'

They turned right, and Maddie led Sable to the Queen's quarters.

'Topaz and I are seeing each other,' Maddie said, as they walked.

'I know.'

'You don't care, do you?' said Maddie. 'You're so wrapped up in your personal problems, that my love-life must seem pretty insignificant to you; but it's a big deal to me. I think I'm in love with him. No, I *am* in love with him. He makes me happy.'

'I'm glad that you're happy.'

'You don't seem it. Ata'nix tried to kill me this morning.'

'Who?'

'The Unk Tannic guy. Topaz and Ahi'edo managed to stop him, then Shadowblaze ripped his head off. It was pretty disgusting, but I guess he deserved it.' She pushed open a human-sized door. 'Well, here we are.'

Sable entered a dimly-lit hall. A huge black dragon was resting along the far wall, on an enormous heap of cushions.

'Blackrose,' said Maddie; 'I've brought you a visitor.'

The dragon looked up, and her red eyes burned. 'Sable.'

'Hello, Blackrose,' she said.

'She wants to talk to you alone,' said Maddie, 'so I'm going to leave. Please don't kill each other; alright?'

Sable and Blackrose watched as Maddie turned and left the hall.

'Do you have something you wish to say to me, witch?' said the black dragon.

'Yes,' said Sable. 'I'm sorry that I was a bitch to you in Throscala. I think killing that Ascendant unhinged me a little.'

'Thank you. I accept your apology, and rescind my earlier statement. You are welcome to visit Udall.'

Sable narrowed her eyes. 'Just like that?'

'Yes, Sable – just like that. I have no desire to prolong our quarrel. Do you?'

'No.'

'Then it is settled. Furthermore, I have an offer to make to you. If you wish, I would be prepared to allow you to make your home here, within my realm. We are stronger together, and...'

'Stop,' said Sable. 'Before you make any promises, you need to know exactly what I've done.'

'Do I? It is bad enough knowing that you unleashed greenhides upon the islands of this world. Is there more I need to hear?'

'Yes. I have intervened in the affairs of Wyst.'

'I see. Tell me everything.'

Sable took a breath, then poured out every detail, from her first attack on Yearning, up to what she had witnessed in Nankiss that morning. She left out nothing – the sailors she had forced to detonate explosive devices, the Wystians' slaughter of the inhabitants of the three cities on the Home Islands, the death of the Ascendant, and the anarchy she had caused throughout the Western Rim by releasing the Eighteenth Gylean. Blackrose sat in silence throughout, her head tilted to the side as she listened.

When Sable had finished, she hung her head, feeling as though part of her burden had been lifted.

'You have made a deep and indelible mark upon this world, Sable,' said Blackrose.

'That's one way to put it,' she said.

'I sense that your rage has burned itself out. All I feel from you now is guilt, shame, and loneliness.'

'You missed out tired,' she said. 'I feel like I could sleep forever.'

'You need a home.'

Sable started to cry. 'After all I've told you; that's your response? You would let me live here, despite the thousands who have died because of me?'

'You sought vengeance for the death of Badblood. I understand. In fact, your rampage was the most dragon-like thing you have done in your life, Sable. Your raw grief blinded you, as it would blind me, if Maddie were to die. And now your rage has passed, and your enemies lie broken and trampled beneath your heel. If you wished to rule this world, it is within your grasp.'

'I have no desire to rule Dragon Eyre.'

'What do you desire?'

'To live alone, isolated from the rest of this world, on a remote island, where no one will know me.'

'My dear Sable, you can run from others, but you cannot run from yourself. After the rage of grief, it is time to heal. You need time, and you need friends. Here, you can have both.'

'Why are you being so nice to me?' Sable sobbed. 'Have you forgotten how many times I've lied to you?'

'No, but I can sense that you are being honest with me now. You proved your worth a hundred times over when you agreed to help me search for Maddie. Do you not recall? You gave up your peaceful life on Haurn, to help me, after I had cast you out of Ulna. And then, you suffered greatly on our journey to Ectus. I shall not turn my back on you now, not when your hour of need has come.'

Sable said nothing.

'Ulna is a large island,' Blackrose went on, 'and there are many lonely places where you could reside for a while, in peace. You do not have to live in Udall, if you do not wish. Think about it, at least.'

'I will.'

Blackrose nudged her with her nose. 'Are we friends again?'

Sable wiped her eyes. 'Yes. Thank you, Blackrose. I'd better go. I'm taking Austin back to Implacatus.'

'Why?'

'So that he can find his mother. Then, with your permission, I'm going to bring them both back here. Can Austin and his mother live in Ulna, too?'

'Of course they can. Go. Do what you have to do, and we shall speak again upon your return.'

Sable nodded, then strode out of the chamber. Maddie and Austin were standing outside the door, waiting for her.

'How did it go?' said Maddie. 'Have you been crying? Is that a good sign?'

'It went fine,' said Sable. 'Austin, the Queen says that you and your mother are welcome to live here.'

'Are you really going to Implacatus?' said Maddie.

'Yes,' said Austin, 'but not for long. You're not getting rid of me that easily.'

'Can I borrow some clothes?' said Sable.

'I assume you're asking me?' said Maddie. 'Sure. We can go to my quarters now, and you can pick out something.'

Sable smiled. 'If we can find anything among the mess.'

'What mess?' said Maddie. 'I have a Topaz now, and he's highly skilled at tidying up. He even sorted out my socks.'

'I can see why you love him,' she said. She glanced at Austin. 'Go and say your goodbyes to Ashfall. Tell her that you'll be back in a few days, and I'll meet you here in half an hour.'

Austin grinned. 'Is it really happening?'

'Yes, Austin, it really is. Don't be late.'

———

Half an hour later, Sable and Maddie were back outside the Queen's quarters. Sable was wearing a loose summer dress, and had a pack slung over her shoulder, with weapons, food, a pouch of gold, and more clothes stashed inside.

'You will be careful, won't you?' said Maddie.

Sable smirked. 'I'm always careful.'

'Yeah, right.'

'I'm going to trigger the Quadrant from here,' Sable went on, 'so here is where I'll return. I might be alone, or I might be with Austin and his mother, if we can find her quickly. If it's taking too long, then I'll come back, and arrange to collect him later.'

Maddie nodded. 'Here he comes.'

Sable glanced up, and saw Austin hurry towards him.

'I'm ready,' he said.

She took the Quadrant out from her clothes and glanced at it. 'Show me again.'

Austin pointed at the device. 'Press it here, and it will take us to where this Quadrant was first used. It belonged to my father, and I know its history. It should take us into the heart of Serene.'

'Alright,' said Sable. 'See you soon, Maddie.'

She triggered the device, and the air shimmered. Sable and Austin appeared in a dark, narrow street, a foot above the ground. They landed on the cobbles of the alley, and glanced around.

'There would have been a palace here, many thousands of years ago,' said Austin. 'It's long gone now.'

Sable tucked the Quadrant into her pack, and glanced at the end of the alleyway. It opened out onto a larger road, where carts and people were passing. She could see no sign of the outside, and the city seemed to be inside a vast cavern.

'Do you know where we are?' she said.

'Roughly.'

'I didn't realise that Serene was underground.'

'It's not. It's built into the side of a mountain, high above the lowland plains. Each level opens out onto the sky. If we head towards the daylight, then I'll be able to work out what level we're on.'

Sable used her vision powers to scan the neighbourhood. In the distance, she saw a faint glimmer of sunlight, where the cavern opened onto the outside world.

'Alright,' she said; 'let's find your mother.'

CHAPTER 27
THE COST OF LIVING

Off Tunkatta, Ulnan Archipelago, Eastern Rim – 17th Arginch 5255 (18th Gylean Year 6)

Lara poked her head out of her cabin. 'Has the rain stopped?'

Topaz nodded. 'Yes, Captain.'

Lara emerged onto the quarter deck, and glanced up at the predawn sky. She yawned, and lit a cigarette.

'There are still a few clouds about,' she said.

'The wind is blowing them to the west, ma'am,' he said. 'It looks as though the morning will be clear.'

Lara nodded, then stared ahead of them, at the two tiny lights in the distance. 'We're still right behind the bastards, then?'

'We are, indeed, ma'am. Give the signal, and we'll increase speed in order to intercept them.'

'I will, as soon as the sun rises,' she said; 'otherwise we'll lose Ann and Tilly. The *Gull's* much faster than their crappy ships.'

Topaz glanced at the master's mate. 'Tommo, fetch me and the captain some coffee.'

'Yes, sir,' said the lad, saluting.

'Make sure it's hot,' cried Lara, as the boy ran towards the main deck. 'Give me a smoke, Master.'

Topaz slipped his right hand into a pocket, and passed the captain his packet of cigarettes.

'This packet's half-crushed,' she said. 'You should have taken that silver case – you know, the one that used to belong to Maddie's old boyfriend.' She frowned. 'I still can't believe that she had a friend who was a Banner soldier. It makes me feel icky.'

'And he's dating a Holdfast, just like you, ma'am.'

'I hope that's the only damn thing I have in common with a bleeding Banner officer.'

The sky to the east was brightening, and the slopes of the mountains of Tunkatta to their right transformed from shades of grey into verdant greens, as the sun appeared on the horizon. Lara walked to the storage box behind the wheel and took out the long eye-glass. She held it up, and peered at the two Sea Banner frigates they were pursuing. She mumbled something, then turned to face the stern of the *Gull* and used the device to check how close her sisters' vessels lay.

'Dear gods,' she muttered. 'The *Fancy* is a slow piece of shit. It's embarrassing, having to go at this speed, just so Ann can keep up. If we capture one of those frigates, I'm going to insist that she scraps her old vessel, and takes it.'

'Captain Ann would never scrap the *Flight of Fancy*, ma'am; she loves it.'

'Then maybe I'll set fire to it one night; give her no choice.'

On their right, they passed a deserted settlement, where a large number of refugees had lived before the greenhides on Ulna had been destroyed. The flimsy houses were falling apart, their roofs in the process of collapsing, and their thin walls leaning at odd angles.

'That place needs a good storm to hit it,' said Lara. 'What a dump.'

'It would be a good place to hide, ma'am; if we were still pirates.'

Lara laughed. 'None of that talk, Master. We're decent, law-abiding citizens now. Respectable, even.'

Topaz narrowed his eyes as he gazed forward. 'The two frigates are turning to the north-east, ma'am. Looks like they're going to sail between Tunkatta and Speen, rather than head up Alg Bay.'

CHRISTOPHER MITCHELL

'Adjust our course to follow them, and increase speed by three knots.'

'Yes, ma'am.'

He called out to a midshipman, and relayed his orders, while Tommo returned to the quarter deck, carrying a tray.

'Your coffee, ma'am, sir.'

'You took long enough,' said Lara, taking a mug.

'Sorry, ma'am.'

She took a sip. 'It's hot, though, so I'll let you off this time.'

The *Giddy Gull* began to turn, following in the wake of the two frigates, as their speed increased. They were starting to pull away from the two Five Sisters ships behind them, but Topaz noticed the *Sow's Revenge* also pick up its pace, its sails fully unfurled.

'Something's not right, Master,' said Lara, as she squinted down the eye-glass. 'Why are the bastards swinging us round Tunkatta? If they'd wanted to flee, they had their chance last night. If they'd made for the Inner Ocean, we'd have lost them in the heavy rain.' She lowered the eye-glass, her lips in a frown, then lifted it again, and began scanning the coastline of Ulna, on their left.

Tommo squinted into the distance. 'What will we do if we catch up with the frigates, sir?'

'Our orders are to eliminate them, lad,' said Topaz. 'That means capture or destroy. With any luck, they'll be running low on pisspots and ballista bolts, but they'll have marines on board.'

Tommo swallowed. 'How many marines, sir?'

'Well, if they're fitted out in the same way as the *Tranquillity*, then each frigate will have forty of the big buggers; but I imagine that neither ship will have its full complement of people on board.'

'Shit!' cried Lara.

Topaz turned. 'Ma'am?'

'There are two more frigates coming at us from the north,' she said, still peering through the eye-glass. 'They must have been hiding between Speen and the Ulnan mainland. This is a bleeding trap, and we've walked right into it.' She turned towards the stern, and glanced at the two ships captained by her sisters. 'The damn *Fancy* is starting to lag behind. Those two frigates will tear it to shreds.'

'The two ahead of us are starting to turn, ma'am.'

'Of course they bleeding are,' muttered Lara. 'They'll hold us in position, while the other two swoop in like vultures.' She strode to the front of the quarter deck. 'Battle stations, you bleeding lazy assholes! Man the ballistae, and bring up the pisspots.'

The crew began to hurry around the deck, as sailors rushed to get into their positions. Young lads scrambled up the rigging attached to the masts, ready to change the sails at a moment's notice, while the tarpaulin water-proofing was hauled from the pair of ballistae on the bow platform. The master-at-arms appeared on deck, and began distributing weapons to the crew, who lined up to receive their crossbows and short swords. Lara paced up and down, stopping every few moments to peer through the eye-glass.

'Send a signal to the *Fancy* and the *Sow's Revenge*,' she said. 'Warn them of the two frigates approaching from the north. After that, they're on their own.'

'Yes, ma'am,' said Topaz. He nodded to Tommo, who ran to the storage box, where he retrieved the signal flags. The boy clambered up the steep steps to the poop deck, and began raising flags of different colours above his head.

Topaz kept his eyes on the two frigates ahead of them. They had spilt, and then turned, and both were now pointing towards the front of the *Gull*, the distance between them falling rapidly.

'What's the *Gull* got that no other ship in these waters can match?' said Lara. 'Speed, that's what. Master, take us between the two enemy frigates at full speed.'

Topaz glanced at her. 'Ma'am?'

'You heard me, Master.'

'Yes, ma'am.'

He passed his orders onto the midshipman, and the *Giddy Gull* tore through the sea, its speed increasing with every second.

'I don't understand, sir,' whispered Tommo, who had returned to the quarter deck. 'Our course will take us into the range of both frigates. It'll be like running the gauntlet.'

'Have faith in the captain, lad,' said Topaz, a hand shielding his eyes from the sun.

The glare from the sun was getting worse, a fact that Topaz presumed had been part of the Sea Banner's plan to entrap the Five Sisters. The two frigates ahead of them were closing quickly, and the passage between them was narrow.

'As soon as we're through the gap,' said Lara, 'drop the left anchor and rotate ninety degrees to the port side.'

'The anchor chain will likely snap under the pressure, ma'am.'

'I know that,' she said. 'As long as it slows us down, I couldn't give a rat's ass.' She turned to face the main deck. 'When we pass between the two enemy ships, everyone take cover,' she yelled to the crew. 'Master, I'm going down to take personal command of the pisspot catapult. You know what you have to do?'

He nodded. 'Yes, ma'am.'

She ran off the quarter deck, and headed towards the bow. Topaz gestured to a midshipman.

'Get yourself to the port-side anchor,' he said. 'Drop it as soon as you see me wave down to you. Got it?'

'Yes, Master.'

The midshipman left the quarter deck, leaving only Topaz and Tommo remaining.

'Find somewhere to hide,' Topaz said to the lad. 'This ain't going to be pretty.'

'What about you, sir?'

'I'm staying by the wheel, lad.'

Tommo's mouth fell open. 'But, sir, you'll be exposed from both sides.'

'That's the job, lad. You've got to take the bad times, as well as the good. Go on; scarper.'

The boy ran to the side of the quarter deck, under the overhang where the poop deck stretched over the entrance to Lara's cabin. He crouched down by the bulkhead, his eyes on Topaz.

'If I get hit, lad,' said Topaz, 'take over the wheel.'

'Yes, sir,' said Tommo, his voice a whisper.

Topaz kept his head low as the *Gull* approached the gap between the two frigates. On the enemy decks, marines were holding their crossbows, aiming at the brigantine, as was the ballistae mounted on the two poop decks. Topaz thrust all worry from his mind. He had to act, without dwelling on the danger he was in. The *Gull* reached the start of the gap, and the crew dived to the deck, or huddled behind any cover they could find, as the shooting began. Swarms of crossbow bolts sped out from either frigate, thudding into the masts or deck, or tearing holes through the sails. A young lad up in the rigging was hit. He cried out and fell, then his foot got tangled in the ropes, and he hung suspended from the ankle, swaying as he died. A bolt whistled past Topaz's nose as the *Gull's* quarter deck entered crossbow range. Topaz remained motionless, his hands gripping the wheel as missiles came at him from both sides. He felt a searing pain in his right leg, below the knee, but ignored it, concentrating on nothing but guiding the ship through. The two frigates loosed their ballistae. One yard-long bolt drove straight through an open hatch, skewering the sailor that had been crouching behind it, while another bolt ripped a great hole in the main sail. A crossbow bolt struck the wheel, just inches from Topaz's left hand, then, suddenly, they were through. Topaz waved down to the midshipman, then spun the wheel fully to port. The *Gull* started to bank, its deck transforming into a steep slope as it began to turn. The anchor was freed from the side of the hull, and the chain rattled and clanked, then went taut. Wooden boards squealed under the strain as the *Gull's* bow rotated to the left, the ship's speed reducing dramatically. The crew were thrown around the deck, and two fell overboard, as the ship's port side moved round the stern of the left-hand frigate.

From the bow, a large ceramic canister flew through the air. It struck the enemy frigate's rear end, which erupted in flames. Another pisspot was launched moments later, striking the main deck of the frigate. The blast waves from the two explosions rolled through the *Gull*, making every timber grind as if being tortured. The anchor chain hadn't snapped, and the *Gull* had slowed almost to a halt. By then, the brigantine had circled halfway round the burning frigate, and was using it to shelter from the other enemy vessel. Lara launched their third, and final, pisspot. It arced high into the air, over the burning vessel, and smacked into the side of the other frigate, ripping a hole through its flank.

'Raise the anchor!' Topaz cried, and a dozen men raced to the capstan, and began turning the great wheel. Topaz righted the rudder, and the deck fell level again. He turned, and glanced at the burning deck of the first ship they had hit. Sailors were jumping over the sides, preferring to take their chances with the dark waters. The sails were ablaze, and smoke was rising into the blue sky.

'Sir,' said Tommo, from his hiding place. 'Your leg, sir.'

Topaz looked down, and saw a crossbow bolt embedded into his right shin. In the midst of the short battle, he had barely felt a thing, but as soon as he saw it, the pain surged up his leg, and he fell to one knee, gasping.

'Hold the wheel steady, Tommo!' he cried, as he gripped the wound.

The lad ran forward, and stood by the wheel.

With the anchor raised, the *Gull* burst back into life and, seconds later, they were a hundred yards from the two stricken frigates. The right-hand vessel was sinking, holed in its starboard flank, while the other was burning, and had started to drift with the wind and tide.

'Did you see that?' Lara cried. 'That bleeding third shot!'

Topaz glanced up, and saw the captain bound up the steps onto the quarter deck. She noticed Tommo at the wheel, and frowned, then saw Topaz sitting on the ground in a pool of blood.

'Shit!' she yelled, then ran to his side. 'Is it bad?'

'It bleeding hurts, ma'am, if that's what you mean.'

She called for a couple of crew members, and they hurried up onto the quarter deck. One yanked out the crossbow bolt, then the other tied a belt round Topaz's lower leg to staunch the bloodflow.

'Can you stand, Master?' said Lara, her gaze on the view ahead.

'Not at the moment, ma'am,' he said. 'Tommo can take over. I'll guide him from here. What are your orders?'

Lara stood, lifted the eye-glass, and aimed it towards the bow.

'My sisters are battling the other two frigates,' she said. 'Tilly's lost a mast, and Ann's piece of crap is taking a pasting. We'll swing round, and come alongside the bastard attacking the *Fancy*.' She glanced down at Topaz. 'Well done for staying at your post, Master.'

'Ma'am; it's me. Did you think I was going to run away?'

She smiled. 'Of course not. We are the greatest damn team on Dragon Eyre. Just try not to get yourself shot next time, eh? What am I going to tell Maddie?' She beckoned to a midshipman. 'Get the master a large gin.'

She strode away, and began organising a boarding party. A chair was brought over for Topaz, and he was helped up onto it. He scanned the scene in front of him. Two separate, small battles were taking place. The *Sow's Revenge* had one of the frigates on the run, but the *Flight of Fancy* was burning from a fire in the stern, and looked dead in the water, as the final frigate attacked. The midshipman handed him a mug of gin, and Topaz relayed his instructions to him. The young officer saluted, then hurried away.

'A little to starboard, Tommo,' said Topaz; 'fifteen degrees. That's it; nice and steady. Good lad.'

As they got closer to the *Flight of Fancy*, Topaz could see that the frigate's marines had stormed the smaller vessel, and Ann's crew were fighting hand-to-hand across their own deck. Tommo guided the *Gull* to the frigate's other side, and closed, as Topaz continued sending his orders down to the crew. The *Gull* slowed, then bumped against the frigate's starboard flank. Lara let out an ear-splitting cry, and fifty of her crew leapt across the gap, half with swords, the other half with cross-bows. With the marines busy on the *Fancy*, the frigate's unarmed crew were soon overwhelmed, and within moments they had surrendered, their arms raised in the air. It took the marines a few more minutes to realise that the battle was over, but one by one, they threw down their weapons. Ann and Lara met on the deck of the *Fancy*, and embraced. Ann had a cut down her face, and an injury to her left arm, but she was in a better way than much of her crew. At least thirty lay dead upon the bloody deck, and a similar number were injured.

Topaz slugged down the gin, as the cries of the wounded echoed across the waters.

One hour later, Topaz's leg had been bandaged up, and he was helped into the captain's cabin. The three Five Sisters vessels were anchored alongside one another, with the captured frigate still tied up between the *Fancy* and the *Gull*. Its crew had been disarmed and led below decks, where they were being guarded by armed sailors from the *Gull*. Lara, Ann and Tilly were sitting in Lara's cabin, along with a few other senior officers, and they gestured for Topaz to sit. Two sailors supported him, and he was lowered onto a chair. Sitting alone was the captain of the surrendered vessel, his hands tied behind his back.

'What have I missed, ma'am?' said Topaz.

'Nothing,' said Lara. 'We were just getting started.' She glared at the Sea Banner captain. 'Why?' she said. 'You had nothing to gain from today's attack. From your pathetic performance, it's clear to me that your crews were hungry and demoralised, and you had no pisspots – not one among four vessels. I destroyed two of your ships in two minutes, on my own.'

'Quit bragging,' said Tilly.

'But it's true,' said Lara. 'I mean, I know I'm good, but come on. Not only were these assholes in Ulnan waters, just begging us to attack them, but they had a trap prepared for us. What was the point? If I was them, I'd have set off for the Western Rim ages ago. Out of their four ships, two have sunk, and one is in our hands. I don't get it.'

'Are you going to execute my crew, ma'am?' said the captured captain.

'No,' said Lara. 'We're going to take you back to Ulna. We ain't pirates no more – we're working for Queen Blackrose. What about you? Who gave you the orders for today's battle?'

'My orders came from the top, ma'am.'

'What? You mean Lord Bastion? What interest does he have in a few former pirate vessels? You'd have thought he'd have more pressing concerns on his mind.'

'I don't know, ma'am. Our orders stated that we were to draw you away from Udall, but I don't know why; nor would I tell you if I did know.'

Topaz narrowed his eyes. 'Lord Bastion's going to assault Udall.'

'How do you figure that, Topaz?' said Tilly.

'Wait; he's right,' said Ann, whose face was half-covered with a large bandage. 'It's the only thing that makes sense. Why else would Bastion want us out of Udall's harbour? He knows that we have the only ballistae and explosive devices among the defences of Udall. He knows the damage we could do to any invasion force, and the greenhides wouldn't be able to touch us.'

Lara and Tilly shared a glance.

'We need to go back,' said Topaz.

'Hold on,' said Tilly. 'I have a broken mast, and Ann's ship will need extensive repairs. Besides, we'll probably have to tow the captured frigate, as the *Fancy* lost so many crew in the battle.'

'Scuttle the *Fancy*,' said Lara. 'I'm with Topaz on this. We should get our asses back up to Udall as quickly as possible.'

'I ain't scuttling the damn *Fancy*,' said Ann. 'We need to take a breath, and think.'

'There's only one thing we can do,' said Lara. 'I can take the *Gull* back, alone, while the rest of you limp along after. That way, we can go a lot faster than if we were in a convoy. Topaz, how soon could we be back in Udall?'

'It's a little under a hundred miles from here, ma'am,' he said. 'We could do it in seven hours. If we leave now, we should be back well before sunset.'

'This is crazy,' said Tilly. 'Say you're right, and Bastion is launching an attack on Udall – you'll be slaughtered. You haven't even got any pisspots left.'

'We can transfer ours to the *Giddy Gull*, sister,' said Ann, 'along with any spare ballistae bolts. That will give them a fighting chance.'

Tilly frowned. 'Are you sure this isn't about trying to rescue Maddie Jackdaw?'

'It's about doing our job,' said Lara. 'Didn't Blackrose employ us to protect Ulna? If Udall gets flattened, who's going to pay us?'

'Fine,' Tilly muttered. 'Let's get moving; we're wasting time.'

It took nearly eight hours for the *Gull* to reach the approaches to Udall harbour. The ship's integrity had suffered more in the battle than either Topaz or Lara had realised, and their speed had suffered as a result. Topaz had felt his frustration mount with every passing hour. His injured leg had ached for the entire voyage, and it had been a struggle to stay calm as he had talked Tommo through what the lad needed to do. Several times, he had tried to get up from the chair behind the wheel, but each time his leg had buckled beneath him, and he had sat back down, his face clenched with pain.

The sun was low in the western sky as they approached the break-waters protecting the harbour basin. Lara was on the quarter deck, and she and Topaz stared out at the town.

'Everything seems fine,' she said. 'Maybe we were wrong, Topaz.'

'Maybe, Captain.'

'It would be annoying to be proved wrong in front of Tilly and Ann,' she said, 'but I'd rather that than the alternative. At least we'll get to sleep here tonight, while they toil through the seas, eh? It'll be dawn before they reach Udall. We'll get the bosun and carpenters to give the *Gull* a thorough going-over as soon as we dock, and try to get a better idea of any damage we suffered in the battle. Still, I'll be telling the story of how we managed to take out two damn frigates in every tavern in town tonight. And how we had to come to Ann's rescue. Poor Tilly never even managed to sink the one frigate she was up against. That bastard will still be out there, somewhere.'

'They will be fleeing for the Western Rim by now, ma'am.'

'Yeah, probably. Did you notice that they fled when they saw us coming to help? Tilly's claiming credit for chasing them away, but I know what I saw. I'm the best captain among the Five Sisters, and today I proved it.'

Topaz smiled, despite the pain coming from his leg. 'That you are, ma'am.'

He gazed at the peaceful town of Udall. The rays of the lowering sun were causing the roofs and walls of the houses to glimmer in the light, and the bridge palace was resplendent, its polished domes shining. He issued a few orders to the midshipman, and the sails were taken down, and the brigantine slowed as it neared the entrance to the harbour.

'Take us in, Tommo,' Lara said to the young lad. She smiled at Topaz. 'This has been good experience for him. Maybe you getting injured wasn't all bad, Master. And think of all the attention Maddie will lavish on her poor, wounded man. There will be no more sailing for you until you've fully recovered; you can tell her that.'

The young master's mate turned the wheel a little, and the *Gull* entered the harbour.

'Take us back to the same pier we left from,' Lara said, and the lad nodded, his face scrunched up in concentration.

The *Giddy Gull* inched through the harbour, passing a collection of fishing vessels that were about to leave for the evening. They were a few yards away from the pier, when a loud scream echoed across the harbour. Lara turned to look, and her mouth fell open.

Topaz shifted position on his chair to glance over at the source of the scream. At first, he wasn't sure what he was looking at. A shimmering black square had appeared on the long quayside, three yards high, and four wide. A man was standing next to it, while a body lay at his feet. The dock workers were staring at the strange black void, then some started to run, dropping their tools and sprinting away from it.

'What is it?' said Lara.

A whistle sounded, and armoured soldiers began running out from the black void, their steel breastplates and helmets shining in the dying light.

'It's a damn portal!' Topaz cried.

'Holy crap!' yelled Lara. 'Tommo, keep us away from the pier! Stop the ship!'

The lad spun the wheel, and the bow of the *Gull* started to drift back towards the open harbour basin. On the quayside, dozens of Banner soldiers had already appeared, while more were charging through. A woman in dark red robes strode out of the portal, and spoke to the man who had been there from the start. They exchanged a few words, then the woman turned towards the harbour, and raised her arms. Sparks appeared in her hands, then they transformed into flames. The fires rose up from the woman, growing into a roiling mass of flame, then she swept her arms across the harbour, and the flames leapt from her hands. A stream of fire hit the closest fishing vessel, and the deck erupted in flames. The woman moved her fingers, and the flames jumped to the next vessel, and then the one next to that, until the entire fishing fleet was ablaze.

'Battle stations!' Lara cried, for the second time that day. 'Loose everything we've got at those bastards!'

The portal shimmered and vanished, after some three hundred Banner soldiers in heavy armour had charged through, then another portal appeared, on the far side of the harbour. A hideous shrieking and clacking noise reverberated from it, then greenhides poured through – a constant stream of the beasts. They raced through the harbour district, cutting down anyone too slow to escape their claws.

'Launch the pisspots!' Lara yelled. 'Launch them all, before the fire god hits us!'

The catapult on the bow of the *Gull* thrummed, and a large ceramic canister shot out from the vessel. It struck the quayside and exploded, ripping through the armoured Banner soldiers as they fanned out from where the first portal had been. The god in red robes turned, and saw the *Gull*. She raised her hand, just as a second pisspot flew off the bow of the ship. It exploded next to the woman, and she disappeared in a cloud of smoke and flames. Dragons appeared in the sky, circling over the harbour. Two soared down, and the man who had opened the first portal lifted a hand. The two dragons cried out in agony, then their heads disintegrated into twin flashes of blood and bone. Their bodies plummeted from the sky, and crashed into the housing district next to the harbour with a noise that shook the ground.

The ballista crews on the *Gull* were loosing bolt after bolt into the ranks of the Banner soldiers, while, on the other side of the harbour, the greenhides were still pouring through the new portal. Then, from the midst of the dust and confusion, the woman in red robes reappeared, striding along the quayside. Her robes were in tatters, but she looked unharmed. She glanced at the *Giddy Gull* for a moment, then raised her hand. Flames from the burning fishing boats leapt through the air, and smashed down onto the deck of the brigantine. By the front of the ship, the catapult had been loaded with their last pisspot, and as soon as the flames reached it, an explosion tore the bow to pieces. The fires reached the masts and sails, spreading along the deck with unnatural speed and fury. Sailors screamed as the fires tore through them, setting the clothes and hair alight.

'Abandon ship!' Lara cried, as the fires reached the quarter deck. 'Swim for the shore!'

Tommo stared at her. 'But, ma'am...'

'Don't bleeding well argue with me, lad!' she yelled, as the flames rose higher over the burning deck. 'Get your ass over the side!'

Tommo ran for it. He leapt up onto the railings on the port side of the deck, and dived into the water. Lara helped Topaz stand.

'My ship,' she groaned. 'My beautiful ship.'

The main mast cracked, the wood straining and screeching as the flames devoured it. It split halfway up, and the top fell, bringing tons of rigging and sails down with it, and trapping several sailors on the main deck.

A tear fell down Lara's cheek as she watched, then she shoved Topaz towards the side, and pushed him into the dark waters of the harbour.

He plunged under the surface, the pain from the bolt wound intensifying. He kicked out with his good leg, and rose up again. He took a gulp of air, then went back under.

He had to get to Maddie. They had to escape from Udall, before the town was destroyed. He kicked out again, and moved his arms, his survival instincts taking over as he struggled towards the rocky shore across from the main quayside. His left leg hit something, and then his hands felt rocks under him. He pulled himself out of the water, gasping for breath, and dragged his injured leg up onto the side of the road that ran next to the harbour basin.

A clacking noise above his head made him look up, and he saw a group of greenhides charging towards the shore. They reached another sailor from the *Gull*, who had also managed to swim to the road, and their claws tore him to shreds in seconds. Topaz plunged back into the water, as a greenhide raced towards him. It halted by the water's edge, its insect eyes staring at him as it shrieked in frustration. Then, its head turned, and it ran away, back towards the town. A man in dark grey robes strode down the road, his left hand clutching a Quadrant. Topaz took a deep breath, and submerged himself, waiting for the god to pass.

A hand reached into the water, and he was dragged out by the shoulder and thrown onto the road, spluttering, and shaking from the agony in his leg. He opened his eyes, and saw the god in grey robes smiling down at him.

'Oto'pazzi,' he said. 'You are Sable's friend. Don't try to deny it; I read it from your mind.'

'Who are you?' Topaz gasped.

'Come now; you know perfectly well who I am. Sable may have destroyed half of this world, but today she will learn that all things come with a cost.'

'Bastion?'

The god frowned, and Topaz felt a blast of pain rip through his body.

'That's "Lord" Bastion to you, mortal. Today is a day for revenge, and what better revenge could I take, than forcing the Holdfast witch to watch as her friends die?' He nodded to a squad of armoured Banner soldiers. 'Take him; this one's coming with us.'

'Yes, sir,' said one. 'Where next, my lord?'

Bastion smiled. 'The palace on the bridge. By the time this night is through, Udall will be nothing – a lifeless, smoking ruin. The graveyard of Sable's dreams.'

CHAPTER 28
ALL THE TIME IN THE WORLD

Serene, Implacatus – 17th Arginch 5255

Austin glanced around the busy market, keeping an eye out for any gods who might be lurking nearby. He had been shopping for half an hour, but no one had paid him the slightest attention as he had purchased food from several stalls, along with a flask of wine and some cigarettes. To the mortal inhabitants of Serene, he was just another man, passing through the busy streets of the enormous city. A couple of Banner soldiers were loitering by the entrance to the market, but they were there to keep the peace, not to root out any potential rogue demigods.

Austin kept his eyes down as he passed them on his way out of the market. He was in one of the lower districts of the city, and, as he had quickly learned, the lower the level, the poorer the citizens became. A vast slum of narrow, winding alleyways lay behind the bright, open and sunlit area where the market was located, and Austin headed into the shadows, tall stone tenements on either side. He walked for ten minutes, going by a different route to the one he had taken on his way to the market. He was wearing drab civilian clothes, but even those seemed better than the rags most of the local inhabitants had wrapped round themselves, and he earned a few glances as he strode down the narrow lanes.

He looked over his shoulder, then entered an abandoned building, its roof gone, and its walls blackened with grime. He crept down into the basement, and squinted in the light of a solitary candle. Sable was sitting on an upturned crate, her eyes glazed over.

Austin watched her for a moment, then sat on the dirty floorboards and lit a cigarette. It felt strange not to be on Dragon Eyre, and he was already missing the sunshine and islands, despite all of the horror and destruction he had witnessed. When he had been walking down to the market, he had passed a row of maimed Banner soldiers sitting by the roadside, their handwritten placards stating that they had been wounded while serving on Dragon Eyre. Austin had dropped them a few coins, and had then walked away quickly. How many more wounded soldiers would be arriving in Serene, their lives forever blighted by the woman sitting on the crate in front of him?

It was war, and these things happened, he told himself. He had to remember that he had also killed many Banner soldiers, leaving an unknown number of widows and orphans in Serene. It hadn't all been Sable.

The Holdfast woman blinked and coughed. She glanced down at Austin, and he offered her a lit cigarette.

'Thanks,' she said. 'Did you find food?'

He patted the bag next to him. 'Are you hungry?'

'Yes.'

He opened the bag, and withdrew a parcel wrapped in brown paper. He laid it out on the floor, and passed her a small leg of meat.

She peered at it. 'Which animal is this from?'

'It's roasted poultry,' he said. 'They're a kind of bird.'

'I think I might have eaten something like this in Rahain,' she said, then took a bite.

'How did the search go?'

'I've finally found the archive office, where the slave records are stored,' she said. 'It's only taken half the night.' She alternated between taking a bite, and smoking the cigarette.

'Where is it?'

'On an upper level.'

'And it has the records of every slave in Serene?'

She shook her head. 'Don't be silly, Austin. What a waste of paper that would be. Have you any idea how many slaves there are on Implacatus? No? A lot. The archives only deal with the present and past ownership records of slaves owned directly by the gods. Your father will be listed somewhere, and through him, we'll find where you mother is.'

'Thanks,' he said. 'I wouldn't have known where to start if you weren't here.'

She nodded. 'I've already stayed longer in Serene than I'd planned. I need to get back to Udall soon; Bastion is still on the loose.'

'You can go now, if you want,' he said. 'Just tell me where this office is located, and I'll take it from here. You can come back to collect both of us, once I've found her.'

'I might, but only if I think it's safe enough for you, and we're not at that stage yet. So, what's your mother's name?'

'Salah,' he said.

'Is that it? No other names?'

'Not as far as I know.'

'And how old is she?'

'Um, forty-two, or maybe forty-three? I'm not sure, Sable. I was only a child when I last saw her. I can't even remember when her birthday is.'

Sable nodded, then threw the poultry bone into a corner of the dark basement. 'Have you considered the possibility that she might already be dead?'

Austin's gaze fell to the filthy ground. 'Yes. Of course I have.'

'We'll work on the assumption that she's still alive, and see what we can find. There is another possibility, however; one that might be hard for you to hear.'

'What?'

'The possibility that she's alive, but that her life has been so traumatic, that she no longer remembers who you are. The lives of the slaves here in Serene, from the limited amount that I have witnessed, are short and brutal. Her mind may have gone.'

He shivered. 'I don't want to think about that.'

'She might also have been forced to carry other children.'

'Enough, Sable,' he said.

'Sorry. I guess I'm trying to lower your expectations. Believe me, I want things to turn out for the best, but you should be prepared for the worst.'

They finished the rest of the food in silence, then they shared the flask of sour wine. Sable blew out the candle, and they made their way up the stairs, and back out into the narrow alleyway that fronted the abandoned building. Sable glanced in both directions, then they set off, keeping to the thick shadows. A couple of men whistled at Sable as she passed, but she uncharacteristically ignored them, a fact for which Austin felt grateful. They needed to attract as little attention as possible while in Serene, and Sable's usual recklessness would only draw trouble.

They passed a few Banner soldiers, and emerged into a huge, cylindrical cavern that reached up through several levels of the city. A long staircase spiralled along the inner wall of the cylinder, while in the centre stood a colossal statue of two gods.

Austin halted on the marble paving slabs, and gazed up.

'Who are they?' said Sable.

'You should recognise the one on the left,' he said. 'It's Lord Kolai.'

'He looks older.'

'These statues were constructed well before anyone knew about salve,' he said.

'Why has the other one's face been hacked off?'

'It's Lord Simon, the Tenth Ascendant,' he said. 'He rebelled against Lord Edmond millennia ago, and then disappeared.'

Sable raised an eyebrow. 'These statues have been here for millennia? That can't be right. They would have decayed by now.'

'Not if they were built with the powers of the gods,' said Austin. 'They look as brand new as the day they were carved.'

A large group of civilians were starting to ascend the first flight of steps, and Sable nodded to Austin.

'Let's tag along with them,' she whispered. 'We need to get past that god standing by the next level.'

They joined the back of the group, and kept their heads down as they climbed the steps. Banner soldiers were also standing at the top of the flight of stairs, and Sable stared at their armour.

'What are those soldiers wearing?' she whispered.

'Stone armour,' Austin said. 'It's pressed into thin sheets by gods, and then moulded to fit. It's the hardest material ever discovered.'

'It's also the prettiest,' she said. 'Look at those pink and orange swirls on that guy's breastplate. How do I get myself a set?'

'You would need to capture a god who possessed stone powers,' he said. 'Meader could have made you some.'

Sable's eyes fell. 'I wonder if your father knows what happened to him.'

'I doubt it,' said Austin. 'I imagine that the gods think my brother's still on the loose.'

'I hope you aren't tempted to try to contact your father while we're here.'

'No,' he said. 'My father will be locked up somewhere within Cumulus, probably with a restrainer mask strapped to his face. It would be suicide to try to reach him.'

'Belinda will be up there, too,' said Sable; 'getting ready for her wedding. I hated that stupid bitch for a long time, but now? Now, all I feel for her is pity.'

The large group passed the soldiers at the top of the stairs, while the god glanced over them. Sable and Austin followed the group for a few more moments, then they slipped down a street as soon as they were out of sight of the god by the stairs.

'This is the level we want,' said Sable, as they walked down a wide road. 'The Banners have their headquarters here, and the records office is close by.'

Austin glanced around at the large buildings on either side of the road. Some looked like offices, while others had a fortress-feel to them, and each was flying a standard from their front gates, displaying the name and crest of their Banner. There was also a smattering of recruitment offices, their wages and conditions displayed outside on billboards.

'Do you not feel nervous, walking down this street,' said Austin; 'considering how many Banner soldiers we've killed?'

'No,' she said. 'None of them have the slightest clue who we are. I would doubt that anyone in Serene will have heard of me. I remember Meader once telling me that the gods heavily restricted bad news from reaching the citizens.'

'He was right,' Austin said. 'That's what happened with Lostwell. The worse it got, the less news was allowed to circulate. And, when that world was finally destroyed, the news was kept from every mortal, so that they wouldn't be disheartened. The gods invest a lot of time in presenting themselves as always being successful. They trumpet their victories, and ignore their defeats. I wonder if anyone here knows that Kolai is dead.'

Sable slowed as they approached a large, windowless office block. They waited until the road was clear of people, then slipped down an alleyway that ran to the rear of the huge building. A rat scurried past their feet, and they came to a back door. Sable paused, and her eyes went hazy for a few moments; then she grasped the door handle, and wrenched it open, breaking the lock. She glanced around again, then they entered a dark passageway. Austin followed her deeper into the gloom, their boots tapping over the marble floor. They reached a set of stairs, and descended into the building's basement, where Sable took out Meader's lighter, and lit a wall lamp.

'The staff work upstairs,' she said in a low voice. 'We should be safe down here for a while.'

She lifted the lamp clear of the wall sconce, and they entered a vast room, its ceiling held up by regular lines of slim pillars. The chamber was filled with shelves that lined the walls and ran down the middle of the room. Austin walked up to the closest shelf, and saw that it was full of papers, all marked by a god's name. He picked up the nearest bundle of papers, and read the name Antoninus at the top of the first page. Beneath the god's name was a long list, of every slave that he had owned.

Sable sighed. 'No fancy powers are going to help with this search. Grab yourself a lamp, and we'll get started.'

Sable and Austin spent hours rummaging through the endless shelves of the archives room. At first, it had seemed as though the names were sorted in alphabetical order, but that had been an illusion – there appeared to be no clear organising principle behind the haphazard collection of documents. Sable's impatience began to grow, and she had muttered her desire to return to Dragon Eyre several times during the search.

At last, he heard a cry of joy come from her lips, and he hurried over to where she stood. She was brandishing a thick bundle of papers, with the name Ferdinand written at the top in clear letters.

'Thank the gods,' Austin said; 'I was beginning to lose hope.'

He took the bundle, and flicked through the many pages, as Sable held up the lamp to provide some illumination. The slaves were listed in chronological order, and the first few pages were yellowed and tattered at the edges. He went through more pages, and began to feel disconcerted. Just how many slaves had his father owned over the ages? There were a hundred names per page, and the list went on and on. He skipped to the last page, and began working back from the present, his finger running down the faded paper.

His finger stopped. Salah. His eyes welled and he nearly wept at the sight of his mother's name. He read the full entry.

'Meader was right,' he said. 'My father sold her the moment I was sent to school. That bastard. He sold her to an armaments factory. They're based two levels below us.'

'Is she still there?'

'It doesn't say.'

'Let me take a look.'

He passed her the bundle, and she examined the entry next to his mother's name.

'Bought when she was fifteen, sold when she was twenty-six,' said Sable. 'She was marked down as capable of performing heavy labour. Austin, she wouldn't have lasted this long doing that kind of work. She might well have been sold on.'

'But there are no records beyond that,' he said. 'If she was sold privately, then she could be anywhere.'

'We'll check out the factory,' she said. 'You never know, we might be wrong; she might still be there.'

Two hours later, the factory manager confirmed their suspicions. Sable had tied him to a chair, and scoured his mind, until the man had been reduced to a sobbing wreck.

'I don't remember any Salah,' he wept; 'please stop hurting me.'

Sable sat down in the manager's small office, and lit a cigarette. Outside, in the main part of the factory, work was going on as normal, as hundreds of slaves toiled to produce uniforms and equipment for the Banners. They were making a loud racket, which had masked the sobs and cries coming from the manager.

Tell me,' Sable said to him; 'once a worker becomes too old, or too weak to keep working for you, what do you do with them?'

'We try to sell them on,' he whimpered. 'We usually only get a pittance for them, but it's better than nothing.'

'Who do you sell them to?'

'Anyone who wants them.'

'Do you keep records?'

'No.'

'Why not?' said Austin.

'To avoid paying tax on the transactions,' the manager said.

'I'm going to have to go in deep,' said Sable. 'There might be a fragment of a memory lodged somewhere inside his brain; somewhere his conscious mind can no longer reach. Keep a watch on the door.'

Austin nodded, then Sable moved her chair until she was right in front of the manager.

'Please,' he begged, then he made a choking noise. Sable's eyes glazed over, and the man's face turned red, his eyes bulging out of his head. Sweat poured down his forehead, and the veins on his neck looked ready to burst. Austin tried not to look, but he was unable to pull his gaze away from the man's suffering. Blood trickled down from his nostrils, and the smell of excrement reached Austin's nose as the man soiled himself. He let out a final strained, choking gasp, then his head lolled forward.

Sable stood, took out a knife, and slit the man's throat.

'I've found her,' she said. 'She was one of three slaves that he sold four years ago, to a man who lives on the lowest level of Serene. I have the address.'

Austin gazed at the dead body, unsure whether to cheer with joy or throw up.

'Come on,' she said. 'We need to hurry. It'll be early evening in Udall by now, and I need to get back.'

The streets were quieter when they made their way to one of the enormous stairwells that connected the various levels of the city. Sable had told Austin nothing about the man to whom his mother had been sold by the factory, and her impatience was almost tangible.

'You'll be back in Dragon Eyre soon,' he said to her, as they neared the stairs. 'Is it Lara that you're desperate to see?'

'I'm not desperate,' she snapped. 'And Lara wasn't even in Udall when we left. No, it's Bastion's attack on the town that I can't get out of my mind. With the Home Islands collapsing into anarchy, I'm worried about what he'll decide to do next. You and I are two of the most powerful people on Dragon Eyre, Austin. I hope you realise what that will mean for our futures, if we decide to live in Ulna.'

'I thought you wanted to live on your own?'

'I do, but Blackrose said I could stay anywhere on Ulna that I liked. I'm not sure what to do any more, but a quiet corner of Ulna might be ideal.'

A lone god was standing by the top of the stairs, along with more Banner soldiers wearing brightly coloured suits of stone armour. Austin glanced around, but there was no one else approaching the stairs on their level.

'Keep your head down, Austin,' Sable whispered.

'Maybe we should go another way,' he said.

'It's too late for that. If we turn around now, they'll only get suspicious.'

They reached the stairs, and the god gave them a long glance as they passed him. They began descending the steps, and a voice cried out.

'Stop them! One of them is a rogue demigod!'

Sable took off, jumping down the stairs, and Austin ran after her, as the sound of heavy boots thudded behind them.

They reached the next level, and darted along a street, passing groups of civilians.

'Down here,' Sable said, then she veered off to the right, down a long alleyway. They went round a bend, and Austin glanced ahead, then groaned. It was a dead end. He turned, and saw the Banner soldiers at the corner of the alleyway. The god strode past them, and stared at Sable and Austin.

'Who are you?' he shouted.

'I...' Austin began.

'Not you, demigod,' said the man. 'I know perfectly well who you are, traitor. It's the woman that puzzles me. Why can't I read her mind?' He glanced at the soldiers. 'Arrest them both.'

Sable raised her hand, and the four soldiers toppled over, their eyes closing as they crashed to the ground. The god remained standing, but his face was straining, as if he were battling an unseen power. Sable strode forward, and the god fell to his knees.

She smiled down at him, the knife in her hand. 'Prepare to die.'

'No!' cried Austin. 'If you kill him, then this level will be swarming with gods.'

Sable hesitated, then lowered the knife. 'You're probably right,' she said. She placed a hand onto the god's face to hold it steady, then stared into his eyes. The god let out a gasping noise, then collapsed to the cobbles. Sable then went to each of the four soldiers, prising open their eyes and staring at each in turn.

She nodded to Austin, and they crept back onto the main road, and rejoined the crowds.

'What did you do to them?' Austin whispered, as they walked.

'I removed all memory of us from their minds,' she said. 'When they wake up, they will have no idea why they were lying in an alleyway.'

'I really thought you were going to kill that god,' he said. 'Thank you for not doing it.'

Sable sniffed. 'This place stinks. In fact, most of Serene stinks.'

'It's a lot cleaner and brighter on the upper levels,' Austin said. 'That's why guards are posted on the stairways; to prevent the people in the lower levels from going up there.'

'While beneath us is nothing but a desert wasteland?'

'A poisonous desert wasteland; and not a single mortal here realises it.'

They walked on for a further twenty minutes through the slums of the lower levels, then Sable came to a halt. She pointed at a dilapidated old building.

'Here we are,' she said. 'Pass me the bag of gold.'

'Why?'

'Because I'm going to buy your mother from the man that lives here. I know what she looks like; well, I know what she looked like nearly twenty years ago, when you last saw her.'

He opened the pack and passed her the pouch filled with Dragon Eyre gold. 'Should I come in?'

She gave him a few coins back. 'No. I might need to kill everyone.' She glanced across the street. 'See that tavern? Get a table inside, and wait for me there. I'll have some wine, but if they haven't got anything decent, then a gin will do.'

She turned to leave.

'Wait,' said Austin. 'What are you hiding from me?'

Sable looked him in the eye. 'Your mother is living like an animal inside that house. She's chained up inside a box, and is only let out to scrub the floors, and to do anything else the owner demands of her. It's not pretty, Austin, and I don't want you to see it.'

'But, how do you know all that?'

'I've been scanning our destination for the last ten minutes. Go. Wait for us in the tavern.'

She strode away, leaving Austin staring at her back. He watched her knock at the front door of the crumbling old mansion. An old woman opened it, and, after a few words were exchanged, Sable went inside, and the door was closed.

He walked over to the tavern, and entered. The inside was as filthy as the outside, and Austin realised immediately that it was not the sort of establishment that would sell wine that Sable would consider 'decent'. He noticed a quiet, unoccupied corner, then walked to the bar.

'Three large gins, please,' he said to the barman.

The man glanced around. 'Three?'

'My... friends will be joining me shortly,' he said.

The man poured the gin from a grimy ceramic bottle, and Austin took them over to the quiet corner table. He sat, his foot drumming off the floor with anxiety. There were no windows facing the street, and he had no idea what was happening inside the old mansion. The minutes passed, and he felt like screaming. He took a sip of gin, and nearly gagged from the horrific taste it left in his mouth.

The door of the tavern opened, and Sable walked in, her arm supporting an older woman. Austin stood. Sable looked up, and saw him, then guided the woman over to the corner table.

'What are you going to do with me?' said the older woman, as she sat down, her rags almost falling from her thin shoulders.

'Mother?' said Austin.

The woman blinked, then glanced at Austin's face. For a moment, her expression remained frozen, then she burst into tears, and reached out for him.

'Austin?' she wept. 'My boy; Austin. Is it really you?'

'It's me, mother,' he said, as he pulled her into a tight embrace. He noticed scars and bruises down her arms, and on her face. He pulled away, then glanced at the two women in front of him. There was little over ten years between Sable and his mother, but the difference in ages seemed far greater. His mother looked like a frail old woman.

He raised his hand, and summoned his healing powers.

'What are you doing?' said Sable. 'If you use your powers in here, any god who is close by will be able to detect you.'

'You've used your powers.'

'That's different. My powers are undetectable; yours will shine out like a beacon.'

'I don't care,' he said. 'I can't leave my mother in pain. It's worth the risk.'

He sent healing powers into his mother, who clutched the edge of the table as she shuddered. The cuts and bruises on her skin disappeared, and the stoop in her back straightened. She gasped, then stared at her son.

'Thank you,' she said, her voice stronger than before. 'I didn't know you had healing powers.' She glanced at Sable. 'Thank you for bringing me to my son, mistress.'

'You don't need to call her that,' said Austin. 'We came to free you.'

'But, son,' his mother said; 'that can't be right. This lady here owns me now.'

Sable sat down, and picked up her gin. 'No, I don't,' she said. 'Your son's right – you're free.'

'I'm free? But, I've been a slave all my life.'

'Not any more, mother,' said Austin. 'It's over, and you're coming home with me.'

Salah stared at him.

Sable downed her glass of gin in one. 'Let's go, before I go back into that house and slaughter every bastard in there.'

'Go?' said Salah. 'Go where?'

Austin lowered his voice. 'To Dragon Eyre, mother. I have a home there, where we can be safe.'

The woman looked confused. 'Dragon Eyre? We can't go there; we'll be killed.'

Sable took out the Quadrant. 'We can explain all this when we get there.'

'What about my sister?' said Salah. 'She's a slave too, and I know where she lives.' She turned to Sable. 'Please, I beg you; can you free her too?'

'Out of the question,' said Sable. 'We haven't got time for that.'

Salah turned to Austin. 'You remember your Aunty Sunnah, don't you? She helped me look after you in the harem.'

Austin shook his head. 'All of the women there were like aunties to me. I can only really remember you.'

'The family that own her are cruel. My boy; I'm sorry, but I can't leave her.'

'You have no choice,' said Sable. 'I can't free every damn slave in Serene.'

'I'm not asking you to free every slave,' said Salah; 'just my sister. Save her, and I'll go anywhere you like.'

Sable frowned in exasperated frustration. 'My answer is no.'

'This can be easily resolved,' said Austin. 'Give me what's left of the gold, and I'll buy her. Sable, you can go back to Dragon Eyre, then collect us in a few days.'

'I don't know, Austin. Remember what happened at the stairs. If another god reads your mind, you'll be arrested.'

'It'll be fine,' he said. 'Mother, where is Sunnah?'

'She's on this level, in a house about two hours' walk from here.'

Austin nodded. 'Are there soldiers or gods on the way to this house?'

Salah gazed at her son. 'Are you in trouble?'

'I need to remain unnoticed. I'm supposed to be on Dragon Eyre, not here.'

She nodded. 'I don't know if there are any soldiers. It's been six months since I was allowed to see Sunnah.'

Austin turned back to Sable. 'Go. We'll be alright. I'll find somewhere temporary to rent for a few days, and my mother can stay there while I deal with my Aunt Sunnah. Two hours is a long walk. Unless... what if you use the Quadrant to take us directly to where my aunt lives?'

'I can't,' said Sable. 'I don't know how to make the Quadrant take me to Dragon Eyre. The only way to get back is to prompt it to go to the last place it was used.'

'That settles it,' he said. 'You go back, and then you can return here in, say, three days?'

'Let's make it four, just in case,' she said. 'Meet me in the alleyway where we first appeared in Serene, at noon on the twenty-first of the month.' She passed him the bag of gold. 'There's plenty left over; spend whatever you need.'

'Thanks.'

She shrugged.

'I mean it, Sable; thanks for everything.'

Sable stood. 'Just make sure you're all in the right place, at the right time. See you soon, and be careful.'

She turned, and headed towards the bathroom, the Quadrant clutched in her right hand.

'She seems like a nice young lady,' said his mother, 'though she frightened my former owner; I've never seen him so scared.' She gazed at Austin, her eyes drinking him in. 'Did you really come all the way to Implacatus just for me?'

'Yes, mother. I'm so sorry that it's taken me so long to come and find you. I was naïve. I had no idea that father would sell you after I left the harem to go to school. I have a hundred questions to ask you.'

'Austin,' she said, smiling; 'don't worry about that. We have all the time in the world.'

CHAPTER 29
THE LAST THROW

U dall, Ulna, Eastern Rim – 17th Arginch 5255 (18th Gylean Year 6)
'I understand your concerns,' said Blackrose, 'but I feel it is worth the risk. Sable has been an extremely useful ally, regardless of whether or not you like her.'

'But, my betrothed,' said Shadowblaze, 'this is not about my personal feelings concerning the Holdfast witch. It is true that I do not like her, but, more importantly, I do not trust her. Nor did you, until a short while ago, it seems.'

'I found her to be reliable when we journeyed from Haurn to Ectus,' the Queen said, 'but I am aware of her previous transgressions. For the services she has rendered, and due to the respect in which I hold her, I am prepared to overlook whatever may have occurred in the past.'

'She forced me to attack you, my Queen,' Shadowblaze said, his temper rising.

'I, too, dislike her,' said Ahi'edo, 'but the Queen is not asking us to be friends with Sable. Think of the benefits of allowing her to live on Ulna.'

'My rider,' said Shadowblaze; 'what is this I am hearing? After everything that Sable Holdfast did to you, are you saying that you are prepared to forgive her?'

Ahi'edo glanced down for a moment. 'Yes. If it comes to that, then yes. The safety of Ulna is more important than an old grudge, and I'm tired of hating her. Sable is possibly the most powerful human on Dragon Eyre, and she would be better as an ally, rather than an enemy.'

Maddie smiled, but held her tongue.

Blackrose tilted her head. 'Well said, Ahi'edo. Uncle, what are your thoughts on this matter?'

'I agree with Shadowblaze's rider, my Queen,' said Greysteel. 'One only has to look at Enna to see how useful Sable could be, if we welcomed her back to Ulna. The Wystians there have been forced to withdraw north to Geist. With Sable based in Ulna, they would never dare touch our island. With Austin too, we would have a formidable defensive force at our disposal. The Wystians fear them both, and with good reason.'

'May I speak?' said Ashfall.

'Of course,' said Blackrose. 'I have missed your counsels of late, Ashfall.'

The slender grey dragon bowed her head. 'Sable is highly unpredictable, my Queen. She has a reckless nature, and seldom thinks through the consequences of her actions. She told us that it was her desire to live alone, far away from the populated areas of Dragon Eyre.'

'I discussed this with her,' said Blackrose, 'and offered her the chance to dwell in any remote location on Ulna, if she so chooses. There are plenty of places upon our island where she could live alone, and yet remain close enough to be called upon if required.'

'That seems a reasonable compromise, my Queen,' said Ashfall. 'If that were the case, then I would be happy for her to live in Ulna. Not only would it give the Wystians pause, but the gods of Implacatus are terrified of her powers. She slaughtered many gods and demigods on her long rampage.'

'And an Ascendant,' said Maddie. 'She killed one of the best gods Implacatus has to offer. I know that you're all focussed on Ulna, but Sable is protecting all of Dragon Eyre, just by being here.'

Blackrose eyed her. 'I assume that you would be content to see her live on Ulna, my rider?'

'More than content. Unlike a lot of you, I do like Sable. Yes, I know that she's lied to each of us at one time or another, and what she did to Ahi'edo and Shadowblaze was terrible, but now that her rampage is over, it would be generous of us to offer her a fresh start.'

'And it would be dangerous if we didn't,' said Greysteel. 'Do we really want Sable to be banished to some remote island, with the power she is capable of wielding? Might not her resentment fester?'

'It sounds like blackmail,' said Shadowblaze. 'If I understand you correctly, you seem to be saying that we should appease the witch, lest she turn her wrath upon us.'

'I did not reconcile with Sable out of fear,' said Blackrose. 'In truth, I pity her. Think of the grief you felt when Ahi'edo was injured, or the madness that threatened to overwhelm me when Maddie was abducted. Sable lost her dragon, and their bond cut deep. I do not intend to cast blame at those whose actions were dictated by grief. She has done terrible things, but those terrible things have driven the occupying forces to the brink of extinction. I shall not turn my back on her.'

'It seems your mind is made up,' said Shadowblaze.

Blackrose looked at her betrothed. 'Do you remain implacably opposed to my decision?'

'I do,' he said. 'I regret that this is the case, my Queen, but Sable is a danger to us all. Those who embrace a snake cannot complain when they are bitten.'

The huge hall fell into silence.

'With your permission, your Majesty,' said Greysteel, 'I shall compile a list of locations upon Ulna that might prove suitable for Sable's needs. There is an old hunting lodge a few miles from Seabound Palace, for instance, that could be made habitable again.'

'Thank you, uncle; please do so,' said Blackrose. 'We can present her with the list when she returns from Implacatus.'

'I think she would like to be near the sea,' said Maddie. 'You know, so that Captain Lara could visit.'

'The Osso girl might well prove to be the key,' said Blackrose. 'Sable appears to have a genuine affection for her; if nurtured, it could provide her with a healthy reason to live a peaceful life.'

'Was that a long way to say that love might fix her?' said Maddie.

'I doubt Sable is capable of feeling love,' said Shadowblaze.

'She loved Badblood,' said Maddie.

Shadowblaze's amber eyes burned. 'I see that I am heavily outnumbered in this debate. Very well, I shall say no more. You all know my feelings on the subject.'

'Perhaps you will come round in time,' said Greysteel. He turned to a large open window. 'Wait. I think I heard a scream come from the harbour.'

'I heard it too,' said Blackrose. 'Go and see if anything is happening that should concern us.'

Greysteel strode to the window, and Maddie and Ahi'edo walked with him. They gazed out over the town, and Maddie's eyes widened. Several things were happening at once. By the breakwaters, the *Giddy Gull* was entering the harbour, but there was no sign of the other Five Sisters vessels. More concerning was the strange, quivering black void that had opened up along the quayside. Soldiers were charging through it, and attacking anyone who stood in their way.

'We are under attack!' cried Greysteel. 'A god has opened a portal on the quayside, just as before.'

'Greenhides?' said the Queen.

'No, your Majesty; soldiers. When exactly is Sable Holdfast due to return?'

Blackrose strode over. 'She did not give a precise time.'

Maddie stared down at the harbour. Someone was raising their hands on the quayside, then fire streamed down, enveloping the town's fleet of fishing boats. The portal then snapped out of existence, and re-appeared on the far side of the harbour. The *Giddy Gull* launched a missile from its bow, and an explosion tore through a dozen Banner soldiers, as greenhides began pouring out of the second portal.

'Send the guard patrol down,' said Blackrose, 'and assemble every dragon able to fight.'

'At once, your Majesty,' said Greysteel, turning and striding away.

A second device loosed by the *Giddy Gull* exploded on the quayside, then Maddie gazed in horror as the flames from the fishing boats diverted towards the brigantine. A torrent of fire crashed down onto the *Gull's* bow, then the flames swept along the deck.

The two dragons on guard duty above the palace swooped down towards the harbour, but they were struck by the powers of a god, and their heads disintegrated.

'Bastion is here,' said Blackrose.

'We have to help the *Gull*,' cried Maddie. 'Topaz and Lara are on board. We can't let them burn.'

'We will not abandon our allies,' said Blackrose. 'Follow me.'

The Queen led the others from the hall, and they ascended a ramp onto a high platform. Several dragons were perched upon the many other platforms that crowned the palace, and they turned to Blackrose for guidance.

'Defend Ulna!' the Queen cried. 'Drive the invaders into the ocean!'

Maddie climbed up onto Blackrose's harness, and the great black dragon extended her wings. She soared up into the darkening sky, the sun low at her back, then hurtled down towards the harbour. Blackrose opened her jaws as she dived at the greenhides, and flames flooded the road on the far side from the quay. A dozen greenhides screamed as the flames tore through them. All over Udall, the Queen's dragons were attacking the forces that had entered through the portals, but one by one, they were being struck down by Bastion.

'We are being slaughtered, my Queen!' cried Shadowblaze, as he swooped beside Blackrose.

Maddie felt a powerful presence tear through her mind.

I see you, Queen of Ulna, said the voice. *It is time to settle Sable's account. Today, Ulna burns.*

Blackrose and Shadowblaze cried out as Bastion's death powers struck them. The god was standing by the roadside with his arms in the air, a squad of armoured Banner soldiers surrounding him. Shadowblaze shoved Blackrose to the side, and placed himself between the Queen and the Ancient, as blood streamed from his amber eyes, then both dragons fell from the sky. Maddie could sense that Blackrose was still conscious, but her wings seemed useless, and she crashed into the wide river. Maddie was plunged underwater with her, the straps on the harness keeping her secured to the dragon's shoulders. She closed her eyes and mouth, and felt water go up her nose as she tried not to panic. Beneath her, Blackrose's limbs were scrambling against the bottom of the river, then the dragon crawled her way up the bank. Maddie's head rose above the water, and she took a breath, then Blackrose collapsed on the muddy bank.

'Shadowblaze,' the black dragon gasped, then she closed her eyes.

Maddie unbuckled the harness straps, and slid down into the brown waters of the river. Her boots sank into the deep mud, and she gripped onto Blackrose to avoid stumbling. She waded through the river, and clambered up the gentle slope of the bank, glancing around for Shadowblaze. There was no sign of the red and grey dragon anywhere, but she could see plenty of other dragons. Greysteel was leading a retreat away from the centre of the town, and out of Bastion's range. Maddie turned, and saw the *Giddy Gull* in the harbour, its sails burning. On the far bank of the river, greenhides were swarming along the road in the direction of the palace. Maddie felt numb. Had she really believed that the war was over?

'Raise your arms!' cried a gruff voice.

She turned, and saw a squad of armoured Banner soldiers aiming their crossbows at her. She lifted her empty hands.

'Inform Lord Bastion that we have captured the Queen and her rider,' the soldier said; 'and fetch chains for the dragon.'

A colleague saluted and ran off. Two of the soldiers strode towards Maddie. They each took an arm, and twisted them behind her back, then she was pushed up the slope to the road at the top.

The officer looked Maddie up and down. 'Name?'

'Maddie Jackdaw.'

'I'm going to ask you this once – where is Sable Holdfast?'

'I don't know,' she said.

'If you're lying to me, miss, we'll soon discover it, and you'll be sorry.'

'I'm not lying; I have no idea where Sable is. However, here's what I do know – if she comes back to Udall, she'll kill you all.'

The officer glanced down the slope. 'Is the beast alive?'

'Yes, sir,' said a soldier, who was knee-deep in water next to Black-rose's head. 'She's breathing.'

The officer and soldiers stood to attention as a man in dark robes approached. He smiled as he glanced at the unconscious form of Black-rose on the bank of the river, then he stared into Maddie's eyes, and she felt an intrusion into her mind.

'Sable is on Implacatus,' he said.

'Implacatus, sir?' said the officer.

'Yes, and she has taken the demigod with flow powers with her. Udall is undefended.'

'What are your orders, sir?'

'We shall continue as planned, Captain,' said the man. 'Block the bridges, to ensure that the greenhides remain on the western bank of the river, then take our prisoners to the palace. I shall transport the Queen of Ulna myself.'

'There are still around eighty or so dragons in the skies, sir.'

'I am aware of that. They will not approach, Captain. They fear me too much. Go to the palace and I will meet you there, and then, we shall await the arrival of the Holdfast witch.'

The officer's face paled. 'Sir, should we not destroy the town and then leave?'

'Had I known that you were so weak-willed, Captain,' said the robed man, 'I would have selected someone else to lead the Banner soldiers on this operation. There will be no retreat from Udall this time. Where is there to retreat to? Dragon Eyre is burning, and this is the last throw of the dice. Either we prevail today, or our time on this world is over. Are you up to the task?'

The officer straightened. 'Yes, sir.'

'Then take Miss Jackdaw to the palace, and never question my orders again.'

'Yes, sir. Sorry, sir.'

The soldiers shoved Maddie along the road, leaving the robed man staring out over the ruins of the harbour.

'Was that Lord Bastion?' Maddie whispered to one of her guards.

The soldier to her left nodded, then glanced away. Maddie was led to the palace gates, which were deserted, the militia guards dead or gone. They entered, and ascended the stairs to the dragon levels. The palace seemed even emptier than it normally did, and the only sounds were coming from outside. The soldiers stopped at a stout door, and one of them unlocked it. Maddie was pushed into a dark chamber, and the door was shut behind her. She tripped, and fell to the floor, then felt a hand touch her arm. She jumped in fright.

'It's me,' said Topaz.

She leapt at him, and threw her arms around his neck. He cried out in pain.

'My leg,' he groaned.

'Sorry,' she said; 'sorry. What happened?'

'I got shot in a battle near Tunkatta, this morning.'

She glanced down and, in the dim light, caught a glimpse of a sodden bandage wrapped round his right shin.

'You're all wet,' she said.

'So are you.'

'When I saw the flames reach the *Giddy Gull* I thought... well, I'd hoped you'd made it overboard in time.'

'I did, but I don't know what happened to the rest of the crew. Lara shoved me off the quarter deck, and that was the last I saw of her. I'm only in here because Bastion knew I was one of Sable's friends. He said he was going to kill me in front of her.'

'Is that why we were captured?' said Maddie. 'Lord Bastion read my mind, and he knows that Sable is on Implacatus.'

'What? Why is she there, of all bleeding places?'

'She's helping Austin with something.'

'Wait; does this mean that Blackrose has also been captured?'

'Yes. Bastion's bringing her up to the palace.'

'Shit. We're screwed, aren't we? The one time we really need Sable, and she ain't here. Bastion could make our heads explode with a snap of his fingers.'

'Maybe Tilly and Ann will arrive soon.'

'They won't be here until tomorrow at dawn, at the earliest. Both of their ships were damaged fighting the Sea Banner. They ain't got any weapons left, neither. They gave all of their pisspots to us.'

'All the same, I'm not giving up.'

He took her hand. 'Neither am I. If we're going down, then we'll die fighting.'

'I don't want to die, Topaz. After everything I've been through, to finally find someone like you...' She shook her head. 'We are not going to die. I refuse to accept it. Yesterday morning, we were talking about starting a family, and now this happens.' She narrowed her eyes. 'Bastion said that if they don't win here today, then it's over for them on Dragon Eyre. He admitted it, right in front of a squad of Banner soldiers. They're so close to giving up; we just need to survive for a little bit longer.'

A key sounded in the lock, and the sturdy door was shoved open.

'Right, you two,' said a soldier. 'On your feet.'

'This man has an injured leg,' said Maddie. 'He needs assistance.'

The soldier nodded to one of his colleagues, who stepped into the chamber, and helped Topaz stand. Maddie got to her feet next to Topaz, and they were led through the quiet hallways of the palace. Groups of Banner soldiers were resting, or standing guard by the main junctions, but there were no signs of any dragons or militia guards. They came to the huge reception hall, and were brought inside. Blackrose was lying unconscious in the middle of the floor, her wings bound in chains, and a large muzzle covering her jaws. Next to her, Lord Bastion was pacing up and down, a sword now hanging from his belt.

'Here are the prisoners, sir,' said one of the soldiers.

'Bring them over, and have someone fetch my armour.'

'Yes, sir.'

Maddie and Topaz were pushed towards Bastion, until they were standing two yards in front of him. Another door opened, and Millen was brought into the hall, his hands bound behind his back. He was shoved forwards, and fell sprawling onto the ground.

Bastion raised an eyebrow. 'I didn't realise Sable had so many friends. We're just missing the pirate captain, and then we'd have the full set.'

Millen glanced up from the floor. 'Sable's going to kick your ass.'

'It's touching, the faith you have in that misguided mortal,' said Bastion. 'I wonder if you'll retain that opinion once she is lying dead at my feet. Silly me. Of course you won't, for I intend to kill you all slowly in front of her. Seeing her friends suffer hardly seems to be an adequate punishment for her many crimes, but it will have to do. And then, once Sable is no more, we can begin the reoccupation of this world, though, I daresay it will be greenhides for Ulna again.'

'We're not scared of you,' said Maddie. 'What happened to Lord Kolai? Tell us.'

'You have a big mouth for someone so fragile, Miss Jackdaw,' said Bastion. 'I look forward to closing it permanently.'

'Oh, shut up,' said Maddie. 'I'm so sick of you stupid gods coming here and ruining everything, just like you did on Lostwell. Nothing's ever enough for you, is it? No matter how many worlds you conquer, you always want more. Oh, and how's your search for salve going? You found it yet?'

The smallest trace of a smile edged round Bastion's lips.

'One rarely hears a mortal address an Ancient in such terms,' he said. 'You are to be commended for your courage, Miss Jackdaw, or perhaps it is stupidity? If we were on Implacatus, I would have killed you out of hand, but, alas, we are on Dragon Eyre, and my purpose here is to slay the Holdfast witch. You are a mere afterthought.'

The Banner captain entered the hall, and saluted Lord Bastion.

'The eastern bank of the river is under Banner control, sir,' he said. 'Lady Vettra is requesting permission to burn the town to the ground.'

'Are the bridges blocked?'

'Yes, sir. The greenhides are currently confined to the western bank. The civilians have been seen fleeing into the outer suburbs, while the dragons have retreated.'

Bastion nodded. 'Inform Lady Vettra to commence the razing of the town. Ensure that all Banner soldiers are pulled back to the palace first, before the inferno begins.'

The captain saluted again. 'Yes, sir.'

Bastion turned to Blackrose as the officer hurried out of the hall.

'I think it's time to awaken the beast,' he said.

He laid a hand onto the dragon's black scales, and her eyes opened.

'Look around, lizard,' said Bastion. 'These three mortals are all that remain of your realm. The others were too cowardly to stay and fight. They have deserted you, false Queen, precisely when you needed them.'

Blackrose turned her red eyes to the Ancient. 'Why am I still alive?'

'To teach Sable Holdfast a lesson,' said Bastion. 'I want her to watch as I kill you all. She needs to learn the cost of interfering with the designs of Implacatus. Then, after she has seen you suffer, I shall remove her head, and present it to Lord Edmond as a wedding gift. I think he'll appreciate the gesture. After Lostwell, his sacred Majesty has developed a strong dislike of the Holdfast clan. To be frank, I'm not overly fond of them myself.'

'Go back to your own world while you still have the chance, god.'

Bastion laughed. 'Dragon Eyre belongs to us. If you people had accepted that basic fact decades ago, then thousands of lives would not have been thrown away in a pointless conflict. Sable may have set us back, but we can rebuild what she has destroyed; and this time, we shall be more thorough. The dragons will be utterly exterminated, like vermin, while the humans of this world will be hunted down and slaughtered. This is what we should have done from the very beginning. Mercy is a meaningless concept when dealing with sub-created species.'

Two soldiers entered the hall, bearing a suit of armour. Bastion beckoned them closer, then stood with his arms extended to each side as the soldiers strapped the steel plating onto the Ancient's body. A helmet was placed onto Bastion's head, with a full visor that covered his face.

'Frightened, are you?' said Maddie.

Bastion lifted the visor. 'It's a simple case of learning from our mistakes, Miss Jackdaw. I saw how Sable ensnared Lord Kolai. She will not be doing the same to me. It happens that I have read the last conversation you had with the witch before she left for Serene, and know exactly where Sable will re-appear.' He pointed a steel gauntlet towards an entrance. 'She will walk through that door, and then the games shall commence.'

'We could be here for days,' said Millen.

'I can wait,' said Bastion. 'I have no pressing business elsewhere.'

Millen frowned. 'Isn't your capital city burning?'

'Cities seem ephemeral to one who has lived for twenty-five thousand years, Millen of Alea Tanton. Whatever has been built will end up in ruins one day, and even the mightiest palaces crumble to dust. I remember what Implacatus was like long before Serene or Cumulus were constructed, and even those two great cities will eventually fall. Everything dies; except us.'

'Tell that to Kolai,' Maddie said.

'Don't try to hasten your death, Miss Jackdaw. It will come in due course.'

A soldier ran in from the hallway outside. 'She's here! Sable's here, my lord.'

'Guard the prisoners,' said Bastion to the Banner soldiers in the hall. 'Sable is mine.'

Maddie felt hands grip her arms, as she turned her head to face the doorway. Time seemed to stand still for a moment, as everyone stared at the entrance. Bastion drew his sword.

Sable appeared by the doorway, unarmed, and wearing the same flowery dress from before. She glanced into the hall, then smiled, folded her arms, and leaned against the doorframe.

'Well,' she said; 'this is a nice surprise.'

'I try to be considerate,' said Bastion, pulling his visor down to shield his eyes and face. 'Has the mighty Ascendant-killer entered the palace without a weapon to her name?'

She patted her waist. 'I have a knife.'

'And a Quadrant,' said Bastion. 'Do you intend to take the coward's way out, and use it to flee?'

'No, Bastion. I intend to beat the crap out of you, and then, if I'm feeling generous, I shall allow you to go home.'

Bastion raised a hand, and Blackrose groaned in agony. Her red eyes closed, and she cried out in pain, her body shuddering.

'Stop it!' yelled Maddie.

'I shall,' he said, 'as soon as Sable fights me.'

'Send him to sleep, Sable!' Millen cried out.

'She can't,' said Bastion, 'I am wearing eye-shields. Do you think I would come here unprepared? No. Unless Sable faces me, I shall slowly kill you all, starting with the lizard.'

Sable walked into the hall. 'Shall we begin?'

CHAPTER 30
NO MERCY

Udall, Ulna, Eastern Rim – 17th Arginch 5255 (18th Gylean Year 6)
Bastion lowered his hand as Sable entered the vast hall, and
the black dragon's cries faded away.

'We have chased each other across this world,' Bastion said, from
behind the steel visor. 'You are a worthy foe, Sable Holdfast. I can
recall when Lord Renko first mentioned your name, after he had
been defeated upon Lostwell. At the time, I mocked him, for how
could a mere mortal be responsible for defying the will of the gods?
When Lord Edmond and I arrived on Lostwell, we focussed our
attention on locating your niece – Kelsey Holdfast. You were of very
little interest to us. It seems we were wrong. If we had hunted you
down, then Dragon Eyre would have been spared the misery you
have caused.'

Sable eyed the locations of the soldiers as she approached Bastion.
They had been ordered not to touch her, and their crossbows were
pointing at her friends. They also had swords strapped to their belts,
she noticed.

She extended a hand.

Give me your sword.

One of the soldiers stepped forward. His eyes were conflicted, but his actions calm and assured. He pulled his sword from its scabbard, then held it out for Sable, offering her the hilt.

She smiled, and took the weapon.

Bastion laughed. 'Were it not for Lord Kolai's murder,' he said, 'I would be tempted to take you back with me to Implacatus, so that your family's unique gifts might be studied by the lore masters of Cumulus. Did Nathaniel understand what he was doing, I wonder, when he created the Holdfasts? It should not be possible for a god to bestow powers that he does not possess for himself, and yet here you are, walking proof that such an impossibility can exist.'

'Did you come here to fight, or talk?' said Sable.

'I came here to kill, Miss Holdfast.'

Sable sprang at Bastion, her sword flashing through the air. The Ancient moved his feet and parried, his speed matching hers. He swept his own blade sideways, and Sable ducked under the blow, then jabbed out with her sword, the tip deflecting off the steel protecting the Ancient's body.

'You are not as fast as your nephew,' Bastion said, 'nor as strong. I watched you fight in Old Alea, next to Corthie and Lady Belinda. You were out-classed by both. Perhaps this fight will not take as long as I had imagined.'

Sable put a hand on her hip. 'What? I could kick Belinda's arse in a fair fight.'

'That's not what she told us,' Bastion went on, his voice rich with mockery. 'Lady Belinda said she defeated you outside Yoneath; with ease, apparently. Maddie Jackdaw was there; shall we ask her what she saw?'

'Don't listen to him,' cried Maddie. 'He's just trying to distract you.'

'I know what he's doing,' said Sable.

'Lady Belinda told us everything about you,' Bastion said. 'She mentioned your horror at discovering that you were a member of a family that you hated; and that you were skilled at nothing, except lying. You betray everyone in the end, don't you, Sable? You are the lowest of the Holdfasts; an unwanted and unloved bastard child;

despised by your own family. Daphne hates you; Karalyn hates you – they all hate you.'

Anger filled her as she listened. He was toying with her, trying to pick off the scabs that covered her heart.

'The Holdfasts don't want you, Sable,' Bastion went on, his sword raised as they faced each other; 'you are an embarrassment to them. Lady Belinda overheard them discuss you behind your back many times. You were sent to Lostwell not because you were worthy of redemption, but because you were expendable. They could not bear to look at you, so they cast you away.'

Sable cried out, and leapt at Bastion. He parried her wild strokes easily, barely moving his feet as he pushed her back. He struck out, and the tip of his blade missed her face by an inch. She swung her sword down at his arm, but the blade did nothing but leave a dent on his armour. He strode forward, and she backed away.

Sleep, she called out to the soldiers in the hall. They fell to the ground with a clatter, their weapons hitting the stone floor next to their unconscious bodies. She sent out a strand of her powers to Maddie, as she blocked another attack from Bastion.

Get out of here, Maddie, she said. *Free Blackrose and run.*

She had to sever the connection as Bastion advanced. He was as strong and fast as Belinda had been outside Yoneath, despite the heavy armour weighing him down, and she had to use every ounce of her battle-vision powers to keep her head on her shoulders. She backed away again, heading towards the ramp leading to one of the high dragon platforms.

'Where are you going?' laughed Bastion. 'There is no escape. Submit to me, and I will make your end a quick one.'

He lashed out again, his right arm driving the sword down at her. She parried, but the blade tore across her upper thigh, slicing through the thin dress and cutting deep into her skin. Bastion was left unbalanced for a split second, and she stabbed out with her own blade, finding a gap in the Ancient's armour by his waist, and drawing blood.

Bastion grunted, and took a step back, as Sable's legs nearly buckled from the pain.

'One strike apiece,' he said. 'And yet, my wound has already healed, while yours looks nasty. Are you tempted to use the Quadrant, Sable? If you are, you'd better be quick, for if I see you reach for the device, I will slice your arm off.'

Sable clutched her wound with her free hand, and felt the blood trickle through her fingers. She backed away, her boots finding the start of the ramp. He advanced, step by step, and she retreated, until they emerged into the open air. Night had fallen, but the dark sky was lit up, as flames rose from the centre of Udall. The entire town was burning, and the palace was like an island, rising above a sea of flames.

'Lady Vettra has done her job well,' said Bastion. 'Did I not promise that Udall would be destroyed this day?'

He resumed his attack, his blade flashing through the air as she ducked and parried. The pain in her thigh was growing. She thought about trying to distract him for long enough for her to make the trip back to Serene, where Austin would be able to heal her wound, but Bastion was too fast for her. She had managed to lead him away from the others in the hall, but his sole reason for coming to Udall had been to kill her, and he didn't seem to care that Maddie and the others might be fleeing. She glanced over her shoulder. The platform was ringed by a low wall, and the wide, brown river was flowing fifty feet below.

'Thinking of jumping?' he said. 'There are soldiers on every bridge, and I possess my own Quadrant. Yield to me, Sable, and I will forego the torture I had planned for you. One stroke from my sword, and it will be over.'

She raised her weapon and attacked. He parried her blow, then kicked her in the stomach, sending her flying backwards onto the platform. He surged forward, and stamped a boot down onto her sword, then kicked it from her grasp. He stood over her, the edge of his blade hovering over her neck.

'Lord Maisk removed that finger from your hand,' he said. 'Do you remember the pain it caused? That was nothing compared to what I am going to do to you. You will plead with me to end it.' The tip of his sword traced a bloody line down her cheek. 'We shall start with the face, I think.'

She ripped the knife from her belt, and drove it into Bastion's left elbow, between the steel plates and through the layer of chain mail. He cried out, and she scrambled to the side as he brought his sword down. She leapt onto his back as he reached across to grasp the handle of the knife, and he pushed himself backward, driving her against the wall that surrounded the platform. She felt her ribcage compress as her hands reached his helmet. She pulled it from his head, and scratched her fingers across his face, trying to reach his eyes. He screamed, then grabbed her by the throat and threw her down onto the platform.

'You bitch!' he cried, as blood streamed from his cheeks. He knelt beside her, and placed his hands round her neck. She tried to enter his mind, but the eye-shields were still in place. She raised her hands as he choked her, but he was too strong, and she felt herself weaken.

'That's it,' said Bastion. 'You feel it, don't you? Your life is ebbing away. Where are the Holdfasts, now that you need them? Are they coming to save you, Sable?'

Her eyes started to close as his grip tightened. He was strong enough to snap her neck in an instant, but she knew he was enjoying watching her die. She could smell his breath, his face was so close to hers, and his eyes were savouring every moment of her suffering.

A dragon's forelimb flashed across the platform, sweeping Bastion to the side, and wrenching his grip from her throat. Bastion raised his hand, then was enveloped in flames, his form disappearing for a moment within the inferno bathing the platform. Sable felt something clutch her feet, and she was dragged away from the flames. She glanced up amid the blistering heat, and saw Ashfall standing over her body, her jaws open as she poured fire over the Ancient.

The dragon closed her jaws, and the flames died down, revealing the body of Bastion. His steel armour was blackened and discoloured, while his head was a mass of burnt and twisted flesh. Ashfall stared at him, then his eyes snapped open. Ashfall raised her claws, then cried out in pain as Bastion lifted a steel-covered hand. Sable reached out, and grabbed the hilt of her sword from where it lay on the platform. She raised it over her head as Ashfall collapsed, then flung herself forwards, driving the blade into Bastion's face. Sable staggered to her feet, and pushed down, forcing the steel through his nose and out through the back of his head. Bastion flailed about, foam coming from his lips, and Sable was thrown to the side as the Ancient convulsed.

'Kill him, Sable,' Ashfall gasped.

Sable crawled over to the Ancient, leaving a trail of blood from the wound on her thigh on the marble slabs of the platform.

'Do it, Sable,' said Ashfall, her voice hoarse.

Sable glanced at the dragon, her form silhouetted by the flames rising from the city. She leaned over, pulled the knife from the Ancient's elbow, and brought it up to his throat. The convulsions had steadied a little, but Bastion was moving his head, the sword embedded through his skull. His healing powers had slowed, and his head was still charred and burnt. She poked a finger into his right eye, and scooped out the shield that had been protecting him from her powers. She entered his mind, and felt the panic and fear that was surging through him.

You have lost, she said. *Beg for mercy.*

He screamed in her head, an inchoate cry of terror.

Feel fear, Bastion; you are under my power now, and I could make you slit your own throat.

'What are you waiting for, Holdfast?' said Ashfall. 'End him.'

'No,' she said.

'Are you insane, witch?' said the dragon. 'Kill him, or I will.'

'Trust me, Ashfall, please. If we kill Bastion, then Edmond will send others. Only Bastion himself can persuade Edmond that it's over for them on Dragon Eyre.'

Do you hear me, Bastion? It's over. You are finished here. You shall leave, and never return. I protect Dragon Eyre, and while I live, the forces of Implacatus will never be able to rule this world.

She sensed his defiance, despite the sword in his head, and unleashed her full powers of persuasion into his mind.

You will obey me. If you try to resist my orders, you will feel nothing but pain and fear, for all eternity.

She dug beneath his armour, and took out the Ancient's Quadrant. She placed it into his hands.

Go back to Implacatus, and tell Edmond that Dragon Eyre is forever beyond his reach. Tell him that if he tries to invade this world again, I will go to Implacatus myself, and hunt down every Ascendant who lives there. I will do to Edmond what I did to Kolai. The only way you can prevent this is by persuading him to leave Dragon Eyre alone. Go.

The Ancient's fingers touched the Quadrant, and his body disappeared.

Ashfall howled in frustration, then Sable collapsed onto the platform, the pain and exhaustion overwhelming her. She closed her eyes, and let oblivion take her.

Sable awoke in a clean, comfortable bed, the white sheets cool against her skin. She opened her eyes, then coughed. Her throat was aching, along with the wound on her thigh.

'Try not to move,' said a voice.

'Maddie?'

'Who else would it be?' said the Jackdaw woman. She was sitting on a chair next to the bed. 'You're in my apartment, after all.'

'This is not your apartment,' said Sable, resting her head against the pillow. 'I can see the floor.'

'I told you that Topaz was tidy. The only thing stopping him from cleaning up now is the fact that he's injured. Like you, he has a sore leg.'

'Where is he?'

'In my bed. This is the spare room.' She passed Sable a mug. 'Here; drink something. It's only water.'

Sable raised her head a fraction, and gulped down the cool liquid. It hurt to swallow, but her thirst outweighed the pain in her throat.

'The dragons will want to talk to you soon,' said Maddie, 'but I won't tell them that you are awake; not just yet. Why did you do it, Sable?'

'Why did I do what?'

'Why did you let Bastion go? Ashfall is beside herself with rage. She said that she saved your life, and allowed you to wound Bastion, but then you gave him back his Quadrant. The dragons are having a hard time understanding it.'

'It was always my plan,' said Sable. 'Did everyone in the great hall get away?'

'Yes. After Bastion disappeared, the dragons rallied, and killed the last of the soldiers and greenhides; they were at it all night. The fires are out, but the town has been destroyed. You know, you'll have to come up with a better explanation when the dragons question you. Everyone's on edge, wondering if and when Bastion will return.'

'He won't,' said Sable. 'Lord Bastion will never return to Dragon Eyre, and he is under my orders to do everything he can to persuade Edmond to leave this world alone. That's why I let him go, Maddie. He's far more useful to us alive.'

She gripped the sheets and pulled them from her, then placed her feet onto the cold floor.

'Get back into bed!' yelled Maddie.

Sable ignored her. She took a dressing gown from the back of a chair, and slipped her arms into the sleeves. She stood, wincing, and staggered over to the window. The town of Udall was a smoking ruin. Her eyes sped past the gutted buildings, and settled on the harbour. The *Giddy Gull* was still afloat, but its deck had been swept by fire, and little remained above the waterline. Sitting by the quayside were three other vessels.

'Tilly and Ann are back,' Sable said, as she put her weight onto the window frame.

'They arrived at dawn,' said Maddie.

Sable bowed her head. 'If something's happened to Lara, tell me, Maddie. Don't hide bad news from me.'

'Tilly is looking for her now,' said Maddie. 'Topaz would be too, if he could get out of bed. A lot of the crew managed to jump overboard, so Tilly is checking the grounds of the infirmary, to see if she's there.'

Sable glanced over at her pile of clothes. Sitting on the top was her Quadrant. She took a breath, and stumbled towards it.

'Oh, Sable, please sit down, or better, lie down,' said Maddie. 'You shouldn't be moving, and I'll get into trouble if the wound opens again.'

'Where's the infirmary?'

'I'm not telling you.'

Sable sighed, then went into Maddie's head. The location of the infirmary was foremost in her mind, and Sable plucked the information out of her. Sable let the dressing gown drop to the floor, then she picked up her clothes.

'You never listen to me, do you?' said Maddie. 'I mean, you never have, so why should you start now?'

The dress went over Sable's head, and she reached for her sandals.

'You look funny in my clothes,' said Maddie. 'Almost ladylike.'

'Tell the dragons that they'll have to wait,' said Sable. 'I need to find Lara; I need to know if...'

'I understand. But, please, Sable – don't leave Ulna again. Blackrose wants to defend you, but that will be hard to do if you run away.'

Sable picked up the Quadrant. 'Are Shadowblaze and the others angry?'

'They're furious, Sable. Some are saying that you were secretly working with Bastion all this time, plotting with him to destroy Dragon Eyre. Blackrose knows this is nonsense, but you have to speak to them, to explain why you did it.'

'I will,' she said, 'but Lara comes first.'

She swiped her fingers across the Quadrant, and appeared in the heart of the burnt-out city. In front of her were rows of the dead – dozens of bodies lined up along a muddy patch of ground, each with a blanket or sheet covering their heads. Many of the limbs were scorched or bloody, and a sickly sweet scent was pervading the air. Sable staggered between the rows of the fallen, heading towards an area where the injured were being treated. The infirmary building had been gutted and the entire garden surrounding it was full of the wounded and the dead.

'Do you need help, miss?' asked a young man, glancing up at Sable from where he was wrapping a bandage around an old man's arm.

'No,' she said. 'I'm looking for Captain Lara of the *Giddy Gull*.'

'I haven't seen her, miss. Try the other side of the infirmary.'

Sable nodded, then started walking. The pain in her thigh exploded, and she fell to the ground. The man rushed to her side.

'You need treatment,' he said, eyeing the patch of blood seeping through her dress.

'Sable?' said a voice.

A young woman ran to her side.

'Tilly?' said Sable.

The man's eyes widened. 'Is this Sable Holdfast?'

Everyone turned to stare at her, and the grounds of the infirmary hushed, leaving only the groans of the wounded. Onlookers crowded round the space where Sable was lying on the ground, each trying to catch a glimpse of her.

'Move back, assholes!' cried Tilly, shoving them aside. She gestured to a few of her crew who were close by, and they piled into the crowd, and formed a ring around Sable. Tilly and the man helped her stand.

'Where's Lara?' said Sable. 'Is she here?'

Tilly nodded. 'This way; come on.'

They forced their way through the masses of people, the sailors clearing a path for them. They came into the shadows on the other side of the gutted building, and stopped by a row of the wounded. Sable's eyes frantically scanned the line of people, then she cried out as she saw Lara, lying with her eyes closed, her chest and head wrapped in bandages.

Sable sunk to her knees next to her, and took her hand. 'Lara?'

The captain opened her eyes. 'Sable?'

Sable burst into tears, and reached out for her. Lara lifted her arms, and they embraced.

'You're hurt,' said Sable.

'I hit my head on something after I jumped from the *Gull*. Are you alright?'

Sable kissed her. 'I am now, Lara. If you want me, I'm here.'

'Of course I want you, Sable. Will I be enough for you?'

'Yes,' she said. 'The war is over, and I'm going nowhere. I love you, Lara; don't leave me.'

Lara tightened her grip round Sable's shoulders and closed her eyes. 'I'll never leave you, Sable.'

Sable opened her eyes, and heard the sound of Lara breathing next to her in the small cabin. Three days had passed since she had found the pirate captain in the grounds of the infirmary, and neither women had left the cabin much during that time. Their only forays outside had been to smoke up on the quarter deck of the *Sow's Revenge*, from where they could gaze at the hull of the *Giddy Gull* as it sat berthed by the pier. Workers were crawling all over the brigantine, and Lara had designs on reconstructing it back to its former glory. Sable had listened to the captain describe in detail how everything was going to be, down to the layout of the new cabin that would be built for her.

Sable turned in bed, and glanced at Lara for a moment, then she nudged her.

Lara groaned, then opened her eyes.

'Today's the day,' said Sable. 'I need to return to Implacatus at noon to collect Austin, his mother, and probably his aunt as well. Before I leave Udall, though, I'm going up to the palace to speak to the dragons. Ashfall is desperate to get Austin back, so they'll probably let me leave the meeting in one piece.'

'Everything will be fine,' said Lara. 'Just tell the dragons what you told me about Bastion. You did the right thing.'

'Let's hope they agree.'

'They knew you were here, on board Tilly's ship,' she said. 'If they really wanted to punish you, then they would have dragged you back to the palace. The folk in this town love you, Sable; they aren't going to hurt you.'

Sable stood, and began to get dressed.

'I'm more worried about Implacatus,' said Lara. 'Please be careful. They might have captured Austin, in which case there could be soldiers and gods waiting for you, and with that injury you shouldn't even be walking.'

Sable picked up her walking stick. 'I have this. I used a stick to get around for nearly two years on Haurn. I'll manage a few days here. If any gods come, I'll bash them over the head with it.'

Someone thumped on the door, then the sound of an argument filtered into the small cabin. Lara groaned as the door opened. Olo'osso marched in, a red-faced Tilly by his side.

'Here you are, my little princess,' said Olo'osso. 'Still in bed, eh, at this hour?'

'She was bleeding injured, father,' said Tilly, 'and so was Sable. Sorry, sister; I tried to stop him.'

'Why are you out of jail?' said Sable.

'Blackrose released me,' he said. 'Perhaps they needed somewhere to put you, witch. I hear you let Bastion go.'

'Yes. I did.'

'I knew you were a filthy little traitor,' he said.

'Shut up,' said Lara. 'You don't know what you're talking about.'

'Blackrose commuted his sentence,' said Tilly. 'She announced that the war was over, and that the death of a Banner officer was no reason to keep him locked up.'

'I would have thought that my daughters would be happy to see me walk free,' said Olo'osso.

'What do you want, father?' said Lara.

'A ship; what else, my treacherous little flower? I want the new frigate that you girls captured, so Dina and I can return to Olkis.'

'If I say you can have it, will you piss off?'

'I want you both to come with me to Ani's vessel; so we can sort it all out, as a family.'

'How am I supposed to get dressed if you're all in here?' said Lara. 'Give me ten minutes and I'll meet you on board the *Fancy*.'

'I'll see you later,' said Sable, leaning on the walking stick.

Lara caught her eye, then nodded.

Sable hobbled from the cabin, and Tilly and her father also left. Tilly closed the door, and gestured to her master.

'Vitz,' she said, 'you're in charge of the ship while I take my father to the *Fancy*.'

The young man smiled. 'Yes, ma'am.'

'Good lad.'

Olo'osso glared at him. 'Is that the damned settler boy?'

'Leave him alone, father,' snapped Tilly. 'That young man has the makings of an excellent master, and where he was born has nothing to do with you.'

'My,' said Olo'osso, as they walked down onto the main deck. 'Touched a nerve, have I, my dear Atili? Are you and the boy close?'

Tilly's face went red, and she looked away.

'What has happened to this family?' said Olo'osso. He sighed. 'One is in love with a witch, and now you, Atili?'

'I'll walk you to the *Flight of Fancy*,' said Sable, as they approached the gangway.

'Should you be walking?' said Tilly.

'It was barely a scratch,' said Sable, grimacing. She clutched the stick, and made her way down to the quayside.

They walked for a few yards, then stopped to gaze at the new frigate.

'It's almost identical to the *Sow*,' said Tilly. 'A fine prize.'

'Indeed,' said Olo'osso. 'I look forward to sailing it to Olkis.'

'If I were Ann,' said Tilly, 'I'd take this ship, and give you the *Fancy*.'

'Maybe Lara should take the frigate,' said Sable.

Tilly winced. 'I hope you haven't suggested that in front of her. Her heart is set on repairing the *Giddy Gull*. She loves that ship almost as much as she loves you.'

A cluster of men appeared on the quayside behind them as they glanced over the new frigate. Without warning, one of them shoved forward, and pushed Tilly into the waters of the harbour, then two large men grasped hold of Olo'osso's shoulders and began to drag him away. Sable turned, and had her walking stick knocked away. She grunted, and fell to one knee, as Tilly yelled up from the water a few feet below them.

One of the men raised a club, and aimed it at Sable's head.

Sleep.

The man crashed onto the quayside. Sable read the mind of one of his colleagues, as they hauled Olo'osso away.

Unk Tannic.

Sable powered her battle-vision, and set off after the men, who were charging their way through the quayside. They ran up a side street, half-carrying, half-shoving Olo'osso along, and Sable followed them. They entered a deserted square, and a dragon limb lashed out, striking Sable across the chest and sending her flying through the air. She hit the side of a burnt-out building, and fell to the ground, winded and barely conscious.

The dragon stamped down onto Sable's body, pinning her to the ground, her face pressed into the gravel. She gasped for air, then tried to reach for the Quadrant, but her arm wouldn't move.

'Unarmed and injured,' said the dragon, 'Sable Holdfast walks into my trap.'

'We have Olo'osso too, Lord Earthfire,' said one of the Unk Tannic.

'You feeble insects have done well,' said the brown dragon, 'and Wyst shall reward you for your services.' The dragon lowered his head, until Sable could feel it brush her ear. 'Your crimes have finally caught up with you, witch,' Earthfire whispered. 'You shall answer to the dragons of Wyst for what you have done.'

'What about me?' yelled Olo'osso. 'It's her you want, not me!'

Earthfire turned to the pirate. 'You know what you did, insect.'

'I only killed one dragon,' cried Olo'osso. 'Sable killed dozens.'

'It matters not,' said Earthfire. 'You have both deprived my kin of their lives, and you shall both answer for it.'

He glanced at the Unk Tannic agents. 'Hood the two prisoners, and bind their wrists.'

Two men ran towards Sable. They pulled a dark hood over her head, and tied it at the neck, then bound her wrists behind her back. The dragon curled his long talons around the Holdfast woman's body, and held her tight.

'Help!' cried Olo'osso, his voice muffled by the hood.

'Silence, insect,' said the dragon. 'You will have time enough to plead your case in Wyst.'

'My lord,' said a voice. 'Sable Holdfast has a Quadrant.'

'Take it,' said the dragon, 'and keep it safe.'

'Yes, my lord.'

Sable felt her body prodded, until a hand clasped onto the Quadrant, and pulled it from her clothing. She felt herself be lifted from the ground, the dragon's forelimb clutched round her abdomen.

'Go to the palace,' she heard the dragon say, 'and tell Queen Blackrose that it was Earthfire of Wyst who has taken the Holdfast witch to meet her judgement. If Ulna attempts to rescue her, it will mean war, and the destruction of Blackrose's realm.'

The dragon lifted into the sky, and soared away, bearing his two prisoners out of the ruins of Udall. Sable tried to cling on to her consciousness, knowing that, if she succumbed, then she might never awaken again; but the pain was too much, and she slipped into the cold embrace of oblivion.

CHAPTER 31
THE LONG ROAD

Talbot, Enna, Eastern Rim – 29th Arginch 5255 (18th Gylean Year 6)

Topaz, Maddie and Tilly stood on the deck of the *Sow's Revenge*, gazing at the ruined buildings of Port Talbot.

'I used to go drinking in that tavern,' said Topaz, pointing.

'Which tavern?' said Maddie. 'All I see are ruins.'

'We'll have to rebuild the water front soon, if we're going to be living here for a while,' he said.

'We don't know that yet,' said Tilly. 'Let's wait for the dragons to finish talking, and then we'll see what's what.'

Lara emerged from her cabin, her eyes bleary. Her body had recovered from the injuries sustained in the attack on Udall, but her mental state seemed fragile.

'Any news?' she said, lighting a cigarette.

'No,' said Maddie. 'We're still waiting.'

Topaz glanced at the hillside overlooking the port, where over two dozen dragons had gathered. Humans had been forbidden from attending the meeting, and he knew that Maddie was angry about being excluded.

'This is so unfair,' Maddie said. 'I should be there.'

'The dragons of Wyst would have refused to negotiate,' said Tilly. 'We just have to be patient.'

'I'm sick of being patient!' Lara cried. 'It's been days since those bastards took Sable and father. I can't bear to think of them suffering in Wyst.'

'I know, sister,' said Tilly.

Shadowblaze flew over the harbour, then landed on the quayside, where he spoke to Ahi'edo. They talked for a minute, then the dragon returned to the hillside. Ahi'edo watched him leave, then ran up the gangway and onto the *Sow's Revenge*.

'The meeting's over,' Ahi'edo said, as he approached Topaz and the others. 'The dragons are just going through their farewells.'

'What was the outcome?' said Maddie. 'Are Sable and Olo'osso going to be released?'

'I don't know. Shadowblaze didn't give me any clues.'

Topaz turned back to the hillside. A dozen dragons lifted into the sky, circled once over the town, then sped off to the north, in the direction of Geist and Wyst. The other dragons remained where they were for a few moments, then Blackrose ascended, and swooped down to the quayside. She landed in a clear area, then turned her long neck until her head was level with Maddie.

'We have agreed a new treaty with Wyst,' she said. 'There shall be peace.'

'I don't care about peace!' shouted Lara. 'Where's Sable?'

Blackrose tilted her head. 'I understand your frustrations, Captain Lara; however, I cannot go to war over Sable and your father – for that is what it would mean. She lost the trust of most dragons in Ulna when she released Lord Bastion. Some believe she deserves to be punished, and I am almost alone in retaining a good opinion of her. My realm would be overwhelmed, and my subjects annihilated, if I attempted to rescue the Holdfast witch.'

'Are we just going to leave her and Olo'osso in Wyst?' said Maddie.

'I managed to extract an oath from Lord Earthfire – he has sworn that neither Sable nor Olo'osso will be killed or tortured while in the custody of the Wystians. I'm afraid that was the best that could be achieved. They have also sworn to abandon their dreams of annexing Enna. This island is now under my protection. Geist, however, I had to concede to them.'

'I'm not sure I understand,' said Topaz. 'The Wystians outnumber us twenty-to-one. Why would they give up Enna?'

'They believe that Austin is still on Ulna,' said the black dragon, 'and I did not disabuse them of the notion.'

'You mean you lied to them?' said Maddie.

'Of course not; I merely declined to correct their erroneous view. They greatly fear Austin, almost as much as they feared Sable. His loss is a sore blow; not only for Ashfall, but for Ulna.'

'Did they admit to having Sable's Quadrant?' said Maddie.

'No,' said Blackrose. 'Lord Earthfire swore that it was not in his possession, but he refused to say if he was aware of its location. I suspect that Unk Tannic agents took it, though I doubt if any know how to use the device.'

'None of this matters,' said Lara, weeping. 'They have Sable. She was going to live with me; she was going to give up fighting. I've lost her forever.'

'The future is unknown, Captain Lara,' said Blackrose. 'Sable is alive and well. The Wystians are using the Unk Tannic to modify a cavern deep in the heart of Wyst – somewhere suitable to hold Sable and your father indefinitely. Under the circumstances, I am relieved. I had feared they would announce that they had already killed Sable. She caused the deaths of over two hundred Wystians, including some of their most renowned and celebrated warriors. In many ways, she is lucky to be alive.'

Lara cried out in frustration. She clenched her fists and strode back into her cabin.

'Poor Lara,' said Maddie.

'What about Dragon Eyre?' said Topaz. 'If Implacatus finds out that Sable is locked up, they might come back.'

'We must hope that whatever Sable did to Bastion works,' said Blackrose. 'In truth, our world now stands undefended against the Ascendants, should they try to retaliate.'

'So, our safety is based upon bluff?' said Maddie. 'Wyst thinks we have Austin, and Implacatus thinks we have Sable?'

'Such is the way of things, my rider. What Sable has given us is hope, and time to rebuild this world from the ashes of destruction. The natives are now in control of Gyle, and the Eighteenth Gylean sits upon his throne, but there are still pockets of Banner resistance on several islands. Stranded by the gods, they are desperate, and may cause trouble for some years to come. In time, I shall go to Gyle, and meet with the new rulers of that realm. Peace is achieved one step at a time, and there is a long road to travel before Dragon Eyre will truly be at ease with itself.'

'What do we do now?' said Topaz.

'Now,' said the black dragon, 'we need to find somewhere in Talbot to live, for I intend to move my capital here for a while, to show Wyst that I am serious about Enna's defence. The refugees will return from Ulna, and I will need the assistance of the Five Sisters to escort them here. Then, the long work of reconstruction shall commence. This world has seen nothing but conflict and despair for nearly three decades; together, we shall make a brighter future for all – dragons and humans alike.'

'Why does it all have to be so messy?' said Maddie. 'I thought that when the war ended, everything would be fine.'

'That is not how the world works, my rider. We have many more compromises and difficult decisions ahead of us. The war tested us, and now we have to prove ourselves worthy of the peace.'

Maddie nodded.

'Pack a bag,' said Blackrose.

'Why?'

'Because I wish to inspect my new protectorate. If I am to govern Enna, then I need to become familiar with its terrain. We will fly from one end of the island to the other, and visit the caverns on the eastern coast, where the old rulers of Enna reside.'

'Are they happy about you taking over Enna, your Majesty?' said Topaz.

'It was their idea,' said Blackrose. 'They felt that a union with Ulna offered the best chance of resisting the power of Wyst.' She glanced at Maddie. 'Lords Greysteel and Shadowblaze will prepare a new dwelling place for us in Talbot while we are away.'

'When are we leaving?' said Maddie.

'In an hour or so,' said Blackrose. 'Pack enough for two nights. I will now speak to my betrothed, and say my farewells.'

The black dragon extended her wings and ascended into the blue sky, then banked, and flew back towards the hillside.

'We have peace,' said Tilly, 'but at a cost. My father, and Sable Holdfast. Bleeding dragons.'

'I wish there was some way we could free them both,' said Maddie, 'but you heard Blackrose. It would mean another war. Without Sable and Austin, the Wyst dragons would win, and the world would be in a worse position than it was under the Banner forces.

'I know,' said Tilly. 'Still, Lara's going to take a long time to recover from this.'

'I think I'll go down to the quay,' said Ahi'edo, 'and help Shadowblaze select a new palace in Talbot.'

'Why?' said Maddie. 'So you can pick the rooms with the best view?'

Ahi'edo laughed. 'Good luck on your trip, Maddie. I'll see you when you get back.'

He turned, and strode away.

'I'll leave you, too,' said Tilly. 'I'm going to see Lara. I doubt I'll find any words to say that will make her feel better, but I want her to know that I'm there for her.'

Topaz turned to Maddie, once Tilly had entered the cabin. 'I'll be the one left behind this time, while you go off with Blackrose.'

She smiled. 'You need to find yourself a nice dragon.'

'I think I'll stick with boats, if it's all the same,' he said. 'Right now, I feel a bit lost without the *Gull*. Ann offered me a place on her ship, but she's already got a master, and I think I'm going to wait until the *Gull's* been fixed up.'

'That could take a while.'

'Yeah. It means that I won't be at sea for a few months, at least. By the time the *Gull's* ready to sail again, you'll be sick of the sight of me.'

She took his hand. 'I very much doubt that.'

'We did it, Maddie,' he said, as he looked into her eyes. 'We made it through the wars alive. We can talk about normal things again, like starting a family, and finding a house where we can bring up children; without worrying if we'll still be alive tomorrow.'

She leaned into him. 'That sounds nice. I think I'd like a boy and a girl. We could call them Corthie and Aila.'

'Old friends?'

'Yes, from the City. So much in my life has changed since then. The one constant has been Blackrose. My old captain told me that the dragon would change everything, and she was right. I wonder if Captain Hilde is still alive.'

'Do you miss your old life?'

'Sometimes, but I prefer my new one. Dragon Eyre is so beautiful, despite the terrible things that have happened.' She glanced up at him. 'And you're here.'

'You're everything I've ever wanted, Maddie.'

'I have you, and I have Blackrose. I know that we still have an awful lot of work to do, and it's terrible what happened to Sable; but at the same time, I can't help feeling...'

'What?'

Maddie smiled up at him. 'Happy. Is that wrong of me?'

'No.'

'It feels wrong. Look at Ashfall and Lara – they're both in pain; and think about Sable. After everything she did to save this world, her reward is to be locked up in a Wystian dungeon with Olo'osso. It seems selfish to feel happy, when others are suffering.'

'You're not selfish, Maddie. You're the kindest person I know. You deserve a little happiness.'

'We still have an hour,' she said. 'Do you want to help me pack?'

'Packing will take five minutes,' he said.

She smiled as she led him to their cabin. 'Then I guess we'll have to find something else to do to pass the time.'

EPILOGUE

S erene, Implacatus – 20th Duninch 5255

Austin trudged along the busy street, keeping his head down. For two months, he had been living with his mother and aunt in a rundown tenement block, on the same level of Serene as the alleyway where Sable had failed to appear. In some ways, it had been easy to blend in with the mortal inhabitants of the city. Gods seldom entered the warren of housing blocks, and he had been keeping usages of his powers to a minimum. On the other hand, it was no longer possible for him to either ascend or descend to any of the other levels of the city – to attempt to do so would mean having to pass the cordon of gods stationed by each enormous stairwell, which would result in his inevitable capture.

The gods had been on edge in recent days, as if something had been disrupting their powers, but Austin had no idea what it could mean. He stopped by a street corner, and paid a few coins for a news sheet. He lit a cigarette and scanned the headlines. The main story was the same as that on the previous day – the horrific murder of Lord Sabat. Apparently, his head had been removed, and his heart ripped out. The crime had taken place in broad daylight, on a level close to where Austin lived. Suspicion had fallen on the other gods of

Serene – for who else would have been capable of killing an Ancient? Austin had hoped that Sable had carried out the murder, but she hadn't appeared in the alleyway that day, or on any other day, for that matter.

There was nothing in the news sheet about Dragon Eyre. The topic was clearly being avoided, which could only mean one thing – the forces of Implacatus had been defeated. There was a rumour that Lord Bastion was back in Serene, which reinforced Austin's opinion. So had the increase in the numbers of wounded and maimed Banner soldiers who had appeared on the streets in the previous two months.

If Sable had been killed or captured, then Austin had no doubt that the news sheet would be trumpeting the fact; so why hadn't she returned for him?

He folded the news sheet in half, and carried on walking down the street. He turned right at a junction, and knocked on the front door of a grimy apartment building. Eyes appeared through a slit, then the door was opened.

'Morning,' said a man.

'Good morning, Sergeant,' said Austin.

The man glanced up and down the road, then let Austin enter the building. He led him into a room where three other men were sitting. They were all in civilian clothing, but each had the air of the military about them. Two had crutches leaning against their chairs, while the other had an arm in a sling.

'This is the... man I was telling you about,' said the sergeant. 'If any of you speaks a word about this outside these walls, I'll know who it was, and I'll find you. Understand?'

The three sitting men nodded.

'How much does he want paid?' said one of the men.

'I don't want your money,' said Austin. 'In return for healing you, I want information. You are all ex-Banner, yes?'

The three men frowned, then nodded.

'And you have all recently returned from Dragon Eyre?' Austin went on.

'That was two months ago,' said one of the men. 'That's when we all got back.'

'And that was the problem,' said another. 'With so many wounded soldiers returning to Serene at the same time, the Banner support system has practically collapsed, and we haven't been given any salve for our injuries. Not that anyone in the city knows about what happened in Dragon Eyre. The Banners have been told to keep quiet about it.'

'Where were you based?' said Austin.

'I was in Port Edmond,' said one. 'It was a nightmare. The bastard dragons killed most of my company, and one of them nearly tore my leg in half.'

'Do you know what happened to a woman named Sable Holdfast?'

The three men eyed each other.

'We're not supposed to talk about her,' said one. 'We're under strict orders.'

The sergeant frowned. 'Do you guys want to be healed or not?'

One of them shrugged. 'The truth is, we don't know what became of the Holdfast witch. A few boys in my regiment claimed to have seen her in Ectus, but that was well before we were pulled out.'

'She's probably the damn queen of Dragon Eyre by now,' said another. 'That bitch is the reason we were evacuated.' He lowered his voice. 'There's even a rumour that she killed the Fifth Ascendant.'

'Lord Kolai?' said the sergeant. 'I don't mean to doubt you, lads, but that sounds a little unlikely.'

'That's not all, sarge,' said another soldier. 'I heard she can control greenhides.'

'Does anyone know what happened to her after the fighting stopped?' said Austin.

The soldiers shook their heads. Austin nodded then raised his hand, and healed the men of their wounds. They groaned for a moment, then grinned, and slapped each other on the back.

'Is that all?' one of them said. 'Can we go now?'

The sergeant glanced at Austin, who nodded.

'Remember, lads,' the sergeant said, as the men got to their feet. 'Don't breathe a word of this to anyone. If someone asks how you were healed, tell them that you were issued with a small amount of salve that someone had saved from Dragon Eyre. Got it?'

'Yes, sarge,' said one, then the three men left the room.

'Was that information any use?' said the sergeant to Austin, once they were alone.

'Not particularly.'

'I can rustle up a few more soldiers, if you like. Say, in three or four days from now?'

'No,' said Austin. 'It looks like they were all brought back from Dragon Eyre at the same time. I don't think any of them know what happened after the fighting came to an end.' He passed the sergeant a pouch of gold. 'Thank you for your help; and thank you for not asking any awkward questions.'

The man took the pouch. 'I'm just happy that some of the boys are getting a chance to be healed. It's like the Banners have abandoned them. Have you finished with today's news sheet?'

Austin nodded, and handed it to the soldier.

The sergeant took it, and put it under his arm. 'With all those questions you were asking about Sable Holdfast, I assume you read the news a couple of days ago?'

'I don't think so. Why?'

The sergeant frowned. 'I think I still have a copy sitting around.' He walked over to a table, and picked up a folded news sheet. 'Here it is. Take a look at page two.'

Austin took the news sheet, and unfolded it. On page two was a drawing of a woman's face. Under it was a caption – Kelsey Holdfast. Austin's eyes widened as he read the short accompanying article. It stated that an 'aberrant mortal' was the cause of the strange disruptions that had been affecting the gods' powers in recent days. If seen, she was to be immediately handed over to the Banners.

'Is she a relative of Sable, do you think?' said the sergeant.

'I don't know,' Austin lied. 'I'd best be going. Thanks again for your help.'

Austin hurried to the door, trying to digest the news that Sable's niece was in Serene. What did it mean? For a brief moment, he considered the possibility that Kelsey had been sent to find him, but he dismissed it. Sable had no means of communicating with the members of her strange family, which could only mean that her niece's appearance was a coincidence. He left the building, and vowed to himself never to return. The sergeant had seemed trustworthy, but it was too risky, especially if the gods were searching for Kelsey. The sergeant didn't know his name, but if questioned, then the gods would probably be able to deduce his identity. There wouldn't be many demigods with healing powers who possessed recent knowledge of events on Dragon Eyre. He would need to lie low for a while; and hoped that Kelsey would be able to slip through their fingers.

He made his way to the small apartment he was renting. The supply of gold that Sable had left was starting to run low; he would need to get a job – something menial, no doubt, where he would pretend to be an ordinary mortal. He turned down a side street, and entered a tenement block. He climbed to the third floor, and unlocked a door.

His mother smiled at him from the kitchen, where she was preparing dinner. Her sister was sitting at the dining table, chopping vegetables, and Austin walked over to them. He kissed them both, then picked up a knife and began to help out.

'Did you have a nice day?' his mother asked.

'Yes. I'll need to find some work soon, though.'

'I can help with that, Austin,' said his aunt Sunnah. 'I know a few people. I can ask around for you.'

'Thanks,' he said, as he began chopping a pile of tomatoes. 'Remember...'

'What? That you're a mere mortal?' said Sunnah, smiling. 'Don't worry; I won't forget.'

His mother glanced over from the stove. 'Did you go up to the alleyway today?'

'Yes,' he said. 'At noon, as usual.' He sighed. 'Today was the last day, though. If I keep going up there, someone will get suspicious. If Sable comes, then she'll have to find us.'

'Will she be able to?' said Sunnah.

'That worries me too,' said Salah. 'How would she be able to track us down? It's not as if we have our names on the front door.'

Austin smiled to himself. 'Don't worry about that. If Sable comes, she'll find us.'

'How can you be so sure, son?' his mother said.

He thought back to all that Sable and he had achieved on Dragon Eyre.

'Because,' he said, 'Sable Holdfast can do anything.'

AUTHOR'S NOTES
MAY 2022

I hope you enjoyed Dragon Eyre Blackrose – and thanks for reading it!

Unlike Ashfall, which was a particularly troublesome book to draft, Blackrose poured out of me as quickly as I could type the words. I always plan my books out thoroughly in advance, but, as is often the case with well-laid plans, the books sometimes veer off course in unexpected directions. This did not happen with Blackrose. I knew almost every detail of what would occur before I touched the keyboard, and stuck to it. Sable's rampage had been swirling round my thoughts for a long time before I had even begun the Dragon Eyre trilogy, and it was a joy to finally be able to let it all out.

One last thing – for those worried about Sable – please be assured that we most certainly haven't seen the last of her…

RECEIVE A FREE MAGELANDS ETERNAL SIEGE BOOK

Building a relationship with my readers is very important to me.

Join my newsletter for information on new books and deals and you will also receive a Magelands Eternal Siege prequel novella that is currently EXCLUSIVE to my Reader's Group for FREE.

www.ChristopherMitchellBooks.com/join

ABOUT THE AUTHOR

Christopher Mitchell is the author of the Magelands epic fantasy series.

For more information:
www.christophermitchellbooks.com
info@christophermitchellbooks.com

Printed in Great Britain
by Amazon

80739244R00274